She didn't know who she was . . .

"There's a way to tell if you're Marti or not. It's an instinctual kind of thing. Are you willing to do it?"

Hallie narrowed her eyes at him. What could it be? "Fine, do what you have to do."

As Hallie prepared for him to turn the truck around, Jesse leaned forward and kissed her, pressing her against the window. For a moment, she felt dizzy, and her stomach did flip-flops. Where his hand rested on her thigh, a warmth spread. Why was he kissing her like this? her mind asked. Who cares? her body answered, drowning in the sensations.

PRAISE FOR *ON THE WAY TO HEAVEN*:

"A truly marvelous debut . . . Ms. Wainscott [is] an author to watch."

—*Romantic Times*

SHADES OF HEAVEN

TINA WAINSCOTT

St. Martin's Paperbacks

SHADES OF HEAVEN

ISBN: 0-312-95671-1

Printed in the United States of America

St. Martin's Paperbacks edition / October 1995

10 9 8 7 6 5 4 3 2 1

To Billy Dean, country music singer, for inspiring me as Jesse came to life, and to Mike, who gave me a glimpse into the racing life.

Prologue

~

The two carat diamond on her wedding set sparkled as Hallie DiBarto ran her fingers across the black velvet surface of the sofa. Not the appropriate distraction to avoid her husband Jamie's eyes, she realized, and shifted her vision to her silk stockings. She deserved the bitterness those blue depths radiated at her, she knew that. But if she didn't go through with this, who knew what Mick would do to her. Or to Jamie.

"I want a divorce, Jamie," she said softly, her words absent of emotion. She would have to put more meaning into them to convince him. If only the migraine would subside enough for her to summon her acting skills.

As it turned out, she didn't need to.

"Absolutely," he told her.

That word sent a chilled rush to her bones in spite of the warm California sun pouring through the windows.

Her voice quivered. "Just like that?"

Jamie sighed, running a hand through his blond hair in frustration. It was a gesture she had seen many times, had *caused* many times, if she was honest with herself.

"What do you want me to do, Hallie, drop down on my knees and beg you to stay, so you can keep making a fool of me by seeing that maniac? I'm done with that business. Don't cry or accuse me of not caring. You'd be right. I don't care anymore."

Pain shot through her skull like an iron lance. She'd had horrible headaches all her life, but this sense of fear enveloping her was new and the pain sharper. Her head dropped down into her hands, and her thoughts scattered like ants on a trampled hill. Dimly, she heard Jamie's concerned voice, but his words were unintelligible, as if spoken through layers of gauze. Her body convulsed under tremors of cold, and she slid onto the tile floor, unable to stop herself from falling.

"Make it stop. Make it stop!" her voice cried out through a fog of pain.

The touch of Jamie's hand, tight on her arm, seemed to tingle, then disappear. She tried to move her hand, her arm. With sheer horror, she realized she could not. Black dots clouded her vision, and she heard her heartbeat slowing to nothing as the darkness closed in. A whistling sound, like a faraway train, pierced the blackness. As the pain lessened, Hallie welcomed the dark cloud of death that took her. Anything to make the pain go away.

Chapter 1

~

$\mathcal{H}$allie DiBarto had come back from the brink of death a changed woman. That in itself was not unusual. Coming back in a different body was.

And not just a different body, but a different life. Someone else's life. Marti, they kept calling her. Who was Marti? Hallie felt the surge of panic that enveloped her every time she realized that *she* was Marti. Before she'd had a chance to ask where Jamie was, or to tell them they'd made a mistake in her identity, she realized something was terribly wrong.

Hallie glanced down again at short fingers and stubby nails, at the body of a stranger. She took a deep breath, willing the panic away. How had she ended up in Chattaloo, Florida? In this bruised and aching body? She remembered dying as if it were years ago, remembered jagged pieces of a life in California. During her stay in the hospital, those memories melded together to form a past that did not coincide with what she'd found here. She had never been to Florida, been a brunette, been short. She had never seen the tall man who helped her out of the wheelchair after they went through the hospital doors, watching her with a worried expression. The man who claimed to be her husband, Jesse.

Jesse's thick brown hair lifted in the fat breeze as they bid the doctor farewell and walked into humid sunshine. He was twenty-five years old; she'd seen his date of birth on a form. He studied her openly, and for that she could not blame him. After all, he'd been told that his wife had been assaulted, nearly raped, and hadn't spoken to anyone since the attack. She didn't know how the man with those dark green eyes would take her crazy story:

that a tall, blue-eyed, blond stranger lived inside his wife's petite body. Hallie had to cling to the only truth she knew: that woman still existed.

She would have to tell him eventually. For now, playing the part of silent trauma would serve her best. She hoped fervently for a sign. It was not God who spoke, but Jesse.

"I don't know what's going on," he said, softer than she thought a man of his size could speak. He held out a hand to her. "But let me help you."

She glanced upward, catching a glimpse of thin clouds against a washed-out blue sky. A sign? Jesse's hand remained in midair, unwavering as she contemplated. Then, very slowly, she reached a thin arm toward him. Somewhere deep inside her, down where she still existed, a small coal of warmth sparked to life as his fingers wrapped solidly around her own.

"The truck's parked over there."

Hallie nodded, maintaining the silence that had seen her through the ordeal of being questioned by Deputy Thomas, the doctor, and Jesse. It bought her time, if nothing else. She stuck her finger in her mouth to nervously chew on a nail, but found with dismay she had no nails to chew; they were already clipped short. Jesse helped her climb into a dusty, red pickup truck.

"Marti, if you want to talk about"—he glanced uneasily at her, then looked ahead—"what happened, I'm here. Dr. Toby said not to press you, and I won't." He reached over and lightly grazed a spot on her cheek where she knew a violet bruise blossomed. "I want to make it better, but I don't know how. Will you tell me?"

Give me back my body and my life! she wanted to scream out, but clamped her lips shut instead. Keeping the panic from her eyes was harder than keeping her silence. Could he see the confusion she saw whenever she looked in the mirror? Jesse sighed softly as he turned back to the steering wheel and started the engine.

After spending most of her life nestled between the Pacific Ocean and the mountains of Southern California, the small town of Chattaloo seemed flat, boring.

She picked idly at the lace that edged her jean shorts. A thin scar edged along the top of one knobby knee, and she wondered how it got there. She loosened the scarf Jesse bought to hide the bruises around her neck. The sight of them had aroused a queer sense of fear in her, though Hallie had not suffered the attack herself.

Trying not to look overly interested, she pulled the worn-out wallet from the vinyl purse lying next to her. One library card and a driver's license. The brunette gave the camera a forced smile. Next to the photo read, "Marti Jeane May." The birth date indicated Marti was twenty-three years old. Four years younger than Hallie! Marti had an identity, a life, a husband. Now Hallie had those, and she didn't want them.

"Is anything missing?" Jesse asked, breaking into her thoughts.

A strangled laugh escaped, which she quickly disguised as a sob. Her life and identity, that's all. At Jesse's concerned look, she shook her head.

The orange groves flanking the two-lane highway grew gradually into downtown Chattaloo. Tiny frame houses snuggled under oak trees, kids raced each other on bicycles, and groups of teenagers gathered idly around trucks and Jeeps. Normal life, going on as if the strangest thing in the world hadn't just happened to her.

Jesse turned onto a dirt road. Distant barking materialized into one of the ugliest dogs she had ever seen. It was speckled, stocky, and worse yet, large. It chased alongside the truck as they passed under a canopy of oak trees to a house in the middle of the hammock.

The dog jumped all over him when he got out of the truck, but Jesse didn't seem to mind the grubby paws. He opened the passenger door and held out his hand, but Hallie didn't move. The dog looked hungrily up at her, flinging its tail from side to side.

"What's wrong?" He followed her stare to the dog. "You're not afraid of ole' Bumpus, are you? You've been living with him for two weeks."

She opened her mouth to say something, then caught herself. Yes, she was afraid of ole' Bumpus. Terrified. But that ugly dog was the least of her problems, she thought, trying to put him in perspective. Bumpus cocked his head, his wrinkled brow looking thoughtful as he waited for some acknowledgment. Jesse whistled, then gestured. Bumpus moved to where Jesse pointed and sat down with an internal whining noise.

"He's just concerned about you, is all."

Hallie took his outstretched hand this time and carefully climbed down. Jesse led her up the stone walkway to the small gray house washed pink by the dying sunlight. Bumpus followed, his tail wagging wildly as he sniffed around her ankles. She moved away, but he followed, trying to jump up in front of her.

"Bumpus, what's your problem? Maybe he knows you're hurting."

Maybe he does, she thought, eyeing him. And maybe he knew she wasn't Marti.

Inside, the house looked larger than it seemed from the outside. A ceiling fan whirred slowly above, barely stirring the wilted leaves of an ivy. Marti obviously hadn't had much of a chance to feminize the place, and a brief glance at Jesse left Hallie little doubt as to where the bride's time had been going. Enjoying marital bliss obviously. He was a kicker, as she used to call the good-looking ones. In a country sort of way.

The blue plaid couch looked lumpy, but it reminded her how little sleep she had gotten last night. Jesse was watching her, perhaps thinking she might faint, cry, or worse. She tried for a moment to put herself in his place. His wife is almost raped and nearly strangled. When she wakes at the hospital, she is so withdrawn that she appears not to recognize either him or the doctor. And she has not spoken a word since. He might reasonably expect her to fling herself out the nearest window.

"You look tired," he said.

Again, he held out that large, strong hand of his. She only hesitated a moment before reaching out and letting him lead her someplace where she could hopefully let sleep wrap her in the comfort of familiarity.

He led her to a room that held a king-size water bed, one long dresser, and not much else. She sat on the padded edge of the bed while he dug through a disorganized drawer and pulled out a long nightgown splattered with blue flowers. Hallie hadn't worn a nightgown like that since she was five years old, but she wasn't in the mood to be picky. Jesse stood by the door, shifting from one foot to the other.

"Do you . . . should I . . . do you want me to sleep out on the couch tonight?"

It took an effort for her jumbled mind to put together what he meant. Well, of course, if he and Marti were married, they probably slept in that king-size bed together. The thought of his body lying next to her was unsettling. She wrapped her arms around herself and nodded.

A strange light shone in his eyes, deep and protective. "If you need anything, anything at all, let me know."

But he didn't leave. Jesse looked at her, obviously weighing something.

"Marti, can I ask you something?" He swallowed loudly. "Why haven't you asked about the baby?"

She could only give him a blank expression. Was there a baby in the house? His shoulders drooped, and he stepped closer.

"Don't you even remember that you're pregnant?"

Hallie slid off the railing and fell into a heap on the dark green carpet. "P-pregnant?" she croaked out, then realized she'd broken her silence.

Jesse pulled her to her feet and helped her sit on the bed. His green eyes held a mixture of confusion and surprise. He still held her hands tightly in his, kneeling in front of her.

"Thank God you can still talk." He gently touched the bruises that ringed her neck, causing an aching tingle. "Dr. Toby was worried that the man who . . . that he had damaged your vocal cords." He removed his hand and looked intently at her. "Did you really forget about the baby?"

Her stomach flip-flopped inside her as she tried her best to compose herself. Could he tell her hands were shaking within the confines of his grasp? She took a deep breath, hoping for some divine intervention in the form of a real good reason his revelation had shocked her into talking. Damn, but this complicates matters, even more than they were!

"Things are . . . muddled right now," she whispered in a hoarse, strange voice. "The past isn't clear to me. Nothing is." Her hand slipped from his and touched her nearly flat stomach. "Are you sure?"

"Oh, I'm sure all right. You're only two months pregnant. Didn't Dr. Toby tell you that the baby was all right?"

Hallie shrugged. "She might have, I don't know. My head was spinning most of the time." She tilted her head back. "Oh my gawd, I'm pregnant."

"Maybe I'd better call Dr. Toby—"

"No!" she blurted out. "I . . . I'll be fine. Really. Just give me some time."

"Time," he repeated with a slight nod. "Okay, I'll give you some time. But this not remembering stuff is spooky, Marti. Are you sure you're okay?"

She nodded, then walked into the adjacent bathroom so Jesse wouldn't see the panic in her eyes. Her heart sank when she saw Marti's face in the mirror. She had looked at that reflection a hundred times in the last day and a half, but it was always the same. The swelling was going down a little, making the purple bruises look more pronounced. There was one bruise, or mark really, that was different from the others. It looked like a sideways "V" with two little marks below it. The skin was broken where a sharp object had dug in.

"Oh, how I wish this were all a nightmare, and if I screamed, I would wake up in a familiar bedroom with a pounding heart and realize it was all over. But it's not, is it?" She'd pinched herself so many times to wake herself up, there were red marks all over her arm.

She had to remember a life she had not participated in. Or run like hell away from this place. But run where? Home to her husband, Jamie, and tell him that she had somehow gotten herself into the body of another woman, a *pregnant* woman?

She thought of Jamie, her *real* husband back in her *real* life. It had been two months since she last saw him.

Two months during which she had lived in some abyss. She couldn't dare to hope that he missed her. And she couldn't dare blame him if he didn't.

Jesse flipped on the television and settled onto the couch. The room was dark except for the bluish glow from the set. Two weeks ago he had married a woman he hardly knew because she had manipulated him into getting her pregnant. He couldn't deny the protective instincts this attack aroused, but he didn't much like them. Could she have staged the whole thing just to elicit some sympathy from him? Jesse shook his head. No, Marti wasn't gutsy enough to pull off something like that.

Through the night Jesse kept moving, twisting, sighing deeply every time he realized he wasn't asleep. It didn't take much to put him on alert, even the sound of quiet footsteps walking past him and the front door closing softly. He wondered if he'd really heard Marti go outside alone, after what she'd been through.

Swinging to an upright position, he eyed the digital clock: 5:49. What the devil was she doing up at this time of the morning? Jesse located where he'd dumped his jeans and slid into them as he walked toward the window. He spotted her silhouette on one of the swings that hung from the large oak tree out front.

She was slumped over a little, moving slowly back and forth. He watched her for a while, trying to imagine what it would feel like to be overpowered and attacked in such a vicious way. He couldn't. What he really wanted to do was find out what son of a bitch had done it to her and rip him apart.

Jesse glanced at the clock again: 6:10. He wasn't going to let her wallow in self-doubt, or whatever else she was dealing with any longer. He walked out into the damp, foggy morning.

"What the devil are you doing out here by yourself?" he asked.

She shrugged, staring down at the toe that kept her swing moving. He dropped down in the swing next to hers. They sat in silence as the early morning glow of pink filtered through the oak trees. She looked at him for a few minutes, studying him. He held her gaze, wishing he could read what her eyes were saying.

"Jesse, do you believe in God?"

He narrowed his eyes at her. "Sure, I do. Do you?"

"I do now."

"You think it was God who helped you get away from the . . . creep who attacked you?"

"It's a lot more complicated than that."

He wasn't following her line of conversation, but he wanted her to get her anxieties out. "Sometimes near-death experiences bring people closer to God, or give them religion when they didn't have it before."

She laughed, a strange, thick sound. "I'm not talking about a near-death experience." Marti pressed a clenched fist against her lips. "What do you think happens to people when they die?"

"They go to Heaven. Or hell." He shrugged. "But you didn't die, Marti."

"Do you think it's really cut-and-dried like that? I mean, is your only choice Heaven or hell, or is there another option?"

He crinkled his eyebrows, wondering if she had sustained a little brain damage or something. "I've never heard of any other options."

She seemed to study him again, as if weighing whether to go on.

"Marti, what are you talking about?"

She took a deep breath. "Let's just say, for example, that a person dies, but they don't go to Heaven or hell." He raised his eyebrows at her, but let her continue. "They knew for certain they were dying, and then they woke up again. But it wasn't their body they were in anymore."

"Marti, you're not making sense."

"Jesse, listen to me. *If* that happened, what would you think had occurred?"

He was becoming more and more sure that something had gotten knocked loose in her brain. "It couldn't happen."

She bit her bottom lip, nodding slowly. "I knew you wouldn't understand."

"What you're saying is crazy. It would be incredible, amazing."

"But God can do anything, right?"

"Right, but things like that don't happen."

"Yes, they do. Something . . . crazy, incredible, and amazing happened to me. I don't know why, but it did." She took a deep breath. "I am not Marti. My name is Hallie DiBarto, I'm from California, and I'm married to a man named Jamie."

She might as well have been speaking a foreign language as far as Jesse was concerned. It had to be delirium! Encouraged by his silence, she continued.

"Two months ago something happened inside my brain and I died. I think God gave me a second chance here, in this body, this life." She gestured vaguely around her.

There was no hint of craziness about her, no odd light in her eyes. But she was sure talking crazy!

"Marti, you've been through a lot. It's just the stress—"

She stood and faced him, taking the chains of his swing in her hands. "It is not stress! I know it sounds crazy, it *is* crazy!" Her voice dropped down to a whisper. "But it's true."

"Wait a minute, let me understand this." He ran his fingers through disheveled hair, trying to make his brain understand. "You're saying that you're someone totally different in Marti's body?" He was trying to put it together, but it sounded so . . . she had the right word: *crazy.* "You died and came back in Marti's body?"

"That's what I'm saying."

Jesse stood up and paced a few feet before turning to face her. She dropped into her swing again and twisted nervously, watching his reaction.

"If you're really some woman from California, then where's Marti?"

Hallie touched the bruises around her neck. "I don't know. She must be dead."

"Nolen Rivers did swear you were dead when he

found you by the side of the road, but—no, it's crazy! I'm calling Dr. Toby—"

"No!" she said as loud as her hoarse voice could manage. "There's nothing she can do about it. Do you think I'd make something like this up?"

"I don't think you're making it up. The problem is you believe it."

She looked so fragile, sitting there on the swing with desperation in her eyes. Like a battered doll. But it couldn't be true. And yet, it could explain why she didn't know she was pregnant with their baby. And why she didn't look at him with annoying adoration the way she had before the attack. He shook his head.

She stood up and crossed her arms over her chest. "Well, it doesn't matter if you believe me or not, I won't be around much longer anyway."

He realized then that the woman before him was like a stranger. Those were not Marti's words. "What do you mean by that? Where are you going?"

"Probably home to California. I can't stay here, with you. I'm married to someone else, for Pete's sake, and I don't even know you!"

Those words made him smile. "You didn't know me before the attack either, doll." The endearment had slipped by.

She relaxed her tensed shoulders. "What do you mean?"

He shrugged. "I hardly knew you before . . . well, you know. It just sorta happened, and you said you were on the pill to make your periods lighter. A month later, you found out you were pregnant. That was two weeks ago."

Hallie thought about the situation for a few minutes. She didn't want this baby, and he probably didn't either. The question of whether or not it was too late for abortion crossed her mind. Then she looked upward, chastising herself for the thought. How could she use her second chance to take away an innocent baby's first chance in life?

"Marti, enough of this bizarre conversation. Let's go inside."

* * *

After breakfast, Hallie watched him clear away the dishes. "Tell me about Marti. What was she like?"

He dropped his head. "Marti, this conversation is making me crazy." He lifted his head and looked at her. "You work at the Bad Boys Diner with my sister, Kati. She brought you home for dinner at my ma's a few times. You were quiet, nice enough."

"How'd you, um, get with her?" Hallie asked, interested in knowing everything she could about the girl who used to be Jesse's wife. "I mean, if you didn't know her very well."

He gave her an exasperated look. "One night after dinner, you looked like you really wanted to talk, and Kati had to take off for class. So we picked up a six-pack of beer and headed down to the river. You were lonely, weren't making many friends. You got another six-pack, we kept talking. We were both feeling pretty buzzed when you leaned over and kissed me. That's how it started."

"Sounds romantic," Hallie said derisively.

"Drunk sex is not what I'd call romantic." He stuck his hands in his jean pockets, tilting his head. "Marti, are you doing this because you want out of the marriage? Because if that's what you're after, you don't have to make up all this crazy stuff—"

"You still think I'm making this up? How can I prove that it's real?"

"Why don't you call home, this place in California where you supposedly came from?" he asked in a challenging tone. "You've got to have family there, someone who knows you."

Home. What was home to her anyway? She dropped back onto the chair.

"Oh, sure, just call home and say, 'Hey, remember me? I died, but now I'm in some other body in some godforsaken town in Florida.' " She felt a frown creep over her face. "Besides, there is no home! My mom's a bitch, I've never even met my father." Her tears, previously pent-up with disbelief, slipped down swollen cheeks. "I was a lousy wife." She sat up, facing Jesse.

"Look at me! I'm a brunette, shorter . . . and pregnant! How can I tell them I'm really alive? They'll think I'm crazy!"

"No-o-o, why would they think something like that?"

"I thought you would understand."

He laughed in disbelief. "You thought I would buy a zany story like this just because you say it's true? I could tell you I'm the ghost of Elvis. Would you believe me?"

"Where's the phone, oh, king of rock and roll?" she snapped.

Jesse got a cordless phone from the living room and handed it to her. She looked at it, then him. He was waiting for her to make the call. Testing her. If she talked to Jamie, told him who she was, would he believe her or just slam the phone down? Would anyone believe her? Another look at Jesse's smug expression prompted her to start pressing buttons.

First she called the mansion in California. Solomon, the butler, sleepily informed her that Jamie was at Caterina. Jesse leaned against the door frame, watching her with curiosity. She punched in the number for Caterina.

"'Mornin', Caterina." a singsong voice answered.

"Jamie DiBarto's office, please."

"Certainly, just one moment."

The accent brought back memories that seemed like only days ago.

"Good morning, may I help you?"

Hallie's heart stopped midjump when she realized it wasn't Jamie's voice. Her hands didn't stop shaking, however.

"May I speak to Jamie DiBarto, please," her hoarse voice whispered. It was Miguel, Jamie's brother. He had never liked her, especially after the time she'd gotten drunk and flirted with him.

"He's out on the boat all day at Sting Ray Point. Can I—"

"Sting Ray Point?"

"Yeah, his wife started swimming with the stingrays on the west end, and now it's our biggest attraction. It's great if you're adventurous—"

She choked out the words, "H-his wife?"

"Yeah." Miguel's tone changed. "Is there something I can help you with?"

Roaring hot flames engulfed her face. Holy toledo, Jamie had already remarried!

"His w-wife, is her name Renee?"

Miguel laughed. "No, her name is Hallie. Who is this?"

Her voice dropped to a lower whisper as she tried to catch her breath. "Is Hallie there? Right now?"

"No, she's out with Jamie. Look, if you want to leave a message . . ."

Even with using two hands to hold the phone to her ear, it slipped out of her grasp. Jesse lifted it to his ear for a moment but didn't respond to Miguel's voice. He hung up, giving Hallie a curious look.

"Are you all right?" he asked.

She swallowed the huge lump in her throat, shaking her head. "Hallie is there. She's there with Jamie."

"So this Hallie person didn't die then. And if she didn't die, then you couldn't be her, right?"

Hallie vehemently shook her head, taking deep breaths to calm herself. "I did die. I was Hallie. But how is she still alive? How can that be?"

"How can it be that you're here if you died?"

Her eyes widened. "That's it! Someone got a second chance in my body! With my husband!"

"That's not what I meant."

"But you're right!" Hallie pulled her hair away from her face in a tight ponytail, staring at the blanket. "I'm not the only one! See, there's more of us, getting second chances in other people's bodies. It's possible. God, does Jamie know?"

"Marti, you're talking crazy again. So now you're going to tell me that you're jealous and want your husband back, right?"

She shook her head, the reality sinking to the bottom of her soul. "It doesn't matter; we were getting divorced anyway. I asked him just before I died."

"Oh." He searched for something to say, looking

around the room. "I'm not really sure what to tell you. I'm sorry?"

"You don't have to be sorry. I'm sorry enough for both of us."

Chapter 2

~

For the rest of the day, Jesse kept busy around the house, staying close in case Marti needed him. What a heavy story she'd laid on him that morning! He couldn't ignore the possibility, crazy as it seemed, that it might be true.

Wherever she had called that morning, she'd talked to real people. And knew the numbers by heart. Marti didn't know anyone in California, or some place called Caterina. His curiosity got the better of him, and he figured he deserved some answers. He pressed the redial button on the phone.

"'Mornin', Caterina. May I help you?" a voice sang out.

"Caterina, huh? Where are you located?"

"We be just east of Jamaica, on da Isle of Constantine."

That threw him! That was nowhere near California. "I see. And is there a Hallie DiBarto there?"

"Yah, 'dere is. I can put you through to the house, or to her husband Jamie's office. She do the books in 'dere. Which you like?"

"Uh, no, don't put me through to either. But can I ask you another question? Did Hallie . . . die two months ago? Something to do with her brain?"

"Yes, she be in California when her brain explode, but she come back to life. It was a miracle from God."

So she was from California.

"This is going to sound a bit crazy, but since the brain thing, is she . . . different now?"

"Oh, yah, very different. She and Jamie have da light

of love in dere eyes, you know? You don't want to talk with her?"

"Maybe I already have. Thanks for the information."

Jesse hung up. Hallie DiBarto did exist, she had suffered some kind of stroke in California, and she did have a husband named Jamie. Jesse sauntered over to the front window. Marti wasn't sitting on the swing with slouched shoulders anymore. She was . . . *swinging?*

Every time she reached the bottom of her swing, her shoulders rose up to give her more height. At first he was glad to see her doing something besides moping. When the swing went so high that there was slack at her upward reach, a pang of fear shot through him that she might jump.

He strode across the leaf-strewn ground toward the swings, camouflaging his worry with a smile. "What'cha doing?"

Marti grinned. "You know, I haven't done this since I was in grade school."

She did look as though she were enjoying herself. Her face was regaining its normal shape as the swelling went down. On the forward swing she closed her eyes in the sun; on the backward swing she got lost in the sun-dappled shade beneath the oak tree's upper branches.

"Who built these swings?"

"I did. I put them up for my brother Billy's kids. They haven't gotten much use since his ex-wife, Debbie, took the boys and left town two years ago."

"Why did she leave him?"

"He was a jerk. Spent more time with his fishing buddies than her and the boys. Debbie was going crazy, raising two little hellions by herself, so she dropped 'em off here now and then. When they started thinking of me as their daddy, she put her foot down and moved to Georgia. I get a postcard from 'em every month."

He ducked around her and sat on the other swing. Starting with a casual movement, he maneuvered his swing in sync with hers.

"You look like you're feeling better," he ventured.

"I feel a little more in control. I've accepted that I'm Marti now, no matter who I was or who I am inside."

"So what would make you be in control?"

She shrugged. "Figuring out exactly what I'm going to do."

A thought pushed itself into his mind. *What if she really leaves?* He would be free again. Not that he'd planned on settling down, but he wouldn't have to wait until the baby came before getting back into the racing scene.

Another thought, a surprising one, crept in, too. That was his baby inside her. His. And no matter what inconvenience that baby represented, it was still his responsibility. No, he couldn't let her leave until she had the baby. Then she could do whatever she wanted, and he'd work the rest out somehow.

Hallie sat on the swinging bench out on the front porch that evening. Jesse's question still echoed in her thoughts: What would make you be in control? She'd put that question to deep thought. Certainly waking up from this nightmare would do the trick, but she already knew that wasn't going to happen. Getting back to her home turf would help, but she had some planning to do before she could hop on a bus heading to California. Losing her identity was the hardest part. Hallie looked down at herself. Well, she had an identity, just not her old one. But she was pretty much stuck with this one, and the first step, she decided, was to make it her own. She kept repeating the phrase in her mind: *I am Marti now. That's me, Marti. Marti.* And Marti glanced up as Jesse walked out the front door and sat down beside her, making the whole thing creak and swing.

"Chuck called today, wondering when he could expect you back to work. I told him when you were good and ready. Don't let him push you."

Work? Marti remembered mention of a job before but couldn't remember what it was. Work meant money, and money meant escape to California. That was the second step to gaining control over her life again. She'd already discovered that Marti had only twenty-nine dollars in her savings account, and not even one humble credit card.

"Where did Marti work?"

"She—you work at Bad Boys Diner."

She wrinkled her nose. "A diner? Don't tell me I was a cook."

"No, you're a waitress."

"Oh, gawd. How mundane."

"It was good enough for you before."

"Before was a completely different story. I didn't deliver other people's food and clean up their dirty dishes."

"Well, la-tee-da. Maybe you should have picked a princess' body to pop into."

"I didn't have a choice. I didn't even know what had happened until I was already here." She narrowed her eyes at him, sitting there in the crook of the swing, a smug grin on his face. Marti didn't let herself notice how the muscles bulged beneath his white T-shirt with his arms crossed in front of him. "I personally think I'm being tested." She gave him a pointed look.

"You're being tested?" He gave a hearty laugh, making the swing rock. "If you hadn't been nearly raped, I'd think this was one of those practical joke shows." He rested his ankle on the other leg, clearly enjoying her frustration. "Okay, miss priss from California. What did you do in this other life? CPA? Attorney?"

"I'm not talking to you about it." She looked away from him, concentrating on a squirrel hanging upside down to steal from a bird feeder.

"Ah, you might as well tell me. Maybe you'll have some useful skills."

Her nose wrinkled involuntarily. She met those green eyes of his and realized he was still having fun on her. "I, well, I went to college. And I modeled."

He raised an eyebrow. "You were a model?"

"Don't look so surprised. I didn't look like this. I was tall, blond, and I had a chest."

Jesse regarded her appraisingly. "Nothing wrong with the way you look."

"But this isn't me! I wasn't petite, I was sexy. I even did ads in major magazines. That's how I met my husband."

Jesse leaned back on the swing and propped his feet up on the porch railing. "So this Jamie guy was a model, too?"

She smiled, remembering the first time she'd seen him. A redhead was brushing his hair, flirting freely with him. Jamie's eyes were on Hallie, though, she in a sleek blue sequinned number.

"Yeah, he was a model. He was rich, good-looking, and fun. We got married soon after we met. About a year later he bought part of an island and turned it into a resort."

"If he was so great, why were you a lousy wife?"

Marti's shoulders tensed before she remembered she'd used those exact words earlier. "I didn't appreciate what I had."

"Sounds like you still have that problem."

She glared at him. "What do you mean by that?"

"Well, if I died and got a second chance, I'd be happy in the body of a midget, just to see the sunshine and smell the fresh air some more. Playing along with your crazy game, it seems to me you should be pretty grateful you got a second chance, no matter where you are or what you look like, but all you keep talking about is how rich and gorgeous you used to be."

She ignored his remark about craziness. "I'm thrilled I got another chance, but is it ungrateful to want my old life back? I had a great life, a great husband, more money than I knew what to do with . . . of course I want it back!"

Jesse crossed his bare feet on the railing, leaning back farther on the bench. "If your life was so great, why were you going to leave your good-looking, rich husband?"

She stood up and leaned against a nearby wooden post. "You listen too much, you know that? I said I wasn't smart enough to appreciate what I had when I had it." She sighed. "I wasn't all that smart anyway."

"I thought you went to college."

"I went to three classes, all right? That's when I got into modeling. That seemed a lot more fun than sitting in a classroom. And I made good money at it."

He looked at her, shaking his head almost imperceptibly. She looked away. Why did he put her on edge just sitting there beside her? They sat in silence for a while, static electricity between them. Her past was nothing to be proud of, and she didn't want to share it with anyone, particularly Jesse.

All the times she and Joya went out dancing, flirting . . . *oh, be honest with yourself, picking up men, that's what you were doing*. The day after, on the phone with Joya, they'd talk about how great or how lousy their man had been in bed. Only Hallie had lied most of the time. She'd varied the stories enough so that Joya wouldn't pick up on the fiction of her bedroom tales. The boring truth was that she chickened out most of the time. When she looked like she used to, men expected her to be wild and uninhibited in bed. She just couldn't live up to that image, not even with her husband. Being called a tease was a whole lot better than being called a disappointment.

Jesse rocked the bench, reminding her that he was there. His head was leaning back, a dreamy look on his face. He actually looked kind of cute, when he wasn't irritating her.

"I can't believe my name is really Marti May. At first I thought it was some godawful nickname."

Jesse pulled his gaze away from the oaks where it lazily rested on her. "It's not godawful. That's your maiden name. I almost didn't want you to take my last name, cause yours sounded so cute. But that sorta worked out nice, too."

"What do you mean?"

He looked at her as if she should know all this. "Now your name's Marti May West."

She raised an eyebrow. "Oh, how quaint. And that makes you Jesse West?"

He grinned, bowing slightly. "Jesse James West, if you please. My brother's Billy the kid. And my sister's Calamity Jane West, although my parents didn't want to actually name her Calamity, so they shortened it to Kati."

Marti forced a smile. "Well, it sounds as if your parents had a sense of humor, anyway."

"My pa was obsessed with old Westerns. You're not going to want me to call you Hallie now, are you? I couldn't get used to that."

"No, it'll make things easier if I just adopt Marti's name." Her breath hitched as she realized what he'd said. "Jesse, do you believe me? That I'm really Hallie?"

He shrugged. "I won't say that I do, and I won't say that I don't. But I do know there's something between here and Heaven."

"Why do you say that?"

"It was something weird that happened when I was seventeen. Ah, it was nothing."

Marti sat down next to him. "No, tell me."

He seemed to weigh the sanity of telling her, then probably figured she was as loony as anything he could have encountered.

"It was just before three o'clock in the morning when I woke up out of a sound sleep. My granny was standing there by my bed. She said, 'I'm going now, but don't worry 'bout me none, you hear? God's going to take good care of me. Your pa's up here, too. He says you're doing real good in the races, but you pulled too early in the fifth turn in last Sunday's race. He's proud of you, Jesse.' "

He shook his head. "Then I went back to sleep. It was true; I did cut too early in the fifth turn. The next morning at breakfast I told Ma about the weird dream I'd had. She got the willies, and a minute later, she got the phone call. My granny had passed away in her sleep, they figured around three o'clock that morning." He shrugged. "It's my one claim to fame around the campfire."

"Ooh," Marti said, rubbing the goose bumps from her arms. "That's spooky!"

"I thought that was spooky enough. But then you come along claiming to be some dead woman from California turned up in my wife's body."

"Yeah, I guess that does sound pretty spooky when you put it that way. But it's true, I swear it."

Jesse sank into deep thought again, a contemplative expression on his face. His eyes always seemed to be smiling. After a few minutes, he turned to her.

"So, tell me what dying was like."

Marti pulled her knees up and rested her chin on them. She would make him believe, if it was the last thing she did. "It was scary at first. I'd had these terrible migraines all through my teenage years, and the doctors couldn't find any cause for them. I was . . . talking to Jamie, in California. My head felt like it was going to explode. The pain was worse than I'd ever felt. I went cold, and my arm couldn't move. Then everything went black." She stared off into the bare branches of a nearby oak tree, remembering.

"I didn't wake up until I was in the ambulance. Except it wasn't really waking up. I could see everything clearly, and I could hear the machines beeping. The paramedic said the woman was in a coma; he was moving frantically, giving the woman on the bed shots, feeling pulses. Jamie was there, and he was holding this woman's hand. I was mad at first, that he was holding her hand and not mine. Then I realized the woman was me. My body.

"I panicked at first, trying to get Jamie's attention by yelling, touching him. But no one could hear or see me. I was floating up by the roof of the ambulance."

Marti remembered something else, too, but couldn't share that with him. She was very in tune with feelings, both the paramedic's and Jamie's. From Jamie she could feel concern, his regret and confusion. But not love. He cared, but he didn't love her. She had destroyed that.

She pushed the feeling of loss aside. "When I realized I was dying, I panicked, trying desperately to get back into my body. I wasn't even sure how to do it, but I kept trying anyway. After the initial panic, I felt peace. It's really hard to describe, but it was overwhelming. I have no idea how much time passed while all this was happening. And I remember this whistling sound the whole time, not real loud, but there.

"Then it felt like I was in this dark cave, and I'd gotten there very suddenly. There was someone else with me in this dark place. I say someone, because I don't know how else to explain it. I think it was God. He was a brilliant light, warm and pure. He asked me, but not in a real voice, what I had done with my life. Not in a condemning way, just asking. I'd done nothing with my life, but I felt then that I must do something. I didn't know what, and I still don't. Through this strange kind of communication, I was told that I would get a second chance. That's all I remember. Wherever I was, I was there for two months, until I came here."

Jesse had been watching her carefully the whole time; she had felt his gaze on her.

"I'm glad to know there is something out there, beyond death. I believe in Heaven and God, but I've never heard of anyone getting a second chance in someone else's body."

"Me either. But I did."

Jesse leaned forward to capture her attention. "So there was no angel with a book of names, or a line of people waiting to get into Heaven?"

"No, that's only in the movies."

"And why do you think God gave you a second chance? I mean, did you save someone's life or do something really great?"

"No, I never did anything great. Maybe I got another chance so I *could* do something with my life." Something that didn't involve other people's hearts. She turned to Jesse. "Have you ever been married before?"

"Nope. Didn't plan on it for a while, if ever. I had other things on my mind first."

She tilted her head, finding herself curious about the man who was suddenly her husband. "Like what?"

His eyes sparkled with determination. "Stock car racing. A few months ago an oil company offered me a ride in the ASA." At her blank expression, he added, "They asked if I was interested in driving their car in the American Sports Association. It's to racing what the minor leagues are to baseball. It wasn't final or anything, but that was before you told me you were pregnant. I just couldn't see juggling all the hassles of setting up house and you having a baby while I was on the road every weekend. You can't have that kind of fuzz on your brain while you're driving a hundred and fifty miles per hour."

"So you gave all that up when Marti got pregnant?"

He held a finger up to her. "I didn't give it up. I just put it on hold for a while. I'll get back to it as soon as the baby comes, and I can get another ride. I turned the oil company onto a friend of mine, Mike Ankins, and now he's driving for them."

Marti could see that spark of anger, held so carefully in check, in those eyes of his. She wondered if he would have ever forgiven Marti for getting herself pregnant. "Do you race around here?"

"We've got a track on the edge of town. It's a good starting ground, but I didn't think I'd be back to it so soon." He sighed. "For now I'll just keep beating the local boys."

"You must be pretty good."

"When it comes to racing, I'm not modest—I'm damn good. Cars have been part of my life since I was three years old. Making 'em run and making 'em run fast, that's what I live for."

"Is that how you make your living? Racing cars?"

"I wish. For now"—he shot a meaningful look at her stomach—"I've got to keep fixing other people's cars down at Harry's Garage."

She glanced at his hands, remembering the black grease encrusted in the ridges of her Porsche mechanic's fingers. Jesse's were spotless.

Long after the sun went down, she and Jesse walked inside. Gravity pulled her down, making her eyelids feel like concrete. She glanced toward the bedroom, then at Jesse. The couch looked a bit too short for his tall frame. She thought of the water bed, warm and comfortable.

"Jesse, why don't you let me sleep on the couch? I don't want to kick you out of your bed again."

He stretched his arms upward, his untucked shirt revealing a slice of tan, flat stomach. "That's awfully nice of you, doll, but I thought we'd both sleep in the bedroom. We're adults, and that's one big bed in there. We can find a bed and put it in the second bedroom for you later."

Marti nodded, not sure how at ease she would be sleeping with a strange man. She wasn't tempted, she assured herself. Jesse was good-looking, strong, virile . . . but he just wasn't her type. He was too country-ish, too good ole' boy. And those good ole' boys were gentlemen, weren't they? What could possibly happen? And why did her stomach tingle every time he called her "doll"?

"Sounds fine. Maybe we can get a bed this weekend."

"Yeah, we can do that."

When Jesse walked out of the bedroom, she slipped into the oversize Garth Brooks T-shirt she'd found earlier. She slid over to one side of the bed and wrapped the sheets around her, facing the dresser. Everything felt so much more real tonight—the scent of Jesse's cologne from the bathroom, the feel of the cotton sheets against her skinny legs. Just as real were her memories of the past, of Jamie. He was a good man, and once he'd been warm and affectionate. In the last year of their marriage he'd become cold, withdrawn. Had she caused that?

Yes, she probably had. She was self-destructive. Love had been hers once, and she'd destroyed it. Would it be any different just because she was in a new body? Doubtful.

It could have only been a few hours after Jesse had finally drifted off to sleep when he heard her scream. She was sitting straight up in bed, the sheets pulled up to her chin, her eyes wide. Then he heard Bumpus barking and growling as though he had cornered a demon.

"Somebody's out there!" she whispered frantically.

"It's probably just a coon, but stay here just in case." Jesse was up with his rifle in hand by the time he'd reached the bedroom door. Bumpus raced back and forth in front of the large window, leaping up on the couch to peer out and snarl.

"Why is he doing that?" an urgent whisper asked behind him.

He whirled around. "Geez, you could get yourself shot sneaking up on a guy with a rifle!"

She looked at the gun, then up at him. "What is going on?"

He leaned forward and opened the door. "Check it out, boy." Bumpus made the sound of eight elephants as he charged across the damp leaves.

Jesse looked out the window, watching the dog race into the darkness, his barks fading out. What had he seen? His fingers tensed on the rifle as he fought the urge to walk out there and find out for himself. But he didn't want to leave Marti alone in the house either. A few minutes later, Bumpus trotted back, his mouth stretched in that funny grimace when he missed his quarry. Usually a lizard or mouse.

Then Jesse turned around to face her. "Didn't I tell you to stay in bed?"

She put her hands on her hips, looking up at him indignantly. "I'm not staying in there by myself when that crazy dog of yours is barking up a storm."

"Come on, let's go back to bed."

She stared out the front window for a second before letting him lead her back to the bedroom. "What did he go after?"

"I don't know. It was probably a raccoon." He wasn't so sure.

He didn't want to talk anymore, to let on how fired up the thought of confronting Marti's attacker had him. He had been ready to find someone standing out in the hall, waiting to finish what he might have already done: kill Marti. Jesse's finger was still crooked, ready to pull the trigger. The rage had him shaking.

Chapter 3

~

Marti hadn't gotten much sleep after Bumpus's barking attack. Shadows had her jumping, frightened of some faceless man with his fingers outstretched.

As soon as Jesse stirred, she sat up and stretched. He turned over on his back, and she found herself grinning at his early morning hairdo. Just as she was about to say something, a strange twinge lighted in her stomach. Hunger? Ooh, the thought of food turned the twinge into a full-blown twist.

"Crackers are in the top drawer over there."

She looked at Jesse, then at the drawer he was pointing to. Inside was half a package of saltines. She grimaced as another wave of nausea washed over her, then quickly stuck one in her mouth.

"Please don't tell me I have morning sickness," she said through a mouthful of crackers.

"Okay, I won't."

As she swallowed the lump of chewed-up cracker, she held her stomach and ran with as much dignity as she could muster into the bathroom.

"You okay in there?" Jesse called from the other side of the door a few minutes later.

"Sure, just fine and dandy," she mumbled into the towel pressed against her face as she emerged.

He rolled out of bed, making it move up and down, up and down. She looked elsewhere.

"You ready for some breakfast?"

She shot him a dirty look. "You've got to be joking. I don't feel like eating anything for the next two days."

He leaned close and put his hand on her stomach. "I don't think he'd like that too much." With a smile, he disappeared into the hallway and was soon clattering pots and pans.

She looked down at herself, then called out, "What makes you think it's a boy?"

"That's what I want it to be. And I always get what I want," he called from the kitchen.

She shook her head. Exasperating male, she could already tell.

Jesse poured two glasses of orange juice and put them on the table as she walked into the kitchen. Marti dropped down into the chair and took a sip. She found herself studying the line of muscling down his arms, his broad shoulders and the faint spray of dark hair that sprouted from the indent in his chest. With every movement, his muscles moved and rippled beneath his tan skin. She used to enjoy watching Jamie swim his laps, marveling at how beautiful the male body could be. This time she marveled at Jesse. No doubt his muscles didn't come from swimming laps in a pool.

"Do you work out?"

He gave her an odd look. "I don't lift weights at the gym, if that's what you mean." He flipped the eggs, then asked, "What makes you ask that?"

"Just wondered. You're . . . you've got a nice build."

He shrugged. "I don't much think about it. Working on engines and pushing cars into the garage are my weights." He lifted hands cleaner than most of the pampered men she'd known had, though they had their fair share of callouses. "My boss gives me hell for putting more effort into washing my hands than anything else."

Good grief, let's stop talking about his body, Marti. Food's safer. "You're not making grits, are you?"

"Not unless you want 'em. I hate 'em."

"I thought everybody down South liked grits."

"I guess I'm not everybody, then. I've always hated 'em." He leaned on the counter separating the kitchen and eating area. "And speaking of cooking, my gourmet abilities end with breakfast."

"Meaning?"

"I could use your help in the kitchen."

"Well, as far as cooking goes, I'm useless. I forget about boiling water and it all burns out. I can't even get Jell-O to set! Why don't you get a cook?" Then she realized what she was saying. "I mean, we could eat out a lot."

Jesse smirked. "In case you haven't noticed the fine selection of restaurants Chattaloo offers, we have one pizza place, two diners, and a deli. I think we'd get tired of that real quick."

"I'm telling you, I cannot cook."

"We'll have to fix that, won't we?"

She did not want to cook, did not even want to talk about it. Time to change the subject again.

"I want to go back to work," she told him as he set down a plate of toast and jam in front of her, waffles and bacon in front of him.

"Are you sure you're ready?"

"As ready as I'll ever be."

He shrugged. "When? Tomorrow?"

"Yeah. I don't suppose you could give me any training tips on the waitressing part, huh?"

"Oh, that's right. A model from California wouldn't know much about that working-class thing."

As if he really believed her! "My experience ends with a six-month stint at a beachside burger joint, and the customers came to me for the food and threw away the plates and utensils when they were done."

"Being on the receiving end of the restaurant process, I wouldn't be much help. Kati'd be your best bet. I could just stick to the story I already told them, which is you don't remember much since the attack. I was going to ask you if you wanted to have dinner over at Ma's tonight anyway. She and Kati have been calling and asking when they can see you."

"Might as well get it over with tonight." As if meeting his family wouldn't be hard enough. Now she was facing her first speaking part as Marti May West.

As they drove over to Jesse's mother's house that evening, Marti was starting to feel a little nervous. Money, escape. She kept telling herself that she had to go through this process before she could get back to California.

"Does your mother like Marti? She probably hated the woman who trapped her son into marrying her."

Jesse sent her an odd look, then shook his head and concentrated on his driving again. "I don't know. She's definitely not used to the idea of me being married and expecting a kid and all. Heck, I'm not either." Marti saw the almost imperceptible tightening of his fingers around the steering wheel. "Besides, none of us could prove you got pregnant on purpose."

"We'll never know now." She leaned over and turned down the radio. "Can't we listen to something other than country music?"

Jesse turned the volume up again, giving her a stern look. "Never, ever, turn down Sawyer Brown in my truck."

"Oh, excuse me. I didn't know the rules."

"Well, now you do."

How was she supposed to discern between Sawyer Brown and all the other crooning country singers? Prince, En Vogue, L.L. Cool J: She could have an intelligent conversation about them. She wondered if her fidgeting hands in her lap betrayed her nervousness.

He took the curve rapidly, his hands firmly on the wheel. Strong hands and long fingers, she noted. Hardly nothing sexier than strong hands. She averted her attention to the dirt roads that spread out like fingers to the right. On the left was a country-club style golf course.

"I wouldn't expect to see a golf course around here," she said.

"Didn't think country hicks liked golf, did you?"

She shot him a look. "I didn't mean it like that." Well, she did, sort of.

"Me and Mike and Alan play golf here in the summer, when the snowbirds go back up north."

"You play golf?" She tried to picture Jesse teeing up in yellow pants and a green checkered shirt, but the image was incongruous.

Jesse's tone dropped to a low, Southern drawl. "Yep, 'magine that, a redneck like me playin' that there golfin' game. 'Course, for a while we thought hittin' a birdie was aimin' fer a blue jay or somethin'. Poor birds didn't know what hit 'em! H'yuck, h'yuck!"

She slapped his arm, trying to keep the smile from her lips. "Yeah, yeah." She still couldn't see him playing golf. And she couldn't figure out why her fingers tingled where they'd touched his bare arm.

When he stopped at the one traffic light on the main road, he turned in his seat. "I've heard of people having strokes, and certain areas of their brain getting zapped so that they don't remember their past. Do you think that while you were being strangled, those parts of your brain were deprived of oxygen too long? I'm serious, Marti," he added at her impatient expression.

"Have you ever heard of those people remembering pasts that were not their own? I know you're looking for some logical explanation; I was looking too, that whole time I was in the hospital. But I remember my other life, up until the time my brain felt like it exploded and I saw the brilliant light."

He bit his lower lip, tapping a beat on the top of the steering wheel before shaking his head slightly.

"I know a way to tell if you're Marti or not. It's an instinctual kind of thing. Are you willing to do it?"

"Do what?"

"Uh-uh, can't tell you. You'll just have to go along with it. That is, if you want me to believe your story."

She narrowed her eyes at him, weighing the sanity of it. What could it be? Probably taking her to the place Marti had been attacked to see if she had any reaction.

"Fine, do what you have to."

As Marti prepared for him to turn the truck around, he leaned forward and kissed her, pressing her against the window. His mouth engulfed hers, his tongue instantly thrusting inside her mouth. For a moment, she felt dizzy, and her stomach did flip-flops. As her mind told her hands to push him away, her mouth became independent, responding to him in that instinctual way he had spoken of. Where his hand rested on her thigh, a warmth spread to tickle her erogenous zones. Why was he kissing her like this? her mind asked. Who cares? her body answered, drowning in the sensations.

In a second, those sensations ceased abruptly, and Jesse leaned against his side of the truck with a resounding thud against the door. The air in the cab seemed supercharged, and she merely stared at him for a second, trying to figure out if that had all been some kind of weird vision or if it had really happened. His expression seemed the same, yet his slightly parted lips, still moist from their kiss, seemed evidence enough to her pounding heart.

She didn't wait to catch her breath. "W-why'd you do that?"

He rubbed his fingers across his lips. "The test."

Marti straightened, feeling abused and humiliated. *"That* was your test? To see if I'm really Marti?" Gathering her pride, she said, "I mean, what kind of test was that? To attack me like some animal?"

"I wasn't attacking you. I just wanted to see how you kissed. In comparison with how you used to kiss."

She felt a pang of disappointment she couldn't explain. "So, did I pass or fail?"

He ran his fingers lightly over his lips again. "I'd have to say it was inconclusive. It was different, but I have to take the element of surprise into it."

"Don't tell me you have to kiss me again," she said, hoping he didn't pick up that ridiculous tremor in her voice.

"No, I don't think it would do much good."

Marti held onto her seat as the truck lurched through the green light. Luckily her hands were occupied or she might have slapped him or something. How dare he tell her that kissing her again wouldn't do much good! How dare he kiss her like that in the first place! Who cared if he believed her or not? She crossed her arms tightly over her chest and ignored Jesse . . . and the tingling of her lips.

She studied the scenery as if her life depended on it, putting her full concentration to it. The tension inside the cab seemed to ease as minutes of silence slid by. Most of the houses in the area were small and quaint.

One had a swamp buggy named "Troublemaker" out front.

Marti saw the Bad Boys Diner before Jesse pointed it out. It was an old building, and the lines of the brick showed through the once-white paint. On the faded sign that stood high next to the road was a pudgy boy in a cowboy hat with a devilish grin. In a small corral, five mannequins clad in vests and ten-gallon hats were in the middle of an old-fashioned shootout. One had a missing arm, but she doubted it had been shot off by the cowboy holding the six-shooter across from him. She wouldn't have thought about eating at a place like that, much less working there.

"It's been around for as long as I can remember, although Chuck's only owned it for a couple of years now since he moved into town. He bought those cowboys from some barbecue place up north, and he's proud of 'em, so don't tease him about 'em. When people talk about Bad Boy's waterfront dining, that's when the parking lot gets flooded after a good rain."

Downtown quickly dwindled away after the Chattaloo River Hotel. Stands of pine and oak trees with the occasional farm seemed to be all there was for a few miles. Jesse pulled onto a dirt road into a quiet area that was less developed than the one in front of Jesse's house. He drove down a driveway overshadowed by oaks and maples to a small, two-story house.

"This is where I grew up," Jesse said as he got out of the truck. As he looked around, he seemed to inhale a hundred memories of childhood. From the smile on his face, she could only guess they were happy ones. Marti envied him that, for she could hardly bring herself to think about her childhood at all.

Two beagles jumped off the front porch and lazily made their way to the truck, barking with tails wagging happily. Though they were smaller and not ugly like Bumpus, she still moved closer to Jesse.

He crouched down to greet them. "Hey, fellows. Come out to greet your ole' buddy, huh?" Leaning to look at Marti, he said, "This one's Trick, and the smaller one's Treat. Aw, don't look at 'em like that, Marti.

They're so old, they'd have to take a nap before even thinking about chomping at a fly. They used to jump all over me when I'd come home. Now they just bark and wag their tails."

She sensed the slight tone of melancholy in his voice, but couldn't imagine why he'd want them jumping on him.

Hallie followed Jesse into the cozy home, feeling like an outsider. The wooden floors creaked a little beneath the braided rug. The television was tuned to a game show.

"Hey, Ma," he called out.

"In the kitchen, hon."

Helen West was standing at the sink. He walked over to her, gently wrapping his powerful arms around the woman, and rested his chin on her shoulder. Hallie wondered why the action made her swell inside, when it didn't even involve her. Still, she bit her lip and stifled a smile.

After a second, his mother turned toward Marti. Helen was tall and curvy, with blond hair and round, brown eyes. She was wearing designer jeans and a lacy, long-sleeved cotton blouse. She walked over and took Marti's hands in hers. Marti vaguely remembered seeing her at the hospital when she was fitfully dozing.

"I'm so glad you're here, Marti. Jesse said you needed some time alone, but it was everything I could do to keep myself from rushing right over to make sure you were okay."

"I—I appreciate your concern, Helen. I'm okay now."

Helen placed a pink, manicured thumb to Marti's cheek. "Those bruises are getting better. You poor baby. It's scary, knowing something like this could happen here in our little town. I've always felt so safe here. Are you all right, really?"

Marti nodded, a lie. Helen still had her soft, warm hands around Marti's. She wasn't at all what Marti had envisioned when they'd pulled up: a haggard woman with gray hair tied up in a bun and hands clean-weary.

"Stop it, Billy!" a voice ordered from just outside the door. When the door opened, two calm people stepped through. From Jesse's description, the man was his brother, Billy, and the girl had to be his sister, Kati. She was Marti's height and thin, with a mane of golden hair that curled and fluffed around her face. Her eyes were almost a seafoam green, bright and fringed with long, golden lashes. Kati walked over to Marti and hugged her hard. Marti hesitantly put her arms around the slender frame.

After a moment, Kati stepped back. "I was so worried about you! Then Jesse wouldn't let us come over"—she shot a dirty look at him—"and we thought the worst. But you look okay, considering. It must have been awful! No, don't tell me about it. Unless you want to, that is." Kati's energy spilled over, filling the room.

"There's nothing to say about it, really. I don't remember a thing."

Kati's hair washed over her shoulders, and coming from it was a skinny, white rope that hung down among the mass. It didn't match the blue handkerchief headband Kati was wearing, and Marti was considering asking what it was when the "rope" suddenly moved up to form a mustache just above Kati's lips.

"Jed! How rude!"

Marti's eyes were wide enough to allow aircraft landings. The "rope" dropped down and disappeared, and from inside Kati's hair appeared a little gray face with quivering whiskers.

"Th-there's something in your hair!" Marti screamed.

Kati smiled, but it was tinged with question. She reached in and disentangled a furry black-and-white creature from her hair. "Don't you remember Jed?"

Marti glanced at Jesse, chastising him for not warning her about this—this thing she was supposed to remember. When she looked back, Kati was holding it out, its four tiny feet and tail extended in all directions. Marti moved back.

"She doesn't remember some of her past," Jesse said.

Kati looked confused. "How could you forget this cute guy?" she asked, nuzzling the creature.

"What is it?" Marti asked, trying to keep the disgust from her face.

"Jed's a rat. Not like the ones that live out in the fields or in the attic. He comes from a pet store."

It was then that Marti noticed Billy still standing by the door. He wasn't as tall as Jesse, and in fact didn't look much like him. He had beady brown eyes, a thin mustache and long wavy hair that was receding in front. She turned back to Kati.

Marti swallowed hard, trying to force a smile. A rat. For a pet. God, get her back to California! Sure, they had pet iguanas out there, but not rats. At least lizards were fashionable.

"Dean's coming over tonight," Kati announced after dinner. After a glance at Marti, she added, "Hope that's okay."

Jesse leaned back in his chair. "So what's Dean coming over for, anyway?"

Billy wiggled his arched eyebrows. "They're gonna neck on the front porch."

"Billy, shut up! He's helping me study for my test next week, as if it was any business of yours."

"What kind of classes are you taking?" Marti asked.

"Don't you remember? I'm taking classes at the community college." Kati smiled with pride. "I'm getting my associate's degree. Someday I'm going to be a veterinarian."

Marti hoped to have that same look in her eyes, as soon as she figured out what she wanted to do.

The sound of the beagles barking outside made Kati jump up and head over to the door. A tall young man with a medium build walked in. He had dark, curly hair and eyes that looked warm and mischievous at once. Dean, Marti surmised.

"Howdy, Kati," he said with a drawl more pronounced than the Wests'. He nodded toward Billy, Jesse, and Helen, but his expression changed when he saw Marti. He immediately walked up to her and gave her a hug.

"I heard somebody hurt you," he said.

Marti was a bit startled by his forwardness, but the

sincerity in his brown eyes made her feel more comfortable.

Kati strode up to stand next to Dean. "You remember Dean, don't you?" To Dean she said, "She lost some of her memory."

"No, I don't. Nice to see you again, though."

"I heard you was attacked," Dean said. "I had an aunt that was attacked, too."

"I'm sorry to hear that," Marti said.

"It was by a herd of bees, though."

Marti's gaze dropped to the floor for a minute to gain composure. "That's . . . really terrible."

"Yeah, it was. She had stings all over her body, all puffed up and red." Dean demonstrated by pointing to areas on his body and puffing his cheeks out.

Jesse interrupted him. "Dean, that's a real interesting story, but I've got to"—he looked around the table, then grabbed a handful of lettuce from the salad bowl—"feed Jed."

Dean's expression was contemplative as he scratched his chin. "Is that a herd of bees, or a pack?"

Jesse merely laughed as he escaped to the living room to drop the lettuce into Jed's cage. The words from the television pulled his attention to where "In The News Today" continued their broadcast. As if held in a trance, he walked over to the couch and sat down in front of the set.

A thin man in a dress shirt and tie looked incongruous amid tropical foliage and people in bathing suits lounging around a sparkling pool. "On our Americans Away From Home story today, Californians Jamie and Hallie DiBarto ran into some serious trouble in paradise last weekend. I'm here on the Isle of Constantine, just east of Jamaica. Mick Gentry, who lives in the same part of California the DiBartos are from flew to Caterina, the resort the DiBartos own, stalked the couple for several days, then broke in and viciously ripped Mrs. DiBarto from her bed as she was sleeping. Gentry slammed Mr. DiBarto over the head with a metal pipe before taking his wife along this beach and over those rocks where he had a sailboat anchored offshore." The camera followed the deadly route along the beach and over a hill of sharp-edged boulders.

"Barely holding on to consciousness, Mr. DiBarto dragged himself to the raft Gentry was struggling with as Mrs. DiBarto fought him. He managed to tilt the raft, then knocked Gentry unconscious and dragged him to the shore.

"The DiBartos, still shaken about the ordeal, agreed to grant us a short interview." A beautiful blond woman sat in one of the swinging chairs that surrounded the bar. She could definitely be a model, Jesse thought, feeling a strange tightness in his chest. Beside her sat a handsome blond man, everything Jesse pictured when Marti described Jamie.

"Did you know the man who tried to kidnap you, Mrs. DiBarto?"

"Yes. He was . . . an old lover from a lifetime ago. He was very jealous when I broke things off. I wanted to leave Mick and that whole life behind me," Hallie said, looking at her husband with determination.

"And what about Mick Gentry, you might ask," the reporter said, now standing outside a stucco building surrounded by a curious crowd of colorfully dressed black people. The camera focused on a hand-painted tin sign swinging in the breeze that read JAIL. "Mick Gentry spent a little time here, in this primitive, four foot-by-four foot jail cell." As the reporter stepped inside the dark room, a thin black man in uniform demonstrated incarceration, waving his hands through the bars. "The most serious crime in this village of three hundred people is the occasional rumsoaker, as they call the drunks here. Strangely enough, Mick was released without any further punishment other than being banned from the island forever."

"Dat loony be gone, mon," Bailey, the jail keep, said. "Dey all make some deal, and send him from our island." The dark man smiled. "But we keep da' sailboat."

"We just wanted him off the island," Hallie said in a clip from the earlier interview. "There's no reason for him to come back again."

"And so," the reporter finished, "the DiBartos continue rebuilding their lives the best that they can, and only time will tell if old wounds heal."

"Wow, the power of obsession," a woman at a round desk said, closing the story. "Coming up, a troupe of bungee jumping grannies . . ."

Jesse tuned out the rest, stunned. Jamie, Hallie, the island resort. All that craziness Marti had told him . . . Jesse now believed it was true. It was hard to imagine that the woman in Marti's body had looked like the Hallie on television. No wonder she wanted her old body back. He closed his mouth for the first time since hearing "Isle of Constantine" and marched into the kitchen.

"There you are," Helen said. "Would you please start on those dish—"

Jesse took Dean's arm with one hand, and Billy's with the other. "Why don't you two fellows take a walk down by the river for a few minutes? I have something to talk to the girls about, and it's kinda personal."

Billy laughed. "What, you gonna talk about periods or something?"

Jesse didn't answer, just steered the two toward the swinging door. Dean looked apprehensively toward the river, then at Billy.

"He won't throw you in again." Jesse gave his brother a meaningful squeeze on the shoulder. "Will you, Billy?"

Billy leered. "No, 'course not." He put an arm around Dean, then looked at Jesse. "You girls have a nice talk now."

Jesse turned to find all three women watching him, waiting. He tried to picture Marti as the tall blonde, but just couldn't. "Okay, sit down. I've got something to tell you."

Marti felt an uncomfortable pressure in her chest as they all sat down at the table, still cluttered with serving dishes and crumbs. Kati and Helen were giving her questioning looks, but Marti could only give them a blank shrug.

"Ma, Kati." Jesse turned to Marti. "I'd like you to meet Hallie DeBarto."

Marti looked at him with mouth agape. What was he doing? "Jesse."

He put his hand on her arm. "I want to tell them the truth."

And he did, from her inability to recognize him at the hospital, to their conversation on the swings, and when he'd called Caterina back by hitting the redial button. Marti herself could only nod to this fact or that, not only because Jesse had taken over, but she couldn't think of anything to say in her shock at his belief. After he'd finished, both Kati and Helen sat back in their chairs with confused expressions on their faces.

"Is this some kind of joke?" Helen asked.

"Would I joke about something like this?"

Marti smiled. So he did believe her. Had that kiss proven it? No, she didn't want to think about that blasted kiss. Then her gaze moved to Helen and Kati. Their expressions were mixed now as they looked at her.

"It's all true," she added.

"The reason I told you is that Marti's going to need help in the next few months, and it'll be a lot easier if you two know what's going on. But I don't want anyone else to know, even Billy. No telling who he'll blab off to. Kati, I need you to give Marti a quick waitressing lesson tomorrow when she goes back to work. Maybe you can get there early and show her the ropes. Kati?"

Kati snapped out of the stare she was giving Marti. "She's really someone different? It's not just a memory lapse?"

Marti fiddled with a napkin. "I'm really someone else. This is all . . . new to me, the small town, being a waitress." She tried not to wrinkle her nose. "I feel like I'm on a different planet, all alone."

Helen hesitantly reached over and touched her hand. "You're not alone." She kept looking at Jesse, maybe to make sure it wasn't all a joke. Or insanity. "We're just glad you're here, and that both you and the baby are all right."

It was acceptance, tentative, but acceptance all the

same. The best she could hope for, considering. She so longed to be a part of a family like Jesse's. She was coming in under more unusual circumstances than the real Marti had, and still they accepted her.

As soon as Marti and Jesse were enclosed in the privacy of the truck cab, she turned and asked, "What possessed you to tell them the truth about me? And why in jiminy's name didn't you warn me?"

Telling her about the story he'd heard on "In the News Today" would only make her worry about that other life, and possibly send her scurrying off to the Isle of Constantine. No, he didn't want that, not just yet. He settled on the half-truth, the best he could do.

"I was watching you all evening, at dinner and around my family, and I realized that you really aren't Marti anymore. I believe you."

"Was it the kiss?" she asked, her throaty voice sounding odd.

The kiss. He knew what he was trying to prove until the moment his lips touched hers, and then he forgot how the old Marti even kissed those few times. The way Marti responded was far different than the way she used to, which lacked anything that would make his heart go as fast as his race car.

"Forget that," he said, wishing he could. "It was just everything, that's all."

She looked away for a moment, then back at him, her expression softer. "You really do believe me?"

"Yes. And I figured that if I believed you, then I couldn't carry on the lie. Now Billy and Dean, I don't know as I'd trust them with this crazy secret, but I trust Ma and Kati. I just didn't have the chance to talk it over with you."

"Oh."

Jesse started up the truck, but he turned to her before putting it in gear. "You know, that was almost as hard as the first time, when I told them you were pregnant and we were going to get married."

"What, telling them about who I am?"

"Yeah. I wasn't sure if Ma would throw me outta the

house or have the men in the white coats haul me away."

She rolled her eyes. "Too much time spent here, and the men in the white coats will be hauling *me* away!"

While Jesse took a shower, Marti wandered around the living room and scanned the photos on one wall. She stopped at a picture of Jesse standing next to a black Nova with a yellow thirteen on the side. He held up a trophy, wearing a triumphant smile. Another black-and-white picture was of the front of a car, parked in a garage with the hood up. Sticking out of the roomy engine was an older man with Billy's beady eyes and same silly grin she'd seen earlier.

"That's my dad," Jesse's voice said from behind her.

"Geez!" she said, turning to face him with her hand on her heart. "And you yelled at me for sneaking up on you the other night!"

He shrugged, looking boyish with his towel-ruffled hair. "You're not carrying a rifle."

She narrowed her eyes at him. "I wish I was." Turning back to the engine shot, she said, "What happened to him? You said something about your grandmother seeing him in Heaven."

"It was a freak accident during the grand finale of the stock car season—demolition derby. A guy from Arcadia hit Dad just right, and his gas tank exploded. There was nothing they could do for him." He was staring at his father's picture.

"And you still race?"

"I couldn't not race. It's my life. I made my car to look like his, so in a way, he's there racing with me."

She looked at him, saw the burning determination in his eyes. "You must have been mad at Marti for getting pregnant."

He shrugged, then leaped over the side of the couch to land in a sitting position. She walked around front, seeing nothing in his closed expression.

"Jesse, it's normal to feel anger at something that takes your dream away."

"That's the way life is," he said, each word a block of ice.

She sat down next to him, wishing he would open up a little. The mixture of deodorant and soap was intoxicating. Since the couch sagged in the middle, she found herself leaning against his bare arm. Why the feel of his skin bothered her, she didn't know. She made a casual movement out of scooting a foot away from him.

When he stretched, he seemed like a lion, strong and intense. His arms reached up over his head, leaving her to stare at the depth of his chest, the rib bones that dropped off to a flat stomach. Her gaze traveled lower where his hips were encased in blue jeans, where the muscles of his legs showed even through the thick denim.

She forced her thoughts and gaze toward the television. *None of those thoughts for you, Marti. Haven't you already learned that you do nothing but destroy anyone who loves you? Not that Jesse would ever love you. And what are you going to do, my precocious libido? Lure me into lust with him so it's harder to leave? No way, I'm smarter than that now. Yessiree, much smarter.* Strangely, the biggest urge she had at the moment was to crawl into his arms and ask him to hold her tight. Just hold her.

"Who's Mick Gentry?"

She hoped he didn't hear her sharp intake of breath at the unexpected question. "Where did you hear his name?" Marti wanted to buy a few seconds to think his question through.

He shrugged, pretending a casualness she knew wasn't wholly there. "You said the name once, in your sleep."

"Oh. What else did I say?"

"Nothing I could understand, just his name. So, who is he?"

She pulled a throw pillow onto her lap, fiddling with the edge of braided rope. "He was . . . a mistake. A man I met in California, the wrong kind of friend to make."

"Was that all he was, a friend?"

Marti looked Jesse in the eye, straightening up a little. "He was the best part of dying. And so you don't think all I ever did was blow my life on mistakes, I'll just leave it at that, okay?"

He shrugged again, but his eyes kept studying her in that thoughtful way of his. "Do you ever wonder what happened to him?"

What was he talking about? "No, not really. I don't know what the woman who took my place is like, but she's obviously smart enough to figure out who the right man in her life is. Mick's probably in France sulking. Why do you want to know?"

"Just wondering, Marti. Just wondering."

Chapter 4

~

It was still dark when Jesse led Marti out to the truck the next morning. He'd told her he was taking her to work until he'd had a look at her car. It only needed gas, but he wanted to have some control over her movements for a while. Bumpus followed them out, wagging his tail. Jesse glanced at Marti's downcast expression, then back at Bumpus. The dog was used to accompanying Jesse to work at the garage.

"Another time, boy."

It was odd, but she didn't look right in the little dress with the Bad Boy on the apron anymore. He knew she hated it, a California model in a polyester waitress uniform, but he'd reminded her how lucky she was to even wear the thing. He reached over and touched her chin, lifting it to face him.

"Cheer up, doll."

Something warm lit in her brown eyes, and she smiled. He didn't know why he was calling her that now. The word just seemed to slip out of his mouth. He removed his hand, suddenly feeling too intimate with her.

"I'll be okay. Once I get used to it."

"You'll be fine."

A few minutes later, he pulled into the dusty parking lot of Bad Boys Diner. Kati's compact car was sitting out front, though only the inside lights were on. As promised, Kati had shown up early to show Marti the ropes.

"Take good care of her," he said to Kati. "She's feeling queasy this morning." He gestured to his stomach and made a rolling motion with his hand.

"Ah, I won't beat her up too hard."

Marti nodded. "I'll do the best I can. As soon as I learn what I need to do." She looked around, scanning the long countertop, the tables scattered around.

Jesse touched her arm. "Good luck. I'll see you at lunch."

He walked away, feeling almost like a father might after taking his daughter to her first day of school. Ah, she'd be fine.

With Kati's good grace, and smaller than usual section, Marti somehow made it through the breakfast crowd. By ten only a few people lingered, reading the paper and drinking coffee, requiring only the occasional fill up.

Kati looked at the clock. "The owner should be here any minute. Chuck usually gets here after the breakfast crowd."

As if on cue, a short, skinny man in his thirties nearly crashed through the door. He surveyed the few people in the diner and headed right to Kati.

"How was the breakfast crowd? Better than this, I hope."

"Chuck, you ask me that every morning. Why don't you come in earlier so you can see us actually feeding people?"

"Yeah, yeah." Chuck stopped when he looked at Marti. "Gawd, you look awful. Do you want to scare the customers away with those bruises?"

With that, he walked back into the kitchen. Marti looked at Kati with widened eyes.

"Do I look that bad?"

"You look fine. Sensitivity isn't his strong point. Before the hour is up, he'll be asking you, in his gruff way, how you're feeling."

Marti glanced at Chuck, now wearing a white baseball cap and moving purposefully around the kitchen as he talked to the other cook. He glanced up at her before quickly looking away. "I hope he doesn't say anything to me at all."

Fifty-two minutes later, Chuck walked over to where

Marti was wiping down the counter. "D'ya know who did it?"

She shook her head, wishing he would go away. "No, I don't remember anything about it."

"Probably better."

"Yeah, probably."

He looked at her for a minute past the comfortable limit. "Do you think you'll ever remember?"

"I don't think so."

He shrugged. "Sick son of a bitch outta pay for what he done. Well, I'm glad you're back. That table over there needs clearing." With that he walked back to the kitchen.

When she relayed the strange conversation, Kati didn't think it sounded out of the ordinary for Chuck. Marti wondered. He did seem concerned about her remembering her attacker. Would it be his face Marti could remember? He was watching her again when she glanced toward the kitchen.

A while later, a woman walked in and sat down at the counter. She had a barrel-body, with short, almost-white blond hair, and a phony smile. Marti glanced at Kati, who sidled over.

"That's Donna Hislope. She's a gossip and general bitch. A while back she had a thing for Jesse, and he pretty much gave her the brush-off. Definitely not his type. Anyway, that's the history. Go see what kind of venom she wants."

"Goody." Marti hesitantly walked over and asked, "So, Donna, what can I get for you?"

She picked up the menu and looked it over. "Um, diet soda—no, make that a chocolate shake. That's all. Gotta watch my weight."

"Here you go." Marti set down the shake a few minutes later. Just as she was about to make an escape, Donna spoke to her.

"You look pretty good. I mean, considering what happened to you."

Marti turned around, forcing a smile. "Why, thank you."

"It must have been awful."

"I don't remember anything about it."

Donna's mouth twitched. "I bet they don't catch him. He was probably just passing right on through. Do you think he was just a drifter? Probably, huh?"

How could she assure the woman? Marti thought bitterly. Wasn't it supposed to be the other way around? "It could be just about anyone. Even someone you see every day."

Marti walked back to the other side of the counter, pretending to clean a dirty spot. The scary truth was that it could be someone in town. She could be fairly certain it wasn't Jesse, not with the tenderness he'd shown. It probably wasn't Dean; he looked too innocent. Only two people stood out as strange so far—Chuck and Billy.

As the clock ticked toward eleven, various people started trickling in for lunch. Kati made a point to clean something nearby and whisper each new person's identity, as she had that morning. Three young men walked in, shoving each other jovially as they dropped down into a booth in Marti's section. Kati scooted over to Marti.

"See the redhead in the overalls?" He was heavy, and his body was littered with pieces of dried grass. "That's Josh. He's probably been mowing lawns. Skip is the skinny blonde with the blue and white hanky around his neck."

"Looks like a German Shepherd I saw once. Who's the other guy?" He was dark-haired, tall, and nicely built, wearing dress pants and a crisp, white shirt.

"That's Paul Paton, the sheriff's son. This week he's selling insurance. He's kinda cute, but a little immature, if you know what I mean."

"He sure looks mature," Marti observed.

"Be careful around him. He and Jesse are like two fighting tomcats; you never know what Paul will do just to piss him off. In fact, don't get friendly with any of them. They're all jerks to the max."

Marti smoothed her skirt down, pulling out her pad and pen. "Why do Jesse and Paul fight?"

"There's bad blood between them, ever since grade

school. Some backstabbing, fights over girls, that sort of thing mostly."

Marti walked over with pad in hand, like she'd watched Kati do. "What can I get you to drink?"

Paul's green eyes were as penetrating as Jesse's could be. "How are you doing, Marti? I heard about . . ." He glanced uneasily at the two men opposite him. "What happened. Are you all right?"

"I'm fine, thanks. Drinks?"

As Marti turned to put their order in, something caught her eye. It was an eagle pendant, wings spread in flight, that hung around Paul's neck. Something about it bothered her, or intrigued her. She wasn't sure which, and without thinking, leaned down and took it in her fingers.

"Wow, that's some pendant," she said, avoiding Paul's eyes now that she realized how close she was to him.

"Haven't you noticed it before? My dad gave it to me last year."

Her fingers briefly traced the edges of the wings before she abruptly let go and stood up. "Maybe I never really saw it." She turned and quickly retreated to clip their order on the chrome carousel.

Kati reached up to clip her own order. In a low voice, she said, "You'd better watch that flirting. You're a married woman, and pregnant no less!"

Marti caught the glint of jest in Kati's eyes, but the warning came through just the same. She started filling two glasses with Coke.

"I wasn't flirting. Have you seen that pendant of Paul's? It's beautiful."

"Oh yeah, he's shown it off plenty of times. It's the only thing his father's ever given him."

Marti returned with the drinks, careful now to avoid Paul's eyes. She didn't want to give him the wrong idea.

"Here you go. Your order should be up in a few minutes."

"You sound kinda sexy, with your voice low and husky like that," Josh said.

She straightened up and looked him in the eye. "It's

from being strangled." She turned her back on the three and walked to the counter.

Josh leaned in. "She doesn't look all that upset considering what happened to her. Maybe she liked it." He sent a leering smile toward Marti, now out of hearing range.

Skip leaned back casually. "Maybe she did, but she says she don't remember anything."

Josh scoffed. "How can a woman forget something like that? No, I think she liked it so much, she doesn't want to put the guy away." He licked his lips. "Maybe she wants him to come back, and—"

"Would you two shut up!" Paul whispered vehemently, keeping his eyes trained on Marti. He got up and walked away from the table.

After taking another order, Marti turned to find Paul sitting at the counter behind her.

"Maybe I shouldn't have asked you in front of them, but I really wanted to know how you were. You seem so, well, different."

She looked away for a second. "Yeah, something like that can change a person, you know." Now that was an understatement!

"We've all heard—I've heard things, but you know how things can get blown out of proportion."

"I'm surprised your father didn't tell you all the gory details."

A bitter laugh escaped Paul's lips. "He doesn't tell me anything about his job since I told him I didn't want to become a cop. I wouldn't even ask him."

Saved by the bell, Marti thought, as Chuck slammed it down twice to indicate her order was up. She turned and loaded the food onto a tray, glad to see that Paul had rejoined his friends. With only a few items on her tray at a time, Paul's table took two trips to make. She was glad when they were taken care of.

As if he'd crept in like a ghost, suddenly Jesse was sitting at the counter, a surly look on his face. It was directed at Paul. Despite his expression, she was glad to see a familiar face.

"Hi, stranger," she said in her whispery voice.

Slowly, he tore his gaze from Paul and his buddies and turned to her. "What did he want?"

Her eyes widened. "Who?"

"Paul. I saw him talking to you a minute ago."

Marti was surprised to see so much malice in the usually easygoing green of his eyes. "Fine, and how's your day going, dear?"

He caught himself, then smiled briefly. "Sorry. How's it going?"

"I hate it, I already smell like a french fry, and I've dropped two glasses so far, making me glad they use plastic here. I would trade government secrets to hear one, just one, song by Janet Jackson. He was asking me how I was doing. Probably to pump me for information to feed the gossips around here."

Jesse leaned forward. "Don't tell him anything, understand? Especially about you being—"

She put a finger against his lips. "I know, I know. I'm not telling anyone anything." His lips were soft, and she quickly removed her finger.

"Good. I'll have a hamburger with pickles and ketchup and an iced tea. Dear," he added, with a smile that was more like his usual self.

Her cheeks warmed when she realized he was reflecting her use of the word. She hurried to get his tea, then took another order. As she passed the large refrigerator, she paused to look at her reflection. God, it was awful! Not the tall blonde she envisioned, but the short, thin girl with the oily face peering back.

By noon, the place was crawling with the working class. Paul and his friends lingered, but Jesse apologetically said he couldn't stay long. He squeezed her hand before leaving, and she wished he would have just pulled her out of the chaos. It was for her escape, she reminded herself. Thoughts of the craziness back in California made her homesick. Carefree, windblown days full of sun and fun. She sighed, bringing her focus back to the diner and the cacophony of voices and laughter.

Harry, Jesse's boss, asked how she felt. Billy sat down at the end of the counter and gave her a faint smile. Most people were friendly, asking how she was, wondering how something so terrible could happen in Chattaloo.

"That's Carl, the sheriff," Katie murmured as she passed by.

Carl approached with that confident air of the law. For a man probably in his fifties, he still looked young. His black hair showed only a few strands of gray, and except for the small paunch, he was in good shape. He walked up to the counter while Deputy Lyle found a table.

"How are you doing, young lady?"

"I'm okay. Any leads yet?"

Carl let out a long sigh. "You want to know what I think? I think it was a transient passing through. I hope he's still around so we can catch the bastard, but I'm afraid he's probably long gone by now." He tweaked his mustache. "Have you remembered anything yet? About the man, I mean."

"No. I doubt I will, Sheriff."

"Mm. That's a shame. It'd be nice to throw that sicko in jail and keep him there a long time." He touched her arm. "I don't think he'll be back. I'm just sorry we haven't caught the guy yet."

"Thank you."

Many eyes watched her, speculating or with concern. She felt terribly uncomfortable. Being in the spotlight was one thing. This kind of attention was something entirely different.

The man watched Marti struggle with the trays as if she'd never waited tables before. In the din of noise and activity of lunchtime at the diner, he could watch her without being noticed. Every once in a while, her gaze would sweep the restaurant, passing over him as casually as it did anyone else.

He chewed thoughtfully. She really didn't remember him. She'd looked right at him, but no recognition had shown. He should have known better than to stop to help her that day. He had fought those erotic, demanding impulses for so long. It was with the best intentions that he'd pulled over to help Marti. She was wearing those cute cutoffs and a tank top that accentuated small, firm breasts. Something about her looking so innocent and helpless summoned those old urges back from the tombs he'd buried them in.

With an embarrassed smile, she'd told him she was out of gas, but he could feel her hesitancy around him. It was the same way his true love, the blood of his heart, had acted after she'd broken off their affair. Marti acting the same way had set something off inside him with that spark of distrust in her eyes and the way she moved away as he moved closer. He'd grown hot, throbbing, and that dizziness overcame his senses. He lunged for her, and her scream of surprise stirred him more.

With his hand over her mouth, he'd dragged her into the woods that bordered the highway. She struggled so hard that he had to pin her beneath his body, his weight on her stomach and hips. She was crying, "Please don't! I'm pregnant, don't hurt my baby!" He'd looked down at her flat stomach, but he'd heard that she was pregnant, with Jesse's baby, no less. He'd smiled. And she'd fought even harder.

He'd been surprised at the kind of strength and desperation that could come from such a small girl. He'd wanted to be gentle, but the harder she fought, the harder he had to pin her down. He ripped off her top—he remembered liking that part the first time he'd raped a woman. The power of control, the shame and fear in the woman's eyes. It was intoxicating. He shifted his weight downward over her thighs, so he could unsnap her jeans and rip open the zipper. She'd lunged up at him, scratching, pulling his hair out. He'd fallen over her, pressing himself hard against the length of her.

His hands had crept around her throat before he'd realized it. She kept kicking fiercely. He wanted her to stop fighting so he could show her how gentle he could be. But he kept pressing harder, squeezing until her eyes widened in shock when she realized she couldn't breathe. He'd let go, but it was too late. He'd looked at her, lying on the mat of leaves. Then he realized what he'd done. Or what he thought he'd done as it turned out. He thought he'd killed her. Panic had beset him, and he'd run stumbling like a coward.

He couldn't understand the violent streak in him. It hadn't been that way when he'd been with the blood of his heart. She'd gentled him, calmed him. When she left him—rejected him, dammit—and gone back to her husband, the cobra of violence had reared its head within him. He'd taken a woman against her will. Not that she would ever talk; he'd threatened her into silence, and she'd left town. He'd held the cobra back since then, but Marti had weakened him.

Noise penetrated his thoughts. Absently, his fingers moved down his chest where beneath his shirt grooves were cut into his skin, made by her fingernails. He watched Marti, wondering if she would ever remember him. Wondering what he should do to make sure she didn't.

Marti expelled a deep breath at two o'clock. Bad Boys Diner was closed. They were only open for breakfast and lunch, and she was ever so thankful for that. She was more thankful for Kati.

"I couldn't have survived without you."

Kati dropped down into the chair she'd just wiped clean. "I don't mind helping out. And the extra money doesn't hurt either. But if I keep up like this, I'll be too exhausted to enjoy it."

Marti picked up the wet rag Kati had tossed onto the table and continued wiping up. "Don't worry. I plan to take my share as soon as I get a handle on this waitressing thing. Besides, I need the money myself."

Kati eyed her curiously. "What do you need the money for?"

Marti sat down. "I'm going home. Back to California as soon as I can. Nothing against good old Chattaloo, but it's just not my style."

"Does Jesse know you're leaving?"

"I'm not sure."

"You'd better tell him. Marti, it's probably none of my business, but you are carrying my nephew or niece in there, which happens to be my beloved brother's baby.

I'd hate to see you do something that might hurt either one. Or yourself."

Kati's support, given to Marti all day, was now shifting away from her. She had her loyalties, of course, and Jesse was her brother. Marti stood and continued wiping down the last tables.

"It's not something I'll decide lightly. And I will tell Jesse. Soon."

A few minutes later, Kati turned off most of the lights and grabbed both their purses.

"I'll drop you by the garage."

They drove up the street a few blocks, then turned left. A large, hand-painted sign showed a car with a happy face beneath the words HARRY'S GARAGE. Kati got out and headed into one of the open bays.

"Here's your wife, safe and sound," Kati said to the car in the back.

As Marti approached, she saw Jesse peer around the front of the open hood. He had a black smudge across his cheek.

"Hi, ladies. How was work today?"

Kati snapped her gum. "Ugh, don't ask. Marti did pretty good, but she definitely ain't made to waitress."

Marti leaned against the car. "Aw, come on, I wasn't that bad." After a pause, she added, "Was I?"

Kati made a so-so sign, then smiled. "You'll get better. You've never worked that hard before, have you?"

Marti's shoulders drooped. "I've never worked before. Except for modeling and a summer at a beachside burger stand. I guess I've had it pretty easy."

"You don't know how easy," Kati said.

Jesse put an arm around Kati, keeping his black hand from her sleeve. "Thanks for showing her the ropes, kiddo. I'll go wash up and be right out."

A few minutes later, he helped Marti climb into the red truck, then slid behind the wheel. They waved good-bye to Kati, and he started in the other direction toward home. Home, Marti thought wryly. For how long?

They pulled in the driveway to the tune of Bumpus's barking. After he helped her out of the truck, his hand still held hers firmly.

"Come walk with me."

"Where?"

"To the river. Come on, I won't throw you in."

She allowed him to pull her a few steps, stumbling a little. "My feet hurt so bad. Can't we just sit down right here and talk?"

Without a word, Jesse swooped her up into his arms. He carried her behind the house, through a thicket of pine trees to the same river that ran behind his mother's house. Bumpus followed noisily behind, his tail pointing to the sky. She felt weightless in his arms, her white shoes bouncing along as they walked. Her hero, her heart sang, but her mind squelched the thought.

The sun cast dancing shadows on the water's surface as it filtered through the tangle of oak branches. He set her on her feet, stripped off his button-down shirt and laid it on the ground for her to sit on. Southern gentleman, she thought with a smile she hid from him. He dropped down on the layer of dead leaves beside her and looked out over the river that flowed lazily by. His air of hesitancy suddenly made her wary. Was he going to ask her to leave? He took a rock and threw it across the expanse of the river, skipping it three times.

"My friends and I used to have contests about who could get their rock to skip the farthest."

Marti nodded, though she wasn't following his words. He was beating around the bush, moving in for the kill. She was too crazy, too different . . . too whatever. He was going to tell her to move out. Where would she go? she thought with a twinge of anxiety. With twenty-nine bucks, plus the twenty-two dollars she got in tips, she wasn't likely to get far. She decided to tell him about her plans before he could say whatever he had to say.

"Jesse—" All the words jumbled forward, then disappeared like a puddle illusion on the highway when you got close. "I can't stay here. I mean, I can't stay long."

"What are you talking about?"

"What I mean to say is, I don't belong here. I don't even belong in this body, but I haven't much choice about that. I can get used to this after a while," she said, gesturing down her body. "But not this town, this life.

It's not me, and inside I'm still Hallie DiBarto. I have to get back to California."

"I thought you had no one to go back to."

She swallowed hard. "I don't. My friends—they weren't really friends." She couldn't stop thinking about how empty her life had been. She'd been too busy partying to notice.

"Then what are you going back for?"

"I don't know. All I know is I have to get out of here."

He drummed masculine fingers on the mat of leaves, looking out over the water before returning determined eyes back to her. "What I brought you out here to talk about was . . . what I wanted to say was that I want you to stay and have the baby."

Her heart tightened. "Jesse that's nice of you, but I can't."

His lips thinned. "I'm not being nice." He placed his palm on her still-flat stomach. "This little guy in here is mine, my responsibility, my blood. I can't just let you take off, never knowing what happened to him. I figured you'd go back where you came from after the baby is born. Until then, I want you to stay here with me."

"Jesse, I'm not going to do anything with the baby. Once I'm settled somewhere, I'll let you know where I am. When the baby comes, I'll call you."

She didn't want to look at him, because she could see his expression of disbelief from the corner of her eye.

"Marti, how are you going to get out of here without money? How are you going to support yourself?"

"I'm going to stay here for a few months, work hard, save up, and drive my car out there."

He reached out and turned her chin so that she had to face him. "Why can't you stay here so we can take care of you, and be with you when you have the baby? What's so bad about this place?"

Face-to-face with those green eyes, she groped. "I was attacked here. How do I know that the attacker was just passing through? Maybe he's still here, lurking."

His reaction surprised her. He got up on his knees and leaned over her, taking her face in his hands. His eyes burned with a mixture of anger and determination. "No one will ever hurt you again, Marti." His voice dropped to a whisper. "I won't let it happen."

She felt a strange squeezing in her heart as his fingers stroked her cheeks. At the same time, an alarm went off somewhere inside her. *I'd be the one to hurt you, Jesse. I can't stay here, not a minute longer than I have to. Please stop touching me.* Yet she didn't move away, didn't take her eyes from his.

She found her voice. "Marti's attack wasn't your fault."

He sat back, but his touch still lingered on her chin. "Yes, it was. I should have made sure you had gas in your car. I should have made you carry a weapon of some kind, I should have—" He punched at the ground. "I should have done something. It's all I can do to keep from tearing up the entire town to find the creep who did this."

"Jesse, stop blaming yourself. You weren't responsible for the attack, and you're not responsible for avenging it. I'm sure the sheriff and Lyle are doing the best they can to find out who did it."

"I'm not going to let you leave until you have the baby, Marti."

She drew her knees up and wrapped her arms around them. "You can't make me stay. What are you going to do, tie me up?"

His expression was dead serious. "If I have to."

She thought for a minute, remembering something he had said earlier. "I thought there was something mechanically wrong with my car. That's why you didn't want me to drive it this morning."

He avoided her gaze. "I'm not sure it was just lack of gas. I'll look at it this weekend."

She knew he was lying. He didn't want her to drive, because he was afraid she'd take off. Well, she wasn't an accountant, but she knew she wasn't going to get far on fifty bucks. Her goal was to save enough to get to California and have a little to get started until she found a job. She didn't want to think about her chances of getting a job with a protruding belly. In California, anything was possible.

"I'll be here for a few months."

"Why can't you wait a few more months?"

"Because I don't want to stay here any longer than I have to."

Jesse picked up another stone and made it skip across the water to the other side. "What's so bad about this place, anyway? Or is it me?"

She raised a hand to his cheek, then pulled it away when she caught herself. "It's not you, and it's not the town really. It's me. I'm out of my element."

He smirked. "Sounds like that's a good thing, from what you've said."

"I wasn't that bad. And I'm not going back to that kind of life. I just want something familiar."

Jesse reclined on the grass, his arms behind his head. Contemplating his next strategy, no doubt. Or maybe considering his threat of tying her up. She had to think he wouldn't do such a thing. If she stayed until the baby was born, she might lose the courage to leave. She'd be stuck in Chattaloo forever. Stuck. It gave her the shivers.

While Marti was deep in her thoughts, Jesse reached out and pulled her down beside him. She allowed him to draw her closer, wondering if he would try to kiss her again, like that test of his. Wondering if she would let him. He lay on his side facing her, tucking a strand of hair behind her ear.

"We made a baby together. Doesn't that mean anything to you?"

She fiddled with a piece of grass, then pulled her hair loose again. "*We* didn't make a baby; you and Marti had all the fun."

He smiled, a devilish light in his eyes. "Fun, huh?"

She blushed. "Well, I'm only guessing that it was fun." She looked away before returning her gaze to him. "Was it?"

"I guess. To be honest with you, we were both sloshed and didn't remember too much of it."

Marti steeled her courage, unable to keep from asking the questions that bugged her. "Was it . . . fun later?"

He looked at a cardinal fluttering from one branch to another, chirping intermittently. "We never slept together after the first time. She told me it would hurt the baby, something about my . . . ."—he glanced downward—"hitting the baby's head. Dr. Toby said that was impossible, but I wasn't going to force her, wife or no. I didn't even want to."

She felt the warmth creep up to her cheeks. Still, she had to know one more thing. "Did you love her, Jesse?"

He moved closer, dropping his head just over her upturned face. "My pa always told me that I'd know it when I loved a woman. He said, 'Can't describe the feeling, but it's a sorta clenched gut, drop down to your knees and die for her feeling, and you ain't in love till you feel it.' I've never felt that way about any woman, and I didn't want to. Racing was the only thing that ever made me feel that way, and I didn't want anything to get in the way of that. No, I didn't love her." Marti could see his anger, but he quickly dropped it from his expression and sighed. "But I didn't want her to die, that's for sure."

"Me either. I didn't want to die either. Sometimes we don't have a choice." She leaned on her side. "So, were you never going to get married, content to be a lone race car driver?"

Jesse smiled faintly, looking at the blade of grass he was twisting between his fingers. "My first ambition was, and is, getting to NASCAR. Maybe even to Indy. But that kind of life doesn't lend itself to the quaint picture of family most women have. Marti figured she'd have me settled down once the baby came, but it wasn't going to be that way. Nothing is going to get in the way of making it." He glanced at her. "And no one.

"Helen and Kati have already volunteered to watch the baby while I race. But in between races, I'll be the best dad I can be. And when the baby is old enough, he'll be part of it all. Aside from that, I don't have any intention of getting messed up with a woman who'll fuss and be jealous because I spend more time with my race car than with her."

"I see." He was telling the truth, she could see that in his eyes. She felt a funny pang as she pictured Jesse letting his son sit in the car and pretend to drive. On the other hand, she could see his point about a woman getting jealous of his racing pursuits. "Love stinks."

Jesse tossed the mangled piece of grass away and plucked another one. "Did you love Jamie?"

"Jamie?" She looked past him, unable to think about Jamie while looking at Jesse. "Yes, I loved him. I think I loved him, anyway. I'm not even sure I know what love is." She returned her gaze to Jesse. "I seemed to screw it up a lot. I had my chance and I blew it."

"You'll have another chance."

She shook her head. "I don't deserve another chance. Life is enough, love is too much, too difficult to manage."

"Who says you have to manage it? It should just flow, like this ole' river."

She watched the leaves drift past, floating on top of the brown water. "I wish it were that easy, Jesse. It's hard to think of it like a lazy river when your life has always been the rapids."

They sat in contemplative silence for a few minutes, facing each other but looking at things deep within themselves. Her own thoughts turned outward as she realized with chagrin that Jesse went around without his shirt much too often.

She wondered if the first Marti had been in love with Jesse, whether she'd been fascinated by the subtle way he smiled, by the deliberate way he spoke. Had Jesse's wife ever run her fingers across the expanse of his chest, trailed down the indent in the middle? They had had sex once, enough to make the baby inside her. Maybe she'd been afraid of failing in bed, of not living up to expectations.

Her gaze traveled down her own thin, tan arms, skinny legs with knobby knees. No big promises here, she thought, sighing inwardly. On the other hand, nothing to live up to either. In her old body, she had been stunning and sexy since she was fifteen. Now she felt like she did at thirteen, before her chest had blossomed, before her hips had become curvy. Before she'd been kissed. She felt awkward and unsteady. Would she ever feel comfortable in this body?

"Marti?"

Jesse's low voice drew her from her disturbing thoughts. His eyes were level with hers, and once she met them, they were locked to his.

"Yes?"

"You have to promise me something. You owe me and God one thing."

She wanted to back away from a forced promise. But she didn't. "What is it?"

"That you won't hurt that baby inside you. That no matter what happens between you and me, you won't do anything to hurt him, or have an abortion. Will you promise me?"

"I promise." That was easy, she thought, letting her breath out. She had already made that decision on her own.

"I'm not going to give you a choice about staying until the baby's born. You're off Sundays, so we'll check out the furniture stores and buy you a bed."

He stood, stretching out his large hand for her to take. There was something secure about his fingers closing around her own. A mental picture flashed into her mind, Jesse with his brawn and muscles gently holding a fragile baby. She found herself smiling at the thought, and quickly wiped the grin away. Still, the picture remained in her mind, and the feeling of security that went along with it cloaked her in a warmth she hadn't felt in many years.

For all his gestures of warmth and security, Jesse James West wasn't letting anyone into his heart except for his family. He'd probably go to any length to protect her, but he wasn't ever going to let himself fall in love with her. Not that she wanted that, she quickly reminded herself. That was some other woman's loss.

Chapter 5

~

*H*ave you ever seen Paul's eagle pendant?" Marti asked as she shoveled a forkful of pancake in her mouth.

Jesse's eyes narrowed across the Formica table at the Someplace Else Cafe, his shoulders broadened threateningly. "I meant it when I told you not to talk to him again. He's trouble, do you understand me?"

Her own shoulders stiffened in response. "Keep your rifle in your jeans, cowboy. Husband or not, you can't tell me who I'm allowed to talk to. The only reason I brought him up was because . . . oh, it's probably nothing. Never mind."

He leaned across the table. "What? What were you going to tell me?"

"I was just going to mention his eagle pendant. Have you noticed it before?"

"Sure. Why?"

"Well, it's just that, when I first saw it, it struck me as being . . . I don't know, there was something about it. Last night, when I got ready for bed, I saw the scratch on my chest. Then I realized why the eagle caught my attention. It looks like the kind of object that would have made that scratch."

Fire lit Jesse's eyes as he leaned closer. "Why didn't you tell me this before?"

"Because, like I said, I wasn't sure it meant anything."

"I want to see the scratch."

Her eyes widened. "Right here? It's kind of low." She pointed to where it was.

"No, not here. Come on, let's get out of here."

After they pulled out of the parking lot, Jesse turned

onto the first street they came across and found a vacant lot.

"Okay, show me the scratch."

His intensity was making her nervous. She tried to make a funny to ease the tension, and cocked her head. "Don't you want to flirt a little first?"

"Marti, this isn't the time to joke around."

She erased her smile and stretched down her shirt to just beyond the location of the scratch. He studied it carefully, pressing his finger on it.

"It's almost gone."

"Dr. Toby took pictures of the bruises. Maybe she's got the photo."

Jesse started the truck and slammed it into reverse. She grabbed onto the strap to keep from flying around.

"You really hate this guy, don't you?" she asked once they were headed toward the hospital.

"I hate the guy who did this to you. And if it was Paul, he's dead."

At the hospital, Dr. Toby explained that she had turned over all the photos to the sheriff after the attack. She remembered the scratch, but not in any great detail. Jesse was just as intent on getting to the sheriff's office, and Marti became very friendly with that strap.

The sheriff's office looked more like a storefront, with reflective windows that mirrored the main street from the outside, and a brick facade. Lyle was sitting at the front desk in the small office, reading through the pile of mail. He looked up, then squinted as the morning sun reflected off the glass door. The blinds on the front windows left the office with a subdued feeling, dim without florescent lights.

"Howdy, Jesse, Marti. How are you two doing?"

Jesse leaned down over the desk. "Well, we might be doing real well if you can help us. Lyle, I've got to see those pictures Dr. Toby took of Marti."

"You'll have to talk to Carl."

"Why? You were the investigating officer."

"I know, but Carl took over the case." Lyle sniffed at the air. "He wanted to investigate the biggest case we've had around here since Mr. Peekin's poodles were kidnapped for those dog fights. I guess he didn't think I could handle it. I couldn've, you know."

"I'm sure you could have, Lyle," Jesse pressed. "As good a job as anyone, even Perry Mason. We just want to see those pictures for a minute."

Lyle shook his head. "You'll have to talk to Carl about it, and he's not in right now. I can radio him if you think you got a lead."

"No, don't radio him. Lyle, it's her body, let us look at the pictures. No one'll know. And we'll give you credit if what I want to look at does turn into something. Okay?"

"What do you have?"

"I'll tell you when I have more to go on. The photos?"

Lyle hedged, glancing down at the papers on his desk, looking out the door behind Jesse. "Okay, one quick peek."

Both Jesse and Marti breathed a sigh of relief as Lyle went searching through the drawers of the spotless desk in back with Carl's name and title spelled out prominently on a name plate. He brought a large, white envelope and pulled out a series of photos. Marti took them before Jesse could grab hold.

"Excuse me, but I'll show you the ones I want you to see." She found the only one that had a close-up of her upper chest. "Here it is."

Jesse snatched it out of her hand and held it under the light at the door. "It's got something spilled on it," he said, turning to Lyle.

"What do you mean?"

"I mean, right where the scratch should be, there's a blotch." Jesse put the photo to his nose. "Coffee!"

Lyle's cheeks flamed red. "Oh, shoot! Carl and me was looking at the photos, all spread out on the desk over there. He bumped me from behind, and some of my coffee splashed out. It was just an accident."

"Damn!" Jesse said, dropping the photo on top of the piles of papers on Lyle's desk. "Why this one? And on that exact spot?"

"Well, there was a few of them that got splashed. See, this one's got a little bit on the corner. And that one."

"Come on," Jesse said to Marti, and headed out the door.

She gave an embarrassed Lyle a shrug, then had to run to catch up with a muttering Jesse.

"Do you think they did it on purpose?" she asked.

"I don't know. Carl might be protecting his son, if he connected that scratch like you did."

"I can draw what it looked like. Will that help?"

"It'll help, but it won't be proof."

After stopping to buy a bed for her, Jesse carried in the bed frame and mattress with Marti guiding him verbally to avoid walls and obstructions. When the bed was positioned, Jesse dropped down onto it, arms outstretched. He was staring at the ceiling, and she was staring at him. Catching herself, she looked around the room that was to be hers for a short while.

It was smaller than Jesse's room, with dark, paneled walls. The only window was bare, so that anyone could look in at night. The closet was just an indent in the room, not even big enough to stand in. Jesse still looked a thousand miles away, and she searched the room for something to break the silence.

She saw the packages of sheets on top of the dresser and grasped at the opportunity to bring Jesse back. "What are these for?"

He looked at the packages she held up, his eyes still tinged with some distant anger. "Marti bought those. We couldn't afford the fancy curtains in the JC Penney catalog, so she was going to make curtains out of those sheets. This is going to be the nursery."

Marti looked at the tiny white lambs on a mint green background and imagined them made into ornate curtains for the bare window. She had no creativity, but maybe she could do something nice with them.

When she looked at Jesse again, he was staring intently out the window. His thoughts were miles away again, obviously some unpleasant place by his expression. The curves of his mouth that usually tilted up in a smile, even when he wasn't smiling, were straight. He stood up suddenly, unaware of her staring at him.

"I've got to go out for a little while," he said, heading toward the door.

Something in his expression made her heart tighten, and she heard herself asking, "Where?"

He swiped something off the dining table, and without looking at her, said, "To see an old buddy of mine. I'll be back."

She watched him walk determinedly to his truck, realizing that the dark fire in his eyes had been there ever since she'd told him about the pendant that morning. The sketches of the pendant and her scratch were gone.

What if Jesse killed Paul? What if Jesse got thrown in jail? The questions numbed her mind. After pacing in front of the living room window for a few minutes, she turned back to her new bedroom and put her nervous energy to work.

Jesse had finally maxed out his self-control. From the moment Marti had mentioned the pendant, he'd wanted to confront Paul—hell, he wanted to beat the crap out of him. Even the irony of bed-shopping with Marti hadn't succeeded in distracting him. Now he couldn't hold it back anymore. Not that he would start pummeling Paul's face and ask questions later. He couldn't do that until he had a little more evidence. But maybe he could gently persuade Paul to admit he'd attacked Marti. Yeah, gently persuade him.

Paul's fancy new truck, black with neon ribbons trailing across the sides, was parked outside. The house was partially hidden by a large banyan tree, roots dripping down from the branches to find a hold. Two stories of brick house stood quietly a short distance away.

Jesse headed right for Paul's truck. He wasn't sure what he was looking for, but he started digging through the piles of receipts, papers, and cigarette packages anyway.

"Jesse, I don't believe there was a for sale sign on my truck, so would you mind telling me what you're doing snooping around in it?"

Jesse swung on Paul so fast, Paul was pinned against the cab of the truck before he could think of fighting back. Jesse had more important things to do before beating him senseless. He grabbed at the pendant and pressed it against the inside of his wrist.

"What the hell are you doing?" Paul screamed, jerking out of his grasp before Jesse could get an imprint.

The rage twisted up in Jesse's throat, and his voice came out strangled. "You son of a bitch, you attacked my wife! You kill—tried to kill her!"

Paul's chest heaved as he tried to gain his composure from the surprise attack. "I didn't touch your wife!" He shook himself free, his white teeth gritted together. "You'll never prove I did it, because I never touched her."

"Don't think I believe that garbage for a minute. Your daddy might tamper with the evidence that proved your eagle scratched Marti's chest, but I'll find another way to prove it."

Paul's eyes narrowed. "What are you talking about? What evidence?"

"Why don't you ask your daddy, Paul? He'll tell you about the little accidental coffee spill on the pictures, the one with the imprint particularly. The imprint that matches your pendant. I will prove it, and you will pay. Not even your daddy will be able to save you when I'm through with you."

Paul moved stealthily around the truck and toward the house. "Jesse, isn't it a little late to go around protecting your wife? Now that it's over, you want to be the big avenger. Why don't you spend your energies making sure your wife has enough gas in her car? Oh, and Jesse? You ever try something like this again, and you'll be the one to pay. I promise you that."

"You'd better be as ready to back up your promise as I am," Jesse shouted.

He watched Paul head back into the house, then looked down to his arm where the faint imprint of the eagle was engraved. It would be faded by the time he got home. Ever since they were kids, Paul had a snake-edged tongue, always slicing through where Jesse was most tender. But he was certain, absolutely certain that Paul was the one who attacked Marti. He couldn't do a thing about it until he could prove it, and without the evidence of her scratch, and without her memory of the incident, there wasn't much hope for it. But Jesse could take just a little bit of hope and turn it into something tangible, like he'd done with racing. He would do it here, too.

Chuck was kind enough to close Bad Boys for Thanksgiving. Then Marti learned that it wasn't so much out of kindness, but because most of Chattaloo's businesses were closed for the holiday.

She awkwardly searched for large pans and serving dishes in Jesse's cabinets, stacking them up on the table for transport to Helen's at two o'clock. When he walked into the kitchen wearing a maroon dress shirt and black pants, she just stared at him.

"Is dinner dressy? I thought it was at your mom's house."

He shrugged. "It is, but we always get dressed up for holiday dinners, ever since I can remember." He looked down at himself and grinned. "We get dressed up, crowd into the kitchen and sweat and get food all over ourselves before dinner even begins. It always did seem silly to me, but Ma insists."

She dropped a large, plastic spoon loudly into the metal bowls. An expression of controlled panic seized her face. They all worked together in the kitchen? Doing what? Talking about what?

Jesse's grin disappeared. "What's the matter?"

"Oh, God, I don't do family get-togethers well. Traditional dinners were usually my mother's latest lover trying to impress us by taking us to some fancy restaurant for dinner. Big dinners with everyone cooking together, chatting gaily about what a wonderful year it's been . . . that's the stuff commercials are made of."

Jesse took her hands in his. She tried to avoid his gaze by staring at the hollow of his throat, but something made her look up into his face.

"As long as you're my wife, you are part of my family. There's nothing to be afraid of, and believe me, it's never as picture-perfect as a commercial. We all work to put a big, sloppy meal together, and we usually have as much fun making it as we do eating it. You'll be fine."

Marti nodded, but inside she was sure she'd fail at her part of the preparation and conversation. She remembered their dinner last week, the lighthearted conversation and smiles. That was an ordinary dinner, though, and this was Thanksgiving. She had so much to be thankful for, but she wanted to do it in private.

The former Marti had few nice dresses. Still, she wanted to wear something special, so she slipped into a high-waisted pink dress plastered with white tulips.

Hearing Jesse's voice outside, she put on white sandals and headed toward the door. Jesse was playing Frisbee with Bumpus. She watched for a moment as he reared back, then threw the disk to the dog who was already in position to start the chase. Jesse's hair was still wet; combed back, it looked slick with styling gel. That was more of the style she was used to seeing on men. But Jesse had nice hair, thick and wavy, and he did little more than brush it.

Jesse headed toward the truck, disk in hand. Bumpus watched him intently, as if waiting for a signal.

"I hope you don't mind if he comes along. He'd be heartbroken if I left him behind for Thanksgiving dinner."

Picturing him riding in the back of the truck, she didn't see what harm could come from it. "Well, I certainly don't want to break his heart."

Jesse helped her in the truck, then gave the signal Bumpus was waiting for: a wave of the disk. Bumpus took a running leap, lunging at the Frisbee. With it in his mouth, he landed on the seat next to her, upsetting the pile of cookware in her lap. She scrunched toward the door.

"Jesse, he's in the truck! Get him out of here!"

Instead of telling the dog to get out, Jesse slid in next to him. "He always rides in the cab."

"Can't he ride in the back? I've seen dogs do that before."

"Not my dog. You don't let your dog ride in back when you see a truck slam on its brakes and watch the dog in back fly through the air and into traffic. Luckily, that dog was able to slink away before he got run over."

"Jesse, what if I gave you an ultimatum? Either the dog comes or I do. What would you say?"

He grinned waggishly. "I'd say, I hope it's not too breezy for you in the back. And don't open your mouth or you might eat a bug."

"Humph."

She stayed flat against the door, seeing that arguing was useless. Bumpus turned to look at her, sending a drop of drool hurtling through the air. As Jesse headed down the road, she opened the glove box and found a package of tissues. She pulled out five and balled them up. Every time she saw the saliva forming on Bumpus's lips, she swabbed it. He was too busy enjoying the ride to pay much attention.

"What are you doing to my dog?" Jesse asked, a little more attentive.

"He's drooling all over! I'm mopping him up. If you'd teach him manners, I wouldn't have to do this."

Jesse just shook his head and returned his attention to the road. She kept swabbing Bumpus's chin.

As soon as they turned on the road leading to Helen's, Bumpus stood up. His tail thumped Marti's shoulder. He was quickly looking back and forth, making it harder to jab the tissues at his mouth. When they turned onto Helen's driveway, he went berserk, whining and dancing a little jig on the front seat.

"Does he have to go to the bathroom?" she asked with a worried expression.

"No, he always goes nuts when he realizes we're visiting Grandma," Jesse said.

"I can see that. And how does Helen feel about being this . . . thing's grandmother?"

He shrugged. "She don't mind. She's used to having critters around. What with Dad and his dogs, and Billy and I catching every kind of creature you could imagine, including baby raccoons and squirrels, she gave up on being squeamish. Even now, Billy's got a pet possum, and Kati's got her rat. She's easygoing."

"I can't imagine getting used to those kinds of animals in the house."

"You know what your problem is?" he said, pulling to a stop in front of the house. "You never had critters when you were little. Every animal we had, except maybe the snakes, gave us as much love as we gave them. Even Kati's rat loves affection. You owe them food and security, and in return, they give you every ounce of love in their little bodies. It's a good way to learn how to love, and how to be loved."

Those last words struck her oddly. Nobody had ever taught her how to accept love. She thought it came naturally, and if you didn't have it, you were just cold. And she'd been called cold enough times.

Bumpus jumped out and joined Trick and Treat, who were barking happily at their arrival. She followed Jesse into the house, ducking under pilgrim and pumpkin decorations hanging over the door. A fat pumpkin was sitting just outside, surrounded by a variety of smaller squashes in gruesome shapes. Inside a football game blared on the television, and the aroma of roasting turkey filled the room. Marti found herself smiling, feeling her anxiety slip away in an atmosphere filled with warmth and love.

"Hi, Ma!" Jesse hollered.

"Hi, hon! Hi, Marti! Happy Thanksgiving!" Helen's voice called from the kitchen.

Helen appeared in the kitchen doorway. "Why don't you come in and help me get the feast process started?" she said to Marti. "Kati's helping Dr. Hislope with one of Nolen's cows. Seems as though Bessie Blue's having a hard time calving, and Donna's nowhere to be found."

"I'd love to help. I will warn you, though, that I can't cook."

"Mom, give her a few lessons, will you? I can't cook all the meals now, can I?"

Helen cocked her head at him. "Aw, that would be awful, wouldn't it?"

Jesse raised his hands in surrender. "I know when to exit gracefully. I'm going to see if Billy needs any help fishing out there. We'll be in shortly to give you a hand."

"I didn't raise my boys to depend on a woman to eat and have clean clothes," Helen said as she headed back into the kitchen. She handed Marti a peeler and several potatoes and set her up in front of the sink.

"Jesse's one of the neatest men I've ever met. Most bachelor pads are pretty disgusting. But not Jesse's place."

"He's always been that way, too. I hardly ever had to tell him to wash his hands before dinner either. He was a strange kid. Billy, unfortunately, was always a slob." Helen laughed, and whispered, "I even put him over my knee and spanked him once after he said it was a woman's place to cook and clean. He was twenty-three years old!"

"That must have been a sight!"

Helen's brown eyes twinkled with mischief. "It was. He never said anything like that again, at least in my presence."

"I guess not. Well, it's a good thing you taught Jesse to be independent," Marti found herself saying. "Being that he's not the marrying type because of his racing."

Helen laughed. "What do you mean? He is married."

"Yeah, but against his will. And I'll be heading back to California soon, so he'll be single again. According to him, he'll be that way for a long time so he can concentrate on his racing."

"Don't let him send you away, hon. A good woman can bring happiness to a man whether he wants it or not. And vice versa."

"Oh, he's not sending me away. I feel the same. We're a perfect match, in that respect."

Helen gave her an odd look, but Marti was watching Jesse stealthily approach Billy from behind. Jesse tossed a small rock into the water. The resulting splash made Billy perk up, then quickly reel in the lure and cast it in the area of the splash. After the third time, Billy turned around and pointed at Jesse with a menacing finger. The two wrestled for a few minutes, then gave up fishing and wrestling for horseshoes. Marti envied them, their brotherly camaraderie.

"Are they goofing around again?" Helen asked, basting the brown turkey with an oversize syringe.

"Just playing horseshoes."

"They never grow up. And frankly, I don't want them to. They're still my little boys when they wrestle and tease each other." She smiled wistfully. "These are the times I miss Bernie the most. Sometimes I'll see him standing in the hallway, or out horsing with the boys. When you love someone like that, it just doesn't go away."

Marti felt a twinge in her heart. She would probably never be able to love someone that much. She'd end up hurting them no doubt.

Helen sighed, bringing herself back to the task at hand. "Once we get the potatoes going, we'll start the green beans and sweet potatoes. A dinner like this is kind of like orchestrating a production."

Marti shook her head as she took in the steaming pots and piles of green beans and tomatoes. "I could never do this. Cooking's just not in my genes."

"Nothing to do with genes, hon. It's just a matter of learning. It's a labor of love, an adventure."

Marti watched as Helen deftly shaved the carrots clean. "Maybe if my mother had taught me how to cook. She was more of the Hamburger Helper type." Even in a lacy apron, Helen didn't visually fit in a kitchen. Yet, she worked like a pro, rolling out the dough and cutting it into little strips.

"Helen, where are you from? Not here, right?"

She smiled. "I still haven't become Chattaloo'd, have I?"

"Well, I can tell you weren't born in any small Southern town, that's for sure."

"No, I wasn't. I was born in Connecticut, in a prestigious community. I went to private schools, attended the dances and all that social poopoo. I had fun, but it wasn't me."

Marti raised her eyebrows. "You look like you'd fit into that kind of world. I mean, you're so pretty and classy."

Helen smiled demurely. "Why, thank you. Everybody

thought I'd marry handsome George McCormick and have three bright, beautiful children and live in a big white house. I did, too. But there was something inside me that was still searching. The summer after I graduated from college I drove down to the Keys by myself.

"On the way, my Jaguar broke down, right here in Chattaloo. Bernie was working that Saturday, and his Southern drawl made me melt. The first moment I met him, I pictured what my parents' reaction might be if I took him home and announced we were getting married. It was a crazy thought."

Marti smiled. "You fell in love? That fast?"

"I'm not sure it was love then. Wild infatuation, maybe. He had to order the part from the dealer, and it was going to take a day or two. I decided to stay on. Bernie took good care of me, making me dinner at his house, taking me horseback riding at a friend's ranch. By Monday afternoon, when my car was ready to go, I wasn't. I was in love then. I didn't have to imagine my parents' reaction anymore—I got their anger firsthand. We made peace when they realized how happy I was, but it took a while."

Marti was trying to pay attention to how Helen was kneading the biscuit dough, but she was too entranced by her story. "It sounds so romantic!"

A melancholy haze fell upon her face. "It was, but it wasn't perfect. I had hoped once Billy was born that Bernie would stop racing so much, but he didn't. We had some problems for a while, and I made some mistakes. By the time Jesse was born, we'd come to an understanding about the racing. And I'd learned an important lesson about the value of love."

Marti blew out a long breath. "I know about making mistakes. I made so many of them in my marriage to Jamie. I sure learned my lesson about love: I'm not good at it, and I don't want to try anymore."

Helen turned to her. "Surely you don't mean that."

"I do. I had my chance, and I blew it. If I couldn't find love with Jamie, who was loving and tender, how can I find it with anyone else?"

"Oh, I think you'll find it again. Or more likely, it will find you. Probably in the most unexpected place."

Billy and Jesse busted through the door then, panting and sweaty. Billy stripped off his T-shirt, baring a tattoo of an eagle stretching from one shoulder to the other on his back.

"Billy, get your naked, sweaty body out of here, wash up and get back in here to help!" Helen said.

Jesse grabbed two bottles of beer from the fridge and put one to his flushed forehead, walking out to hand one to Billy. He did remind her of a carefree boy. Through the wide doorway, she could see him standing in the living room. He stripped his shirt off and ran his fingers through his hair. The tips of his hair were damp, and they grazed his upper back as he moved. His back and shoulders were wide and muscular, tapering to his thin hips. The black pants shaped his tight buns nicely, molding to his legs. When her eyes felt locked to him, he turned around and caught her staring. She couldn't tear her gaze away, and a warm fire burned in her stomach.

"Green beans are easy. You just cut the ends off and put them in the steamer," Helen's voice said, breaking Marti out of her spell.

"Hm?"

Helen smiled. "Are you having a hot flash?"

The warmth of her cheeks flamed hotter. "H-hot flash?"

"Yes, pregnant women sometimes have hot flashes. Your face is all red."

"It's the first time it's ever happened to me," she said truthfully. "That's probably what it is." She wanted to believe that's what it was.

Dean stopped by, and after a quick perusal of the surroundings, pushed his lower lip out a little. "Kati's not here?"

"No, she's out birthing a cow. You're still going to join us for dinner, aren't you?" Helen asked.

"Sure. I'll wash up and help."

They kept everything waiting until Helen announced that the turkey would dry out if it stayed in any longer.

Kati still wasn't home. When the turkey was placed on the table, Dean said, "At least we're not having beef for dinner. Katie'd probably be a little upset after helping that baby cow into the world."

Jesse leaned over and whispered in Marti's ear, "Just ignore him. Everyone else does."

Before a single green bean could be dropped onto a plate, they all joined hands for prayer. Jesse's hand enveloped hers on one side, and Helen's hand took the other one. Billy passed the duty of the "head of the household" onto Jesse, who took charge easily.

"Dear Jesus, thank you for bringing us here together, our health and sanity intact, Billy notwithstanding. We thank you that Kati is absent from our table only because she's helping a living thing come into the world." Marti felt him squeeze her hand as he continued. "We thank you for bringing Marti to us, and for giving the tiny baby inside her health and our love as he grows. Amen."

Everyone repeated the Amen, and for a moment, four sets of smiling eyes·settled upon her. Uncomfortable under their gazes, she reached over to stab a piece of turkey.

Chapter 6

~

The following Monday was another long struggle of balancing trays. Marti saw a lot of the same people she had seen on Saturday.

"Don't these people have anyplace else to eat?" she'd whispered to Kati during the afternoon rush. "The same people keep coming in, day after day, meal after meal."

"There's only three other places in town to eat lunch besides us. At least we offer more variety than Pie in the Sky."

"Yeah, well, I guess you can only eat so much pizza."

Marti caught Chuck watching her again. Often he seemed to be studying her from his steamy place in the kitchen. Was he just curious about the changes in her work habits? Sometimes she'd look back at him, and he'd grin at her, then resume whatever he'd been doing.

Jesse was always a welcome visitor during her day, even though he could only order a couple of sandwiches to go today. He sat at the counter and watched her shoulder a tray of meatloaf specials.

"How's it going, doll? Any better than your first day?"

Whenever he called her that, her senses swirled inside her and her legs went limp. Why he could say it so casually and make her go silly boggled her mind. *Affection comes easily for Jesse. It's nothing personal, nothing romantic. And you don't want it that way, do you?* Her self didn't answer, but she was sure that it didn't. She tried to remember his question.

"Uh, it's okay. I don't think I'll ever get used to this kind of work."

"Wish I could stay for a while, but it's pretty busy today at the garage. I'll see you after work."

As he grabbed his white bag, his smile promised more than his words. She was imagining it, of course. That lazy smile, the way he held her hand and called her doll. They were all natural to him, and he probably did that to all his women friends. And there were probably a lot of them, a whole lot of them! She tried to push the fuzzies dancing in her stomach away with thoughts of reality. And they could have him, because she would be leaving soon.

Once everything was cleaned up and put away, the two locked up the diner and got into Kati's compact. She didn't mind riding with Kati, but Marti resolved to start driving the Datsun on her next workday. Jesse's tinkering with the engine was probably a farce, just to keep her with someone at all times. A little independence sounded good for a change. And she had the can of tear gas to protect her now, courtesy of Jesse. Kati swerved into Harry's parking lot like a speedster, pulling the compact car up short just before they hit the building.

"Do you race cars, too?" Marti asked, prying her fingers off the dash.

Kati's eyes sparkled. "Jesse lets me drive his stock car sometimes, but he'd have fits if I really wanted to race. Well, I gotta get ready for a test tonight in class. See you tomorrow."

"Yeah, tomorrow. Thanks for the ride."

Marti walked into the open bay, but didn't see Jesse at first. He was talking, although his voice was muffled somewhat. She approached a red Chevy facing the back wall with the hood up. The engine was revving, but there wasn't anyone in the driver's seat. When she walked around the hood, she was taken off guard to find a woman leaning on the car and looking down into the engine. She was tall and lean, with short brown hair and dark eyes.

"Hi, Marti," she said. "How are you feeling?"

Before she could answer, Marti heard a scooting noise below, and Jesse rolled out from beneath the car.

"Hey, Marti," he said easily. "Desiree was just asking me how you were doing."

Marti knew he was letting her know the woman's name without actually introducing her. Still, Marti found herself more than curious about the beauty wearing a black tank top and jeans.

"I'm doing pretty good. Considering."

Desiree walked around the car and leaned against the side near Marti. "What an awful thing to happen, especially around here. You grow up feeling safe and secure, and then something like this happens to rock your boots. Your voice still sounds hoarse, but you look good."

Jesse grinned. "She sounds like Demi Moore. I like it, kinda soft and sexy."

Marti turned to look at some tools hanging on the pegboard, hoping to hide her uneasiness. "I just want my old voice back." Hallie's voice, she meant.

"I think I agree with Jesse. It probably sounds worse to you."

Something about Desiree bothered Marti tremendously, but she couldn't pinpoint what it was. Maybe the way she moved—confident, hips swaying as she walked toward the bay door. Yes, that's what it was! Desiree reminded her of Hallie, seductive, with full lips and bedroom eyes. Marti watched Jesse, watched his reaction around Desiree. For some reason, she was curious about his feelings toward her. He was busy putting his tools away.

"See you both later," Desiree said as she walked toward a shiny black Jeep. Her snakeskin cowboy boots thumped on the dirt, kicking up little clouds of white dust.

"Who is she?" Marti asked, telling herself that the strain in her voice was not jealousy. Couldn't be. Jesse wasn't even her type.

"She's a friend," he said, glancing up to see her Jeep pull away.

"Oh."

"Let me wash up and I'll be ready to go."

Marti wandered around the shop, kicking at a tire,

feeling grungy and small compared to Desiree. A spotty mirror concluded what she didn't want to know: She was absolutely no match for someone like Desiree, someone like Hallie used to be. She was no longer in that league. The part of her that was always so concerned with looks still lived inside her. She wished it didn't. Desiree and Jesse looked good together, both tall, Southern. They both fit in here. She certainly didn't. It bothered her far too much for her comfort.

"Ready?"

His voice broke her out of her thoughts.

"Sure."

He came up behind her, smelling of industrial grade soap. "What's wrong? You've been quiet since you got here."

"Long day. Let's go."

What was wrong? she wondered as they drove home. She had been in a good mood up until she'd gotten to the garage. Now she was eager to leave, get her new life started.

When they pulled into the driveway, Bumpus ran out to greet them, barking happily. Strangely enough, his loud happiness at their arrival seemed comforting, familiar. Jesse greeted him with chiding sounds, riling him up even more. Bumpus ran over to Marti and barked, bowing in a play-with-me stance. She picked up a nearby rubber bone and tossed it for Bumpus to fetch. She was getting too comfortable here. So comfortable that Desiree's presence made Marti feel as though her territory was being threatened. She didn't even have a territory! No, something had to be done about this comfort level.

"Jesse, I want to leave in one month."

He stopped midplay and looked at her. "What are you talking about?"

"Just what I said. I'm letting you know. Don't look at me like that. You knew I wasn't going to stay."

"Yeah, I knew that. But I thought you'd at least stay until you had the baby."

"That's seven months away. I can't stay here, living this life, pretending I'm someone else. When I leave here, I can make Marti who I am. Here, I have to play her part."

"It's only for seven months. Don't make it sound like an eternity. It'll chug by faster than you think, then you can leave here and forget all about us."

"Jesse, I can't stay. I'll get settled in California and come back after I have the baby."

"I don't believe you."

"Then I'll come back just before I have the baby. How about that?"

"Marti, the moment you walk out that door, I'll never see you again. I know that, and if you look deep down inside, you know it, too."

He was wrong. What would she do with this baby, anyway? It was his son. "This is so unfair, what you're asking me. I said I'd have the baby and give it to you, but I don't want to put my life on hold for seven months until that time comes."

"I don't think it's unfair. It's only seven months! Where will you go where you'll have people around to help you get through the tough months ahead? Your mother? Your perfect ex-husband, Jamie? Are they going to stand by you?"

She looked everywhere except at him. At that very moment, she hated him for pressing her into a decision like this. She didn't want to be stuck in this no-place town for seven more months!

"I can't stay."

"You are one selfish lady, you know that?"

"Oh, sure, sweet-talk me. If I am, it's because that's the only way I've ever known."

Jesse reached into the truck and pulled a manila folder out from beneath the seat. "Let's go inside and talk." His voice sounded serious. She steeled herself to defend her reasons for leaving.

Jesse sat down at the table. He looked businesslike, sifting through papers with a somber expression on his face. She joined him.

He pulled out a piece of paper, unfolding it carefully, thoughtfully. "I figured I might have to resort to this. It seems the way to your heart is through your purse, so here is my proposition."

She started to organize her rebuttal, but only got as far as looking insulted before he continued.

"I talked to the doctor's office and the insurance company. If the pregnancy is normal, no complications, this is what our bill will be. My bill. The loan officer at the bank said I could qualify for this much money. That leaves a balance of eight thousand seven hundred fifty-two dollars. I'll give you the rest if you stay. How about that?"

She could only stare at him. He was paying her to stay in Chattaloo until the baby was born. "You think you can buy me off? Pay me to stay? That's ridiculous!"

"No, it's not. What are you going to do, drive that piece of junk of a car out there to California with a couple hundred bucks in your pocket? You've never lived on your own, have you? I mean really on your own."

"No, but I can take care of myself."

"That's not the point. By the time you get there, you're going to be broke. Where are you going to live, in a halfway house or a homeless shelter? Marti, you're not going to have any money to get your new life started. Don't you understand, no money for food, for rent. For doctor visits. And what about hospital bills? What if you go into labor early, before you intend to come back here? You want to get out of here so bad, you're not considering reality."

He was right, of course. She hated thinking about reality. In her mind, she was just going to make it, no matter what. But what if she didn't? He was being fair, she reasoned. After all, she needed money to get a new start in life, and that was a good start. More than she'd ever be able to save working at the diner for a month, or even seven months. She'd have the baby and be gone. And Jesse would be in debt.

"But you'll have to pay off that loan," she said.

"That's my problem, not yours. What do you say?"

She looked at the list of numbers, the calculations on that folded piece of paper Jesse had reluctantly pulled out. Where else could she go until she had the baby anyway?

"As soon as I'm released from the hospital, the money's mine and I'm free to go?"

Jesse's expression hardened. "Yes, you can leave and never look back."

"Who will take care of the baby? You by yourself?"

"I have Kati and Ma. We'll get by."

"And you won't ask me to stay? Try to convince me to play mommy after the baby comes?"

There was a second's pause, but he shook his head. "No."

"You have to promise me you won't try to convince me, Jesse. That you won't put a guilt trip on me for leaving you with the baby."

"I promise."

She put her hand on her stomach, the baby's presence still not noticeable. "Okay, I'll stay."

Marti breathed in deeply. "I love the smell of clothing stores! It seems like forever since I've been shopping."

Kati eyed her. "I don't think I've ever seen anyone get so excited about shopping. You buy clothes, you wear them."

Marti looked at her as if she were from another planet. "Shopping is an experience, Kati. The excitement of finding a dress that fits just perfectly, spotting something that nobody else has, something completely outrageous. It's absolutely excellent!"

Marti had talked Kati into going to the mall that evening. If she was staying, she was going to buy some decent clothes. Lugging twenty bags of clothing and merchandise, Marti was finally becoming satiated with the experience. She looked over at Kati who was carrying some of the bags over her shoulder. Marti smiled, realizing that Kati was the first woman friend she'd ever had that hadn't made her feel competitive. Kati was just as attractive as she was, even more so. Yet Kati wasn't concerned with one-upping her, or pretending to be something she wasn't. It was a new experience for her, a true female friend. Without thinking, she leaned over and gave Kati a sideways hug.

"Thanks for keeping me company today. Shopping alone just isn't the same."

Kati smiled wearily. "No problem. It was different. I'm not sure I'm going to get used to that hair, though."

Marti touched the blond curls, her most impulsive purchase. The hair stylist had done wonders with the straight brown hair. "I thought it would make me feel more like my old self."

"Does it?"

She shook her head. "No, not really. But I like it. You don't like it, do you?"

"Ah, it's okay. It's a pretty color."

And that was another thing; Kati meant what she said. There wasn't the second guessing Marti had with Joya. Feeling warm and thankful, Marti spotted a shirt that she thought would look great on Jesse.

"What do you think about this for your brother?" she asked Kati, holding up the purple, teal, and maroon swirly shirt.

Kati cocked her head. "Hm, I don't know. It's not him."

Marti took it to the counter. "It'll do him some good to get out of character once in a while. Look what it's doing for me."

Kati gave a wry grin. "He's going to have enough of a time getting used to that hair of yours."

"You don't think he'll like it?" she asked, handing the clerk her new account information.

"You'll have to find out for yourself."

"I'm staying, you know," she said, signing the receipt and cramming the bag in with the rest of her bags.

"You are? Does Jesse know?"

"Of course. He's the one who proposed the deal."

"What deal?"

"He's going to take out a loan to pay the hospital bills and give me the balance. All I have to do is stay here until I have the baby."

Kati silently processed the information, and suddenly

her opinion of the matter seemed important to Marti. She turned to Kati, halting in the middle of the mall.

"Am I a terrible person for taking his offer? For not wanting to stay in the first place? Tell me, Kati."

She shrugged. "I'm not in the habit of judging people. Everyone has their motives and values. I couldn't begin to imagine what it's like being in your shoes. I think I would have stayed to have the baby without the bribe."

Feeling guilty, Marti found a nearby bench and sat down. "But you have a family, people who love you and whom you can depend on. It's different for me."

"I know it is. You asked my opinion, and I gave it to you. As long as you feel it's the right thing to do, then it is. Nothing's as important as your feelings."

That was the problem. Her feelings weren't particularly thrilled about the deal she'd made with Jesse, and buying a silly shirt wasn't going to allay the guilt for putting him in debt. *But I'm staying here, putting my dreams and life on hold for seven months for him. He made me the deal, so he must think it's okay.* But from down deep his words echoed through her mind: *It seems the way to your heart is through your purse. . . .*

"We went to the doctor this morning, Jesse and I." Marti wanted to change the subject.

Kati's smile returned. "Jesse went, too?"

"Yes, he insisted."

"He's going to make a great father."

"We heard the baby's heartbeat. Dr. Diehl put a doptone, which looks like a little black box, on my stomach and rolled it around until he found it. It sounded so fast and loud, kind of like panting." Marti grinned, then leaned toward Kati as if to share a secret. "You should have seen Jesse's face. He was like a little kid who just found out he's getting a pony for his birthday."

"Aw, that's sweet. What did the doctor say?"

"Well, I'm eleven weeks pregnant, due June twenty-second. Everything's fine so far. I think he took half my blood for all these tests. He prescribed these super prenatal vitamins, and recommended vitamin B for nausea." She turned to Kati, her hand on her stomach.

"Kati, I'm scared. This baby in here is going to go through so many changes. Things could go wrong."

Kati put her hand on Marti's leg. "Everything will be just fine, you'll see. And Jesse will be there with you, all of us will."

There was something else she wanted to talk about, but she wasn't comfortable enough to bring it up to Jesse. She'd been dying to know.

"Dr. Diehl said that he wasn't going to charge us for his services. He said he owed Jesse a lot because he saved his daughter's life. Desiree's life."

"Well, that means more money for you then," Kati said in a tight voice.

"I told Jesse to put the amount he allotted for the doctor back on the loan. I don't want it. What I do want to know is what he did to save her life. And who is she? To Jesse, I mean."

Kati leaned back. "Jesse and Desiree started dating back when he was in high school. I think part of it was the older woman allure. They were pretty hot and heavy. It wasn't love so much as, well, you know. A physical thing. That part fizzled out, but they've been friends ever since.

"About six months later, she up and married some guy who'd just moved into town. Desiree's new husband wasn't just crazy about her, he was insane. He beat her up. A lot. At first she tried to hide it, defend the jerk and all. But Jesse saw right through it, and when he couldn't talk her into leaving him, he did some checking up on the guy. Turns out he was wanted in Kansas for nearly killing his last wife, and Desiree didn't even know he was married before. Jesse notified the police and the guy was arrested. He made sure the guy knew he'd better never come back.

"It took a while for Desiree to get back on her feet, esteem-wise, but Jesse stood by her and talked her into getting counseling. He doesn't think he did anything special, but I believe he did save her life."

Kati's story made Marti feel many different things, some of them she couldn't explain. Her mind threw her a picture of Jesse and Desiree in a hot and sweaty clinch. Then she saw Jesse befriending her, standing by her. He might have been hurt himself if her husband had caught him talking to Desiree. Now Jesse was still friends with her, and they had a special past between them. She pushed the pictures from her mind, unwilling to acknowledge that it bothered her. It was the same way she'd felt seeing them together that first time.

"You ready to go?" Marti asked, gathering her bags up.

"My, yes." She gave Marti a sheepish look. "I'm not cut out for this shopping thing."

Jesse fixed himself some spaghetti, knowing that Marti wouldn't be home until well after nine o'clock. He thought he'd enjoy having the evening to himself, but long before nine he was already getting bored and restless. He wandered down by the river, watching the moonlight ripple along the current. His thoughts were far from the sound of the frogs singing in different pitches, far from the moonlight and the shadows of the trees as they swayed in the cool evening breeze.

He shook his head, remembering the bags of clothing Marti had dumped into the Goodwill container. He pictured her stretching up to push the box of old clothes into the cavernous hole of the Goodwill box, so eager to get rid of them. He had offered to throw them in, but she wanted to do it herself. So he'd wrapped his arms around her and hoisted her up. She had waved good-bye to the bags and boxes, giggling. In his arms, she had felt so small. Inside that delicate body his baby was growing. The feeling had overwhelmed him, and he'd put her down very slowly, so he could savor the feelings that coursed through him.

Her laugh was different, he realized. So was her smile. Before, Marti only smiled tentatively, as if she were breaking some rule and someone might catch her. The only time he'd really seen her smile was when she'd told him she was pregnant. *He* certainly hadn't been smiling then.

Now she was smiling again, a new woman inside. When he'd asked Marti why she was so happy at giving the clothes away, she'd said she felt in control again. She was reclaiming her life. He'd swear she only felt that way since he'd made his deal with her. Maybe he'd given her a path to follow, if for a short while. Then she'd be gone, and he'd have a little boy, or girl, to take care of. That child's life would be in his hands, to guide and love forever. But his heart wasn't pounding because he was afraid of the awesome responsibility; it was the excitement, the change in her.

Headlights slashed across the oak trunks and Bumpus raced toward the house barking. Jesse told himself that he was only glad she was home because he knew she was safe. He headed toward the commotion of Kati's voice greeting the dog and the crinkling of bags.

At first he didn't see Marti, only Kati and some blonde. Bumpus recognized Marti before he did. Jesse stopped and stared at the woman who had left a straight-haired brunette several hours earlier.

Kati watched the two stare at each other for a moment, then asked, "Well, what do you think, big brother?"

He walked closer, touching her hair to make sure it wasn't a wig. "You dyed your hair?"

Marti smiled. "Yep. This is sort of what my hair looked like before. Do you like it?"

Jesse half smiled. "Well, like wouldn't be the word for it. Aw, I don't know. I liked it well enough before. Why'd you change it?"

Marti tossed her hair and stalked toward the house. Kati looked at him, a sheepish grin on her face.

"Well, what did *you* think about it? You were a party to the deed," he asked.

Kati raised her arms. "Not me, no sirree! You think I could've told her otherwise. Nope. I didn't like it at first, but I'm getting a little used to it."

Jesse ran his fingers through his hair. "It's not as if I care. I mean, she can do what she wants. But I have to live with her for seven more months."

"Well, if you want to live in peace, you'd better march in there and tell her it doesn't look all that bad."

"I never tell a woman anything I don't mean. That policy has kept me outta trouble more times than it's gotten me into it."

Chapter 7

~

*A*fter he'd seen Kati off, Jesse ambled back inside and peered into Marti's room. She was sitting on the edge of her bed, staring at her reflection in the mirror over the dresser.

"Hey," he said as a greeting, leaning against the door frame. "I . . . I really like . . ." He glanced at the window and stepped inside to get a closer look. "I really like what you've done with the sheets." Now wasn't the time to change the honesty policy.

Her dark expression lifted when she saw his genuine appraisal. "Do you? I had to do something with that window. It was giving me the creeps."

He looked behind the curtains to see how she'd made the top angular and puffy. The curtains themselves had been cut at angles and draped nicely in the middle.

"This looks like something out of a catalog, you know, from those custom sections."

She beamed. "It's amazing what you can do with a couple of wire hangers and a sewing kit. I poked so many holes in my fingers, I thought I'd leak when I drank something."

He couldn't help smiling at her. Her pride was evident, and she looked cuter than a puppy the way she was looking for the pinpricks in her fingertips. The floor was covered with white, pink, and blue bags of every size. Marti dropped back on the bed, stifling a yawn. He looked at her stomach, now puffed out a tad. The reality of the baby hadn't hit until he'd heard its heartbeat that morning. It was a thundering realization, that his baby, a real human being, lived inside Marti. He sat down on the bed next to her.

"You know," she said dreamily. "I had some ideas about the curtains in the living room. Something masculine, but new and different. Would you let me redecorate a little?"

Only when she looked at him did he snap out of his trance. "Sure, do anything you like."

"What about your room? It's kind of dull in there. Can I . . ." She hesitated when he leaned near her. "Can I do something in there, too? It's actually exciting, getting ideas about redecorating this place. Oh!" She sat up suddenly and starting looking through her bags. "I bought something for you."

When she pulled out the swirly, multicolored shirt and held it up, he could only stare at it for a minute.

"You bought that? For me?" He forced a smile.

Her grin soured. "You don't like this either. Kati said it wasn't your style, but I thought it would look great on you. Try it on."

"I didn't say I didn't like it. I just have to, well, absorb it first." Jesse stripped off his shirt and put the new one on. He leaned over and looked in the mirror. "It's different. I guess I could get used to it." He looked at her hair. "And your hair, too. You're just throwing too much new stuff at me at once. I'm too laid back to accept big changes easily."

She bit her bottom lip, letting her gaze travel down his chest before meeting his eyes again. "It looks absolutely excellent on you."

He leaned across and tucked a blond curl behind her ear. "Thanks for buying it for me. I can't believe you even thought about me."

"It's hard not to think about you." She looked away, loosening the strand again. "I mean, being with your sister and all, talking about the baby."

"You talked about the baby?" Was she accepting her pregnant body?

"Well, you know, telling Kati about the doctor's appointment and all."

"Oh. Marti, can I ask you for one thing?"

She stiffened slightly, her expression closing off the

tender part of her. "Sure, you can ask, but it doesn't mean you'll get it."

"I won't try anything with you. I promise I'll be the perfect gentleman. But I'd like to touch the baby. Through your stomach, I mean."

She looked at him for a few seconds, swallowing loudly.

"Yes," she whispered. "You can touch my stomach."

Hesitantly, he reached forward and placed his hand on the outside of her shirt. After a moment, she untucked her shirt and lifted it an inch. He slipped his hand underneath and pressed it flat against the skin. He watched her reaction. Finally, she looked at him, and her face flushed pink. Not wanting to embarrass her, he pulled his hand away.

"Sometimes, when Debbie was pregnant with Turk and Clint, I felt the baby move. It was something special, to feel that little flutter and know a baby was forming in there. I want to feel my boy's movement, knowing that I made him."

"This baby means a lot to you, doesn't it?"

He nodded. "When I first heard I was going to be a father, I couldn't accept it. Once I made a decision to live up to my responsibility, I realized what it all meant. Heck, I wasn't sure what would happen between Marti and I once the baby was born, and I wasn't going to stop racing, but I was going to give the family thing a try." He laughed. "I'd do anything for that kid, and he's not even born yet."

"You're going to spoil him rotten, I can tell."

Jesse's smile faded. "I'm going to have to. I'm all he's got."

Marti twisted her lips. "Jesse, you promised."

"Promised what?"

"That you wouldn't put the guilt trip on me."

He stood up. "Marti, I already told you how I feel about emotional attachments to women interfering with my racing. And you've told me you want to go back to California. I have no intention of trying to get you to stay after you've had the baby. We're going to get along just fine on that score."

A shadow of disappointment flitted over her face, though he hoped it was only his imagination. That look hardened.

"Absolutely. I don't belong here with you, in this town, and especially with a baby."

He agreed with the words, but for some reason they sounded hollow to him.

The man stood just outside Marti's window. He couldn't see in since she'd hung that silly curtain up, but he could see silhouettes. Bits and pieces of their conversation drifted through the fabric and glass. She and Jesse weren't sharing a bedroom anymore. How interesting.

The wind scattered dead oak leaves across the cool earth, but he stood perfectly still. As long as that damn dog didn't start barking again, he was safe to remain there.

Safe. Was he safe from the burning truth? From what he'd done, or almost done, to Marti? She had been dead when he'd left her there at the side of the road, but she came back. How? At first he thought maybe she didn't remember anything about his attacking her. Now he wasn't so sure. He'd heard that she and Jesse had stormed into the sheriff's office and demanded to see the photos. What exactly had they seen? What could they tell from them? He'd seen Jesse go into two jewelry stores the other day, but he couldn't subtly extract from the salespeople what he'd been looking for.

She was remembering, he was sure of it. Damaged memories could come back, and what then? *Think, man, think. Can I keep lingering on the seesaw, waiting for the heavy truth to drop on the other side and send me flying into prison?* He clenched his fists. No, he couldn't. Sometime soon she would be alone.

The following week, Kati and Marti were sweeping up after the last customer finally lifted himself off the seat and sauntered out. Kati was right behind him, turning the dead bolt on the door.

Marti blew out a loud breath. "Damn, people are

slow here in the South! I thought that lazy pace was just exaggerated on television, but now I know it's for real."

Kati laughed. "Well, we don't run around like a bunch of chickens in the butcher yard like you Californians, that's for sure. How was your first day pulling your share of the tables?"

Marti grimaced. "It wouldn't have been so bad if every time I take a step"—she put her hands over her breasts—"I didn't feel like these things were going to explode."

"Yeah, I know what you mean. Mine get tender too when my aunt flow starts planning her visit."

"You have an aunt who makes your boobs sore?"

Kati chuckled. "My period."

"Oh, gotcha. Well, this is *nothing* like that kind of pain, let me tell you. They even hurt when I breathe." Marti leaned on the broom handle. "Do you think that Marti got pregnant on purpose to trap Jesse?"

"Yes," Kati answered without much hesitation. "I was mad at her for doing it, but if you knew Marti, it was hard to be mad at her. She seemed so . . . I don't know, pitiful. Needy. And we could never prove it anyway."

"Sometimes I think about her, about what she was like. I took her life, and yet I know hardly anything about her."

Kati scooted an army of ketchup bottles toward her as she sat down. "I didn't either. She came into town, rented a room, and got a job here. I didn't think she was hiding from anyone, but it did seem like she was running away."

"From what?"

"I don't know. Whenever I asked about her family, she changed the subject. The only thing she ever said was that they didn't get along, and never would. It's hard for me to imagine being separated from my family like that."

Marti stared off for a moment, thinking of her own father whom she'd never met, of her mother whom she hardly knew. Sometimes it was better to be separated from them, she thought.

* * *

On the way home, she drove to the grocery store to get a ready-cooked chicken for dinner. It was as she had suspected. Marti had trapped Jesse into a marriage he wasn't ready for. Maybe she'd known how family-oriented and responsible the man was. Still, it wasn't fair. She would return to California with stretch marks and extra weight, and Jesse would have a baby to care for by himself.

And Marti already knew that some of that extra weight she would carry back to California would be guilt. It inched up on her already, every time she thought about leaving. She told herself she shouldn't feel guilty—Jesse didn't want her to stay.

She glanced down at her gas gauge, now very conscious of running out. It had snuck down to a quarter of a tank. Did she dare take a chance that the gauge was accurate? One of the things she had promised Jesse was that she wouldn't stop to get gas by herself. She certainly didn't want to relive Marti's terror. But the first gas station on the edge of town was right up ahead, and it was still the middle of the afternoon. What harm could come of it? She pulled into the four pump station and got out to pump the gas. The modern pumps looked out of place in front of the 1940s style wooden building.

"Marti, you should have waited another minute. I could've done that for you."

She whirled around to find Paul dressed in green overalls, leaning against the farthest pump. With a casual stride, he walked over and propped himself up against her car.

"I thought you sold insurance," she blurted out, completely unnerved.

"I do. But business is pretty slow, so I'm earing some extra cash to put neon lighting underneath my truck. What do you think? Purple?"

There was something beneath the green of his eyes that made her think he didn't much care about her opinion of color.

"Purple's fine." She watched the numbers on the gas

pump, waiting to hit the five-dollar mark so she could leave.

He reached out and touched her hair with blackened fingers. "I like this. Sexy, different. Taking a walk on the wild side, Marti?"

"No, just wanted a change." She moved away and found herself tucking her hair behind her right ear. Irritated at herself and Jesse for a second, she yanked it back out again.

"Marti, your husband thinks that I was the one who attacked you. You know that's not true."

She avoided his penetrating gaze. "I don't know who attacked me."

He touched her arm, and she involuntarily flinched. "It wasn't me. Don't you understand that Jesse's just trying to make you distrust me? Hate me? He knows I liked you before he got you pregnant, and he doesn't want anything to flare up between us."

"I didn't know there was anything to flare up between us."

"There wasn't. Yet." His fingers loosened their grip on her arm, and he leaned against her car. His smile was pure, unadulterated charm. "Marti, I know that inside is a wild woman clawing to get out. Am I right?"

Her eyes widened. Could he know? Impossible! "What do you mean?"

"I mean, you don't belong in a pregnant body waiting on Jesse and pumping out babies." He lifted his hand to graze her cheek. "We could have a lot of fun together. You can have babies when you're older and more settled."

She moved away from his touch, turning off the pump and closing the gas door. "Are you suggesting that I have an abortion so I can romp with you?"

He cocked his head at her directness. "I'd make it worth it."

"I don't think you could."

She started to get in the car, planning to toss out five bucks and screech away. His voice stopped her.

"You're carrying a criminal's child."

"What are you talking about?"

"Jesse is a criminal. You're living with a car thief."

"You're lying. Jesse wouldn't steal a car."

Paul crossed his arms and leaned back on his heels. "Oh, but he did. And he was convicted, too. Think about that as you lie next to him at night." Then his smile curved up wickedly. "But you're not sharing a bed with him, are you?"

"How would you know something like that?" She suddenly felt confused and violated.

"Someone saw you bed shopping a few Sundays ago. Something like that can mean only one thing—trouble at the home and hearth."

"It's for the baby." She closed the door and handed him a five.

"Babies don't sleep in regular beds," he stated triumphantly.

Screeching tires drew her attention away from Paul's leer to the face of barely controlled anger: Jesse. His truck pulled to a stop just inches away from Paul and her car. He lunged out and toward Paul.

Before he said anything to him, Jesse turned to her. "Go home. Now."

"Jesse, I—"

"Now!" his voice thundered.

She tossed the five out into the air and slammed the car into gear. Damn men! All she wanted was five bucks worth of gas. In the rearview mirror, she could see Jesse making pointed gestures while Paul stood back unaffected. Arrogant even. Still, he'd imparted some unpleasant news, if it was true. A convicted car thief? Couldn't be. But she couldn't push it from her mind.

Jesse arrived home only five minutes after she did. She steeled herself for his anger. Who was he, anyway, to tell her what to do? She'd never seen him angry before, and his face was bright red.

"Damn it, Marti! What did I tell you about getting gas alone?"

"I didn't want to run out."

"You shouldn't let it get that low, then."

"Jesse, I can't hide away because someone tried to attack me."

"So you position yourself alone with the man who probably tried to rape you and killed Marti? You're a damn fool!"

She felt the warmth rising inside to fill her cheeks with heat. "I am not a fool! It was broad daylight. By a busy road."

He leaned into her face, his voice sarcastic. "And what time of the day was Marti attacked? And by what busy road?"

She felt her face momentarily pale. He was right on that score. "Well, I was handling it just fine. I was about to leave when you stormed in like the army."

"He was probably planning on puncturing your tire. Geez, you don't know what he might have done!"

"You're only speculating it was Paul because you hate him. You don't have proof, except for a similarity in his pendant and my scratch."

Jesse sat down, breathless. "No, I don't have proof. But it just so happens that Paul was off the afternoon Marti was killed."

She dropped down on the couch a few feet away from him. "How do you know?"

"Because my friend Alan is dating the secretary at the insurance company. She checked the sign-in sheets; he left at noon and never returned."

Chapter 8

~

Marti was having trouble conjuring up the Christmas spirit, even though it was only a week away. She'd laid three different outfits on the bed trying to figure out what to wear to Harry's Christmas barbecue, wondering why it even mattered to her. It was unbearably warm for December, not at all suitable for the holiday season. At least it got cold in Southern California, even if they didn't have white Christmases.

Finally she chose a teal top that laced up the front and took advantage of her swelling chest. White, high-waisted jean shorts went well with that. She pulled her blond curls into a ponytail and tied a ribbon around it. Never one to shun a social event, Marti just couldn't conjure up any excitement for this shindig. No pearls, lace, or sequins for this party. An outside barbecue with a roasted hog and a bunch of country hicks was not her style. Burping, dirty-joke-telling, country-music-listening hicks. She stared grimly into the mirror and set her mouth in a straight line. Worst of all, she couldn't even get drunk to numb the situation. The baby was more important than her temporary comfort. Besides, Jesse would never allow it, not even a sip.

Her bottom lip puckered out indignantly at the thought of Jesse. He had forced her into this. This hadn't been the first party they'd been invited to, and every time he brought one up, she told him to go without her. But he didn't want to leave her alone, not with the attack so fresh on his mind. Not with Bumpus's barking fits in the middle of the night, and no raccoons to be found as the cause. So he had declined them, never citing her as the reason. He wasn't so obliging with Harry's shindig. It was his boss, and the biggest event of the year, besides the one Harry threw after the Fourth of July parade. Jesse called her selfish again, and for some reason it bothered her when he called her that more than when anyone else had. The selfless bastard.

When she opened her bedroom door, the country music that had been seeping under in polite volumes now pounded against her. With her hands over her ears, she went in search of the stereo controls. Jesse found her first. He appeared out of nowhere, pulled her into his arms, and danced her across the living room.

"Yeah-eee!" he hollered with a twang.

"Jesse!" she exclaimed, but to no avail.

The room spun around her as his arms held her tight. She could only see Jesse's face, lit with a two-thousand watt smile. On his head was a black cowboy hat tilting low over his forehead. When the heel-kicking song ended, Jesse slowed his pace to match the slower melody. He also pulled her close against his body, and she could feel the heat of his pounding heartbeat against her cheek.

"Jesse," she murmured against the texture of his shirt.

"Shh, I like this song."

A man's voice sang out that he was born to love her, and the warmth froze over in her blood. Of course, he didn't mean anything by it, she told herself. Still she moved out of his arms and turned down the stereo. His dismayed expression only held her attention for a minute before her gaze drifted down over his bolo tie, white shirt with cowboy stitching, black leather belt, and indigo jeans. And black leather cowboy boots.

"I've never seen you, uh, dressed like that before," she said, a smile creeping over her face.

He tilted his head and smiled, those indents in his cheeks not quite full-fledged dimples. "I don't put on the dog very often. Just when I'm in the mood."

"Your cowboy mood, huh?"

He turned the stereo back up and pulled her close again. "Yep, my cowboy mood. Are you afraid to dance with me?"

She stiffened. "No, I'm not afraid to dance with you. Why would I be?"

He started slowly moving her around, swaying to the music. "I don't know. Why would you be?"

"Jesse, I just don't . . . like this kind of music."

His hips were pressed against hers. Suddenly he dipped her, poised just above her.

"Say you like it or I'll drop you," he taunted.

"Like what? Dancing with you or country music?"

He grinned. "Both." He dropped her a little lower. "Say it."

"Jesse . . ." His warm breath pulsed against her throat. "Okay, I like it. Now let me go."

He yanked her up and twirled around the room. "Not a chance! You just said you liked dancing with me."

"Under duress," she stated, trying to ignore the sparkle in his eyes. He was having too much fun at her expense. And even in his getup, he looked devastatingly sexy. Ooh, how she hated admitting that! But it was only in an objective sense since he wasn't anywhere near her type. When he loosened his grip a little, she slipped out and sat down on the couch. He did a little jig ending with a slap to the bottom of his boot and wiggle of his derriere. Finally he turned down the stereo. With a flushed face, he leaned down over her and tucked her hair behind her ears.

"You gotta learn to loosen up a little and have some fun."

She untucked her hair. "When I did that, I got into trouble. Besides, I don't want to have fun."

"Why not?"

"Because . . ." *I'm leaving in six months. Because you're making me feel very funny inside leaning so close to me like this.*

"Well?"

She slid around him and walked to the other side of the room. "Don't we have to go soon?"

He ran his fingers through his waves, shaking his head slightly. "I thought you didn't want to go. Now you can't wait to get out of the house?" He rested his chin on the back of the couch facing her. "Why is that?"

"I just want to get it over with." She reached for her new leather purse.

With a quick leap, he was over the couch and sauntering near her. "I know what it is," he said in a teasing voice. His woodsy cologne wafted over before he got close. Too close.

Marti backed away, her eyes narrowed. "And what is it, mister know-it-all?"

He took a step closer. "I think you've always had a secret cowboy fetish. Oh, you never admitted it to anyone, but down deep inside . . ." He pressed a finger to the middle of her chest. "It's there."

She flung his finger away. "Don't be silly! I've never had a thing for cowboys. I go for the slick California types, blondes with surfboards attached to the roofs of their cars." And not ones with criminal records, a voice added to her thoughts. "You're just a little too arrogant for your own good, Jesse James."

His smile reeked of confidence. "Maybe. But you sure don't trust yourself to get too close to me, now do you? You've moved away from me twenty times in the last ten minutes."

"Your cologne's too strong."

"Come on Mrs. Marti May West," he said with a roll of his eyes, holding out his arm to her. "Be my wife for an afternoon."

Bumpus crawled out of the bushes and followed them as soon as they walked toward the truck. When he opened the door for her, she saw the roll of paper towels on the seat. He smiled.

"See, I didn't forget about you. And you don't have to ride in the back, either."

She slugged him in the arm and climbed up. Did he actually think she was attracted to him because he was wearing cowboy clothing? Or for any other reason? Maybe he was just flirting; part of his cowboy mood. That sounded better.

Harry's place was farther west than Helen's, down a long dirt road. Anxiety set in when she saw the cars and trucks scattered all over the front driveway. All these people. She was going to have a miserable time.

The house was a new two-story with gray wood siding. The commotion was around the back beneath a strange structure with a roof made of dead palm fronds. Country music blared, people laughed, and Marti grimaced.

Jesse stopped just before they reached the house. "Stay nearby so I can help you out with anyone you don't know that you should." He grinned. "That is, if you can handle being close to me."

She slugged him in the arm again, ignoring the pain at contacting hard flesh.

All the hoopla Jesse received when they arrived at Harry's was proof that he really didn't dress up like that very often. It sounded more like a construction site with all the wolf whistles and cowboy calls.

Harry was in his forties with a bulbous nose and an even more bulbous belly. He teetered over to greet them, just a little intoxicated already.

"Jesse, Marti! Glad you could come. Kegs are over there, sodas are in the big red cooler and hog's on the fire. He'll be ready to come to supper about five. Help yourselves."

Marti looked at a primitive brick structure with a whole pig on it, hooves, head, and tail. She wrinkled her nose, wondering if her appetite would ever forgive her for this one.

"What would you like to drink?" Jesse asked.

"A glass of Chardonnay? Martini? Guess I'll have to settle for a Coke, and I'd pay you a hundred bucks if you'd slip something in it."

"Gotcha," he said and walked toward the coolers.

Fat chance that he'd bring her a rum and Coke, she thought. Still, it was nice to think about. Most of the people sitting at picnic tables and playing horseshoes she'd seen at Bad Boys at one time or another. She saw Skip and Josh, but Paul was luckily nowhere in sight. While talking to some guy, Desiree gave Jesse a cutesy wave of her hand. Marti caught herself wrinkling her nose and just settled for rolling her eyes.

"Here you go," Jesse said, handing her a cup of Coke with a peach hibiscus flower in it.

She smiled sardonically. "Gee, thanks."

"Well, you said you wanted something in it. And you don't even have to give me a hundred bucks. Maybe it'll look better here."

He tucked her hair behind one ear and slipped the flower in, looking pleased with the result.

Dean and Kati showed up a little later. Marti was glad to see a face she knew and liked, but Kati was busy telling everyone about the cow she'd calved and just visited earlier. Dean watched her flit from one group of people to another.

"Hi, Dean," Marti said, moving up next to him.

"Hi," he said, his smile almost too wide. "Where's Jesse?"

"I released him," she said. "I told him to wander around to his heart's content. I'm just not in a party mood."

Dean glanced uneasily down at his beer. "Me neither. Hey, I like that flower. My aunt Flo used to eat flowers. She'd dip them in batter and deep-fry 'em."

Marti's eyes widened. "Your aunt flow? You're not talking about your . . . oh, you really have an Aunt Flo!" He was looking at her as strangely as she sometimes looked at him. "Never mind. Did fried hibiscus taste good?"

"They weren't bad if you sprinkled a little powdered sugar on top. That Kati's gonna wear herself out." Dean wandered off to follow Kati around.

Jesse took up a game of horseshoes, he and Billy creaming two other guys. Josh, wearing dingy overalls again but minus the dried grass, moseyed over and planted himself next to Marti on the bench. His red hair stuck out as if he'd just woken up.

"Hi," he said. "Like a beer?" He held up his half-empty cup as if to offer her the rest.

"No, thanks. I'm pregnant."

"Oh, that's right. You gonna dance later?" He pointed to a cleared area strung with lights.

"Not likely."

Josh made her increasingly uncomfortable as he stayed there a little too close for a little too long. The smell of his sweat was making her feel nauseated.

"Do you really think Paul was the one who attacked you?"

She eyed him. "Why, do you have someone else in mind?"

"Could be lots of guys." His glassy eyes leered. "Could've even been me."

She lifted her chin a little. "Was it?"

"It was if you enjoyed it. Did you?"

She stood up and made a beeline toward the house. Josh walked next to her. He looked as though he were casually walking her to the house, but his voice sounded sinister.

"You better tell your husband he's asking for trouble if he keeps tryin' to pin your attack on Paul. He didn't do it, but people's starting to wonder the way Jesse keeps snooping 'round like a hound dog, checking the jewelry stores and Paul's work records. He happens to be a good friend of mine, and it's really buggin' him. You just tell Jesse to lay off."

She turned around just before reaching the door. "Why don't you tell him yourself? He's right behind you." When Josh looked to where she pointed, she ducked inside and quickly hid out in the bathroom for a while. She wished Jesse *had* been standing right behind him. Only when the third voice outside the door lamented at waiting to pee did she finally flush the toilet and walk back outside. Jesse was sitting where she had been earlier.

"Are you all right? You were gone for a while."

"I'm fine. I just needed to get away from annoying company." She decided not to get Jesse's ire up over Josh's lame words.

"They're just about to serve dinner. Are you hungry? Boy, you're gonna love roasted hog, smoking all day long in the pit."

With great ceremony, four men pushed aside palm fronds from the pit. They lifted the black mass out and set it up to start slicing away at the carcass. Marti decided to wait at the table for Jesse and let the whole process remain a mystery.

After dinner, everyone sat around and talked about

how wonderful the hog was. Burping was the next order of business, compliments to the chef all around. Thankfully, Jesse abstained from the rude behavior, although he did laugh at some of the more creative efforts. The next round of conversation was how many men had noticed that the ice cubes were in the shape of a woman's boobs. She glanced at her glass, realizing that she hadn't noticed it and not feeling all that amused.

Deep in her thoughts she removed herself from the lewd conversation and took herself to one of Theresa's parties in California. Her mother-in-law knew how to put on a party, waiters making the rounds with trays of champagne, bars scattered around the huge lawn behind the mansion. No boob cubes or burping. She pictured her old self, drinking a little too much champagne, dressed in black velvet and diamonds.

"Wheeehooo!" Billy hollered, bringing her back to the dreadful present. Marti turned to see someone's white behind glaring from atop one of the tables. She didn't bother to see whose behind it was before looking back at Jesse. Her mood was deteriorating rapidly.

"Come on," Jesse said good-heartedly. "It's only fun and games. We gotta stay for some dancing, at least."

"You can be so optimistic," she said below her breath. "You're half sloshed!"

His smile disappeared. "No, I'm not. Maybe a quarter sloshed, but not nearly a half." He reached over and tucked her hair behind the other ear. "Don't be mad. Have fun."

She turned on him and forced a wide smile. "Oh, Jesse, I'm having a great time! The company is terrific, the hog body gourmet, and the music enchanting. See, I'm getting into it." Her good humor slipped away. With the twangiest voice she could muster, she started singing. "My wife left me for my best girlfriend, my hound dog died on the front porch, and the bank repo'd my land, so I can't even bury him. Woe, woe, woe is me!"

Then she started laughing, howling even. Did she ever think she would be at a party where burping was considered good-hearted fun? Where they had boob cubes, and you were a boob if you didn't notice your cubes had titties? She was doubled over with tears streaming down her cheeks. Her stomach hurt, she was laughing so hard. *Have fun.* Whoo boy, she was having fun now! She tumbled off the bench and onto the grass, and finally gained some control over herself after catching her breath. When she peered up over the edge of the table, everyone in the vicinity was watching her. And they weren't laughing.

Even Jesse looked serious. "You have a strange way of having fun," he stated flatly.

That started her giggling again. "*I* have a strange way! At least I'm not trying to top the biggest, most disgusting belch!"

The others' attention faded away to their individual conversations, but Jesse's gaze remained on her.

"What is the matter?" she asked, getting to her feet.

"At least our way of having fun isn't making fun of others' ways. And others' music."

She sat down on the bench, taking a last deep breath. "So sue me. At least I can say I had a little fun."

He pointed to her, his finger slipping between the lace of her top. "For that little outburst, you owe me a dance tonight. A slow one."

"I don't want to. You know I don't like this music."

"If these people are going to think you were just kidding, you'd better get that cute little butt of yours out there with me. Then we can leave."

She looked out to the patch of ground reserved for dancing. The lights defined the square, and inside several couples were dancing and moving in a circle as they did so. The people who weren't under the tent were mingling outside the dance area watching. Watching? Ugh.

"Well?" Jesse said.

"Then we can leave? You promise?"

"Yes, I promise."

She grimaced, but stood up anyway. He took her hand and led her toward the dreaded square. At Jesse's request, a slow song started, and he walked her out to the far edge. The square quickly filled up with couples, making her feel less self-conscious. And more conscious of being in Jesse's arms again as they were pressed into intimate quarters.

He was still wearing the black cowboy hat which cast a shadow across his cheeks and nose. A cowboy fetish indeed! The whole thing was silly. The hat made him seem taller than ever and gave him a sort of refined roughness. His collar points were tipped in silver, which caught the light as they swayed to the rhythm. And those boots, they made him taller yet! She stared downward, watching them move back and forth.

The singer in the song likened his love to Reno, Nevada, cold, heartless, and playing with his affections. The Hallie of the past might have been perceived that way. Maybe she'd even been that way sometimes. But love wasn't her game now. She pictured the scene earlier in Jesse's living room, him moving up close, her stepping away. Might he think she was still like that? No, she had made it clear that she wasn't interested in him or his way of life. And he had made it clear he wasn't interested either. His flirting was nothing more than that; couldn't be. And her uneasiness? Just like the hot flash at Helen's house, she could explain that away, too. She'd think of something, if she gave it a minute.

Jesse lifted her chin way up to position her face in his view. His soft smile was more subtle than earlier.

"You don't have to watch our feet," he said. "You're doing just fine."

She realized then that she had been staring at his boots while lost in thought. Better to let him think she was unsure of her footing than her heart. He tucked her hair behind her ears. The flower was smashed in the grass where she'd fallen off the bench.

"Jesse, why do you keep tucking my hair behind my ears?" she asked, loosening it again.

He shrugged. "Just seems like it should be."

"Did you used to do that with"—she glanced around—"the other Marti?" She wasn't even sure why she wanted to know.

"No. It was different with her."

"How?" She wanted to bite back the question.

He tucked her hair back again. "Well, for one thing,

there's something different about your eyes. I don't see neediness there, but there's still a wanting. Like you're searching for something, but you don't know what it is yet."

She looked away, wondering how he could see something she didn't even know was there. But she was searching, for a new life. A new identity.

"I'm not looking for love, I know that." It sounded hollow to her, but she believed in those words more than anything else. She expected Jesse to be put off by them somehow.

Warmth burned beneath his green eyes as he let go of her hand and trailed his finger up the length of her throat to rest under her chin. "It'll find you someday, you just wait." *But not with me.*

Marti could hear the unspoken words just as clearly as if he had spoken them aloud. She searched for words to respond but couldn't get past the disappointment. Why was she feeling that way? Silly fool, get your mind out of the bed!

"The song's over," she said, finding it hard to swallow with his finger still touching her.

His hand slipped from around her waist and took hold of her hand as he walked off the dance area. They wound around others who were line dancing to the jaunty tune. *Oh, God, we've been slow dancing through part of a fast song! With half the town watching! They'll think . . . they'll think . . .* The words dropped down on her head. *They'll think you're in love. Too distracted to realize the slow dance was over.* She shook her head, ignoring Jesse's glance at her movement. *I knew the song was over. Damn, I can't lie to myself! Okay, I was distracted, but not in that way.*

Jesse pulled her around to various groups to say good-bye, then to thank Harry for his hospitality, burping and boob cubes excepted. The looks of speculation at her earlier outburst had been replaced by good humor. Hopefully they thought she was drunk. Or just stupid. Hopefully they didn't think she was in love with her husband. How ridiculous!

Bumpus, like a child having fun, was reluctant to

leave his canine pals. Still, when Jesse gave the word, he stood at attention and tromped over to them. All three walked down the drive to the truck in silence, except for Bumpus's occasional slurping noises. When they reached the truck, she armed herself with the paper towels before she got in next to Jesse. With a tiny groan, the dog twirled around and settled down on the seat, nestling his head on Marti's thigh.

Jesse tilted his head at the cozy scene. "I don't understand it, but that dog sure does like you."

She crossed her arms, careful not to disturb Bumpus. "What's not to understand?" A warm feeling curled inside her as she looked at the dog, eyes drooping sleepily.

He shook his head slightly as he put the truck into gear and pulled onto the dirt road. "You're ornery, snobby, and you can't cook worth a damn. I'm gonna have a talk with that dog. Maybe he can enlighten me."

She shot him a look, then rested her hand gently on the dog's head, feeling a sudden kinship with him. After all, it was safer to be around the dog than it was to be with Jesse James West, the outlaw cowboy.

Florida's weather at least had the decency to get nippy two days before Christmas. When Marti thought the diner might be a little slower, it just got busier. All the usual patrons came in with visiting relatives and introduced them to Kati and Marti as if they were family, too. Even her own family hadn't been that friendly.

The warm, country theme inside the diner seemed enhanced by the tinsel and garland draped all over the walls. Chuck didn't much want to perpetuate the Santa Claus myth, being much more religious than he let on. A manger with Mary, Joseph, and baby Jesus sat in the corner, displacing one of the tables. Chuck's usual sullen expression had lifted some; maybe he thought he was safe from her memory of the attack, if he had something to worry about. She hated thinking that way, but the fear lingered at the back of her mind.

Ten minutes after closing time, Jesse knocked on the glass door. Marti felt greasy and shabby after shuffling between tables and the kitchen all day, and didn't want to see Jesse until she'd washed up. She caught herself starting to smooth her hair back and stopped. It was just vanity, not any special desire to impress Jesse.

In the warm diner she'd forgotten how cool it was outside. And overcast. Little puffs of fog appeared when Jesse talked. He looked like a little boy anxiously awaiting Santa's visit.

"Hi, doll. Let's go Christmas tree shopping."

She glanced at Kati. "I can't. Kati and I are going Christmas shopping when we're done. I'm going to shower and change at your mom's place on the way to Fort Myers." When his smile disappeared, she added, "We can go later tonight."

He grinned again. "Kati, want to come along? You and Mom need a tree, too."

"Nah, she wants to put up that fake tree again this year. You know, she complains about the needles and everything."

His eyes lit up with mischief. "We'll get her one anyway. Don't let her put that thing up until we get there later tonight. And don't tell her!" He looked at Marti, still standing in front of him. "See you at home then." He clicked his tongue and winked, then walked back outside and jumped into his truck.

"He's like a little boy," Marti said with a smile.

"This year he is." Kati had a wistful smile which Marti ignored.

Marti didn't get home until six that evening. She sneaked into the house with her packages and put them in the closet. With everybody out of the way, she could relax and enjoy a Christmas she was actually looking forward to. Family celebrations were something she could become accustomed to, although she wouldn't. Couldn't. Still, she'd remember these days with a fondness lacking in her past holiday memories.

"What'd you get? What'd you get?" Jesse whispered from the other side of the door.

"Jesse, don't you dare come in here!" she hollered, shoving the closet door shut.

"Does that mean there's something in there for me?" he asked hopefully.

She threw a shoe at the door. "Only coal for you!"

Jesse was standing at the front door when she emerged. Wearing a white T-shirt and black jeans, his expression radiated joy. She couldn't help but smile. Jamie had enjoyed Christmas, but not as enthusiastically as Jesse seemed to. Maybe that had something to do with her, she thought with dismay. Hopefully he was having a wonderful Christmas with his new wife.

"Hey, hey, what's the frown for?"

She pushed Jamie from her memory. "Nothing. I'm ready."

"Good." He took her hand but blocked the front door when they reached it. "Close your eyes."

She eyed him suspiciously. "Why?"

"Come on, trust me."

"Humph."

When she started to close them, she felt him move up behind her and clamp his palms over her eyes. Slowly he guided her out the front door and into the crisp air tinged with the smell of chimney smoke. Christmas music wafted over from the vicinity of his truck. He turned her around, and she thought she might be facing the house again.

"Ready?" he asked.

"Yes."

Still, he waited, pressed up behind her with his hands firmly planted over her eyes.

"Jesse? What are we waiting for?"

"I don't know. I kind of like standing here like this."

She nudged him, and he removed his hands. The house twinkled every color of the rainbow, vivid against the night air. The lights on the roof spelled out, "Merry Christmas!" The bushes were sprinkled with tinsel, which sparkled as Bumpus moved among them. A big, plastic angel was poised above the front door, holding a star in her hands. She caught her breath, taken in by the magic of the lights.

"Oh, Jesse, it's beautiful! Like a fairy tale!"

He wrapped his arms around her, resting his chin on her shoulder. "Just for you."

She turned, suddenly finding it hard to breathe. "Jesse, don't say that. You probably do this every year."

The boyishness of earlier was gone, replaced by a masculine softness. "No, I don't. I wanted to make this a special Christmas for you. Once you get out to California, you're going to be all alone. I wanted to give you a good memory to think about next Christmas."

She swallowed, feeling overcome by a barrage of emotions. At the moment, with the music and warmth welling up inside her, she couldn't dredge up a foul, underhanded reason for his doing all this. Besides, he didn't want her to stay anyway. Her voice nearly failed her.

"I won't forget you." The lights twinkled in her eyes as she was held mesmerized by them.

He touched her chin briefly, then tucked her hair behind her ears. "Let's go tree shopping, doll."

They stopped at the first lot filled with Christmas trees. There were still plenty to choose from under the yellow and white striped tent surrounded by bare light bulbs. Jolly music filtered through the air as they walked among the trees searching for the two most perfect ones left. The ones in the front were either crooked or had massive bare spots.

"They're more out back," the young salesman told them. "It's kinda dark back there, so watch for holes where the trees have been."

Beyond the last line of trees, the empty lot continued before turning into woods. The music was only faint, and she felt as if she were lost in a magical forest. One of the trees moved slightly, and before she could mention it to Jesse, she saw a man jump out and throw a rope of some kind over Jesse's head, pulling him back. Before she could react, a hand clamped over her mouth and a familiar voice whispered, "Don't say a word, or your husband gets it worse."

Paul suddenly appeared in front of Jesse, who was whipping his fists wildly at the man holding him from behind. Since the man, who she realized was Skip, was shorter, he had Jesse bent backward at an awkward angle. Paul slammed a fist into Jesse's stomach, and he groaned before kicking out. His foot connected with Paul's knee, making him shout in pain. With more anger than before, Paul lashed out and kicked Jesse in the gut, making him drop down to his knees. Marti wriggled, but Josh pinched her hands tighter behind her back, causing a sharp pain. She was terrified for Jesse.

"I'm tired of you snooping around trying to pin Marti's attack on me," Paul growled. "Mack told me you were checking out my tee times at the golf course. People are starting to wonder what you've got on me, and you got nothing. Nothing! I was at the course the time she was attacked."

Paul took another slug, this time at Jesse's face. Marti cringed. With a spear of panic, she bit into Josh's hand. He let go with a curse, and she screamed.

Skip dropped Jesse, and both he and Josh took off into the darkness. Paul took a step back, looking down at Jesse. "Leave it alone, Jesse. Consider this your final warning. I didn't touch the girl." With that he was gone, just before the tree salesman came rushing over.

She ran to Jesse, who was getting slowly to his feet, coughing violently. When she saw that he was going to chase after them, she pulled his arm back.

"Jesse, no! There's three of them, and only one of you."

"Geez, are you two all right?" The young man looked terribly concerned. "I know it's dark back here, but I never figured it'd be dangerous. Tell you what. I'll let you have whatever tree you want, for your trouble. No charge."

Jesse started to say something, but she interrupted. "Thank you, that's awfully nice. We'll take this one here, and we also want that one, for his mother. She's going to be awfully upset when she hears about this. She's so fragile, you know."

Marti reached up and touched the blood oozing from Jesse's lower lip.

The salesman watched with growing concern in his

eyes. "Aw, you can have that one, too. I don't want his mama to get too bent out of shape. It is Christmas."

When the trees were loaded into the back of the truck, and the salesman had apologized for the fifteenth time and left, Marti reached up and dabbed at his lip with a paper towel. He flinched.

"You gonna swab me like you do Bumpus?"

"Stop moving! You're bleeding all over."

"Son of a bitches ambushed me. What kind of slime ambushes a guy when he's Christmas tree shopping?"

The true amazement in his expression made her laugh before she had the sense to bite her lip. "So you've been doing some snooping, huh?" She remembered Josh's remarks at Harry's, but decided not to share them with Jesse just then. "Do you think he really did it?"

"I—ouch! I don't know. He left work at noon. Apparently he'd called the course and arranged a tee time of twelve-thirty. Nolen said he found you at around one o'clock, and . . ." He looked off into the distance for a second before looking back at her.

"Marti was already dead. But she hadn't been dead for long, so that means that the attack happened just before one. Paul had checked in at twelve-twenty, but Mack didn't see Paul and those two deadbeats start the first hole until about twelve-forty-five. That means that Paul had twenty minutes to drive down the road and find poor Marti stuck. It doesn't exactly point to him as the murderer, but it doesn't clear him either. Apparently that dumb-ass Mack mentioned my inquiries to Paul, who had to get his buddies to help him out." Jesse placed his palm on his flat stomach and grimaced.

"Are you all right? God, I was so scared."

His expression was dark. "So was I. For you." He took her face in his hand. "Marti, I wouldn't have let them hurt you. I can take my punches, but if they'd tried to hurt you, they would have been dead."

"I know," she whispered. Somehow, she did. "Jesse, you haven't let this attack go, have you? You've been thinking about it a lot."

"I've got to find out who did this to you. To Marti. I don't want them to hurt you again."

"Jesse, how can you hide your anger and determination so well? Like with the racing. And that Sunday when I told you about the indent and Paul's pendant; you just went about the rest of the day like normal, then you confronted Paul."

He looked off into the distance again. "When my pa died, I wanted to scream and yell and never stop crying. He was everything to me, my whole world. Billy withdrew, and Mom had so much stuff to deal with, I couldn't dump her with that burden, too. So I put it aside until after the funeral. When I could deal with it alone. I do it when I have to."

She put her hand on his arm. "Jesse, please don't go after Paul. I mean, don't get crazy. I know you're mad, but remember, he might be a killer." She smiled, trying to make light of what she was about to say. "What would I do without you? I can't have this baby alone, you know. He needs a father." *And a mother.* Marti pushed that errant thought away.

He turned and started the truck. "I'm not going to do anything stupid." Then, as if remembering something, he laughed. "My fragile mother?"

She shrugged. "Got us another tree, didn't it?"

They dropped one of the trees off at Helen's, who was more annoyed at Jesse's bloody lip than she was at having the live tree forced on her. When they pulled back into their drive, Marti's heart tightened at the lights. Kati had confirmed what Marti didn't want to really know: Jesse had never decorated his house full tilt before. Just a paper Santa on the door and a few strings of lights. She bit her lip, wondering at how the gift of Jesse's decorating could touch her more than a long-ago gift of a red Porsche. He was so sweet. Damn him.

Chapter 9

~

$\mathcal{D}$uring the entire Christmas Eve day, Marti was surrounded by a flurry of activity. First at work, where Chuck gave them fifty dollar bonuses and let them go home without cleaning up. He'd actually smiled.

Jesse ordered her to stay out of his bedroom while he wrapped packages. Dressed in a red and black flannel shirt, he looked like a misplaced lumberjack. Handsome, but misplaced.

"I won't tell Kati what you got her," she'd teased, trying to peek in through the crack of the door.

He had pinched her chin. "But will you tell Marti what I got her, that's the worry here."

She had turned crimson, realizing for the first time that Jesse had actually bought her something for Christmas. It was the perfect time to wrap her own presents, and she scrounged up a pair of children's scissors with green plastic handles and some tape. For once, the country music took a back seat to traditional Christmas tunes by Bing Crosby and Johnny Mathis. It filled the house with the sweet warmth of anticipation.

All those empty Christmases with her mother slipped away with every song that played, with every package she wrapped in red and gold foil. Between her mother and her mother-in-law, even holidays with Jamie had seemed dismal.

This year she would spend the most special day of the year with a real family. As Jesse had said, she would treasure the memory when she was alone in California. She shook her head, flinging the lonely thought from her mind. She wasn't worried about leaving here, or being alone. The moist crinkled paper she'd been clutching in her hand dropped to the floor among the rejected scraps. Besides, it wasn't like she could stay even if she wanted to, which she didn't. Jesse was going to be a race car driver, and he'd made it more than clear he didn't want any emotional attachments to a woman.

Marti saved Jesse's presents for last. They were more expensive than the other gifts put together. But it would be worth it to see his face when he opened the box and pulled out the gray, ostrich skin boots. The other box contained a gray cowboy hat with a matching ostrich band. She'd known the moment she saw them in the window that Jesse must have them. It would be another twenty hours at least before she could watch him open the boxes.

Later in the day, Kati, Helen, and Billy showed up to decorate the tree. Marti had never felt so much like a kid, stringing fresh popcorn and twirling it around the tree. Dinner was eggnog, tarts, and fried cheese. Helen snapped a picture of Jesse wrapping his arms around Marti's waist and lifting her up high to put the angel atop the tree. Bumpus even got into the act, fetching the red velvet balls that got knocked off and rolled away. Marti tied a red ribbon around his neck, although it dangled upside down beneath his chin most of the time. She discovered country Christmas music, but she could live with that. Nothing was going to spoil her evening.

Except Billy. His smiles were tinged with melancholy, and sometimes she caught him staring off into a distant land. Or time. She remembered his boys, celebrating Christmas without their father. He had made mistakes, but he still deserved his kids for the holidays. Marti involuntarily put her hand on the small mound of her stomach. This baby, she knew, would never be without his father. Jesse wouldn't let that happen.

She found Billy standing in the kitchen alone, looking out the window. His wispy hair stuck out in places, reaching way past his collar. He was always either quiet or making jokes, and those wild, beady eyes of his fit both personas. She had all but ruled him out as her attacker.

Marti had never quite connected with him, as she had

with the other Wests. Most of the time she wasn't bothered by that fact, but watching him standing there like a lost boy made her approach him. The part of her that said go back to the fun and forget about his problems lost out to this new side of her.

"Billy?" she said softly.

He turned, smiling just a little. "Nice night out, huh?"

"I'm sure they miss you as much as you miss them."

He rubbed his nose, looking away. "I wasn't . . ." Then he met her eyes and shrugged. "I hope so. How'd you know I was thinking 'bout my boys?"

She put her hand to her belly. "Woman's intuition. We've got a box of tinsel out there that we could sure use your help with."

Jesse's expression was one of curiosity when she and Billy walked out of the kitchen together, sharing a private smile. Let him wonder, she thought with a grin.

After every inch of Jesse and Marti's tree was duly covered with ornaments, everyone packed up the food and eggnog and drove over to Billy's to decorate his tiny tree (because Jesse insisted that he have one), and then to Helen and Kati's house. Even though it wasn't exactly frosty outside, Jesse lit the fire in the fireplace. Billy lifted Kati up to top the tree with a sparkling star. By the time their tree looked as merry as everyone else's had, Marti was exhausted. It was nearly midnight. Almost Christmas.

Billy was settled in for a night in the recliner. Kati was stretched out under the tree, asleep for at least twenty minutes. Jesse was sprawled out on the couch, his bare feet resting on the arm at one end. Helen had retired some time ago. Christmas music floated faintly on the air. After throwing scraps of wrapping paper away, Marti sat down on the floor in front of Jesse. He looked like a sleepy-eyed boy with his head resting on his hand.

"Did you have fun?" he asked softly, trying not to wake the others.

Marti didn't have to worry about whispering. Her voice was still soft and raspy. "Yes, I did."

He glanced toward the tree where Kati shifted in her sleep in front of the fireplace. "When we were kids, we used to sleep under the tree every Christmas Eve. Even after we knew there wasn't a Santy Claus (that's what we used to call him) and Mom and Dad put the presents underneath early, we still spent the night there." His eyes sparkled the reflection of the flames. "Pa used to try to talk us into going to bed 'or else Santy Claus won't come for you' he'd say. That's when we believed. The three of us would conspire to go to bed, then get up and meet under the tree. And we did, although one time Kati fell asleep and didn't come down. She was mad because we didn't come get her, but we didn't want Pa catching us."

Marti watched the amber glow of the fire dance across his features. "Did Santy come?"

"Yes, he did. We were usually asleep when Santy Pa came down to unload the dryer. That's where they hid the presents, we found out later. One time we stayed up late, and you know what? My pa actually dressed up in his Santy costume before he came downstairs. Billy and I had already figured out by then that Santy was Pa, but we didn't want to spoil it for Kati. She was so cute, her eyes were this big." He gestured with his finger and thumb, then glanced Kati's way again. "I'd feel silly sleeping under the Christmas tree now, and so would Billy, I'm sure. But Kati looks just right down there, like she did when she was six. Hey, what's wrong?"

Marti snapped out of the mental pictures she'd conjured of the Wests' Christmases. She didn't even realize tears had been slipping down her cheeks until Jesse reached out and wiped one away with his thumb.

"I wish you could give me your memories for Christmas. They sound so wonderful."

He pulled her close. "I can share mine with you."

"Thank you," she said, her voice a squeaky whisper.

What is wrong with me? she thought as they drove back home. This was Christmas Eve, and the town was cheerily lit up by thousands of lights. She stared out the window and hoped Jesse couldn't see the silly tears that continued to flow. But she did know what was wrong. Christmases without Santy Clauses and family and lots of presents were normal for her. And when she got older, watching people trying to outdo one another with the most expensive presents was normal.

Everything that she'd been told 'was just on the television' had really been happening at Jesse's house. The warmth and love and sharing—it had been going on without her.

When they got home, she walked ahead of Jesse, swiping at her tears. While he was locking up the truck and petting Bumpus, she unlocked the door and went straight to her room. When Jesse walked inside, she was standing by the Christmas tree, a pillow in each hand.

All stuffed up, she sounded like the little girl she wished she was. "Will you sleep with me under the tree tonight?"

He took the pillows from her, laying them down side by side. After stripping off his shirt, he took her hand and pulled her down. He tucked her hair behind her ears, his gaze never leaving hers. She lay on her back, looking up at the glittering tree. Her pulse started racing when he leaned down over her.

"Why are you still crying?" he asked in a soft voice.

She shook her head. "I don't know. For everything, for nothing."

He looked at her for a few moments. "What can I do to make your tears go away?"

Her lips twitched. *Tell him, Marti. No. Tell him.* "Will you hold me?" she heard her full voice ask him.

Without hesitation, he reached for her hand and pulled her into his arms. She nestled her mouth on his bare shoulder, her arms slipping around him as if they belonged there. She realized that she'd wanted this for a long time. Her hands were splayed against his back, and she fought an urge to run her fingers through his hair.

After a moment, he pulled back a few inches and looked at her. His finger trailed down the tracks her tears were leaving.

"You're still crying."

She managed a laugh. "Happy tears."

Jesse leaned close and kissed the tears from her cheeks. He looked angelic, with the colored lights setting off his hair and the curves of his face. Her heart pounded inside her, and suddenly she was very frightened. And elated.

He seemed to watch her warring emotions. His broad shoulders looked strong, and at the same time soft and creamy in the blinking ambers, blues, and greens. She remembered, for a dreamy moment, what his lips tasted like, wondered what his body might feel like lying next to hers naked, holding her close through the night. All that warmth and affection in him might pour into her, fill her with it. Was it a dream, his lips grazing hers softly? Pressing against hers again, capturing her lips? She drowned, lost in the swirl of lights and the dazzling brilliance his kisses shot inside of her. It tickled through her body, warming her as no fire could.

When he stopped, he held her face in his hands. "Don't cry, okay?" he whispered.

She sucked in a deep breath, meeting his gaze. "Is that your cure for crying? To kiss a girl senseless?"

One side of his mouth quirked up. "It worked, didn't it?"

Her senses were too busy to produce any more tears. "Like a charm."

Marti dropped back down on the blanket. She remembered his earlier words and tried to lighten the mood that threatened to crush her under its weight. "Do you feel silly, sleeping under the tree?"

The grin she hoped would materialize didn't. "No. Silly isn't quite the word I would use."

What? Disappointment? Uneasiness? Her heart raced as his gaze stayed locked to hers.

"Do you want to leave?" she asked, terrified that he would leave, terrified that he might stay.

"No."

She smiled, snuggling under the blanket. *Leave it at that, Marti. I don't understand what just happened. I'm afraid to understand.*

"Merry Christmas, Marti," he said, pulling the blanket over his shoulder and closing his eyes.

Great. She didn't want to cry anymore. Now she wanted to jump him. "Merry Christmas, Jesse."

* * *

The crinkling sound of Bumpus sniffing around the presents under the tree woke Jesse on Christmas morning. It was almost seven-thirty. He rolled over to see if Marti was awake. She wasn't. Her left hand was tucked beneath her pillow, and her right hand was lying between them, as if she'd tried to reach out for him in her sleep.

The wan glow of the lights reflected only lightly on Marti's skin. He watched her for a few minutes, wondering about the woman who sometimes seemed like a little girl. Now he understood better what her past was like, and how it differed from his. Her loss had touched him.

But that wasn't why he'd kissed away her tears. Not out of pity, but out of a deep desire to take away her pain. He didn't even want to think about why he'd kissed her lips . . . and why he'd wanted to keep on kissing her. It hadn't been the same as that night when the first Marti had leaned over and kissed him, and they'd made love because he'd felt sorry for her. Still, he was going to make sure he didn't confuse what was obviously a big brother feeling for anything more than that.

Her eyes fluttered open, and she looked at him, then around her in confusion. She smiled when she saw the tree.

"It's Christmas," she said.

"Yes."

As if she suddenly remembered their kiss, her gaze shifted away and her face pinked over. He threw off the blanket and stretched, aware of the thousand goose bumps that rose on his bare chest when the chilly air hit. She wrapped the blanket around her shoulders and sat looking up at the tree.

"It's so beautiful," she said, an almost reverent smile on her face.

"Haven't you had a Christmas tree before?"

"Yes, but not one like this. Not a real one. My mother had an old silver tree, made from tinsel. She only put red and green balls on it, nothing else. Especially not pretty ones like you have, with the trim and beads and bits of jewelry."

Jesse looked at the menagerie of ornaments, made from plastic, glass, and cloth. But the ones she had pointed to were the most special of all.

"My grandmother made all the ones like those. She'd go to garage sales and buy costume jewelry, and get the beads and baubles from the hobby shop. For hours she'd sit at her kitchen table and create little masterpieces."

"They're beautiful."

"She was a beautiful lady, inside and out." He looked at the pile of presents. "I've always packed up all the gifts and taken them over to Ma's house. What do you want to do?"

She shrugged. "This is all new to me. Let's just keep with tradition."

They both took showers and bundled the packages in the back of Jesse's truck. The sun was shining, and the chill in the air was giving way to a comfortable warmth.

The Christmas music was blaring from Helen's white house when they pulled up, and even Bumpus hesitated before approaching. Trick and Treat quickly persuaded him to start trotting toward the back of the house.

"Hey, Bumpus," Jesse called out. "Merry Christmas."

He handed the dog a bone-shaped present, which Bumpus quickly ripped open. Trick and Treat each got one, too. Within a few minutes, all three dogs had decided they wanted the other's bone, and were chasing each other around the yard. He was surprised to see Marti pull out a little bag of beefy bits and give them to Bumpus.

"Don't say a word about it," she said, narrowing her eyes at his shocked expression.

He merely shrugged, wondering again exactly who this woman was.

Jesse opened the front door with the three fingers he had available. Both he and Marti were loaded down with bags. The warm air, mixed with the aroma of baking ham, made his mouth water. Marti stepped inside, and as soon as Jesse followed suit, Kati's holler stopped them.

"Wait a minute!" she said, holding her hand out like a

crossing guard. Then she pointed up, an impish grin on her face. "Mistletoe!"

Jesse raised an eyebrow. "But she's my wife."

"So? You have your orders, Private West. Go to it."

Kati skipped into the kitchen, leaving Jesse to awkwardly turn to Marti. He shrugged one shoulder.

"You heard her."

There was a trace of that same hesitancy he'd seen the night before when he had kissed her. Marti looked away, then back at him again, quirking her lip. She leaned a few inches forward, and he leaned across the bags. When their lips touched, a spark of static electricity popped, and they jerked apart again.

He glanced up at the mistletoe, as he walked to the kitchen. "There must be something to it."

She just stood there for a moment, fingers over her lips. As if startled out of her trance, she followed, hiding behind the big paper bag she carried.

Billy was still in the recliner, and Jesse doubted he'd moved all night.

"Merry Christmas, Billy. Did you call the boys yet?"

Billy wiped his hand down his face, scratching his nose in the process. "Nope. Wasn't sure they'd be up yet."

"Of course they'll be up! They're kids, aren't they?"

Jesse helped set the recliner straight with his foot. Billy was always worried that his sons would forget about him, and yet he was only helping that become reality by not calling them once in a while, especially at Christmas. Jesse turned down the music.

Helen emerged from the kitchen, giving both Jesse and Marti a big hug.

"Merry Christmas, you two!"

Marti gave Helen a sincere hug, closing her eyes and seeming to savor it. His mother seemed particularly sentimental this year. Boy, holidays sure did strange things to women.

Billy tapped Jesse on the shoulder a few minutes later. "They wanna talk to you." He gestured toward the phone sitting on the doily-covered table.

Even though Billy didn't seem too happy about it,

Jesse's heart warmed that the boys hadn't forgotten about him. He talked with Turk and Clint for fifteen minutes longer than Billy had talked to them. They thanked him for the basketball hoop and ball he'd sent them and asked when he was coming up to see them. Then Debbie got on the phone to wish him a Merry Christmas and ask how he was doing. For some reason, he didn't tell any of them about Marti or the coming baby. Somehow he knew the boys would be disappointed and he didn't want to do that to them on Christmas. There would be time to tell them.

"Let's open presents!" Kati shouted.

In West tradition, Kati passed out presents Santy Claus style, giving each of hers a little shake. Even though it had been years, to Jesse, there seemed a great big hole in the day where his father used to be. After wishing him a silent Merry Christmas, Jesse focused in on the celebration again. Nobody opened their presents until the last one was given out. Marti seemed to get redder and redder every time Kati handed her a present. Had she realized there wasn't one under there from him?

She seemed more preoccupied with the presents she'd given than the ones piled in front of her. Helen opened up a box filled with sheets and material.

"You asked me to redecorate your windows like I did with the baby's room. I thought the pink and beige material would go great in here, and we could do your bedroom in the teal and maroon." When Kati opened up a veterinarian reference book from Marti, she explained, "I thought that would help with college. And, Billy, I thought you could use a new set of horseshoes. If you look on each one"—she leaned over to show him—"they're engraved 'Billy the Kidd West' on top."

Billy's expression was a mixture of confusion and guilt. In his usual show of thoughtfulness, he'd given everybody an assortment of sausage and cheese from the mail order catalog.

Jesse saved opening the presents from Marti for last. By the time he turned to the two medium boxes wrapped in red and gold paper, everybody was throwing their scraps of paper in one of the empty boxes.

"Open that one first," she said, a glow on her features.

Everybody watched as he unwrapped a pair of the most beautiful boots he had ever seen. Made from ostrich skin, they were a rich gray color covered in bumps. What was she thinking of, spending her California money on him?

"Wow, they're terrific."

She grinned. "Open the other box now."

The box came from the same Western store the boots were from. Inside was a felt gray hat with a matching ostrich skin band. He put it on and smiled at her.

"For your next cowboy mood," she said.

"I like them. Thank you." He grinned wickedly. "See that big box there."

She glanced at the box brimming with scraps of wrapping paper and shipping popcorn. Her eyebrows crinkled. "The garbage box?"

"Yep. Your present is in there."

Everyone smiled, but she was still confused. "But that was Kati's box."

"I know it. But I put something in there for you, too."

She gave him an indignant look. "You mean I have to dig in there?"

Everyone nodded, holding back their laughter. Marti crawled over to the box and started digging through the wads of paper. When she gave Jesse a look of exasperation, he nodded.

"It's in there, I promise."

"We do this to someone every year," Kati informed her. "You're the victim this year!"

Marti smiled wistfully at those words. With more vigor, she jammed her hands deep down and pulled out a small box wrapped in purple paper.

She opened the box slowly and pulled out the gold chain and looked at the heart that dangled at the bottom. She let it rest in her palm, reading the name "Marti" spelled out in raised letters in the middle of the heart. Before she had a chance to look at him, he said, "Read the back."

In tiny writing he'd had the jeweler inscribe, "Love from your West family—J, K, H, B, and B." She closed it tightly in her palm, then looked at him.

"Who's the last B?"

"Baby. If it's a girl, I'll name her Annabelle. If it's a boy, Eli. I just decided to keep it simple."

"Thank you, Jesse. It's beautiful."

Beautiful like you, he wanted to say. *Sitting there with your face aglow because everybody loved your gifts.* She looked like an angel, next to the tree with the colored lights setting off her blond hair. For the second time in a month, their eyes locked to one another's, and the room and everybody in it fell away to leave only them. There were so many sides to the woman who carried his baby: insecure, childlike, sad, confident, sassy, and sometimes selfish. And when she was gone, he would look at their baby and wonder where she was and how she was doing. Even though it was better for both of them that she was leaving, he would miss her, he realized.

Then the dogs started barking, breaking the trance. Dean knocked on the door and brought in new presents for everyone, getting a few of his own to open. Jesse saw his kid sister blush for the first time when she opened the small box containing an emerald ring, her birthstone. She stammered a thank you and didn't meet anyone's eyes. Jesse knew she didn't want to encounter "hmm . . ." expressions on his and Billy's faces.

"All right, everybody," announced Helen with a clap of her hands. "Gentlemen, why don't you help clean up in here a little and set the table. Ladies, I could use your help in the kitchen. The men can clean up afterward."

All three men made a great deal of fuss at that, but Jesse knew better than to seriously complain. After all, he'd seen his mother put Billy over her knee not all that long ago, and he didn't want that to happen to him. After the chores were done, they took care of the important business of testing Billy's new horseshoes.

Marti followed Kati and Helen into the kitchen, letting the swinging door close behind her. She grabbed for the bags of green beans that Helen pulled out of the refrigerator; those she could do. Kati settled at the cutting board piled with red apples.

"What nice gifts you two got," Helen said with a twinkling smile.

"It doesn't mean anything," Kati retorted. "It's my birthstone."

"I don't know," Marti said. "A ring is, well, pretty serious."

Kati was positively red-faced. "I don't see what the big fuss is about. It's not an engagement ring. And what about you, Marti? A gold heart pendant is not exactly a box of candy either, especially for someone who's leaving town in six months. Anything we should know about?"

Marti thought about the words inscribed on the back. "It's a good-bye gift."

"Humph! That didn't look like a 'good-bye' look you two were giving each other back there in the living room."

"Goodness, Kati, you're acting like a cornered animal. I think you both have a light in your eyes, whether you want it to be there or not," Helen said.

Kati and Marti glared at each other before looking back at what they were cutting.

Forty-five minutes later, most of the preparation was done. Now all they had to do was wait for everything to get ready. As Kati washed her hands, she watched the guys playing horseshoes from the kitchen window. Dean was putting all his weight into a throw, and when it hit metal, he jumped up in victory. Kati glanced briefly at the emerald ring on her right hand.

"Well, if we're just about done here, I'm going to go outside and teach those guys how to play. Want to come, Marti?"

"No, that's okay. Helen and I will just sit in here and talk about you."

Kati made a face before walking outside. Helen set the packages of fabric on the coffee table. Marti sat in the recliner Billy had spent the night in, feeling ready to sleep herself.

"I can't wait to see what you're going to do with this," Helen said, looking at the front windows. "I just love what you did with the baby's room."

"Well, I'm going to practice on Jesse's living room windows first, just to make sure it wasn't a fluke."

"Oh, it wasn't a fluke. I think you're very talented. The best part is, you're doing it on a budget. That's an attractive marketing angle."

"Marketing? You mean selling my curtains to people? For money?"

"Sure, why not? You go in, measure, ask what they want. They can have something as nice as a decorator could do at half the cost."

"I'm not even sure I can do it again. But I've got some neat ideas for those two windows, if it works the way I'm imagining." She looked back at Helen. "I don't want you to get the wrong idea. I—there's nothing between Jesse and me. I mean, we like each other well enough, but that's all. Nothing romantic."

"Maybe I'm just seeing what I want to see. For Kati, too."

"Helen, do you think I'm a terrible person for wanting to leave when the baby comes?"

"Terrible? No, not terrible. If you're really someone else, you didn't make this baby and you didn't want it. You can't help the way you feel. I know you'll do what you think is best for yourself, the baby, and Jesse."

Marti blew out a breath. "Believe me, leaving is the best thing I could do for them. As a mother and a wife."

"Why are you so sure you'll disappoint them?"

Marti looked away. "I just know. My mother didn't set a very good example. All my life I've disappointed people, especially the ones who are closest to me."

"Like your ex-husband, Jamie?"

"Especially Jamie. When I . . . died, I saw all those things I did to screw up my marriage. At the time, I made all kinds of believable excuses for myself, but seeing it as an outsider, there were no excuses. I can't do that to anyone, and I don't want to have a baby involved when I destroy my second marriage."

"You're so sure you'll destroy it. Jesse's tough, you

know. I'm not so sure he wouldn't be willing to give it a try."

"Are you talking about that light again?"

"Mm-hm," she said with a demure smile.

"Okay, I admit there's a light there. But it's not what you think."

"Lust?"

Marti dropped her head, shaking it. "I can't believe I'm talking to his mother about him like this."

"Then think of me as a girlfriend, who's a bit older. I know I've got a good-looking son, who's as stubborn as that river that runs behind the house. So, it's only lust?"

Marti shrugged. "I don't know, and it doesn't much matter. He wants me to leave, I want to leave, and we're two totally different people. We have this . . . current between us sometimes." She thought of the kiss under the mistletoe. "But it doesn't mean anything, not really."

"If you say so. But you've got a few months left before you leave. Think you can hold out?"

"Yes," she answered too fast. "Look at me, getting bigger every day. He's not going to even want to look at me before too long."

Helen smiled in an irritatingly knowing way. "I doubt that, Marti. I doubt that."

Marti sighed, wanting desperately to change the subject. "I wish I had a mother like you. Maybe I wouldn't have screwed up so much."

Helen tilted her head. "You do. Now."

Marti warmed inside. How different would her life have been if she'd had a mother who cared?

"I wish I could believe in myself the way you do. But I can't. I'm just screwed up. Maybe I am attracted to him in some bizarre way. I mean, he is kind of sexy. And, as you so kindly pointed out, good-looking."

Helen smiled. "Yes, he is. More so on the inside."

"That's just the point. He's too good for me. He's had this perfect mother as a role model."

"Don't say that. I'm not perfect, Marti."

"But you wouldn't do the things I've done in my life. You're too good of a person."

"Everybody makes mistakes. You're a different person now, in a new life. You can put those mistakes behind you."

"No, I can't. Because deep inside, I have the same soul. That's been the problem all along."

Chapter 10

~

Most of the town's Christmas decorations were gone by the second week of January. The lunch crowd had dispersed at Bad Boys, leaving Marti time to count her tips and wonder how she was ever going to pay that awful department store bill from her two shopping sprees. Still, she was glad she'd spent the money. It was the most peculiar phenomenon, but buying gifts for other people was more fun than buying stuff for herself.

She looked up when the door opened. Carl stepped inside, smoothing his hair back while he stood at the door. He settled onto a stool in Marti's section. It was unusual that he was without Lyle for lunch.

"How are you doing, young lady?" he asked, green eyes sparkling.

"Fine, thank you."

"I understand you were in the office a while back, looking at the photos of yourself."

"I didn't think it would be a big deal to look at photos of my body," she stated, ready to defend her actions.

"Well, it is official property now." He smiled graciously. "But it's okay. Lyle seemed to think you and Jesse were onto something. An idea, maybe. Would you care to let me in on it, considering I'm the investigating officer?"

She shrugged. "It's just a theory, really. We'll let you know if it pans out."

His smile disappeared. "Don't you think I'm capable of completing this investigation?"

She took a pot of coffee and poured it into a cup in front of Carl, wanting to put the steaming pot between them. "It's not that I don't think you're capable. We just have an idea, nothing more."

His voice lowered. "You think Paul has something to do with it, don't you?"

Of course, Paul's father would be aware that they had checked into his son's whereabouts on the day of the attack. Even as recently as last week she overheard Jesse discussing it with someone on the phone. "Maybe. It might be, well, hard, to investigate your own son."

Carl's eyes narrowed, all traces of friendliness gone. "You think I wouldn't nail that good-for-nothing son of mine if I thought he'd done that to you?"

She stepped back, the anger in his eyes steaming like the coffee in his untouched cup.

"I—I don't know."

Just as suddenly, the anger was gone, leaving remnants of officiality on his expression. "Marti, my son didn't attack you. I know he didn't. Don't you think a father could tell?"

"Maybe, and maybe not. Your son and his friends attacked Jesse just before Christmas. I bet Paul didn't tell you about that, did he?"

Carl's fist tightened. "No, he didn't. Damn kid's got a rocket up his . . ." He looked up. "He's a little reckless, but he doesn't go around attacking women. People are starting to talk about him, wondering why Jesse keeps hounding him. You two don't have a thing on him, do you? You know, Marti, he and Jesse have always had this feuding blood between them, and Jesse took your attack as something personal. Now he wants to pin it on his best enemy. You're a smart girl. Can't you see that?"

She shrugged. "I don't know. But your son was in the area at the time . . . I was jumped. And the scratch on my chest could have matched the kind Paul's pendant might make. And isn't it funny how that one photo got coffee spilled on it, right in that spot?"

Carl stood up, tucking his newspaper beneath his arm. "There wasn't anything there but a regular old scratch, probably made with a button. Both your imaginations are running wild. The guy who did that to you is probably long gone, but if he isn't, I'll find him. Leave the investigating to the police." Just as he was about to walk away, he turned around again. "Don't forget that Jesse is a criminal himself. He doesn't have a lot of right to be pointing fingers." He found a seat at a booth in Kati's section.

After work that day, Marti drove by Harry's Garage to ask Jesse if he wanted to go to the mall with her to shop for (gulp!) larger size pants. Not maternity yet, but her pants and shorts were getting a bit too tight. Kati couldn't go, and Marti hated to shop alone.

Marti had distanced herself a bit from Jesse since Christmas, for his own protection as well as hers. She noticed that he had done the same. Those moments under the tree on Christmas Eve still held her in a spell when she allowed herself to daydream about them. That kind of thing couldn't happen again. Shopping was safe enough.

When she pulled into the dirt parking lot, her heart sank. Desiree's black Jeep sat out front. Marti chewed her lip. What was she doing there, anyway? Didn't it look bad when an ex-flame hung around with a married man? Even if he had saved her life? Well, she certainly wasn't going to ask Jesse to go shopping for larger clothes when Desiree was there. She backed out of the parking lot and headed for the mall.

It was nearly six when she returned home. Jesse's truck was sitting out front, and Bumpus was keeping watch from his usual vantage point in the bushes. With tail wagging, he stepped out to greet her. With her one bag, she had no trouble opening the front door. Jesse was sitting on the couch with his arms crossed over his chest.

"Where the hell have you been?" he boomed without ceremony.

"Shopping."

She started to walk by him, but he grabbed her arm and swung her around to face him. His green eyes flared.

"I have been looking all over for you. Do you know

what I thought? I thought he got you this time. I hunted Paul down, drove to Ma's. I've been all over this damn town looking for cars pulled off the road."

She groped for something to say in the face of his anger. "Your baby's just fine, Jesse."

When she started to walk to her bedroom, he jerked her back, almost slamming her into his chest. His fingers held her chin.

"I wasn't just worried about the baby. Did it ever occur to you that I might be worried about you, Marti?"

"I'm not sure who you really care about," she said, meaning Desiree.

His voice softened a little in anger, but not in intensity. "I care about you *and* the baby, not you because of the baby. Don't take off without telling me. I just about went out of my mind tonight."

She moved out of his grasp, but stayed in front of him. "Well, I tried to check in with you, but you were busy."

He looked as if he were waiting for more explanation. "Busy? With what?"

"No, with whom. So I turned around and went to the mall myself."

Jesse gave it some thought before the light dawned on his features. "Don't tell me you saw Desiree's Jeep there and took off." He waited for her denial, which didn't come. "You thought she was at the garage and went off without telling me?" His expression was one of disbelief.

"Thought she was there? She wasn't?"

"No, her Jeep was making clanking noises, and she dropped it off this afternoon so I could look at it first thing in the morning."

He leaned against the back of the sofa, his arms crossed. She realized what she had just said. She had admitted in so many words that she'd been jealous! Not that she had been, but it sounded that way.

"I just figured you were busy, whether she was there or not, so I left. That's all. It was a stupid thing to do, and I'm sorry."

He wasn't buying it. "Marti, I just can't figure you out."

"Don't try."

"I'll be darned. You were jealous, weren't you?"

She moved away, desperate to put some distance between them. "I was not jealous. I thought you were busy, that's all."

"Then why did you mention Desiree's car out front? No, with whom?" he imitated in her own haughty tone. "I'll be darned," he said again, shaking his head.

"Well, then I guess you'll have to be darned, because I wasn't jealous." His arrogant attitude was making her madder. "Why would I be jealous of a . . . convict?"

The amusement in his features disappeared. "What are you talking about?"

"Oh, I know all about it. You're a car thief, convicted even!"

"Who told you about that?"

So, it was true. Her admiration for him fell into a heap, where it felt much more comfortable. "Paul told me. That day at the gas station."

Instead of getting defensive, he just shrugged. "I was nineteen. Big deal."

"Big deal? I'm living with a common criminal! You're pointing at Paul, and you're the one with the record. You've probably got more of a police record than he does."

Jesse's expression became rigid. "You know why I do? Because Paul's daddy got him off. I'll bet Paul didn't tell you he was the one driving the car, did he? As a matter of fact, it was his aunt's car, up in Sarasota. Paul got pissed off because we didn't want to joyride it down to the Keys, so he took off. Alan, Mike, and I got busted because we were the ones returning the car. Marti, I already stood before the judge on this one. You gonna try me again?"

Every ounce of fight drained from her and formed a self-pity pool at her feet. Before she could say anything resembling an apology, he scooped up his keys from the end table.

"I need some fresh air. See if you can keep yourself from wandering off while I'm gone."

He didn't quite slam the door, but she felt its firm impact just the same. Marti grabbed her bag and walked to her room as fast as she could without actually running. She closed the door and dropped down on the bed, feeling as small as a bug.

It's an omen. I let myself have a few interesting thoughts about Jesse, then I screw it up like this. By the time I have this baby, he'll be glad to see me go.

The quiet of the house lulled her into a light daydream before dropping her into the abyss of sleep. She didn't remember dreaming about anything when the noise woke her. In the dark, her eyes adjusted to the familiar shadows of her closet and dresser. At first she listened for the sound of Jesse's keys, of any sign that he was home. The house was still, except for the peeping of a frog outside her window. She let out a long, soft breath and started to let her eyes drift closed again. A shadow moved. Her eyes flew open, wide and scanning.

A distinct shape evolved from the blankness in front of her, moving closer to her bed. Her lungs were frozen —she couldn't scream, couldn't breathe. It wasn't Jesse, somehow she knew that. But who? The shadow moved closer, but it seemed a deadweight was lying on her.

She didn't see the shadow move upon her, but she could feel fingers slide around her throat. Her arms couldn't move to push them away. Panic seized her. Panic and the knowledge that she would die. The fingers tightened. Her breath came in jagged gasps. And then she could scream, and the terror that was frozen inside her let loose like a wail from beyond the grave. She blinked as she realized the lights were on, had been on. Her bedroom door flew open, and a rumpled but thoroughly awake Jesse barged in.

All she could do was breathe, finally, pulling in one deep breath after another. Jesse took a quick inventory of the room and her before relaxing the muscles in his chest and shoulders.

"What happened?"

She found a laugh in a tiny place the fear had not filled. "You look as scared as I feel."

"When I hear a blood-curdling scream like that, you better believe I'm scared. Are you all right?"

She shivered, wrapping her arms around herself. The laugh was gone. "I had a nightmare. He was back."

"Who, the man who killed Marti?"

"Yes."

"But you never saw him."

"I know, but I could feel him. I saw him standing right there in the shadows. It was dark, and I swear I opened my eyes and saw him. He moved toward me and started strangling me. I felt his fingers around my throat, and I couldn't move."

She buried her face in her hands, afraid of the images she was dredging up. The bed dipped when Jesse sat down beside her.

"You want to sleep in my room? I mean, we've done it before."

She looked around the room, weighing the sanity of that move. "No, I'll be all right. I'm going to leave the light on, though."

He ran his fingers through his wild waves of brown hair. "If you change your mind, don't be afraid to slip in."

"I'll remember that. Thanks, Jesse."

"Well, good night then. Sweet dreams this time, okay?"

She smiled. "You better believe it."

When Jesse closed the door behind her, she got up and checked the closet and beneath the bed, just to be sure. Everything was fine. Except her nerves. It was just a nightmare, that's all.

The man stepped out of the shadows again, standing just outside the glow of light from Marti's window. That scream was so much like the one that day he'd attacked her, when her eyes were wide with terror. When he'd wrapped his fingers around her neck and her eyes bulged with fear. She'd forced him to do it, by resisting, by kicking him. And now she was forcing him to linger in the shadows, wondering when her nightmares would show her that he was the one who had pinned her down. How long could he go on like this, a coward hiding in the dark, once again letting a woman rule his fate? If she and Jesse got even the slightest bit closer to him, he would have to take desperate steps to ensure her silence.

He stiffened his shoulders. Even if she did point him out as her attacker, it would only be her word against his. Would his word stand for truth, he wondered. Or would the questions start, the doubts?

He prayed to every god he could think of that she and Jesse would drop their silly investigation. They were getting too damn close figuring out it had been a pendant that had made the scratch.

"The last time you wanted to talk to me like this, you told me Marti was pregnant. What's bugging you, sweetheart?"

Desiree looked down at Jesse, sprawled out on the ground with his head on her legs. He'd taken the morning off to clear his head of the thoughts that had made him pretty much useless all morning. He wished he could toss his aggravations into the Chattaloo River, flowing only five feet from them, but he couldn't. Desiree owed him a few hours of listening time, he figured. He was cashing in.

"Marti's driving me crazy. She keeps throwing things at me to keep the distance between us. Last night it was the fact that I stole a car when I was nineteen. Paul kindly supplied the information without telling her his involvement in the deal."

"Why would it even matter to her?" Desiree then looked down at him with an open mouth. "Wait a minute. She wants to put distance between you and her? Is this the same girl who followed you around like a puppy a few months ago?"

"No. She's completely different since the attack." Jesse had decided not to tell Desiree the whole story. It was too bizarre. "She's leaving for California after the baby's born."

"Leaving? She's the one who got pregnant!"

"With a little help from me, if you'll remember."

"Yes, but even you're smart enough to realize she manipulated you into making love with her that night. And she told you she was on the pill."

"No matter. I was the fool who gave in."

Desiree shook her head. All he could see was the bottom of her chin. "So she's dumping you with the baby?"

"In a manner of speaking. It's still my baby, no matter how it came to be mine. What else can I do?"

She smoothed some hair off his forehead. "You, Jesse, could do nothing else. You're just built that way." Her voice became soft, nostalgic. "Why couldn't we have made.it? We were so good together."

He laughed. "We would have driven each other mad. But I have to admit, right now I'm catching myself wondering what kind of mother you'd make."

Her skin flushed red, something he rarely saw. "Not me, Jesse. I don't do kids."

He pulled her hand down and held it against his chest. "I know that. I'm going to have Kati and Ma there to help. We'll make it."

"Are you afraid, Jesse?" she asked softly.

He shrugged, knowing that question wasn't easy to answer. "Most of the time I'm fine with it. There are those times, though . . ."

"You won't have any trouble finding a woman to help."

"I don't want a wife. Women are nothing but trouble."

"I beg your pardon."

"You know exactly what I mean."

"There are plenty of women who would be glad to help you out, baby-sitting and stuff like that. Heck, I'd even do that."

"Yeah, but I want . . ." He stopped, not sure what he wanted.

"Marti?" Desiree supplied.

"No. I don't know."

It seemed strange to him that he was the confused

one and Desiree was playing counselor. For so long, it was the other way around. She'd sneak away from her abusive husband and they'd meet by the river, lying together with her head on his lap, her tears on his jeans. The turnabout bothered him.

"You said she's different. How?"

"Well, she used to be quiet, clingy, afraid to speak up or do anything on her own. Now she's feisty, hates living here, listens to rap music. Heck, she even threw out all her old clothes, bought new stuff, and dyed her hair blond."

"And how do you feel about her now?"

"Fascinated," his mouth blurted out without checking with his mind first. "I mean, because she's so different. She laughs different, smiles different. She's started redecorating the house, and she's so cute the way she beams with pride. And she hates being cute. One time I caught her dancing in her room, swaying to the beat with her eyes closed. She didn't know I was there."

Desiree was studying him, but he couldn't identify the expression on her face.

"What?" he asked.

"Your eyes sparkle when you talk about her. I think you're in love with her."

He sat up suddenly, facing her. "I'm not in love with her. I'm just fascinated with her. Heck, she's carrying my baby. I should feel something for her. Sometimes it's just plain irritation."

She narrowed her eyes. "You're in love with her, Jesse James West."

"No, I'm not. Besides, she's leaving after the baby's born."

"So? When does love follow the rules?"

Desiree's observation sent him atilt. What was she seeing that made her think such an impossible thing? He groped for a reason.

"I think you're just interpreting the way I'm looking at you right now."

She slugged him in the arm, but she wasn't smiling. "Jesse, you haven't looked at me like that in years! You used to look at me with lust, but the way you were looking when you talked about Marti, that wasn't the same thing."

He put a skeptical expression on his face and settled back on her legs again. "Even *if* I felt that way, it wouldn't matter. She's leaving for across the country soon."

She thunked him on the nose with her finger and thumb. "Well, get her to stay."

He grabbed her hand. "I can't. I promised that I wouldn't talk her into staying after the baby's born. I can't go back on a promise, you know that."

She leaned over him. "I didn't say anything about *talking.*"

Marti pulled up beside Jesse's truck and made it inside just in time to get to the bathroom. She didn't know why her stomach was rebelling in the middle of the day, but every smell in the diner seemed magnified, curling her stomach by the minute. For Kati's sake, Marti held out until Priscilla could be called in, and then she headed home.

After her retching session, she washed up and wandered through the house looking for Jesse. She didn't know why she'd been so hard on him about that convict thing. Maybe his casualness about it had infuriated her more, but still . . . perhaps she was looking for something negative about the man who seemed so perfect. And she had sure fired him up. All she wanted to do was lie down, but first she wanted to let him know she was home. Maybe he'd see her wan expression and put his anger aside. He'd hardly even looked at her that morning.

After searching through the house, she walked outside. A rustle in the bushes stopped her cold. At first she didn't see anything, then the leaves started quaking. Two light brown paws inched forward under the hedges, and Bumpus's nose peered out and rested on them. His tail thumped against the side of the house.

"You!" she said, then cracked a tiny smile. He almost looked cute snuggled in among the bushes. Almost.

As soon as she headed toward the river, she could

hear the dog disengage from the bushes and follow her. She had to admit she felt just a little safer knowing he was back there.

When she saw Jesse and Desiree, it was as if she'd walked into a block of ice. His head was on her thighs, and she was resting against a tree. They seemed in deep discussion when Desiree reached down and flicked Jesse's nose. He held on to her hand. An uncomfortable tightness in her chest made it hard to breathe. The least he could do was wait for her to leave before reigniting old flames! Or maybe the flame was never out. She turned and stalked back to the house.

Why are you so mad? her inner voice asked her.

Because . . . because he's my husband! He should behave while he's married to me. When I'm out of here and starting my life in California, he can do whatever he pleases.

But it's more than that, the voice taunted. Isn't it?

No, it's not! He's not my type. What would I do with a man like that? Break his heart, that's what!

She slammed the door behind her, slipped the "Phantom of the Opera" tape in the stereo, and headed to her bedroom. Her pale skin now flamed red and hot. The soprano's voice filled the air. She stripped off her uniform, slipped her long T-shirt over her head and pulled out her Hairlady. Pain was good in these situations, especially hair-pulled-out-by-the-roots kind of pain. Normal pain to obliterate silly, irresponsible pain. She turned it on and started running the coil over her legs.

"Yikes! Ouch! Yowee!"

Hallie had never shaved the long legs she'd had before. She had always waxed them to avoid stubble. The former Marti had shaved, but it wasn't too late to get rid of the short, stubby hairs. After a few minutes, she heard the music turned lower.

"Marti, are you all right in here?"

She jumped at Jesse's voice suddenly in her room but didn't take her eyes off the buzzing plastic machine. Continuing with what she was doing, she answered, "I'm *fine.* Go back to whatever you were doing."

She could see him advance closer. "What are you doing home so early?"

"I didn't feel well so I came home. Ouch!"

"And what you're doing is making you feel better? What *are* you doing?" he asked loudly over the racket.

She finally turned it off and faced him. "I'm shaving my legs, in a matter of speaking. This coil here vibrates and pulls the hairs out. Then the hairs don't grow back stubbly and stiff." She started the machine up again.

Jesse shivered. "So, is it making you feel better?"

"Yes!" She was trying to keep the grimace from her face, but the pain of seeing the two of them together was worse than getting her leg hairs pulled out.

"What are you listening to out there? It sounded like people screaming."

"It's opera. I was the only one who liked it back then, too."

He knelt down by the bed and took the machine out of her hand, turning it off. "Marti, what is going on? Why are you upset?"

He was forcing her to look at him, answer him. How could she tell him what she didn't want to admit herself? After all, it was insane to be jealous.

She still didn't meet his eyes, even though he was looking right at her. "I'm just tired of feeling nauseated all the time. Now I'm getting sick in the afternoons."

His voice was soft. "Are you sure that's what's bothering you?"

She finally looked at him, though she couldn't keep the harshness from her voice. "Of course, I'm sure. What else would it be?"

"I don't know. The nausea will be over soon, and so will the fatigue. Hang in there, doll."

His smile zapped her anger then, and she sagged down on the bed. "I'll try."

"Good. Listen, I've got to take Desiree home. Then I'll be back if you need anything."

So he wasn't going to hide it from her. "Desiree's here?" she asked in a voice that desperately tried not to sound jealous. Because she wasn't.

"Yeah. She came over so I could bend her ear. My

head was too clogged to even work on cars. Do you want me to pick you up anything while I'm gone?" She shook her head. "Okay, I'll be back in ten minutes."

A few minutes later she heard their voices outside, and she walked to the front window to watch. Desiree threw the Frisbee to Bumpus, who caught it and brought it back to her. She opened her door and held the disk up like Jesse had, giving the signal that sent the dog jumping into the truck. So, she didn't mind riding with a dog. Well, good. All three of them could live happily together when she was gone. Meanwhile she had made a fool out of herself in front of Jesse, again, and only hoped that he didn't think it was because she'd known Desiree was there.

Failure. The word loomed in her mind, pushing itself forward with every ounce of self-pity that dropped onto her heart. With Marti's past, Jesse was better off with Desiree. Much better off. After all, the man just wasn't her type, and wouldn't that doom her to failure even if she wanted to stay?

Chapter 11

~

$\mathcal{I}$t seemed to Marti that Jesse had been awfully quiet in the last week and a half since she'd come home to find him and Desiree cozied up by the river. She settled onto the bench swing with a sigh, wondering if she would have found Desiree's Jeep parked outside the garage had she driven by. Wondering if he was really working on his stock car on a Sunday morning. He told her he had to get it ready for the point races and something about a transmission.

As soon as he'd left, she'd gone to work on the living room curtains, pulling down the old brown and beige ones and installing crisp linen and blue ones. She only hoped he'd like the new look. A victory was needed to counteract her string of failures of late.

She tried to ignore the bumpy, jumpy feeling in her heart when Jesse's truck rounded the bend and barreled down the driveway. When she stood up, she pulled her shirt down to cover her growing tummy.

"Hey," Jesse said as he jumped down from the truck. "Hope I didn't wake you up this morning."

"Nope. I was already up."

He walked by her and into the house. She wondered if by leaving the front door open he was inviting her to follow. He stopped in front of the curtains, she was sure of it. Then he walked back outside with an icy beer and a small carton of orange juice, which he handed to her. A large towel was draped over his shoulder.

"I like the curtains. Please tell me you did that this morning. I'd hate to think they've been up there all week and I just now noticed."

She smiled. "No, that's what I started doing as soon as you left."

"Mom's been telling everyone what a great job you did with her living room and bedroom. You might have something here with this budget redecorating."

"Nah." She looked at him, finding no teasing in his eyes. "You think so?"

"Sure. You could do anything you set your mind to, Marti."

Everything that didn't involve other human beings, she thought. Especially their hearts.

"Come on down to the river with me," Jesse said, stepping off the front porch.

She hesitated for a moment. Was he going to tell her that he didn't want her living with him anymore? Or maybe that Desiree was moving in? The thought made her feel panicky for a moment, and her hand involuntarily went to her stomach. When he paused and looked back, she hurried to catch up.

They neared the river, and she sat down on the grass.

"God, it's so hot for January! It's never this hot in California this time of year. I can't believe—what are you doing?"

Jesse peeled off his shirt, then started unsnapping his jeans. He stopped midmovement, looking down at his hand that was starting to pull down the zipper. "I'm going for a swim to cool off. Wanna join me?"

She didn't like the glint in his green eyes. "No." She shifted her gaze to the brown water just beyond him. "I'm not getting into that nasty, muddy water."

He shrugged his bare, broad shoulders. "Suit yourself."

She watched his muscles flex as he kicked off his jeans. When he looked at her and grinned, she covered her eyes and looked away.

"How can you just prance around in your underwear like that?"

"I'm not prancing. Besides, there's no one around for a mile."

How prude, Marti. You who used to wear those slinky outfits at parties and prance around the house naked all the time, criticizing him for being in his underwear, around his wife no less!

He grabbed onto the rope that hung from a branch and swung into the water, letting a call trail after him. "Yeah-eee!" She shook her head but found herself smiling as his legs and arms flailed before sending a tidal wave of shimmering water everywhere.

At first she didn't see anything but the ripples Jesse caused. Just when anxiety started creeping in, his head popped out of the water. He flung his hair out of his eyes, sending a spray behind him.

"Whooee, it's nice in here!"

She ignored the trickle of sweat dripping down the side of her face. "Good for you."

"Come on in."

"What if there are sharks in there?"

He laughed at her in that patronizing way. "There aren't sharks in rivers. Especially freshwater rivers."

Marti got up and walked to the edge of the bank, hoping she could sit and dip her toes in the water. The bank was too steep.

"What about alligators?"

"Never seen one yet. Not around this part, anyway. I've seen them farther down." After a minute, he gave up on her and did a back flip.

Jesse reminded her of a kid, diving down, holding his breath for awfully long amounts of time, springing up with a gasp. He was younger than Jamie at the same age, mentally anyway. Maybe Jamie was a bit too serious at times. Someone like Jesse could generate some childish fun. But she was leaving in a few months, so she didn't want to get attached to him.

She found a large sea grape leaf and fanned herself with it. The water glistened off Jesse's tan skin.

"Is it deep?" she asked.

"In places. It's pretty shallow right here. See, I'm standing."

Marti frowned. She used to be taller. The top of her head would have reached his nose. Now it only reached his shoulders, she thought, remembering their dance together.

"Are you coming in?" he asked. "You know you want to."

"Don't tell me what I know. Or what I want."

He raised his arms in surrender, then fell backward into the water. When he stood up, he said, "You're too good for swimming in a dirty ole' river anyway, right? You're used to those aqua oceans you see in ads for the Virgin Islands."

"I am not."

"And I'll bet your ex-husband carried you in."

She pursed her lips. "No, he didn't! And he's not my ex-husband. I'm still married to him."

"No, you're not. You're married to me. I have the certificate to prove it."

She stood and turned away.

"Why don't you just give up that high-and-mighty attitude of yours and come in the water?"

She didn't turn to face him. "I don't have a bathing suit with me."

"Neither did I."

Marti kept staring back through the woods, not wanting him to get the better of her. Yet, the water did look good. She turned back and walked toward the bank. Slowly, she stripped off her top and shorts, leaving only her bra and underwear. She frowned at the tiny pooch that was her stomach. Her body was small and firm, but she couldn't deny that the pregnancy was showing. When she looked at Jesse, he was looking at that same stomach with a grin on his face. Sitting on the bank and leaning her legs in, she was able to touch the water. The initial feel was cold, but refreshing. She advanced a little farther.

"Oh, no you don't. You gotta come in the Southern way." Jesse nodded toward the rope.

"You've got to be kidding."

"I never kid about anything as serious as this."

Not a trace of a grin could be detected, but she knew it was there just the same.

She crossed her arms over her chest. "Then I won't come in."

"Suit yourself. I think you're just afraid."

"Afraid of what?"

"Plunging in—maybe being in the water with me."

"Why would I be afraid of being in the water with you?"

He shrugged, a mischievous light in his green eyes. "I don't know. Maybe you don't trust yourself around me."

She made an exasperated noise. "You're impossible!"

"Am I?"

She looked at him with his head cocked, waiting for an answer. "Yes. No. Sometimes."

She dropped her arms to her side and stalked to the rope. Trying to remember how he had done it, she grabbed high on the rough rope, jumped up and let the swing take her over the water. With a small yelp, she let go and plunged into the brown water. She was sure he had looked more graceful, and that wasn't saying a heck of a lot. When she came up for air, he was standing next to her.

"That wasn't so bad, now was it?"

She glared at him. "Don't intimidate me into doing things, Jesse."

He smiled. "It worked, didn't it?"

She started to head toward the bank, but he grabbed her arm and pulled her back. "Come on, it's not a big deal. Don't you feel great now?"

She did feel refreshed, if she didn't think about the creatures below the murky surface that might be swimming right next to her. Hopefully they'd bite Jesse instead. Maybe they'd nip that arrogance right in the bud.

She turned the conversation away from them and to more neutral subjects. "Did you really like what I did with the living room? Were you telling me the truth or trying to humor me?"

"Yeah, I liked it. I was afraid you'd put something frilly in there, and it's just going to be the two of us men living there after you're gone. That was neat what you did with the material above the window, twisting it like that."

She beamed, though she couldn't imagine why Jesse's praise pleased her so. "It just came to me, while I was looking at the fabric and trying to figure out what to do with it. I was thinking, maybe I could do something with the kitchen. You know, just something small, to add the . . ."

"Woman's touch," Jesse supplied, moving a little closer.

She looked up at him, wondering why her legs felt so wavery. Probably the mud beneath her feet.

"Yes, the woman's touch. For the baby."

"For the baby. Yeah, that'd be nice."

His gaze dropped to her lips momentarily. She felt her heart clench painfully.

"Jesse . . ."

He took her face in his hands and pressed his lips against hers. His eyes remained open, looking straight into hers. She had no idea what he saw there. She tried to force away the fear that surely lingered, wanting to replace it with a "no" signal.

His lips captured hers again, this time more intensely. He tucked her hair behind her ears, then closed his eyes and leaned down once again. Wherever his fingers touched her, the skin beneath tingled.

Her heart thudded around her ribs like a racquetball shot into an indoor court. She couldn't catch her breath between kisses, couldn't swallow. He parted her lips with his, then ran his tongue along her front teeth. Her mind warred with her senses, and her senses were quickly gaining ground. That feeling of refreshment evaporated into steam, and even the current seemed to pick up.

Her body had kicked into second gear without her consent, and she joined the kiss. Jesse deepened the kiss, and ah, what a kisser he was. His tongue stroked hers slowly, enticingly. A kiss with him was better than the whole shebang with other guys. She touched his arms with her fingertips, feeling the silky, fine hairs and firm muscles beneath. That slow seduction of her mouth had other parts of her body all hot and bothered, reminding her how bloody long it had been.

What kind of lover would Jesse be? she found herself wondering in that dreamy state of pleasure. Standing there nearly bare, she imagined them completely naked, pressed together with only droplets of water between them. And if they made love, what then?

At first her senses bemoaned the intrusion of consequential thought. She knew she was headed for trouble, big trouble, and they had only kissed. Her heart seemed ready to burst, and that was not a good sign for one planning to leave in a few months. With a groan, she shook her head and backed away.

"Jesse, what are you doing?"

His eyes opened, looking at her without showing any emotion.

"They call it kissing down here. What do they call it in California?"

The panic started growing inside her. "I thought you weren't going to try anything. You promised you wouldn't."

"I changed my mind."

She moved toward the bank, desperately trying to get away from him. "Jesse, please don't."

He came up behind her, pulling her down and against him. From behind her ear he said, "It was only a kiss."

She squeezed her eyes shut, trying to block out the feel of his strong arms pressing her against his chest. *Only a kiss? Maybe to you, buster, but not to me.* But his words hurt all the same. Only a kiss. She masked the pain and turned to him.

"I'm not interested."

"Sure as shooting didn't seem like it to me."

"Instinct, nothing more."

"Sure. You'd melt into any guy's arms if he kissed you, is that what you're saying?"

"I wasn't melting into your arms," she said a little too vehemently. "I was being pushed by the current."

"Why are you getting so worked up over a kiss?"

"Why start something that will have to end soon?"

He didn't want her to stay. He'd said that more than once. And she didn't want to stay either, she reminded herself harshly. She turned and started climbing up the bank again. Her knees felt weak as she stumbled to get her balance. She dropped down to a grassy area, surprised to find Jesse right behind her. He stretched out beside her, resting his head on his hands. She was building her defense for further attack.

"Marti, what are you so afraid of?"

"I'm not afraid. I just don't want to start anything I can't finish."

Jesse moved closer, dropping his gaze to her lips again. Panic raced through her veins, and she backed away.

"Don't tell me you're not afraid. Every time I come near you, I can see it in your eyes, the way you move away."

She turned away. "Jesse, please don't."

"Fine. If you're afraid to even tell me about it . . ."

"Jesse, don't bait me. I don't want to get . . ." She groped for the words. "Involved with you."

He leaned forward on his hands, his face only inches from hers. "Even in some highly exhausting, unemotional lovemaking?"

She pushed him back to a sitting position. "Especially in some hi—that way." There were certain parts of her body that disagreed with that notion, but she ignored them.

"So what would be so terrible about us getting together and doing the dirty deed?"

"I would. I'm lousy in bed."

She had to hide the smile of satisfaction at his shocked expression. That shock turned to outrage.

"Did that Jamie guy tell you that?"

"No, he was too nice to say anything like that. But it's true all the same."

"Don't you want another opinion on the matter?"

"No. You'll just have to take my word for it."

He eyed her in disbelief, narrowing one eye more than the other.

Water droplets glistened across his skin, occasionally sliding down to drop on the towel beneath them. She suddenly felt self-conscious in her underthings next to Jesse who looked all kinds of interesting in his briefs. He stared at her stomach, then traced a droplet across the curve over her belly button. She shuddered. His fingers then encircled her belly, stroking across the stretched skin.

"I've been thinking. You can stay here if you want. I mean live here, after the baby is born and all."

All she could do was look at him for a second before realizing he wasn't kidding. He was letting her stay, after telling her that he didn't want any woman in his life to tangle him up. "Oh? Just like that?"

He shrugged, looking more casual than she thought he should. "Sure. What do you have in California, anyway? Why not stay here where you've got a home, a kind of family, and the baby?"

She noted that he hadn't mentioned a husband in there anywhere. This wasn't a proposal. "I thought you weren't going to ask me to stay, that you didn't want me to stay."

"I changed my mind."

She narrowed her eyes. "What exactly made you change your mind, Jesse?"

He was looking toward the river, still mangling an innocent piece of grass. "I told you, I just got to thinking that you staying might work out good for everyone. You'd have a family and a place to stay, I'd have help with the baby . . ." He grinned at her. "And you wouldn't have to miss us all so awful much."

She couldn't find it in herself to smile back. Why did his words leave her heart aching for something more? Foolishness, she told herself.

"A marriage of convenience, is that what you're proposing?"

He started to debate that, then nodded. "Yeah, I guess that's what I'm talking about. No emotional attachments, just two friends living together."

She gave him a dumbfounded look. "Then what was that you just did in the river? You don't call smooching emotional?"

He ducked his head, giving her an innocent grin. "Aw, that was just for fun."

She wanted to smack him, but she didn't dare let on how mad she was. Just for fun, when her heart had been hammering in her throat! Only a kiss, that's what he'd told her. Why couldn't he tell her that he wanted her to stay, that he cared about her? Through all of his affection, she knew there was a place in his heart locked away from her, reserved only for racing.

"Thank you for your *concern,* Jesse, but I'll pass on playing housemother to two kids."

He gave her a highly insulted look. "What was that comment for? All I did was offer you a home."

"Well, I'm declining, thank you." She got to her feet with amazing grace and started toward the house as she slipped her shirt on. "Besides, I'm sure it was *only* an offer."

Jesse had given much thought to the conversation he and Marti had had two weeks earlier. In fact, bits of it kept creeping into his thoughts at the oddest moments, like in the middle of giving Mr. Glaser's old Mercury an oil change.

On a crisp Saturday morning, he couldn't go back to sleep after he'd heard Marti leave for work. Now he walked along the riverbank wondering why his mind and his heart weren't coordinating. He thought about their swim and rolled his eyes at his stupidity. Telling her it was only a kiss—geez, what could he have been thinking of?

He *wanted* it to be only a kiss. But even he couldn't deny it was more than that, not if he was going to be the tiniest bit honest with himself. He didn't know why he'd even kissed her to begin with, though it was a thought that was becoming a preoccupation lately.

The asking her to stay part was the only planned out action he'd taken. He still didn't want to get emotionally involved with her, despite what Desiree had said the other day. Racing was more important than that mushy stuff. He wasn't in love with Marti, no way. He was probably just a little horny, he'd convinced himself. Nothing more than that. Jesse would only admit that he sort of enjoyed having her around, and that it seemed logical for her to stay on after the baby was born. He still couldn't figure why she was so hostile about the offer.

The sound of a car pulling into the drive drew his attention as Bumpus tore across the dried leaves. He didn't recognize the car, but he knew the two boys who jumped out and fussed over the dog. Turk and Clint, Debbie's kids. The tall, slim brunette stepped out of the car, and he hardly recognized her.

"Wow, look at you," he said, his attention on Debbie even as the boys jumped into his arms. "You look great. And you two, look how you've grown!" The boys looked more like their dad than ever, but he wasn't going to tell Debbie that.

After a few minutes of greetings, Debbie said, "Turk, why don't you take your little brother down by the river?"

"Aw, Mom, I wanna see Uncle Jesse. We just got here!"

"You can go swimming," she said with a lift in her voice. "And we can spend more time with Jesse later tonight, if he doesn't mind."

Turk trained his hazel eyes on his mother, then shifted them to Jesse. "'Sat okay with you, Uncle Jesse?"

Jesse mussed the boy's hair. "Sure fire it is."

"Okay. C'mon, Clint," the seven-year-old said, taking his little brother's hand. "See you later, Uncle Jess."

He waved to the boys, who were mumbling about being sent away, then turned back to Debbie and gave her a hug. "I can't believe what I see. You back, after two years. And looking like this. A business suit, hair . . ."

She looked down demurely. "Well, you know I can't do a thing with this hair. I gave up on perming it and let it grow straight. I just put a little curl at the ends."

Her dark hair was parted down the middle, fine and straight. Her broad, pale face was subtly made up, and her whole poise was more confident than it had been when she'd left. He sensed an uneasiness in her mood as she leaned against the car.

"I just got tired of the city, so I packed the boys in the car and headed back down. I had an interview with a bank manager today for a position at a branch in Fort Myers." She twisted her mauve lips and narrowed her eyes. "Jesse, you didn't tell me you were married when we spoke at Christmas."

He shrugged. "You didn't ask. Okay, I just didn't feel like saying anything to the boys, and everybody was there."

"Well, I was . . . sort of hoping that we might be able to stay with you for just a few days, until I find a place to live. I remembered that you had a second bedroom."

"I'd love to let you use it, but Marti's in there." At her raised eyebrow, he tried to explain. "I mean, she's using it for—she's got . . . oh, hell, she's sleeping in it. We have separate bedrooms."

Strangely enough, her expression lightened at his awkward admission.

"I'm sorry. I didn't mean to make you, well, you know. And I'm sorry to hear things aren't working out between you."

"It's not that they're not working out. She's leaving after the baby's born."

Debbie's eyes widened at that one. "Leaving? With the baby?"

"No. The baby's staying with me. It's a long story, but I'm okay with it."

"Really?"

Eager to change the subject, he asked, "Have you seen Billy yet?"

"No. I didn't come back to see him. I came back to see you." She laughed nervously. "For two years I've had this fantasy about you. I'd come back, and you'd fall in love with me. Isn't that crazy?" She didn't give him time to answer. "But I couldn't stop thinking about you, especially after we talked at Christmas. So I came down. Your wife didn't quite fit into the fantasy, and neither did a baby. Just don't laugh at me, Jesse. I've been awfully lonely, and I always had this thing for you, even when I was mar—"

Jesse put his finger over her lips. "Debbie, if you're serious, I'm flattered."

"But," she said with a certain finality, "I know you don't feel the same about me."

"It's not even that. You were married to my brother."

She laughed bitterly. "Billy never loved me. I was pregnant with Turk, so he did the required thing. You know as well as I do that I, or our sons, didn't mean much to him. The four of us," she said, gesturing toward him, "were more of a family, even back then. I wanted to see if, with Billy long out of my life, there was anything there for us. But I chickened out when I got here and went to see your mom first, to test the waters."

"What did she tell you?"

"Nothing more than you were married and expecting a baby. Of course, she filled me in on Billy's life, as if I cared. Maybe she figured I came back to reunite with him. I know it would make her happy, but it would be hell for me. I told her not to count on that."

Jesse was trying to assimilate what she was saying. The boys' laughter, drifting on the wind, interfered with his thought process. "So, what are your plans?"

She took his hands in hers, swinging them nervously. "Well, that depends on you, I guess. They changed a little since I got here. But I still have a proposition for you."

"A proposition, huh?" He was trying to lighten the conversation, but her expression was intense. "Okay, shoot."

"I want you to think about your baby, and my boys. Why don't we get married?"

Chapter 12

~

*E*ven before Marti saw the strange car sitting in the driveway, she sensed the intrusion into her familiar territory. Strewn along the path to the front door were children's toys: a red spotted ball, a plastic baseball bat and spongy baseball. Even the odd comfort of having Bumpus there was amiss. Maybe they were inside, she thought.

Someone peering out between the front curtains stopped her. Upon closer inspection, she realized it wasn't a someone, but a something: a bright purple gorilla leaning out as if to see who was there. With furrowed eyebrows, she walked inside. The noise she expected to hear made the silence even more profound.

"Jesse? Bumpus?"

Nothing stirred. Quickly she changed out of her greasy uniform and slipped into jean shorts and a white shirt. As soon as she walked out back, a high-pitched child's squeal pierced the air. She followed it down to the river.

The disquiet that had settled under her skin sunk deeper when she saw a woman sitting next to Jesse on the bank. They were laughing at something in the water. Whoever she was, she felt relaxed around Jesse, touching his shoulder as she giggled. She was wearing crisp white pants and a blue dress shirt, and beneath her was a towel Jesse had thoughtfully placed to keep those pants clean.

Bumpus's greeting barks made the pair turn around. Jesse got to his feet and walked toward her with an easy smile. She wished she could look that easygoing. He put his arm around her and steered her toward the woman.

"Hi, Marti. I want you to meet someone." The woman stood and extended her manicured hand. "This is Debbie, Billy's ex-wife. And those rugrats in the river are her boys, Turk and Clint."

Debbie squeezed Marti's hand confidently, giving her a warm smile. The boys perfunctorily waved and went back to splashing each other. Marti found it hard to imagine the attractive woman married to Billy.

"It's nice to meet you, Marti. I've heard a lot about you."

Marti shot Jesse a look, but he was smiling. "Nothing bad, I hope."

"No, of course not."

Jesse gave Debbie a sideways hug. "When this lady left, she was wearing cutoff jeans and running around barefoot every chance she could." He gave her an appraising look. "Then she shows up here in a business suit, a sophisticated banker from the big city."

Marti felt grubby all of a sudden. If she'd known the visitor was a woman, well then, she would have dressed nicer.

Debbie smiled modestly. "I've been working my way up, slowly, but getting there. I managed the loan department at one of the largest banks in Atlanta."

Marti forced a smile. "Well, that's great. And you're down for . . . a vacation?"

She gave Jesse a look that smacked of intimacy. "I'm not sure yet. It depends. I've interviewed at a bank in Fort Myers for the management position."

"Marti's been working on redecorating the house. I keep telling her she should start advertising. She's really good."

Marti beamed at his compliment, glad he didn't mention the waitress part. The boys climbed up on the bank and flopped their wet bodies onto the dirt and leaves. They were cute, with brown hair and hazel eyes rimmed with long, wet eyelashes. Both studied her openly, with Billy's scrutinizing eyes.

That black feeling gnawed at her stomach, the same way it had the day she'd seen Desiree with Jesse at this same spot. Debbie was nothing like Desiree, though.

She wasn't overly beautiful, nor sexy. But she had a bland beauty and a look of sensibility that came from accomplishment and confidence. Marti felt that Debbie could see the confusion and roller coaster emotions on her with the same clarity.

"Debbie's going to stay with Ma for a while, until she decides what she's going to do. I invited her to stay for dinner tonight; I hope that's all right with you."

Before Marti could even shrug a vague confirmation, Debbie said, "Hey, I can cook up my famous Turk casserole. I used to make it all the time when I was pregnant with my first, so I named it after him."

"Uh, I've already got something planned for dinner," Marti blurted out before she even realized it. Jesse gave her a surprised look, and she smiled. "I thought about it today at work."

"Okay. What are you going to make?"

Marti went blank. I'm just making this up as I go, she wanted to say. "Spaghetti. I have an Italian recipe for the sauce. You'll like it, I think."

"Sounds fine to me," Jesse said.

"I'm looking forward to it," Debbie said with a gracious smile. "The boys love spaghetti." They nodded without a great deal of enthusiasm.

Then she realized that she'd have to go to the grocery store to get the ingredients she remembered Jamie putting into the sauce. That meant leaving them alone for a while longer. But what could happen with the boys there? And why should she worry about it anyway?

Marti raced through the grocery store, but her thoughts went even faster. She was trying to remember what Jamie commandeered from the kitchen on those nights they'd actually had a family dinner. Her mind kept straying from the fresh tomatoes and basil to the woman at home with her husband. What was it that lingered in Debbie's eyes? A wanting, maybe? Marti threw a couple of cans of tomato paste in her basket and scooted to the checkout.

There's nothing to worry about, she reminded herself as she upended the basket. *Besides, Jesse's not my type, and he can do whatever he pleases when I'm gone. But*

Debbie's not his type either. Why is she bothering me so damn much then? She caught herself speeding all the way home.

Dinner was a minimal success, even though the sauce hadn't simmered long enough and the noodles were a little sticky. Nobody mentioned it, and the boys were too busy sucking each long piece into their mouths to notice. They reminded her how little she related to children. Every time she said something to them, her voice sounded phony. *Too cutesy, Marti. Too adult, Marti.* Her inner voice rated every sentence. Her inner voice was becoming a real pain, she realized. She'd never heard it before her life-after-death experience.

When Marti started carting the dishes into the kitchen, Jesse stood up to help.

"Jesse, why don't you let me do that?" Debbie said. "I'm sure the boys would love to spend some time with you."

"Yeah!" cried Turk. "Will you twirl us around again like a helicopter? Please, please?"

"Anything for my nephews."

Marti noticed how easily he left her to Debbie's company and went outside with a squealing boy under each arm. Debbie had a soft smile on her face as she watched him go outside.

"He's good with kids, isn't he?" Debbie asked.

"It looks like it. I think he's just good with everybody."

"He sure is. He would have made a good preacher."

Marti's eyes widened. "Jesse? A preacher?" She couldn't help but remember Jesse in his cowboy mood, holding her close.

"Sure. He has a warmth that reaches out and touches people. They're drawn to him." She turned on the faucet and started rinsing dishes. "How old are you, Marti?"

"Twenty . . . three." Twenty-seven she'd wanted to say.

"God, you're so young. I'm thirty-one. You're going

to have your first about the same time I had Turk. You're not really a blonde, are you?"

Marti stiffened her shoulders, then wondered if her roots needed to be done already. "No, I'm a brunette. Is it obvious?"

"No, but your coloring is more suited for brown hair." She leaned back against the counter with her arms crossed loosely in front of her. "Jesse says you're leaving after the baby's born."

"Yes," she said firmly, more for her own benefit than Debbie's. "I'm going to California."

"Wow, that's far away."

"It's where I'm from. Originally."

"You're about five months along, aren't you?"

Marti glanced down at her belly. "Nineteen weeks last Wednesday."

"Have you felt the baby move yet?"

"Not yet. The doctor says any day now."

Debbie put her hand to her heart. "That's the most exciting moment in pregnancy, when you really know there's a little human being living inside you. You're still so tiny yet. I was *huge* by five months, and I just kept getting bigger."

Marti cringed. "I hate being this big. I already feel like a duck, and I'm not even waddling yet."

"Does Jesse touch your stomach a lot?"

"Sometimes. He looks at it a lot."

"He used to put his hand on my stomach all the time when I was pregnant."

Debbie's smile was free from intent to make Marti jealous. Still, she felt her fingers tighten slightly on the plate she put in the dishwasher.

A peal of laughter drew their attention to the large window facing out back. Jesse jogged slowly by with Clint on his shoulders, making horse sounds and pretending to buck. Marti found herself smiling wistfully and stopped.

"He's going to make a great father." Debbie hadn't yet removed her smile. Her eyes were still trained on the window, although Jesse wasn't in view. She stood half a foot taller even in flats. "I'm going to tell you something. You might be worried that Jesse won't be able to take care of the baby by himself. Or that he might be lonely once you're gone. Maybe it'll take the guilt away if you know this. I proposed to your husband."

Marti stood there with a dumbfounded expression on her face. She ignored the empty space her heart had occupied before dropping down to her toes. After closing her mouth, she asked, "Proposed what?"

Debbie laughed. "Marriage, of course. It makes sense, don't you think? You're leaving. He's going to be alone with a baby. I'm alone with two boys who adore him more than their own father. It's a perfect solution, a marriage of convenience."

Marriage of convenience? The relief that Debbie obviously expected didn't appear on Marti's face. Marti closed the dishwasher door with a little more zest than necessary.

"Oh, maybe I shouldn't have said anything. I just thought that, well, you were leaving anyway. You might feel better knowing."

Marti swallowed hard, trying to put on a casual mask. "I—I do, really. I just wasn't expecting . . . you proposed to him?" And then the question she had to know the answer to. "What was his answer?"

"He said he had to think about it. That he still had a couple of things on his agenda before he could consider my proposal."

Marti's eyes widened. A couple of things on his agenda? What agenda? "I see."

"I hope you're not angry with me. You'll see that it's the best thing for that baby and for Jesse."

"Yes, the best thing," Marti said softly as the boys raced through the front door, followed by a breathless Jesse. He collapsed on the couch, followed by the boys, who snuggled on each side of him. "The best thing," she repeated, knowing that she should see it that way. After all, it was exactly what Jesse wanted, what he had just proposed to her.

* * *

Jesse never mentioned Debbie's proposal, and Marti didn't tell him that she knew about it. In the five days since her surprise visit, Debbie had only been over twice, and that was to drop the boys off. As Marti and Jesse sat across the table from each other after dinner, she couldn't keep away the picture of Jesse and Debbie and the family sitting there on a quiet Thursday evening. In her picture, Jesse was laughing with the boys, not somber and thoughtful as he was now.

The rain outside made a pitter-patter sound on the roof, and the sky outside was a pasty gray. She crossed her arms in front of her, resting them on her belly. Why couldn't she get the thought of Jesse and Debbie out of her mind? In the cozy picture her mind tauntingly created, he leaned over and kissed her. Marti wrinkled her nose at that.

"What's wrong?" Jesse asked, pulling her from her self-torture.

"Why didn't you tell me my hair looked terrible?"

He raised his eyebrows. "It doesn't look terrible. I thought you liked it."

"I do. But my coloring's wrong." It was. She had studied her mirror image and realized Debbie was right. Damn her, the woman was just too sensible!

He shrugged. "I never liked it all that much to begin with, but you were hell-bent to do it. And who am I to say anything? I'm just your husband."

His words bit into her heart a little. A lock of hair was hanging down over his forehead, making him look like the boys he loved so much. She caught herself remembering how soft his hair was as it had brushed her hands while they danced. To distract that thought, she picked up her fork and poked at the elbow noodles on her plate.

"You've been awfully quiet lately," he said. "It doesn't bother you, the boys being around and all, does it?"

She noticed he hadn't mentioned Debbie being around. "No, they don't—" Her eyes widened and the fork dropped from her hand. Jesse was out of his seat and at her side in seconds.

"What's wrong?"

A chill washed over her when she realized what had happened. She smiled. "I felt the baby kick," she whispered. "There it goes again!"

He put his hand on her stomach. "Where?"

She took his hand and placed it under her loose shirt at the spot where the baby had last kicked. They waited a few minutes like that, and the skin beneath his palm grew moist. Her belly looked naked and vulnerable. He was crouched down beside her, his expectant expression never wavering. Finally his patience paid off, and the baby kicked again.

"I felt it! It was like a little . . . push. Like he was testing. My son did that!"

"There's really a baby in there," she said softly, avoiding Jesse's gaze. "And he's moving around, just like a regular person. Debbie was right. She said it would feel more real when the baby started moving."

Jesse's expression didn't change, although he did look down at her belly just then.

"I hope it's a boy, Jesse. For you."

"Well, that's up to the Big Guy upstairs. I hope it is, too, but I wouldn't mind a girl either."

"Do you think you'll be all right, raising the baby alone?"

He gave her an odd look, and she tried to make her expression light. He reached up and touched her cheek, then tucked her hair behind her ear. She didn't untuck it.

"Don't worry about us, doll. We'll be okay. Course, you can always stick around and find out for yourself."

She shook her head quickly: "I can't. And anyway, it seems as if you have a better offer."

It took him a second to realize what she had said. "Debbie told you?"

Marti nodded. "She figured I wouldn't get mad because I'm leaving. She wanted me to know you'd be well cared for. So I wouldn't worry."

Jesse rose to his feet. "That was nice of her. Actually, I'm glad she offered."

She felt a tightness in her chest. "You are?"

"Yeah, it answered a question I'd had on my mind."

"What question was that?"

He looked as if he were going to answer her, then shook his head. "It's not important."

"Are you going to marry her, Jesse?"

He leaned against the wall, crossing his feet. "Would it make you feel better if you knew I had a wife when our divorce is final?"

"No, I . . . yes." She was screaming inside. It was ridiculous, her not wanting him to marry Debbie. But how could she explain that to him? *I don't want you to marry her, because* . . . She didn't even know herself.

Jesse's eyes hardened. "Maybe I will, Marti. Maybe I will."

Time was passing faster than Marti cared to think about. She should be happy, she told herself, that her pregnancy was coming closer to an end. It was the beginning of March, the middle of her twenty-fourth week. The baby was happily kicking away almost a dozen times a day. Still, whenever Jesse saw her expression change suddenly, he rushed over and asked where the kick spot was, as he called it.

Debbie had accepted the bank manager's position, and promptly moved into an apartment a few miles away. She had gracefully backed away from Jesse, but Marti knew the woman was just biding her time until she left. The boys were a constant reminder of Debbie's proposal: a family, a marriage of convenience. What bothered Marti most was the realization that Debbie could offer Jesse so much more than she could.

The sound of a truck door slamming and Bumpus's barking drew her to the front window. Jesse was walking up with three fishing rods over his shoulder. She opened the door so the dog could see the intruder was really his master.

"Hi," he said, leaning the poles against the wall by the door. "I always like to hear him barking when I come up. Makes me feel safer about leaving you here alone."

"I have to admit, he does make me feel safer. But about that barking . . ."

Jesse was already nodding. "I know, I know. He hears something out there, but I don't know what it is."

"For the last three nights in a row?"

For a crazy moment, as he walked toward her, she thought he was going to kiss her. Instead, he leaned over and patted her belly. "Hi, Eli. Kick for me, little guy." Something in his voice made the baby move a little, and Jesse grinned. "He likes me already. I can tell." Jesse sank down on the sofa with a deep sigh. "Those kids sure wipe me out. They're into everything, more interested in exploring around the lake than fishing in it. I ended up having to carry them in when I dropped them off."

Marti stiffened. "So, how is Debbie?"

He shrugged, not hearing the cold tone in her voice. "All right, I guess."

"No proposals tonight?"

He gave her a curious look. "No. Why, you got one for me?"

She turned away. "You have too many women for my taste."

"What are you talking about?"

"You know exactly what I'm talking about. Debbie, Desiree. Is there anyone else out there with their fangs out that I should be aware of? All I ask is that you wait until I leave before you send out the invitations."

"Whoa! Where is this coming from?"

She felt the baby kick, but didn't tell him. The heat of anger rose up to her face. "It's just that, I feel like there are predators waiting to pounce on you the moment I turn my back! I'm the mother of this baby, and it seems like everyone's anxiously waiting to take my place." She couldn't find the right words to convey what she was feeling. Maybe she didn't want to. Threatened, left out. More. She quickly walked to her bedroom, closing the door softly behind her.

"Marti?" he asked from the other side.

"Just leave me alone for a while, okay?"

"Okay. If that's what you want."

It was her hormones, she told herself, that made her

feel disappointed even when Jesse did as she asked him to. Sheesh, what a mess she was!

Marti moved around in her bed for more than two hours before she finally stilled. He had been waiting impatiently for her to go to sleep. Was she dreaming about the attack, finally seeing his face? She never seemed to sleep well. When Jesse was playing golf last weekend, he had timed the trek from sign-in to the place Marti had run out of gas. Timing to see how long it took. Jesse wouldn't rest until he found the truth. Once she remembered his face, it would be all over for him.

Three nights after he'd decided to kill her, he was still standing outside her window. But tonight the dog wasn't roaming the house. He'd seen Jesse lock him in his bedroom. They were stupid enough to think the dog was barking for nothing. Their mistake.

The only sound he could hear were the frogs, celebrating the return of warmth in the night. His feet were bare, better to keep the wet leaves quiet. He would climb in through the window, strangle her in her sleep, and slip away. It would be morning before Jesse knew she was dead. He knew Jesse would throw accusations for her death, and surely he would investigate, but without Marti's memory, it would lead to a dead end.

He slipped the glass cutter out of his pocket and cut a half moon over the window latch. With a suction cup, he pulled the piece toward him, cringing at the crunch of the glass parting. He parted the curtains an inch with his finger. Marti rolled onto her back, and he waited until he was sure she hadn't woken. Then he reached inside and switched the lever.

The one glove he'd managed to find at the house wouldn't give him the traction he needed to slide the window up. He took it off, stuffed it in his pocket, and started to place his bare hands against the glass—and remembered fingerprints. With the suction cup, he managed to raise the window a half inch, enough to get his finger in the crevice and lift it all the way.

Crawling in would be the hard part. He crawled halfway in before losing his balance. With the sill at his stomach, he teetered back and forth, knowing that if he crashed inside, she would awaken. He couldn't have that. Once he had her neck clutched in his grip, she wouldn't be able to scream. She would die quickly.

He was able to reach the dresser and regain his balance. The thought of his task pumped the adrenaline through him. He didn't want to kill her; he had to. There was no choice. He had never killed before. He couldn't fail this time. Last time he had threatened his rape victim into silence. She'd had no one to protect her or back her up. But Marti did.

Steadying himself, he awkwardly climbed down from the window. His heart started thumping. The glow of the nightlight lit the bed with warmth. The only part of her body that showed from beneath the blanket was her face. Her rounded forehead was creased with worry. Not because he was standing there next to her, but from the dream that kept her deep in its grasp. Far from the reality that would soon end her life.

He rubbed his hands together and reached down to her neck, barely visible. As soon as fingers circled her throat, her eyes opened. But she didn't scream. Her arm tried to move to her throat, but it was encased in the blanket. He pressed tighter around her throat, anxious to have it done with before she realized she wasn't dreaming.

From somewhere, her foot escaped the blanket and slammed him in the groin. Her hand shoved at his chest. Then her scream tore lose, filling the room with the sound of terror. A violent fit of coughing ensued. He grasped the injured part of himself before realizing he had to get out of there. She might see who he was through the black makeup that covered his face.

"Jesse!" she screamed through her coughs.

Working with his survival instinct, he locked the bedroom door, just as Jesse slammed into it from the other side. Shoving Marti aside, he dove for the window, scratching his back as he slid through and reached the ground. The crack of the wood around the door sounded as he tore through the woods to the river. He heard the sound of small footsteps tearing through the leaves, and dared a glance behind him. The snarling dog was racing up, as if released from the gates of hell.

His shallow dive landed him several yards from the bank, where the dog was just launching from. The current ran swiftly, already taking the man farther and farther away. The dog seemed to have disappeared in the darkness.

Safe from the dog, he reached the shore and trailed through the woods to where he'd left the truck. He had parked it far away from Jesse's house, but he knew it was closer to where he was now. And he could navigate those woods like a sailor on a lake. He found the truck easily and started it before he'd even closed the door. He tried to shake away the trembling in his hands as he pulled into the front drive and turned off the truck. His heart was pounding, threatening to burst inside him.

If Marti were the blood of his heart, then he couldn't kill her. He remembered when his love carried his baby, and let another man raise his son as his own. Marti was pregnant, as his love had been. Soft and beautiful, carrying high and remaining small. So alike they were. And he'd almost killed her, twice. It was an omen that she'd lived both times. An omen that she belonged to him. Now his only choice was to get rid of Jesse.

Chapter 13

~

Marti wailed and trembled violently in Jesse's arms, holding on so tightly that his muscles started aching. He held her and stroked her hair, trying to calm her so she could tell him what happened and who it was. His eyes never left the open window, his emotions warring between staying with her and going after the son of a bitch with a rifle. Marti's grip was too tight to even think about leaving her.

"Marti, please calm down and tell me what happened. Can you do that for me, doll?"

Her cheeks were splashed with tears streaming down her face. She was still sucking in deep breaths, but she nodded. He tucked the strands of hair that stuck to her face behind her ears.

"I—thought—dream—not a dream—standing there —came at me . . ."

Jesse pulled her close again. "Doll, I can't understand what you're saying. Come on, walk with me to the kitchen. I'm going to call the sheriff's office, then get you something to drink."

He helped her to her unsteady feet, then guided her into the kitchen where he poured her a shot of whiskey. She gulped it down, then coughed and sputtered.

"That should calm you down a little. Now here's some water to wash that down."

With her in his sight, he picked up the phone and called the emergency number. Lyle's voice sleepily answered the phone.

"'Lo?" Then he cleared his voice and seemed to come awake. "Deputy Thomas here."

"Lyle, this is Jesse West. Somebody just broke in and tried to kill Marti. Get over here right away!"

"Oh ma' gosh! Should I call an ambulance?"

He looked at her. "No, I don't think that's necessary. She's just shaken up."

"Okay, let me call Carl and we'll be right over." To his wife's urgent inquiries, he answered, "Marti just got attacked."

Jesse knew Eileen would be on the phone until sunrise telling everyone about it. No matter; it would get around anyway.

Jesse called Helen to tell her what happened and warn her that he was bringing Marti over after the questioning. Then he took Marti's hand and led her to his bedroom. "I want you to stay right here, lock the door behind me and get dressed."

Her eyes filled with panic. "No, don't leave me! Where are you going?"

"I'm going to take a look around. I'll be right outside. Go on, get dressed. Lock the door."

He grabbed his rifle and took his fishing flashlight out of the closet. When he came around back to Marti's window, he found the half-moon shaped piece of glass on the ground. Footprints were nonexistent in the mat of oak leaves. He tried to imagine which path the creep would have taken, then started following it. The sound of flapping ears made him stop, and Bumpus appeared out of the blackness, glistening with water. Jesse knew where the guy went. The river would end tracking completely. Still, Jesse took another few steps toward the river before stopping again.

A single blue glove lay on the damp leaves. He didn't want to touch it, but trained the flashlight on it as he crouched down to investigate. It was a damn golf glove, of all things. His eyes narrowed as he tried to remember if he'd ever seen it before. Who noticed golf gloves, anyway? But he did know one thing: Paul played golf.

His anger boiled as he imagined Paul running through the woods. Jesse stood up when he heard the sirens wailing in the distance. Hopefully it was Lyle. He hurried back to the house.

Marti was still wearing her nightshirt when she unlocked the bedroom door for him. He pulled her into his arms and gave her a brief hug.

"I found a golf glove. Marti, did you see the guy?"

"He was black."

"Black? Are you sure about that?"

"No. I think he had black stuff on his face. He was tall, not heavy, not skinny." She was trembling so hard her teeth were chattering.

"Think. Could it have been Paul?"

She bit her bottom lip, obviously trying to conjure a painful picture. "It could have been, but I don't know. I just don't know."

"Okay, go get dressed. The police are here."

Carl was the first to show up, and Jesse clenched his fists as he walked outside. Carl was as put-together as he always was, even at 1:15 in the morning. Still, his face was stiff with tension.

"What the hell happened? Lyle told me someone broke in and tried to kill Marti."

"What happened is that the bastard who's been running around since November is still trying to kill my wife. Where's Paul?"

"Hold on there, Jesse. Paul's at home asleep on the couch. I saw him when I left. Did she see the man?"

"No, he had black all over his face. There's a golf glove out back. Come on, I'll show you."

Lyle's car pulled into the driveway, lights flashing in silence. He jumped out and met the two men near the front door. Carl took charge.

"Lyle, have Jesse show you where Marti was sleeping and talk with the girl. Find out if she can identify the man who broke in. I'll take a look outside and go over the window for prints and anything else I can find."

Jesse didn't want Carl to walk around back alone, where he could do away with any evidence that could convict his son. But he didn't want to just send Lyle in when Marti wasn't expecting him. Damn, but things were complicated.

Before Carl reached the corner of the house, Jesse

said, "Carl, don't spill anything on the evidence this time."

Carl turned around in a bull-charging stance. "What's that supposed to mean?"

"You know exactly what it means. I think you'll do whatever it takes to protect that good-for-nothing son of yours."

"Paul had nothing to do with this. If I thought he did, I'd throw his butt in jail as fast as I'd throw yours in." He pointed to Jesse. "And I'd watch what I'd say, if I were you, or I'll do just that."

With every passing second, Jesse was more sure that it was Paul. He quickly led Lyle to Marti's bedroom, then went into his own.

"Marti, Lyle's looking around in your room right now. You need to talk to him, tell him what happened." She nodded. "I'm going out back to keep an eye on Carl. Make sure he doesn't lose any clues or anything."

Her eyes widened. "You really think it was Paul, don't you?"

He put his hand on his stomach. "Right here in my gut, I do. Carl would be a fool to get rid of the glove, because he knows I've seen it. But maybe there was something I missed. I'll be right outside if you need me."

"I need you now," she whispered. Then said, "No, go. It's important."

With a last look at her, he left and went outside to monitor Carl. The blue glove was in a plastic bag on the ground. Carl was dusting the window with one hand, holding a flashlight with the other. He gave Jesse a side-long glance before returning to his task.

"Don't see any prints on the outside. We might find some inside. There probably won't be any on the glove, but I'm going to check to see where it was bought."

Jesse watched him work without comment. After they'd dusted the bedroom for prints, Carl and Lyle packed up their kits. Marti had stayed in the living room, huddled in a blanket.

"Lyle," Carl said. "Why don't you go on home. I'll take this stuff in and go over it tonight. Maybe I can find something. It seems that I'll have to find this guy so Mr. West here won't think I'm covering up for my son."

"That's the only way I'll believe Paul's innocent," Jesse said, Carl's comment grating on him.

When the sheriff and deputy left, Jesse packed up a few things and reached down to take Marti's hand.

"We're going to Ma's for the night. Tomorrow I'll fix that window, but it's not going to matter because you're sleeping with me from now on."

She only nodded, instead of giving him the protest he expected. Probably tomorrow he'd hear one, but she wasn't going to win that argument. If she'd been sleeping next to him tonight, the bastard would be dead. The way Jesse felt at that moment, he might be anyway.

Once at Helen's house, she led them up to Jesse's old room and settled Marti into bed with a cup of warm milk. Bumpus curled up at the foot of the bed. Kati was lying next to Marti, holding her hand.

"The warm milk will help you sleep," she told Marti.

"I don't want to sleep!"

Jesse put his hand on her shoulder. "You'll be fine here. He's not going to come after you twice in the same night."

After a moment's hesitation, she drank the rest of the cup, then snuggled under the blankets. Helen looked expectantly at Jesse as he moved closer to the door.

"And where are you sleeping?"

"Right here. When I get back."

Both women looked at him with worry in their eyes.

"Where are you going?" Marti asked.

He tried to keep the hatred from showing in his eyes. "I've got some business to take care of."

"Jesse . . ." Helen warned.

"I'll be back shortly."

"I'll stay here until you get back," Kati said, giving him a knowing look.

Helen followed him into the hall and down the stairs. "Jesse, whatever you're thinking, I know it's trouble."

"It's trouble all right, but not for me. For the guy who tried to kill my wife. And my baby. Don't try to stop me."

She didn't. But the look of worry gnawed at him. The anger gnawed harder, bit into his skin and down to the bone. Ever since he could remember, Paul had tried to invade Jesse's life, sports when they were kids, car racing and golf later, and even Desiree, although that hadn't succeeded. Now he was trying to destroy his future. Now Jesse was going to invade his life.

There were no lights on outside the brick colonial. Paul's black truck was the only vehicle parked out front. Jesse felt the hood, but it had been too long since the attack to tell whether it had been used for a getaway vehicle. The doors were locked, and it was too dark inside to see anything out of the ordinary.

He pounded on the front door over and over again, until finally a disoriented Paul opened the door. He blinked twice, as if he couldn't believe who he saw. Before he could react, Jesse shoved him inside and slammed a punch to his jaw. Paul went down instantly, almost too easily. Jesse picked him up and shoved him against the wall.

"You son of a bitch, you tried to kill her!"

Jesse drove a fist into Paul's stomach. He groaned, then slid down to the floor.

"Jess—what's this about? I didn't . . ."

Jesse pulled him back up again. The smell of liquor was still strong on Paul's breath.

"You got drunk and did it. What'd you do, sit there and keep drinking and thinking that she might remember you were the psycho that tried to rape and kill her by the side of the road? Did it get to you?"

Paul was more cognizant now, standing on his own. "I was drinking, but I wasn't thinking about that. I didn't do anything to Marti. I had too much happy hour and came home. I don't even remember lying down on the couch."

"Where's your golf glove, Paul?"

He gave Jesse a confused look. "My golf glove? It's at the club with my irons. What does that have to do with anything?"

"What color's your glove?"

"Gray and white. I just bought it last week. You can go down and check if you want."

Jesse leaned back on his heels, daunted only for a second. "What about your old one?"

"Uh, blue I think. Light blue."

"It's your glove, Paul, isn't it? You left it in your hurry to get out of there before I got hold of you. But you're not safe yet. Not by a long shot. We have some things to discuss."

When Marti woke up the next morning, her head was still fuzzy from sleep. She sat up suddenly as the room came into view. White walls, dark blue curtains covering two windows facing the rising sun. A queen-size bed and white ceiling fan overhead. Not her bedroom! Kati sat up and yawned, sprawled out at an angle on the bed next to her. Then everything came back to her, the horrifying nightmare that was real.

"Where's Jesse?" she asked, searching everywhere.

Kati shrugged. "Maybe he's already up. It's almost seven. Seven? Oh, my gosh, I'm late for work! Priscilla's going to kill me!" She lunged from the bed, then stopped just in front of the door. "Are you all right, Marti?"

"Not until I know where Jesse is." She was already grabbing the clothes they'd taken from the house much earlier that morning.

Helen was on the phone when Marti walked into the living room. She was kneading her blond hair with nervous fingers, pacing frantically.

"How much? Sheriff, that's ridiculous. I know, I understand that, but surely you can understand what he's been through. Fine." She slammed the phone down, then was startled to see Marti standing there.

"Something's happened to Jesse, hasn't it?"

Kati came downstairs, half-dressed, with a pale expression on her face. "They arrested Jesse?" At Helen's surprised look, she added, "I was going to call Priscilla to tell her I'd be at work in fifteen minutes. I heard the last part of your conversation."

"Oh, my God," Marti muttered, falling back onto the couch. "He killed Paul, didn't he?"

"No, he didn't kill him, but he nearly did. Paul's at the emergency room now. If his ribs are broken, it could be a felony. Jesse's been in jail since four this morning, but Carl didn't want to wake me up any earlier than now to tell me. He's so thoughtful, that one. Jesse is scheduled for his twenty-four-hour hearing at ten-thirty. Bond will be set then. Carl's going to press for seven thousand dollars if it's a felony."

"What?" Marti stood up and curled her hands into fists. "That jerk deserves everything he got, even if he wasn't the one who broke in last night. Jesse didn't want you to know so you wouldn't worry, but Paul and his two fiendish friends jumped him the night we were Christmas tree shopping. Jesse didn't let on, but I know he was in some pain."

"So the story about the tree falling on him was a lie," Helen said.

Kati started heading upstairs. "That's it! I'm going down there myself, and I'll show that sheriff—"

"Oh, no you're not," Helen said. "You go into work. I don't need two of my kids in jail, with Billy sure to jump on the bandwagon. Lord knows he's been in the tank enough times already. Marti and I will head down and straighten this whole thing out. If we need your help, we'll call."

"But—"

"Go to work!"

Kati sputtered in anger before stomping back upstairs. Helen sat in silence for a minute, weighing the situation. Marti wanted to join Kati's army and head down to the jail to raise some hell, but something in Helen's quiet deliberation showed more strength. She only wished she had that strength.

Helen stood up. "I'm going to get dressed. You get some food in your stomach, so that babe doesn't think the whole world is coming to an end. Last night was probably enough of a scare. Then we'll go down and see what we're in for. After that, I can talk to the lawyer I work for and see how we're going to get out of it."

Helen calmly went to her room, and Marti walked into the kitchen. She put her hand on her belly.

"I didn't even think about how all this affected you. It's not that I don't care, but I think you're in this little cocoon all sheltered and snug. We'll have to see Dr. Diehl tomorrow, just to make sure. It's okay, though. Your daddy's going to take care of us at night from now on. Well, after he gets out of jail."

Marti buttered a piece of bread and forced it down. She thought of those strong arms wrapped around her while she slept, his bare chest pressed against her back. Then she thought about him spending the morning in jail on an old, stained mattress without a pillow. She could have died last night, and the last conversation between them was about Debbie. Why did the thought of his marrying Debbie after she was gone drive her mad? How could she explain that she was jealous? He would ask, "What does it matter if you're leaving?" What else could she tell him but the truth: "I don't know, but it does, dammit. It does."

"Are you ready?"

Marti jumped at Helen's voice, then turned to see her standing in the kitchen doorway dressed in a coral suit. Marti felt like a ragamuffin in the jeans and long-sleeved top she had on.

Kati came sliding down the wooden banister. "You have to let me know the second you find out anything. I'll go nuts wondering."

"We will."

Helen and Marti followed Kati down the road until she turned off at Bad Boys Diner. Marti knew Kati was using her utmost self-control not to keep going to the jail. The Wests were nothing, if not strong.

"Helen, how do I become like you, so strong and calm?"

Helen's coral-painted lips softened into a smile. "It takes time. Every time you resist doing the wrong thing, you become stronger. It keeps building on itself. When you do the wrong thing, you fall down a notch; but you keep striving."

"What if you're not good at resisting temptation? What if you have nothing to build on?"

"You have to start somewhere. Something small, like not eating the doughnut when you want it badly. Then you keep growing, taking on bigger challenges."

"Oh, how I wish you'd been there to teach me this stuff when I was growing up. All I keep thinking about are the mistakes I've made, over and over again. Weakness is like strength, Helen. It keeps building too, small things at first, then larger and larger."

Helen's smile became wistful. "I always think about what I have to lose by acting on my impulses. Flab, hurting someone's feelings. I weigh whether the deed is worth the price."

They pulled into the parking lot next to the sheriff's office. Marti took a deep breath.

"I wish I could be so confident. I want to scream and kick something. You look completely in control."

"I want to scream, too. You're stronger than you think. You're holding it in just as I am."

The sheriff's office smelled piney, as if the cleaning service had recently vacated the premises. While Helen talked to Lyle, Marti walked to the door behind him, hoping to glimpse Jesse. All she could see was a hallway off to the side of the back room and a hint of bars.

"Sorry, Marti, but you can't go back there. As I was saying, Helen, I can't let you see him until we're through processing him."

"Processing him? He's been here for hours."

He shrugged, avoiding her eyes. "Well, Sheriff Paton has his ways. But if it makes you feel any better, Paul doesn't have any broken ribs. He'll be on his way down to sign the papers, but all Jesse will get is battery. Forty bucks'll do it for bail, probably." Lyle sat back in his chair, enjoying his official duty.

"I don't suppose it matters that Paul and his friends ambushed my son at Christmas."

"Not if he didn't report it. Why didn't he do that, you think?"

"He's not built that way," Marti said.

When the women walked outside, Helen looked at

Marti. "Self-control is slipping fast. When I can't see my own son, I start feeling panic. Like something's not right."

"What do you mean? Like he's hurt and they don't want us to know yet?"

Helen shook her head. "No, I don't want to think about that. Let's go down to Bad Boys and let Kati know what's going on."

Marti stopped before opening the car door. "Can you do me a favor? Drop me off at the hairdresser's down the street. I'm going to undo one of my earlier impulses."

At ten o'clock, Helen and Marti showed up at the sheriff's office. This time they were prepared to bulldoze any roadblock they had to, even one named Lyle.

But as it turned out, they didn't have to. Carl walked out from the back room as they stepped inside. His expression was grim, his lips pulled into a tight red line.

"We're filling out the paperwork now. Then you can get him the hell out of here."

Helen flinched slightly from the tone of his voice. "I don't understand."

"There is no bail. If it were up to me, I'd have Jesse in jail until I finish this investigation. But it isn't up to me. Paul isn't pressing charges. The kid wimped out on me again." He leaned close to Helen, and Marti was surprised to see Helen back down by looking away. "Maybe if Paul had had a mother, and Jesse a father, we wouldn't be standing here like this."

"Carl, stop it," she muttered under her breath. "I want to see my son."

Carl gave her a curious look. "*Your* son will be out momentarily."

He stepped back into the room, leaving Helen and Marti alone up front. Just as Marti was about to ask her about the strange comment, Helen said, "I don't understand why Paul isn't pressing charges."

"Maybe he wants Jesse to lay off his case, so he's being nice."

Carl appeared in the doorway, and Jesse walked

through behind him. He had a black eye, and his brown hair was disheveled. The sparkle that usually lit his eyes was gone, replaced by a dull look. Marti's heart ached for him and she rushed into his arms. Even in his surprise to her reaction, he hugged her close, kissing the top of her head.

She had dreamed about those arms around her all morning, waited for him to return and comfort her. He had been sitting in a cold jail cell locked away from her. Now he was here, and she squeezed back the tears of relief. But it was more than that. Rumpled, tired, and smelling slightly sweaty, she realized the awful truth: She was in love with him. Drowning in the feel of him, seeking the strength he so freely offered her, the warmth and affection he gave without asking for anything in return. No, she couldn't drown! She cleared her throat and moved away from him, hoping he didn't see the film of moisture on her eyes.

"I, er, missed you."

Helen moved up to hug him. "Let's get out of this dump," she whispered, though Carl still heard it.

"Jesse, you're looking for clues in clear water," he said in a stiff voice. "There's nothing to see."

"That's what you want me to think. But the truth will come out."

They stopped at Bad Boys on the way home. Kati squealed and rushed into his arms. The midmorning crowd was small, but everybody turned to look, then talked speculatively. Marti was sure they already knew about the attack and Jesse's arrest.

"I heard you broke two of Paul's ribs. Good for you, big brother!"

"Kati," Helen admonished, looking around at the listeners nearby. "He didn't break anything."

Kati lowered her voice. "What did they set your bail at?"

When Kati heard that Paul hadn't pressed charges, she took back her ill comment. Jesse was unenthusiastic about the whole ordeal, quiet even. She was sure he was tired. Just looking at him made her realize how tired she was, how little sleep she'd actually gotten.

Helen held up the conversation for the ride back to her house. Marti and Jesse were too quiet. When they reached home, Helen checked in at the office and found that she was needed for a special case.

"I'm only part time, but they get to choose which part. Relax here if you want."

Jesse groaned softly, then took Marti's hand, leading her up the stairs. It gave her a funny feeling, him leading her up to his old bedroom. Not that she expected anything to happen. He was too worn out for that. And it wouldn't happen anyway, she added tersely.

The bed was still rumpled from where she and Kati had slept last night. Sunlight filtered through the curtains, lighting the room softly. He stripped his shirt off and lay down, pulling her down beside him. His green eyes were sleepy, yet something kept them from slipping closed. He smiled slightly, reaching for a strand of hair.

"You dyed your hair back."

She nervously tucked her hair behind her ear before realizing what she was doing. "Now you have me doing it! Yeah, I dyed it back. Easier to take care of."

She looked away, then back again. His smile was gone, replaced by that faraway look. He still held her hand, moving and bending it, studying it.

After a minute she asked, "Jesse, what's wrong? You don't feel bad for what you did to Paul, do you?"

"No, I feel bad for what I did to you."

"To me?" There was a strange pounding in her heart, put there by the way he touched her hand, the way he looked at her with quiet agony in his eyes.

"I let you down. My anger got the best of me and got me put in jail. I promised to take care of you, and it's damn hard to do that when I'm locked up. All I kept thinking about in there was what if something happened to you. If he knew I was locked up, he'd know I wasn't there watching over you." He squeezed her hand, finally looking up to meet her eyes. "You're my life right now. I can't let my emotions override your safety. Never again, Marti."

She found it difficult to breathe when he'd said those words, "You're my life right now." What to say to him after he'd said that? What to say to take away the self-incrimination in his eyes?

"You didn't let me down, Jesse. I know you were trying to put an end to this . . . this man who's trying to kill me. You were trying to protect me. I was safe here, you knew that. You even said he wouldn't come after me twice in the same night. You knew I'd be okay."

He looked at her for the longest moment, weighing her words perhaps. She tried to catch her breath without letting him know he'd taken it from her. Before she could accomplish it, he leaned over and kissed her. Like under the tree that Christmas Eve, he pressed his lips softly to hers, not in passion but in tenderness. Passion she could fight. Maybe. But how could she fight tenderness?

He kissed her again, then closed his eyes as if savoring the feel. Or deciding whether to kiss her some more. She was poised at the edge, hoping he wouldn't, wishing he would. He didn't. Without opening his eyes again, he lay back, pulling her along with him. Her head nestled against his shoulder, and she could feel his breath on top of her head. She waited, holding her breath. His heart beat healthily beneath her, lulling her to a dreamy state. His hand still held hers, although his grip had loosened as he'd fallen asleep.

What would she do with a lifetime of this, she wondered sleepily. It was too much to think about. Too wonderful, too scary.

Chapter 14

~

Donna Hislope walked into the diner, flashing Kati and Marti a phony smile before prissily sitting at the counter. She licked her finger and ran it down the hair that tapered to a point at her temple.

"She either wants to know something, or wants us to know something," Kati whispered before slowly making her way over. "Hi, Donna. How's your dad?"

"Oh, the usual. And speaking of that, can I have my usual?"

"Chocolate milk shake," Kati said with a nod, turning to start preparing it.

"Oh, you're funny. No, a glass of tomato juice. Got to watch my figure."

Marti lifted an eyebrow at Donna's barrel torso leaning against the counter. Not that she felt particularly shapely, but at least she had a good reason.

"Marti, how are you doing? I heard about the break-in last week. The creep broke into *your* bedroom, I understand. Too bad he picked the time you and Jesse are, uh, having problems."

Either the sheriff or the deputy had a big mouth, Marti thought, cursing the gossips of the small town. She smiled. "Yeah, well, backache or no, *our* waterbed will just have to do until the baby's born."

Donna showed her large, flat teeth in a lascivious smile. "If I had a husband like him, I wouldn't let him sleep alone for a minute. Speaking of that, guess who asked me for a date next Friday? Paul Paton."

Kati's eyes widened. "I hope you didn't accept it."

Donna pulled at her polyester miniskirt, shifting around on the stool. "Oh, come on. You don't really believe he's after Marti, do you? He's too good-looking to be that evil. And he's a lot hotter than the other guy who's been flirting with me lately."

Donna examined her fingernails, forcing Kati to ask, "And who's that?"

"Dean Seeber."

Marti saw Kati's spine stiffen. "Dean asked you out?" Kati asked in a thin voice.

"Well, not asked out directly. Yet. But he sent me flowers today. I have to call and thank him, I suppose, but that's all he gets. I wouldn't be caught dead with him."

Kati's face was flushed, a mixture of disbelief and betrayal in her eyes. Marti spoke up before Kati could give away the affection for Dean she always hid, even from herself.

"What's so bad about him?"

"He's just weird, that's all. Not bad looking or anything, just too strange for me." She took a sip of her tomato juice, left a dollar on the counter and stood up. "Nice chatting with you, girls."

"Be careful on that date, Donna," Marti said.

She held out her arm and dropped her wrist. "Oh, pooh. I think you two aren't getting enough. You're just too uptight."

Marti just shook her head as the glass door swung shut. "I'm uptight not because I was almost killed last week, but because I haven't had enough sex lately. There's logic for you."

Kati just stared out the window with narrowed eyes, watching Donna get into her new sports car. "Do you think Dean really sent her flowers?"

"There's one way to find out: ask him. Um, your concern wouldn't be anything other than friendly, would it?"

Kati met her eyes. "Of course not. But I'd break his nose if he went out with her."

Later that evening, Marti sat across the dining room table from Jesse, watching him pick at his food. Mostly he was stirring it around, and she couldn't take the blame for lousy cooking; the peas were canned and the roasted chicken she picked up at the grocery store. With her pointed toe, she tapped his leg.

"What'cha thinking about?"

"A lot of things. I've asked Paul twice why he didn't press charges. He doesn't even meet my eyes, just shrugs and turns away. That just isn't like him. It's not that he's even acting guilty, just preoccupied. He knows I'm still on his trail, even if I couldn't prove the glove was his. I just don't get it."

"Do you think that maybe Paul isn't the one? I mean, whenever I've seen him in the diner, he never acts like he'd murder me if he had the chance."

"Don't be fooled by his appearance. Paul has always been superb at masking his emotions. But I'm going to have all day Sunday to watch him. You're coming with me, aren't you?"

"To where?"

"Racing."

She shifted in her seat. "I don't know. I'm not really into that racing stuff."

His flash of disappointment turned smug. "That's okay. I'm sure I'll have a couple of females in the stands to cheer me on."

She stood up and threw her napkin across the table at him. "Desiree and Debbie can wear little cheerleading outfits and wave pompons for all I care!" At his slight grin, she added, "I didn't say I wasn't going to go, just that I wasn't sure. And don't use your *women* to manipulate me into doing things, Jesse!"

He shook his head slowly. "You're something else, you know that? I was referring to Kati and Ma."

She threw a bun at him, smearing his nose with butter when he didn't duck in time. "I know exactly who you were referring to, Jesse James West. It was not them!"

When she grabbed her plate and glass and headed into the kitchen, he came up behind her, next to her ear. "I just wanted to get you there. I don't want you here by yourself while I'm at the race. Besides, I want to keep an eye on Paul's reactions to you all day."

"Sure, use me." She turned on the water.

Sliding his arms around her belly, he whispered, "Don't tempt me, Marti. Don't tempt me."

It seemed like hours before Marti drifted off to sleep. Jesse had shifted and moved for a while, but she lay silent and still, not wanting him to know she was awake. There was something intimate about sharing a midnight conversation in bed in the dark.

But now she was awake again, and it was still dark. It wasn't the fear of waking up with somebody standing over her bed that she felt. Not with Jesse beside her. Something had woke her, and then she realized what it had been. She felt his warm hand on her belly and knew he was awake. The bottom of her shirt was bunched up just under her chest, baring her belly. The blankets were covering her waist. Her eyes adjusted to the ghostly light streaming through the curtains. She slowly turned her head toward him, finding him lying on his side very close to her.

"Jesse? Are you awake?"

He looked at her, but she couldn't see his eyes. "I couldn't sleep," he whispered, his voice velvety in the darkness. "I felt the baby move and I kept thinking about him in there."

She felt a shifting in her stomach and smiled. "What were you thinking about?"

Jesse trailed his fingers lightly over her belly, and in the moonlight she could see the smile on his face. "What his life is like in there, what he feels. I mean, is he happy, or does he know what happiness is yet? I wish I could remember what it was like."

She remembered his kiss the week before in his old bedroom, and her heartbeat quickened its pace. Did the baby feel that, too? Part of her wanted to feel Jesse's lips on hers again, desperate to experience that new sensation of tenderness and masculine sensuality. Part of her wanted to pack up that very moment and get to California as fast as she could.

He reached up and touched her cheek. "You are so beautiful, Marti."

"Jesse . . ."

His finger grazed across her lips, skin rougher than his lips would have been. "You are."

"I feel like a duck," she murmured against his finger. "I look like I swallowed a bowling ball."

He removed his finger, shifting so that his face was near hers. "You look great. You're a walking miracle, carrying a living little human right here in your tummy. There's a glow about you, and your eyes sparkle. Your belly is one of the most beautiful parts of your body."

The glow, the sparkle, they were from the baby. Only from the baby. Her dry throat, the warm flush on her face, that was all from the pregnancy, too. He was touching her chin, drawing her closer for another devastating kiss that would rock her insides and her resistance. She squeezed her eyes shut as he moved closer.

"Don't kiss me, Jesse."

He stopped where he was, not moving away. "Why not? I like kissing you."

"I just . . . can't handle it." Well, at least she was being honest. He had kissed her four times, and each time she had felt it farther down in her heart, pushing away reason and fear of failing him. Lulling her into a sense of false confidence that she could change somehow and deserve a man like Jesse.

"What's there to handle? I kiss you, you kiss me back. Are you afraid I'm going to jump you?"

She found herself adopting that awful habit Jesse had started, tucking her hair behind her ears. This time she left it there. "No, actually, I'd be afraid that I'd jump *you*. You know, pregnant women, hormones, all that."

He leaned closer again. "Hm, I think I could deal with that risk." His lips grazed hers before she backed away.

"Jesse, I don't want to . . . I mean, I *want* to, but I can't. Physically I want to, but emotionally I can't. Do you understand what I'm trying to say?"

"You don't want to make love with me because you're afraid it might be so wonderful, you couldn't leave."

"No!" Yes. "Jesse, don't pressure me."

When he leaned and touched her lips with his, she

didn't back off. "Who said that if I kissed you, we'd have to make love?"

"Well, we are in bed. It always seems that way, that men can't just kiss or hold a woman without expecting more. To men, kissing means sex. . . ." He was kissing her then, and more than kissing, but teasing her lips with his tongue. Her heart tightened, wanting to resist, unable to. Her mouth opened at his invitation, against her will. Without hesitation, his warm tongue moved along her teeth, tickling the roof of her mouth. All in an agonizingly slow, lazy way. After ravishing her mouth, he kissed across her chin and down her throat. She was caught breathless, drowning again . . . not thinking about the consequences for once.

"What if," he murmured against her skin, "I didn't expect to make love to you, but I wanted to pleasure you in other ways?"

His hand drifted down across her belly to beneath the blankets. He slid his fingers over her underwear, sliding them down, making her legs tense in reaction. Even tensed, they moved easily apart for him.

"Jesse . . ." she managed until his hand cupped her hair, and his fingers slid down to explore.

He took her sharp intake of air as consent and trailed kisses along the same path his hand had taken earlier. She clenched her hands, wanting him to stop there and not take her to the brink of pleasure. A brink he could easily take her over, and her body was aching with readiness. It had been so long, too long. When his tongue trailed down the tender skin of her inner thighs, she ceased thinking about the past and the future.

She tried to keep her eyes open, as if to somehow distance herself from what he was doing, but it didn't work. He teased and taunted, bringing her close, then nibbled a path to less sensitive areas. Just when she caught her breath again, his tongue trailed back, washing her body with chills. When she got closer, nearly ready to fall over the edge, fear crept in. She felt exposed, vulnerable, as she always did at this point. She squirmed away and sat up.

"Come here."

"What's wrong? Aren't you enjoying it?"

"Yes, it feels great."

"Then let me finish."

"No." She felt foolish, like a child.

"Why not?" Despite her words, he pulled her lower body down close to him again and started kissing her belly.

"I'm not sure. I never . . . finished this way. It makes me feel uncomfortable."

"Do you think I'm going to hurt you?"

"No."

He gently pushed her back down. "Then lie down. Now repeat after me: Jesse, I trust you."

"Jesse . . ." She faltered, feeling even more foolish.

"Repeat it. Come on."

She took a breath. "Jesse, I trust you."

"Jesse, I'm going to let you take me as far as I can go."

As he spoke, he ran a finger down her wetness, making her shudder. "J-Jesse, I'm going to let you take me as far as I can go."

"And just say my name. I want to hear you say it again."

"Jesse . . . Jesse . . . mmm, Jesse."

The impulse to move away, to stop him, vanished as she kept repeating his name, as his tongue moved slowly, teasingly around and around, until the warmth exploded within her and her body tensed in one earth-shattering tremor. She had fallen over the edge. And survived.

Jesse covered her up again and slid up next to her. "Are you glad you trusted me?" he whispered.

"Yes." No. Now she wanted him more than ever. If he even suggested making love now, she *would* jump him.

But he didn't. Instead he pulled her into his arms, forming himself to her back and holding her close. "Do you think the baby felt it?"

She giggled. "I'm sure he did. I just hope he didn't know what it was."

* * *

Marti and Jesse drove into the speedway midafternoon, the truck straining under the weight of pulling number thirteen. If anything had changed between them as a result of last night, she couldn't tell. Except that they regarded each other with a measure of shyness that didn't exist before.

Billy was there, talking to one of the other racers. They parked in the pit area in the middle of the track, a large circular area covered in dirt and tire tracks. There were several other trailers loaded with race cars of every type, including Pintos, Buicks, and even tiny little cars that hardly seemed as though they could accommodate a grown man.

"Those are the midgets," Jesse explained when she asked. "They're the special feature tonight."

"What is your kind of car called?"

"I'm in street stock."

Jesse hopped out of the truck, then held his hand out so she could slide along the seat and get out on his side. She wondered if Billy could tell something had happened last night. Nah, she decided.

"Hey, little brother. Marti. You ready to get the beast going? Steven's got a new Camaro over there. Says it'll beat anything."

"It doesn't look new to me," Marti said after glancing at the car.

"New to the racing circuit," Billy corrected. "You gonna race in the Lady Road Warriors, Marti?"

"Me? You mean women race these cars?"

"Yep. 'Course, I don't think they'll let a pregnant woman do it."

"Gee, that's too bad."

Jesse just shook his head at the bantering as he removed some metal ties and lifted the entire hood off the car. He pulled out a toolbox and started fiddling with the massive engine. A young man with a battered face in dingy jeans and a faded T-shirt that read "I'm not arrogant, just better than you" sauntered over.

"Well, Jesse James, didn't think you'd be back with us so soon. Maybe a sponsor'll spot me as his driver this time."

Marti could see Jesse's expression harden. Without looking up at him, Jesse said, "He ain't just looking for a pretty face, Dwayne. You actually have to know how to drive."

"We'll see 'bout that, West. I think they outta send you back to the dirt tracks." Unsatisfied, he walked back to his Camaro just a little faster than he'd walked over.

"You probably hate coming back here, don't you?" she asked quietly.

He stopped and looked at her. "Ah, the guys around here will jab at you for anything, but they're just funning. It's all head games." He glanced at the track. "I'll just beat these guys to stay in shape. Dwayne knows I can beat his tail end on the dirt, too. That's what this track was before they decided to become a real race-track and pave it. Asphalt racing is one thing, but racing dirt is a thrill all its own. Marti, you just can't imagine the feeling when you're charging down the straightaway, jumping into the left turn. You can feel your back end sliding around, then the car's sliding sideways, and just when you think 'aw, heck, this is it,' you jerk the wheel the other way and straighten the beast out again.

"Or when you're really feeling your Wheaties and end up sliding around a turn on three wheels, and everybody tells you later that you were kicking up dirt twenty feet in the air, but you didn't have time to enjoy it because you were too busy making sure the fourth wheel stayed on the ground." He smiled at her. "Nothing like it. Better than sex, or at least any that I've had."

Marti shook her head, imagining the scary scenario as he spoke. "You must be trying to kill yourself, Jesse."

"I'm having too much fun to have a death wish. I want to be the best someday, Marti. Right up there with Richard Petty and A. J. Foyt. My dad knew what he was doing when he built me my first race car when I was a kid. It only had a lawn mower engine, but it was a start."

He went back to his work, but Marti wasn't fooled. Jesse hated being there, and she knew it. Why wouldn't he let his anger show? If only he would share it with her.

"Yee-haw!" a guy yelled out of a stripped Yellow cab, complete with the light on top. She recognized Alan beneath his black cowboy hat as he pulled his car off the trailer and next to Jesse's. He nearly lost himself climbing out of the window, but regained his composure quickly.

"Hey, Jesse! Marti. Billy, that you under there?" Billy belched in response. "Nice to see you, too." Alan took his hat off and wiped the sweat from his brow with his shirtsleeve. His blond hair was matted in a ring where the hat had been sitting. "Hey, well I'll be! Another one of our prodigies come back to their old stomping grounds."

A long-legged man about Jesse's age with brown hair and brown eyes sauntered over to the car. Jesse walked over and shook his hand.

"Damn, Mike, what brings you around here? Why aren't you racing?"

Mike? The guy Jesse gave his ASA spot to when he found out Marti was pregnant?

"Serious car trouble, that's what." He shrugged, looking around the track. "Since we were down this way, I thought I'd stop by to see you. Figured you'd be around here."

Jesse leaned on the roof of his car. "Last time I talked to you, it was your third race. Now that you're an old-timer, how is it?"

Mike laughed. "It's cool, Jesse. I feel like I'm on my way. You'll get there too, bud."

"Yes, I will," Jesse said with fiery conviction.

"Maybe sooner than you think," Mike said meaningfully.

That got Jesse's attention. "What do you mean?"

Marti sat on the back bumper of the car, feeling as good as invisible. No wonder Jesse didn't want to be involved with anyone while he made his way up in the racing world. He was much too focused to pay attention to any attention-needing female.

"Minski's going to build another car. He wants you to drive it."

There was no hesitation. "I'm there. When's he going to have it ready?"

"In a few months. How long has Marti got?"

When Marti looked at them at the mention of her name, she saw that same fierce determination in Mike's eyes that burned in Jesse's when it came to racing. *Men,* she muttered in her thoughts.

"A few months," Jesse answered. "I've got to wait until she has the baby. Then I'm free."

Mike gave Jesse a strange look, but didn't delve further. "I'll let Minski know. What if he wants you to start racing before the baby comes."

"He'll just have to wait. I can't leave Marti for days at a time, and she'll be too big to come along."

Mike nodded. "It'll be good driving together again, Jesse."

"Yeah," Jesse said, drawing the word out. "It sure will."

Billy crawled out from beneath the car and leaned in to start it. The roar of the engine was deafening. Mike braced his hands on the side of the engine and asked Billy something about the engine. Jesse walked to the back of the car.

"Did you hear that, Marti? Minski's going to build a second car. I could have another ride."

"I heard." She smiled, knowing how much it meant to him. "I'm happy for you, I really am."

"It's what I want most in the world."

She wondered where she fit into his list of wants in the world. If she fit there at all. Feeling crummy, she changed the subject.

"Why doesn't Billy have his own car?" she asked over the noise.

"Not since Dad died. He says he'll never race again, but he's determined to make sure the same thing doesn't happen to me, so he's my mechanic on race day. Listen, doll, we're going to start qualifying soon. It's going to get pretty crowded around here, and you're not going to want to hear their trashy language, so it'd probably be a good idea for you to sit up in the bleachers." He pointed to the line of bleachers that ran along one side of the track, then flashed his teeth in a grin. "That's my cheering section right there. Ma and Kati should be here anytime." His smile disappeared. "Stay away from Paul when he gets here. I mean it."

"You don't have to tell me, Jesse. You think I want to see you in jail again? No way. Good luck."

He grimaced. "Don't wish a race driver good luck. It's bad luck."

She gave him a confused look, then shook her head. "Men." After she started walking toward the bleachers, she looked back again. "And what a man," she whispered. In tight, faded jeans and a T-shirt cropped short on the bottom with the sleeves cut off, he cut an impressive picture. He crouched down to commiserate with Billy and Mike, already busy at winning.

"Hey, little lady," a heavy man she'd never seen before called. "You want to be my pit crew? My old lady hit the road last night."

He was leaning over his engine, sweaty and red-faced. She tried not to notice the two-inch butt crack showing above his faded jeans.

"How can I be your pit crew if I'm rooting for another driver?" She flashed him her wedding ring. "My husband."

"Oh. Who's your husband, anyway?"

"Jesse James West," she said, feeling an odd kind of pride.

"Hell, forget I asked."

She did.

Marti had only been sitting on the sparsely filled bleachers for a few minutes when she spotted Paul's black truck pulling in with a trailer. Jesse was aware of him too, but he didn't approach him. In fact, Paul chose a spot at the far end when he saw Jesse's setup in the front section. Even from a distance, a week later, Paul's face looked a little bruised. She wished she could be sure he was the one. Her insides jumped when Paul looked to the place she was sitting, but she couldn't tell whether he was looking at her or just somewhere near her. Just as quickly, he turned and went to work on his car, soon joined by Josh and Skip. Josh said something, and all three glanced up at her. She shifted uncomfortably under their interest.

A short while later, she watched Debbie walk through the gate and across the track to Jesse's car, boys in tow. Billy stayed discreetly beneath the car, although he motioned for the boys to crawl under with him. Debbie held onto her floppy yellow hat as the breeze picked up. The pit was now packed with cars and people all busily making last minute adjustments. Marti concentrated on everyone else but Jesse for a long time, and when she looked back, Debbie wasn't there. Only the boys were.

Debbie picked her way through the bleachers toward her, wearing a deep blue shirt and white jeans. She had a slight flush on her face, and Marti had a feeling it wasn't from the trek up the stairs. She sat down next to Marti as easily as if the two women had planned to meet there.

Only after she sat down did she turn to Marti and ask, "Is it all right if I sit here? The boys are going to stay down there with their father."

Marti shrugged, giving more attention to what was going on down below than to Debbie. Jesse was showing the boys something inside the car, tracing the roll bar and illustrating how the four point harness worked on Clint. Jesse's blue-jeaned derriere stuck out in their direction when he leaned in the car and pulled his helmet out, settling it on Turk's head.

Debbie sighed happily, leaning back against the seats behind her. "It seems like forever since I've been here, watching Jesse race. It's a shame, about ASA and all." She glanced subtly at Marti's belly. "But Jesse told me the sponsor is building another car so Jesse has another chance. I'm so happy for him. It must be hard to come back to this after getting so far."

"He doesn't seem to mind that much," Marti said, trying to keep the defensiveness out of her voice. Jesse was joking around with a group of men.

"I think he does."

"I know he does," Marti said, refusing to have Debbie know more about Jesse than she did.

Debbie watched Jesse with a wistful expression. "He could do anything well. I told him that later, when he was ready, I could watch the baby while he traveled the

ASA circuit, and eventually NASCAR. The kids and I could even travel with him, cheer him on. The boys would love it, and . . ."

"Debbie, don't talk to me about this."

Debbie's smile disappeared when she pulled her gaze from Jesse and her sons. Marti realized then that her proposal of marriage wasn't just for a marriage of convenience on her part; Debbie was in love with Jesse.

"You're in love with him, aren't you?"

Marti was startled to hear Debbie voice her own thoughts. "What makes you say that?"

"I should have realized it when we talked in the kitchen that first night. But I didn't see it then, the way your eyes follow his every move, the way they drink him in when you're close to him. I wonder if you even see it yourself."

Marti shifted uncomfortably on the hard metal bench. Of course she saw it; that didn't mean she was going to admit it to Debbie. And she didn't want to explore it much, in any case.

"You think just because I appreciate him physically that I'm in love with him?"

"No, it's not just that. All I know is that you walk in, screw up his life by getting pregnant and marrying him, and now you want to leave. I'm not condemning you, believe me. It's just that, any other woman in that position would be feeling some amount of guilt if she was human at all. So when someone like me comes along and offers him his dreams again, it should be a big relief. When it's not, there's a reason. Or maybe you're not planning to leave anymore."

Marti felt trapped, searching for an answer to give Debbie—and herself. When she looked up to see Helen, Kati, and Dean walking toward them, she stood and waved, effectively ending their conversation. Then she further ensured it wouldn't start again by directing Kati and Dean to sit between her and Debbie.

"Why don't you race, Dean?" Marti asked once everyone was settled.

"I do."

She waited for him to explain why he wasn't out there, but he seemed content with his answer.

"So-o-o, why aren't you racing today then?"

"Oh, I don't race cars. I race frogs. Big, warty ones. They don't give you warts, you know." He nodded knowingly. "It's all a myth."

Marti started laughing, but Dean obviously didn't realize the depth of his humor. Or even that it was humor.

When Dean was involved in a conversation, of sorts, with Debbie, Marti leaned over to Kati and whispered, "So, did you ask him about the flowers?"

"Yes. He said he did it because she looked depressed the day before when he took his hounds in for their shots. I guess I don't have any reason to get mad at him. I don't own him or anything. I went over to Dr. Hislope's office and she had that bouquet of daisies on her desk. I didn't see any card at a glance. Not that it matters, really."

"But it does," Marti finished, and turned to Helen. "This is probably a pretty familiar place to you."

"Oh, yes. I try to come whenever I can. Still, it's hard sometimes."

Marti grew silent for a moment, realizing that Helen lost her husband to this sport. "Was it here? That Bernie died?"

"No, this track didn't even exist then. He traveled all over the state. I couldn't go with him, not with three kids to raise."

Marti wanted to tell Helen that was Debbie's plan, but she kept quiet about it. She wondered if Helen knew about the proposal at all. That probably depended on how seriously Jesse was taking it.

Then the other woman plaguing Marti these days showed up: Desiree. Wearing her standard boots, jeans, and tank top, she settled in two rows behind them. Marti bit her lip, trying not to let her presence, and Debbie's, bother her.

Kati leaned over. "Don't worry. She always comes to cheer Jesse on, always has. Even when she's seeing one of the other racers."

"I'm not worried about it," Marti said, almost too fast.

"But you are," Kati quipped, turning to intently watch something in the pit and ignoring Marti's glare.

When Jesse climbed in the car through the window, she realized that there wasn't any outside hardware on his car, or any other. Door handles, hubcaps, and trim were all missing. The doors were welded shut. Even the headlights were gone. Some of the cars were like Jesse's, shiny and nice looking, with only a few dents. Others looked like inner-city victims, stripped for parts and left for dead. Except that they were painted with sponsor names, mostly body shops and mechanics. Hm, wonder why, she thought. One had "T&A racing" painted on it; another had "Crash and burn racing." The last one fit the dented car it was painted on well.

The menagerie of old cars organized on the track, and before long the qualifying was underway. After a while, when her buns were half-numb from sitting, and her hearing half-gone from the announcer's speaker above them, the first race began.

When Jesse nearly went into one of those spins he had told her about, she found herself clenching her fists. Paul's gold car purposely bumped into him in the third turn, and Jesse's back end slipped before he got it under control. Jesse retaliated by passing him on the next lap. Marti spent most of the time tensed up watching the cars all clustered together on the turns. One car went into a spin, hitting another and sending it toward the wall. The man who did his flag dance in the box way up high jumped up and down with the yellow flag.

Could she be one of the wives she saw vehemently cheering their spouse or boyfriend on, chasing the straying baby, attending every race? Or would she get bored, become a straying wife? If only she could be sure that things would be different with Jesse.

With Jamie, she had been swept away by his good looks, money, everything. Jesse was good-looking in a different way, not glamorous, but strong, warm, and carefree. He hadn't meant for her to fall in love with him; it had just happened. Thinking back, she realized it was inevitable.

That was Jesse, a cowboy, willing to do anything for the woman he allowed himself to love. Not that he loved her, she thought, startled by the direction her daydreams were leading her. Leading her down the path of the broken-hearted. She couldn't bear to see a betrayed look on his face, like the one that day when she was talking to Paul at the gas station. Her heart would shrivel up and wither if she caused Jesse real pain. And she would; it was inevitable as falling in love with him had been.

Chapter 15

~

The drone of the engines continued throughout the evening, and heat off the racetrack made Marti think about the day she had gone swimming in the cool river with Jesse. She was now more relaxed, more confident in his driving abilities. He was just finishing his feature race, and he'd be done with the business for the night. It was only the very close calls that made her tense up and grimace. And with Paul out of the race, after his car started making guttural noises, she felt even more relaxed. The first group of four cars raced around for the last lap, and Jesse roared beneath the checkered flag first. Their whole section, and a lot of other people, stood up and cheered.

Bugs swarmed around them, dive-bombing the bright lights above. The smells of french fries and onion rings permeated the air in waves.

"I'm going down to get a soda. Anyone want anything?" Marti asked, standing and stretching. Really she just wanted to stand up and walk around.

After getting everybody's orders, she carefully walked down the bleachers to the concession stand near the entrance. Before the girl loaded six cups into a carryout container, Marti wolfed down a greasy, forbidden hot dog. Then she balanced the drinks with four more hot dogs for the others. When she turned around, she nearly dropped everything. Paul was standing there. His face was ashen, and not a trace of his usual arrogance could be found.

"Can I talk to you a minute?"

"No, we shouldn't even be talking at all."

"Marti, I did not break into your house last week, nor

did I attack you the first time. I wish to hell I knew who did. And if Jesse wants to keep investigating it himself, that's fine. I hope he finds the guy, but it isn't me. How can I get you to believe that?"

"I can't talk to you," she said, hurrying away with her load. Helen wouldn't have talked to him in the same situation, and Marti wouldn't either. As she walked up the bleacher stairs, she realized that she was doing that more often lately: asking herself whether Helen would do this or that in the same situation. Her own mother's antics seemed like some movie now, so very far away. California, beaches, Jamie—it all seemed like a dream. She made a mental reminder to get some travel litera- ture on California, just to remind her of her destination.

When all the racing was done, they opened the gate to the pit area again. Marti walked down with the rest of Jesse's cheering section to congratulate him on winning. She had to admit that he didn't look all that thrilled and realized he had probably won many, many times. Marti reached up and kissed him on the cheek, a gesture that raised Kati's eyebrow. Well, Kati probably kissed Dean's cheek when his warty frog won.

After the ruckus was over and the cars were all loaded up, Marti and Jesse walked out to his truck. She shivered in the cool evening air, after getting too much sun during the day. Jesse walked behind her and rubbed her arms, giving her more goose bumps than warming her.

"I don't think I could handle watching you race all the time. It's too nerve-wracking."

He stopped, leaning down to look at her. "Are you thinking about staying?"

"No, no. Just talking theoretically. I don't know how those women do it, watching their men in dangerous situations all day every week." She tried hard to look neutral. "How would these guys feel if their wives raced? In the Lady Warriors, let's say?"

"I don't know about the rest of 'em, but I'd find the best damn car we could get and cheer you on louder than anyone else."

He's way too good for you, she told herself. But from

somewhere deep inside, a tiny voice asked, "But can you live without him?" The answer was too complicated to even ponder.

The following Saturday Jesse was at the garage doing a little work on his car. Only with Bumpus's protection and her promise to use the shotgun was she able to stay at the house alone. A small ad in the local newspaper had gleaned three new decorating jobs. She had given two of Helen's friends estimates, and one had called this morning telling her to get started. The idea was taking shape in her mind, a budget decorating service.

Over the "Phantom of the Opera" music that poured through the rooms, she heard Bumpus bark once, then the front door close. She stopped sewing, grabbed the shotgun she wasn't sure she had enough guts to use, and walked into the living room. Jesse's truck was parked outside, and the bedroom door had just closed. A few seconds later she heard the shower running and went back to her sewing machine. But her concentration was lost now.

She looked into the mirror opposite her, tilting her head. The brown hair did suit her better, she realized. This was who she was now, not Marti, not quite Hallie anymore. Somebody new and surprisingly strong. But always she questioned, how strong?

Whenever the Phantom hit a low note, the baby kicked. She put her hand where his foot had just been, wondering how big it was now. Would he look like Jesse, or more like Marti?

"What is going on around here?"

Jesse's voice jerked her out of her thoughts. His hair was wet, and he wore nothing but a dark blue towel firmly wrapped around his waist.

"What do you mean?"

"This . . . *music* blaring again! It's awful!"

"Well, now you know how I feel about your country music. And anyway, your son sure likes it. He's been kicking up a storm through the whole tape."

Jesse sat down on the bed beside her, moving the sewing cart aside. "He's probably protesting." He put his hand over her belly, and when the bass sounded again, the baby kicked. "He's going to make a great dancer, you know that?"

"You're thinking of the two-step, maybe?"

"Well, you can't dance to this stuff. Can you?"

Jesse got up and tried to fit country dancing to "Masquerade." The harder he tried, the sillier he looked. Giving up on that, he acted out the trill voices in a parody of the opera. Marti busted out laughing, making the baby kick more. All of a sudden, Jesse stopped and looked at her. They stayed that way for a long minute, Marti swallowing hard beneath his gaze. He held his hand out and she took it, wondering if he was going to ask her to dance. Instead, he turned her around to face the mirror. The glow from her laughter still showed on her face, and she smiled at his reflection.

"You are so beautiful."

Her heart tightened inside her, and her face flushed red. "Jesse, I'm not." *You're the beautiful one,* she wanted to say. With his intense green eyes staring at her in the mirror.

His voice was velvety smooth. "Yes, you are."

She looked at the mirror, at her reflection. She was amazed to see something she had probably never seen on her face before: contentment. The thought scared her, and she turned away. She couldn't stay here, content or no. Jesse didn't want a real wife, and Marti wasn't sure she could be one.

"Jesse . . ." she started again, but he leaned down and held her face in his strong hands, forcing her to look at him.

"Why are you so blasted sure you can't be happy here?"

She wasn't going to tell him what she wanted to hear, because then he'd know how much she'd fallen in love with him. He only wanted her to stay for practical reasons, not reasons of the heart.

She left him standing in the bedroom and walked as fast as she could to get away from him, from his words. She stood in the living room, fighting the tears and feelings that threatened to flood her. Her heart tightened inside, but she told herself it was because the baby was moving. The baby he wanted a mother for so badly. That was the only reason he wanted her to stay, she tried to convince herself.

But he can have a mother for his child, her inner voice reminded. *Debbie is more than willing. He wants you, fool. Can't you see that?*

"No!" she answered aloud, startling herself with the voracity of her words. He didn't want her. He'd never said that, never. She couldn't stay there.

Why not?

"Because I want to go back home, to California."

Home is here.

She put her hands over her ears, as if that would stifle the horrid inner voice that had taken Jesse's side. But it was his voice she heard, just behind her.

"Marti, what would be the worst thing that could happen if you stayed? Would you at least tell me that?"

"It's not an option," she said through tightened lips. "You promised me you wouldn't try to talk me into staying!"

"I'm not asking you to stay, just asking you a question. Answer me, and I won't bring it up again." He moved to encircle her in his arms. "Tell me you'd be miserable here, that you don't feel a thing for that baby inside you. Tell me that you honestly believe you'd be happier alone in California than here. Tell me, Marti," he asked softly, looking directly into her eyes to gauge for lies. "Tell me, and I'll believe you."

She dropped her head, because she couldn't meet his eyes. "I-I'd be happier in Califor—" The sobs tore through her, and she pushed him away.

He pulled her close again. "You can't even say it, can you?"

Holding her face again, he rubbed away her tears with his fingers. Then he leaned close to kiss her, and the passion he kept under control pushed through as he claimed her mouth with ferocity. The world spun around her as she was swept into a whirlpool of emotions. At the end, her barest self was left, only needing him and what he was offering her at that moment.

He kissed her endlessly, his fingers entwined in her hair. She held onto him, clutched his shoulders, afraid to let go lest she drown completely. His hands trailed beneath her shirt, over her belly to the softness of her breasts. He caressed gently, though she knew he had the power inside him to crush her. She wanted him to crush her. Beneath his towel, she could feel him pressing against her, hard and ready. Her hands moved down over his tight rear end covered in soft terry cloth. A tiny growl emanated from somewhere inside him as she squeezed and caressed. He smelled of soap and male and aftershave, deliciously Jesse.

"Marti," he whispered breathlessly. "If you don't stop me now, I'm going to want all of you. I'm not strong enough to stop this myself."

She could stop this, she thought. No, she couldn't. She wanted this more than anything, even if she regretted it later. Even if they both regretted it later. She found the knot where the towel fastened together and wrestled it free with her fingers. The towel slipped down to the floor, sliding past her legs. She wanted to touch him, feel his smooth skin beneath her fingertips, tracing around both sides of his waist to encircle what was pressed against her stomach.

The second she touched him, he groaned louder, closing his eyes. He swept her up into his arms where he carried her to the bedroom, and the crescendo of the music built with the anticipation. As he stripped off her clothes, he admired her body with his eyes, his hands. What she found bulging and unattractive, he found beautiful, miraculous. Beneath his gaze she was transformed into a swan.

If she had thought lovemaking would be awkward with her belly, it didn't occur to her then. She was too overtaken with him, with the feelings that rushed in like a foamy wave. Crashing over her, receding gently, crashing forward again. His kisses made her ears roar, and like a tidal wave, they swept her away beyond all thought and reason.

Her hands were everywhere on him, sliding down his back, over his smooth buttocks, then around to his flat stomach. She wanted all of him, wanted to touch and experience every inch of his body. He was hers, for that precious time, even his heart. She saw that in his eyes, eyes that seemed open to his soul.

Her breath came in shallow gasps, between kisses and sighs. His fingers were in her hair, tracing around her ears, her chin. He murmured her name softly, then captured her lips again. She felt the tip of him prodding, exploring. Then slowly, he moved inside her. Her breath hitched, and when he was fully in, she forgot how to breathe. He watched her expression as he became one with her, hesitated at her sharp intake of breath until she squeezed his shoulders, urging him on.

"Jesse, Jesse, Jesse . . ." she murmured as the wave built slowly to enormous heights, towering over her. "Jesse." She loved the sound of his name as it rolled off her tongue. It sounded so natural to say it, over and over again. His hands seemed everywhere on her, touching, caressing her skin as he moved inside her, fought his climax, and continued on to satisfy her.

The feelings inside her built, rising to envelop her in a rush of warm water. She allowed herself to drown in him, in the feelings that made every nerve ending come alive. Marti didn't have to fight off thoughts and inner voices; she thought nothing. Her senses needed nothing but to simply enjoy what was happening to her body. She felt so high, giddy, entranced. She towered above Heaven on the crest of the wave. And then the wave crashed down, filling her with such elation, she was sure her insides would explode. She gasped for air as Jesse shuddered, and he swooped down to capture her lips as vibrations encompassed her body. Finally, he collapsed beside her, taking her hand with him and pressing it to his chest.

They laid in silence for several minutes, breathing heavily, smiling softly. When he caught his breath, he reached out and caressed her cheek.

Marti moved her cheek into his palm, moist against her skin. She still tingled inside, from her toes all the way to her heart. Their gaze met and held for several long seconds, and she wondered if he could see the question in her eyes. His eyes only reflected dreamy satisfaction. She was on a roller coaster, wondering when the next drop would be.

"What happens now?" she finally forced herself to ask.

"What do you mean?"

The words slipped away from her like goldfish in a pond. "I . . . I don't know. This shouldn't have happened."

He rolled onto his side, facing her. "I know. I didn't plan on it happening. It just did."

She wasn't sure what she wanted him to say, but those words disappointed her. They were both going in the wrong direction—toward each other. Wrong, wrong, wrong, she told herself. He had his racing, she had California. Falling in love would only get in the way.

He rolled back over to face her again, his expression serious. "Don't get me wrong; I don't regret it happening."

Marti forced out the words, "I do." She steeled herself to face him, to convince him. "You should, too. That could have been you visiting Mike at the track, talking about having dinner with one of the NASCAR sponsors discussing future possibilities."

He shrugged, though his shoulders were tense. "What's your point?"

"My point is . . ." *that I don't want to be in love with you when you won't let yourself ever feel the same way about me.* "We're headed for trouble."

When she looked at him again, he had that faraway emerald look in his eyes. He rolled off the bed and slid into his jeans.

"You're right. I do regret it," he said without looking at her. He ruffled his fingers through his hair in an attempt to straighten it, then looked at her from the doorway. "Do you really think you have to remind me that I could have been the one on my way to NASCAR? If you think I'm going to lose my head and give that up because we had a good time in bed, you're way off track."

She was so angry, she wanted to throw something at

him. Lacking anything substantial, she shouted, "I wasn't the one who started this!" She wildly gestured to the rumpled sheets. "I'm not trying to sway you from your racing career. Go off and race! Get yourself killed if you want, I don't care! I'm just trying to keep your head on straight about it."

He smiled sarcastically. "Why, thank you, missy. But you didn't have to bother."

She could tell his pride was wounded, but so was hers! "You're the one who keeps asking me to stay. If you don't want any entanglements, why do you want me to stay?"

He looked thoughtful, and oh, too delicious in his bare chest and tight jeans. "I don't know, Marti. Right now, I just can't imagine why." And he walked out the door to leave her wondering the same thing.

Over the next three weeks Jesse was more indignant and irritable than he'd ever been. He concentrated on rule books for racing, *Car and Motor,* and anything else that took his whole concentration. He slept on the edge of the bed, and hardly grunted at her in the mornings.

Marti had never wanted a man so much, never lusted after a man with her body, soul, and heart as she did Jesse. She could not get their lovemaking out of her mind, though sometimes it was hard to imagine the grumpbag being so tender, so passionate, so very concerned with her pleasure. If he'd felt anything for her, and she wasn't sure that he had, then he had squelched it completely. She knew she'd deliberately pushed him away, a panic reaction to that feeling that she would never be able to live without him. It was for the best, she told herself. It just didn't feel that way at the moment.

That morning they lay in bed, both awake, but pretending to be asleep. The sound of the doorbell intruded. He was up and into his jeans before she could even get out of bed.

"I'll get it," he said, grabbing that ever-present shotgun.

Kati pushed her way in, motioning them to sit on the

couch. "I thought you should know this, both of you. Donna Hislope was raped."

"What?" Marti couldn't stop the frantic beating of her heart.

"When?" Jesse asked, his muscles tensing.

"They've kept it under wraps, but Dr. Hislope had to ask for my help because she's too upset to work. He tried to tell me it was something else, but he's not a good liar. Finally he broke down and told me. It happened last Friday night."

Marti's eyes widened. "Last Friday? After her date with . . ."

"You got it. She doesn't want to press charges, and she's terrified of anyone finding out."

"After her date with who?" Jesse asked.

Both women answered simultaneously. "Paul Paton."

"Jesse, calm down. Dr. Hislope said she doesn't know who it was. She didn't point Paul out as the rapist."

He jumped up and paced, glancing at his shotgun. "She was out on a damn date with the guy. Who else would have done it? I need to talk to her, find out what she knows."

Kati stood up. "You can't do that! You're not even supposed to know about it."

"I'll talk to her," Marti said calmly, remembering Helen's poise in such situations. "After all, I've been in the same situation, or so she thinks. I won't tell her who told me."

Kati threw her hands up in the air. "Great! She'll think everybody knows!"

"What if her dad asked me to talk to her? Because I would understand? We could clear it through him first."

Kati shook her head. "I don't know. Let me talk to him about it."

After Kati left, Marti walked to the window and wrapped her arms around herself, wishing they were Jesse's arms. She thought of the man who had tried to strangle her—twice. The man standing in her room was still on the loose, and no one would be safe until he was caught.

* * *

It was the following Wednesday before Kati could talk Dr. Hislope into letting Marti see his daughter. Jesse drove her over to Dr. Hislope's house. Marti mulled over what she wanted to say, to ask. The truck rumbled to a stop beneath a shade tree on the other side of the road.

"I'm going to wait for you here. Take all the time you need."

Jesse had taken the day off, insisting on going with her because Dr. Hislope's house was so near Paul's.

"Hello, Marti," Dr. Hislope said without much of a smile. "I sure hope this is a good idea. Maybe you can bring her out again. She hardly eats, doesn't talk to anyone, not even me. Don't be surprised if she doesn't talk to you either."

Despite the wooden floors and white walls, the house seemed dim. Outside birds sang and butterflies danced on the wind, and a breeze rustled through the flowers. Inside, the air was quiet and musty. She followed him down a hallway to the room at the end. He tapped on the door.

"Donna? Marti's here."

Marti stepped inside, with Dr. Hislope standing beside her. The room was set up for a teenager, with a lacy, canopy bed, frilly curtains, and a fancy, old-fashioned telephone. Donna sat in the windowseat, her knees pulled up to her chin. She kept staring ahead into nothingness. When Dr. Hislope started to say something again, Marti held her hand out to silence him.

"Why don't you leave us alone for a little while?"

He hesitated, then backed out and closed the door. Marti stood there for a few minutes, hoping for some kind of invitation to step closer. She thought then about leaving, but remembered Jesse waiting across the street, desperate for answers. Answers she could get from Donna. She spotted a wicker chair and pulled it to within a few feet of Donna's still form. Again she waited for some acknowledgment, but it didn't come.

"Donna? It's Marti. Do you want me to leave?"

No response. Donna kept looking out the window at

nothing in particular. Nothing because the curtains were drawn closed in front of her.

"I'm not going to ask you how you're doing, because I know you're feeling pretty awful right now. The reason I'm here is because I thought you might want someone to talk to, someone's who's been there. Almost."

Marti tried hard to imagine what she would have felt if she had been nearly raped. She could easily imagine the fear of being attacked, though. That fear was still fresh. Donna didn't have any bruises around her neck. She waited for some kind of reaction, but none came.

"Well, I just wanted to let you know I'm here if you need to talk."

Marti started to get up when Donna spoke in a deadpan voice.

"Everyone knows, don't they? They're all talking about it, saying how stupid I was."

Marti drifted back down into the chair. "Nobody knows. I haven't heard anything about it and remember, I work at Gossip Gourmet. And you're not stupid. You thought you were safe with Paul." She was fishing for a reaction, but none came. Marti waited. Finally, she asked the question she most wanted to know. "Donna, do you have a . . . scratch, right here?" Donna didn't look to see where she was pointing. "A weird scratch right . . ."

Donna reached up over her left breast, placing her palm over her T-shirt. She didn't say anything about it, but Marti knew it was there. Finding a small pad and pen, she drew the indents she remembered. She walked it over to Donna and stuck it in her face.

"Does it look like this?" she asked quietly.

Donna squeezed her eyes shut, and a tear slid down her broad cheek. Marti pulled the pad away and set it on the desk.

"I'm going to go now. Call me if you need anything. I'd like to come back again. Shake your head if you don't want that." No reaction. "Okay, I'll be back."

Marti visited Donna twice a week over the following two weeks, keeping her visits short, learning little with each one. Donna now seemed to expect her, and even acknowledged her existence. That was about it. Marti was always disappointed that Donna wouldn't share anything, or even point out Paul as her rapist. The cut, if it had truly existed, was now long healed.

Marti arrived later than usual that afternoon, after running some errands when she got off work. Marsala, the Hislopes' housekeeper, opened the door, an expectant look on her face.

"Oh, I thought you were Mister Doctor Hislope," the Spanish lady said, stepping aside to let her in.

"He isn't here?"

"No, a farmer on dee edge of town have sick horse, and he go to fix it. I must go now, to my mother's house. Can you stay until he return?"

"Sure, I'll stay."

"Gracias, señora."

"Hello, Donna," Marti greeted as she entered the bedroom. The curtains were open this time, but Donna was still where she always was, in the windowseat. She was hugging a pink teddy bear between her chest and her legs.

"I wish he had killed me." Her words seemed to drop with heavy thuds.

"No, you don't mean that. You'll be all right. I can't promise you that it'll go away, but you will take control of your life again."

Donna dropped her head on her knees and wept, deep, guttural sobs that made Marti wish Jesse were there. It went on like that for a long time, as if she had broken the dam and let the barred tears flow. Marti put her hands on Donna's shoulders, not feeling comfortable enough to hug her. Later she called Jesse to let him know she would be a little later than usual. She was tempted to take him up on his offer to meet her there, but she knew it would upset Donna if she knew.

"Call me if you need me," he said before hanging up.

She smiled, feeling that he at least cared about her still. "I will."

It was almost nine o'clock before Dr. Hislope arrived. Donna's renewed sobs reached them in the living room, and he rushed in to comfort her. Marti gathered her purse and let him know she was leaving.

"If you'll wait a few minutes, I'll walk you out," he offered, but Marti knew by Donna's heaving chest that it would be longer than that.

"Thanks, but I'll be all right. The moon's bright out, and I'm parked just outside the door."

The crunch of the mango leaves beneath her feet obliterated her thoughts as she walked toward the car. When she reached for her keys, a voice scared her into dropping them.

"Marti, don't be afraid. It's me, Paul."

She stiffened, ready to run back inside. But she'd locked the door before stepping outside. Would Dr. Hislope hear her screams over Donna's sobbing?

"What are you doing here?"

"How is she? Donna, I mean?"

"You're always so concerned about your victims, aren't you?" Her anger pushed adrenaline through her veins, making her less afraid.

"I didn't do that to her, to you, to anyone. But I've got to talk to you about something. This is going to sound crazy. Hell, I'm probably crazy for even thinking it."

Something in his voice made her listen. A confession, maybe? "What is it?"

"I noticed it the night someone broke into your house. I—" The sound of a truck approaching made Paul stop and look.

"It's Jesse," she said, not sure if she was relieved to see him or not.

"Damn."

"You'd better get out of here."

Paul turned into a silhouette in the darkness, then disappeared just before Jesse's headlights cut across the yard. She ran to his truck, feeling as though she was betraying him by not alerting him to Paul's presence. The old ways, coming back. No, this was different! Her sixth sense told her that she hadn't been in danger, but Jesse wouldn't believe that. He'd just kill Paul, and she had to admit, his waiting for her in the dark didn't look good.

"What are you doing out here alone? I was getting worried about you so I drove by."

"I was just walking out. Donna's crying up a storm, and I didn't want to wait for Dr. Hislope to calm her down so he could walk me out."

He hesitated for a moment, assessing the situation. "Next time wait for him. Let's go home."

Chapter 16

~

*H*e sat in the dusty, dark attic. Alone. Filling his lungs with stale air and the aroma of ghosts lingering nearby. Ghosts that haunted him, taunted him. He was a failure, a weak, rotten son of a bitch—good-for-nothing failure. He thrashed around in the darkness, shoving boxes onto the floor. A box filled with old china dropped with a muffled shatter. Spent, he dropped down to the floor and let himself cry for two seconds. Then he stopped and listened. Nothing.

Clutching at his head, he rolled it about, wishing he could make the buzzing and the words go away. *Failure! Weak!* It wasn't his fault! If only the blood of his heart would have married him. If only his love would have seen that he was the only man for her. None of this would have happened.

Marti had looked so helpless, so female. Like that day long ago when his love had broken down on the side of the road and he'd given her a ride to the service station so many years ago. She had smiled nervously, the same way Marti had after admitting she'd run out of gas. Somehow he'd felt he had another chance to win his heart's blood—and he wasn't going to let her get away that time, no matter how hard she resisted. And he'd nearly killed her in his rage. But if he convinced her that he loved her, she would forget about all that. This time he'd keep careful control over his fury. No matter how much she fought, no matter how fiercely she rejected him. He ran his fingers through his short hair, tearing at his scalp, scratching until he drew blood. Pain, yes, pain would temper the rage.

Hell knew Donna had not. She had been so scared,

she'd just lain there and let him do it. He pretended it was Marti, submissive, wanting him.

He shook his head violently. None of the past mattered now. Marti would be his soon. He had to find some way to make her understand how much he wanted her. Once Jesse was out of the way.

When Marti returned home from her shift at Bad Boys, she felt dull, huge, and achy. Squatting down, she picked up a piece of paper that was lying in the driveway and trudged inside. The thought of driving to the Port Charlotte race track didn't thrill her, but Jesse had insisted, in light of Donna's recent attack. He'd headed up to the track, along with Kati and Helen, a few hours ago. In fact, she'd promised him that she'd have Priscilla come home with her while she changed. Priscilla wasn't feeling well, so Marti let her off the hook.

Marti changed into pants and gathered up her oversize pillow for sitting comfort. Bumpus tilted his head at her as she made a groaning noise.

"Oh, I'll live, I suppose," she said to him. "Only a little while longer, and then I'm out of here." Bumpus made an internal whining noise. "Oh, stop it. Your master will be more than happy to see me go."

As she gathered her things and readied to leave, she remembered the piece of paper. It was sitting on the table, just a small square of white paper. Marti leaned over her pillow and read the scrawled pen. "Jesse, meet me behind the old Jenkins place before you go to the races. I want to settle this suspicion thing once and for all." It was signed from Paul. She looked around for signs that Jesse had seen the note, or left her a note, but there was nothing. Maybe Paul had left it on Jesse's car, and he hadn't seen it before pulling away. She fingered the note, wondering what to do. If he'd seen it, he would have gone over to the abandoned house north of Helen's place. And what if he had gotten into trouble?

After debating for a minute, she grabbed the note and headed out the door, feeling a great deal of trepidation about going to some abandoned place alone. Once she was heading over, her fears eased up a bit. Paul had wanted to talk to her about something, and she had a feeling it was important. Maybe he decided it was safer to talk to Jesse about it instead. That seemed logical.

It was bright and sunny, not at all foreboding as she drove down the dirt road and pulled into the gravel driveway overgrown with weeds. Jesse had pointed the place out to her once, telling her a story about how he and Billy had spent the night there on a dare when they were kids. She shivered at the thought of walking in the run-down wood house.

Paul's slick black truck was parked over to the side, but Jesse's truck was nowhere to be found. So maybe he was racing. If the two had met here earlier, why was Paul still here?

She knew she should turn around and leave then, but her hand put the car in park and turned off the engine. What if something had happened? What if Jesse had gone crazy and Paul was lying here hurt? She opened the car door, telling herself it was for Jesse as she stepped out. She couldn't bear to see Jesse go to jail again.

A breeze made the leaves rustle and brushed through the tall grasses all around. A blue shutter, hanging from a corner on the house, scratched against the cracked wood.

"Paul?" she called out, though the wind took her words in the opposite direction.

Although the yard was a miniature forest, Marti spotted a well-worn pathway leading around back. Obviously kids still hung out here, probably still dared each other to sleep there. As she walked around Paul's truck toward the path, she noticed the quickened pace of her heartbeat. Jesse would be furious if he knew. But she remembered that night when Paul had wanted to talk to her. She hadn't felt threatened then. Her shoes crunched softly on the rocky gravel beneath her feet.

Her eyes scanned the area as she walked, her ears tuned to pick up anything beyond what the wind caressed. Everything looked serene. Until she saw the knife lying there in the path. It was a pocketknife, and the blade reflected the sunlight filtering through the trees. She knelt to examine it, and her heart stopped when she saw "J J W" etched on the ivory handle. Instinctually she picked it up to look for signs of blood, then dropped it when she saw faint smears. Dear God, what had Jesse done? Or had Paul done something? No, it couldn't be blood.

Again she searched the area behind the house, walking farther back without thinking. She ignored the thoughts that Jesse might be hurt, but her steps grew more quick and her glances more frantic. When she saw him lying there by a tree, she fought the black spots that threatened to take her to unconsciousness. Her hand went to her mouth as she trodded through the high grass and choke vines to the body sprawled out in the shadows. Paul.

"Oh God, no."

She stared at him for a full minute, making sure her mind wasn't conjuring him up because she'd expected the worse. His neck was twisted strangely. And her mind wouldn't have imagined the blood that surrounded a hole in his shirt. Still, there wasn't a lot of blood. She pushed herself forward to grasp his wrist, but she didn't have to even check for a pulse. His hand was cold and stiff and she dropped it.

"Oh, my God."

Marti heard her own shock voiced aloud behind her, and spun to find Lyle Thomas standing on the pathway. Relief soured through her as she stood and made her shaky way toward him. His gaze had been locked on the body, but it quickly shifted to her, his hand going to the butt of the gun on his hip.

"Marti, stay where you are. Don't make me have to use this."

She came to a slow stop, bewilderment dazing her thoughts. "What are you talking about?"

"You're under arrest for"—he glanced at the body, so obviously dead—"the murder of Paul Paton."

Numbness set in once she reached the sheriff's office as she was escorted to the back rooms where Jesse had spent a morning not long ago. That ever-present smell of cleaner permeated the air, and the bright, florescent lights made everything seem sterile. Lyle took her fingerprints and photo. He didn't say anything until he locked the jail door behind her.

"Think about who you want your one call to be to. I've got to process this paperwork, and then I'll be back." Before turning away, he paused, looking more like a hound dog than a deputy. "Marti, I hope this is all one big mistake. But I can't deny what I saw."

What he saw. She'd picked up the knife, dropped it, then walked over to Paul's body. She'd touched the knife, put her fingerprints on it! Her thoughts had been on Jesse, not incriminating herself.

"Lyle, it is all one big mistake!"

"Remember, you don't have to say anything until you get an attorney."

"I don't care about an attorney! I didn't kill Paul. You've got to believe me." It all seemed so unreal to her, standing behind bars, pleading her innocence.

"I want to, Marti." He looked thoughtful. "Do you think Jesse saw that note?"

"No. He wouldn't have left it behind if he had."

She wouldn't believe that Jesse had killed Paul. It was as unlikely as her killing him. Lyle nodded, then walked away.

"Lyle?"

He turned around.

"What were you doing out there, anyway?"

"Carl saw Paul writing the note to Jesse. Since he was going to be gone today, he'd asked me to kind of keep an eye on the place, check to see if Jesse's truck was there. He didn't want any trouble."

"Does he know? About Paul, I mean."

"We've called him in, but he doesn't know why."

Chattaloo didn't have much of a crime rate, and she was the only one in the twenty jail cells that night. Company didn't have much appeal anyway, except for Jesse. He would come get her out of this, she knew. Win the race, rescue her from jail. Until then, all she could see was the horrid image of Paul. It made her stomach turn like worms in dirt.

Marti knew she hadn't drifted off, but a large amount of time had passed since she'd been arrested. Struggling to her feet, she paced back and forth for a few minutes, then called for Lyle. The door leading to the outer room was open. It wasn't Lyle who came, but Carl. His face was blank, eerily free of emotion.

"Where's Lyle?"

"He's gone. His shift is over."

She backed away from the steel bars as Carl neared, but kept her shoulders squared.

"I didn't kill your son. And neither did Jesse."

He leaned even nearer. "I think you were both in on it. But I think it was Jesse who did it."

"He couldn't have done it. He left for the races at five this morning. That's probably why he didn't see the note Paul had left for him. The guy who let him in at the track can verify his arrival time." Marti only hoped all these things. A wave of irritation swept over Carl's features. "I want my phone call."

Carl's smile was flat, but his green eyes sparkled with evil. "Doesn't matter. Nobody's home."

"What are you talking about?"

"Jesse got into an accident at the racetrack."

"I don't believe you," she said, although the blood rushed to her face.

Carl shrugged. "I guess I don't care what you believe."

He pulled out his revolver and unlocked the door, nodding for her to walk ahead. She stepped out and followed his nod toward the phone on Lyle's desk.

"I don't know the racetrack's phone number."

"Shucks, neither do I, honey."

"Can I call information and get it?" She started dialing.

"You can, but that's your one call."

She determined quickly that he wasn't kidding. He still held his revolver at his side, finger at the ready. She dialed home and left a message on the answering machine and was escorted back to her cage without another word. She didn't give him the satisfaction of knowing she was worried about what he'd said. Jesse was a good driver. He wouldn't crash.

At nearly midnight Marti was roused from a light slumber by Carl.

"Helen is here."

"To bail me out?" she asked hopefully, ignoring the question of Jesse's absence.

"No, to see you. Your bond hearing is tomorrow. The bail hearing won't be until next week. *If* you get bail. Until then, you're mine."

Her skin crawled at his words, at the strange glimmer in his eyes. She followed him to safety and warmth, to Helen. Carl escorted her to a series of phone-booth-size cubby holes with a telephone on each side. Helen was standing hesitantly on the other side of the slate of thick glass. But where was Jesse? Helen's pale face told Marti more than she wanted to know. Marti slid onto the vinyl chair between the partitions and picked up the phone.

"Are you all right?" Helen asked, fidgeting with a white handkerchief.

"I'm fine. Is Jesse all right?"

"Yes, he's going to be fine. It wasn't as bad as it looked."

All the hope and energy drained from Marti, leaving her shoulders to sag. "Then it's true? He was in an accident."

"Yes. But don't worry about him, Marti. You have enough right here to think about."

But she wasn't thinking about herself. "What happened? Where is he?"

"All I could understand was that he lost his brakes. He went off the track, hit the wall, and flipped the car. The doctor says he probably broke a rib or two and suffered a mild concussion. They're checking him for internal injuries, and he'll probably be in for another day or two." Helen shook her head. "Then I come home to find a message on my answering machine from Lyle. What in God's name happened?"

Marti paced, aching to be at Jesse's side. Her own plight seemed insignificant at the moment. She relayed the gruesome events of that afternoon, ending with, "I know I shouldn't have gone there alone, but I was afraid for Jesse. I didn't kill him, Helen." Panic pitched her words in a higher tone.

"I know you didn't. Stay calm. Tomorrow is your bond hearing, and my boss is going to represent you. Bill Everhart plays bridge with the judge and his wife, so he pulled some aces out of his sleeve and got your bail hearing moved up. We'll get you a reasonable bail and get you out of here."

"Don't tell Jesse. He'll just worry."

Helen looked away, then back. "He's pretty out of it right now, but tomorrow he's going to want to know where you are. Don't you think he'll worry when you're not there?"

Marti nodded, realizing her request was unrealistic. "When will my bail hearing be?"

"Tuesday morning. Bill will be in to talk to you about what to expect. I've got to go. It's not really visiting hours, but I made Carl let me in for a few minutes. Are you going to be okay?"

Marti shook her head, then nodded. "Just get me out of here. And give Jesse . . . my love." The words came out, and Marti swallowed hard.

Helen smiled knowingly. "I will."

Once Helen was gone, Carl pushed Marti back along the corridor toward her cell. He didn't say a word to her, as if he had some sinister plan to carry out after hours. The glint in his eyes was the only thing to indicate he was alive in there mentally.

"Carl, please let me out of here, just for a few hours. Jesse's in the hospital."

"I know."

"Please let me see him. He needs me!"

"You murdered my son and you want me to let you out so you can see your husband?"

"I didn't kill Paul, and you know it!"

He pushed her in and slammed the door shut. "We'll see about that."

He left her alone to kick at the walls and hate him for keeping her when Jesse needed her.

* * *

The bail hearing was held Tuesday afternoon. It was the first time she saw Jesse since his accident, and his pallor told her at what expense he was sitting there waiting through traffic violations. She saw him try to hide the grimace whenever he shifted.

Even with Bill Everhart standing before the judge with pressed suit and perfect hair, it didn't look good. Carl was pushing for denial of bail altogether, repeating "risk of flight" over and over. Somehow he'd gotten hold of the information that she was leaving after the baby was born.

Judge Oldburn studied her, as if weighing her integrity. He set the bail at $150,000, and Marti felt the thud as her heart dropped to the wooden floor. So much for bridge-playing loyalties. Helen maintained her determined stance: shoulders straight, mouth in a firm line. Marti wanted to cry but drew strength from her. Jesse seemed to draw strength from her too, as he started to his feet to protest. Her softly spoken words made him slowly sit down again. Kati whispered frantically, but those same words made her calm, too.

Deputy Lyle Thomas escorted Marti back to the jailhouse. Jesse was already waiting to see her when they pulled up. He glanced at her cuffs, but his eyes carefully cloaked any emotion that threatened to show.

Twenty minutes later Lyle escorted her to the visitors room. "You have fifteen minutes." At her distressed expression, he added, "Sorry, Marti. Gotta follow the rules."

Once alone, she rushed to the confining booth and leaned toward the glass.

"Jesse, I'm so sorry I couldn't be at the hospital. Are you all right? What happened?"

He looked tired, dreamy almost. "Marti, how are you doing in here? God, it's good to see you."

They spoke simultaneously, stopped to let the other talk, then smiled.

Her lower lip trembled, wishing to comfort him, and wanting his strength. The last weeks of cold politeness slipped away. "I just wish you could hold me," she murmured into the phone, holding back tears.

His gaze shifted away before meeting hers again. "Marti, I know the bail sounds like a lot, but we're going to get it. We only need to come up with ten percent; we'll let a bail bondsman come up with the rest. Ma has money, I'll try to push through the loan for the baby's expenses."

"No, I don't want you to do that. You won't be able to pay the hospital."

"Don't you think we're going to clear you and get our money back?"

"I don't know. It looks bad, and I've seen small town trials on television." She took a deep breath. "I'm so out of everything in here. Have they talked to you about being at the track? It sounded like they were going to try to drag you into this."

"Lyle talked to me and to Bud, the guy at the track. They don't have anything on me, though I know Carl wants my blood bad." His expression changed to something she couldn't identify. "Did you think I'd killed Paul?"

"No. When I got to Jenkins's place, I wasn't sure what I'd find. Then I saw the knife with your initials on it, and I got scared."

"That's a weird one, too. How'd whoever did this get that knife? My dad gave that to me years back, and I keep it in my truck. It's almost as if—"

"Someone was trying to frame you," Marti finished, relieved that Jesse wasn't a killer, not even aware that she'd wondered. "The note, your knife, and your past with Paul. And then I found the note instead of you. . . ."

"Marti, I don't think I need to tell you how stupid that was, going there by yourself, especially when it was only Paul's truck there, so I won't tell you."

"Gee, thanks, Jesse. It was stupid, I know. But you didn't see him that night . . ." She trailed off, but Jesse's interest was too high for her to slide over that one.

"What night?"

She quickly found a lie to cover her mistake. "At the racetrack. I went down to get drinks, and he was there. He said he had to talk to me, that he hadn't attacked me. Have you noticed how different he'd been since the night someone broke into my room?"

"Probably scared thinking what might have happened if I'd gotten hold of him."

"No. Oh, I don't know. I keep thinking, now that Paul's dead, I'll be safe." She glanced around. "Well, once I'm out of here. But something just doesn't feel right about it."

"You'll feel better once this is all resolved. And it will be."

"Sometimes I think that, but sometimes I think about actually getting convicted. What if I'm in jail when the baby comes? What if Carl is here, and he doesn't take me to the hospital? I could spend the rest of my life in some penitentiary!" Her voice was rising, gaining traces of hysteria.

"Calm down, doll. We'll get you out of this, believe me."

The word *doll* instantly filled her with longing. And hope. He hadn't used it for a long time. "Okay, I don't want to talk about this anymore. Tell me what happened at the race."

"It wasn't much, really. We were toward the end of a long race and my brakes wore out. When I realized it, I was right behind Alan and Josh. Now, I wouldn't have minded hitting Josh so much, but he was right up on somebody else's butt, and that would have hurt three of us. Hitting Alan was out of the question too, so my only other choice was to jerk it to the right and go into the wall. I hit it harder than I thought I would. The car flew up against the wall, tipped up on the front end and real slowlike, dropped back on the other side."

She ran her fingers through her hair, the dangerous picture filling her mind. "But you're all right? Please tell me you are. It sounds like you shouldn't even be here."

"I gotta be here. Just like the crash, no choice. But I'm okay. Really," he added to her disbelieving expression. "I broke some ribs, bruised my heel, a little bump on the head, that's all."

"That's all? Broke *some* ribs? How many?"

"Three," he said with a shrug, trying to be cavalier about it. But his grimace at the action betrayed him. "Okay, it does hurt. But it ain't fatal."

She dropped her forehead against the glass, feeling overwhelmed.

"Hey," he said softly, tapping on the glass. "Stuff like this doesn't happen all that often. But it's part of the game."

He placed his hand on the glass, and she pressed her hand against his, aching to feel more than the cold glass. His expression was intense, his gaze seemed to swallow her up. Their exchange didn't end when Lyle noisily opened the door behind her. After a few seconds, he cleared his throat. Jesse slowly leaned back into his chair again.

"Sorry, you two, but time's up."

Using the table's edge, Marti pushed herself up. Jesse used the table for leverage, too. They remained there for a few seconds, communicating in a language all their own through their eyes. She wanted to cry. Then Jesse motioned for Lyle to pick up the phone. Lyle looked around nervously before doing so.

"When are you going to clear my wife, Lyle?"

"Well, first we got to get a report from the medical examiner from Fort Myers to get official cause of death. He's on vacation, but we're trying to get hold of him. I'm sure it'll happen pretty fast after that."

Fast, Marti thought with a frown. Nothing happened fast in a small Southern town.

Throughout the week, Marti got plenty of visitors. Each visitor brought a report on how much bail Helen and Jesse had collected so far, and even Marti's friends in town were donating. The list was growing every day, and she was touched when she saw names of Bad Boy patrons who didn't even know her that well. By Friday they were still five thousand nine hundred dollars short.

"I want you out of here by this weekend," Jesse said on the phone.

She leaned against the partition. "You're almost there. Maybe by Monday or Tuesday."

"No," he said harshly. "By this weekend. There's one way to raise the whole amount by Sunday afternoon."

He looked at her, and she instantly knew she wasn't going to like it. "A race?" she asked cautiously.

"Yep. It's up in Georgia. The qualifying starts Saturday, and the race is Sunday. First place is eight thousand dollars."

"No, Jesse. You can't do it."

"I've got a ride."

"No, that's not what I mean! Look at you, you're still all banged up from the last race! What does your doctor say about this?"

"She says it's fine," he said through tight lips.

"You're lying, Jesse James West! I'll bet you haven't even asked, have you?"

"You're right, I haven't. She's my doctor, not my mother."

Marti stood up and paced a little. "What *does* your mother say about it?"

"She knows I'm going to do what I have to."

Marti leaned down over the table, her emotions warring. He was risking his health for her. She wanted him to get her out, but not that way.

"What do you mean you have a ride?" she asked, realizing he'd said that earlier.

"A friend of Harry's needs a driver. Chigger's an independent in the ASA; the minor leagues, remember? He registered for a race in Georgia, but he's in the hospital. With pneumonia," he added at Marti's expression. "He's seen me race a few times, so Harry asked if I could race for him. I think I could win you the hell out of here. The deal is, I take what I need from the prize money, and he gets the rest."

"Does he know you just wrecked?"

"Yes, he knows. Harry and I are pulling the car to Georgia tonight."

She released a breath she didn't realize she was holding. "So it's a done deal, then?"

"Yes. You gonna give me hell about it?"

She sighed, leaning against the partition. "No. I learned a while back that it does no good." For either of them.

"Time's up."

Carl's presence behind Marti startled her. He didn't intrude noisily like Lyle did. Marti turned around to face him.

"How long have you been standing there?"

"As long as I want. This is my jail, isn't it? I am the sheriff, am I not?"

"That's what they say."

Carl narrowed his eyes at her, then turned and led her away. She had a funny feeling about this race, though she couldn't pinpoint why.

"I won't wish you good luck!" she shouted, her voice echoing in the empty rooms.

"Thanks." she could see his lips mouth the words. "I won't need it!"

I love you! she wanted to shout, but caught herself short. Surely she couldn't mean that. She was just worried. Yeah, that was it. Loving Jesse was futile anyway; he wouldn't let himself love any woman, especially not her. He'd made that more than clear.

Things were not working out as he'd planned. He didn't want to do it, but it was coming down to the ultimatum of his life: Jesse's life or his freedom. The setup sure didn't work the way he'd planned. Since he couldn't get Jesse out of the way by getting him put in jail for Paul's murder, he'd have to resort to another more permanent way. He didn't want to hurt Jesse. He dropped his head down on the table. No, he had to do it. Just like he'd had to kill Paul.

Once Jesse was gone, Marti would be putty in his hands as he comforted her. It was too bad she was so in love with him. That would make it harder, of course. But he could overcome that, just like he'd overcome everything else.

The question now was how to get rid of Jesse. He was stronger and smarter than Paul. He would definitely be harder to take down physically. Too bad the accident last Saturday wasn't more . . . fatal. Yes, fatal. It happened all the time, race car drivers losing control of their brakes, steering, whatever was convenient. Going around and around at over one hundred twenty miles per hour, and what if the steering cable snapped? And Jesse couldn't make the turn? He'd smash into the wall but good.

He took a deep breath, holding it in, letting it out as if it were cigarette smoke. Anything could happen if the steering went out. It would be easy enough to find Chigger's car at the racetrack. He'd go up tomorrow morning, wait until Jesse was through qualifying and tinkering with it Saturday night. Then he would tinker with it a little himself. Just enough to last through some of the race on Sunday morning. And wouldn't Jesse be pleased to die like his old man? By the same hand as his old man? Last time it didn't get him what he wanted. This time it would.

Chapter 17

~

Lyle Thomas stopped in at the Someplace Else Cafe for a quick dinner before returning to the station. When Carl had asked him to cover the weekend shift so he could spend some time alone, Lyle almost breathed a sigh of relief that the sheriff was acting like a normal, grieving man. He'd been almost unemotional at his own son's murder. No man should be that unmoved by such a tragedy.

"Hey, Nolen," Lyle mumbled to Nolen Rivers as he headed to his favorite booth in the far corner. He settled in and scanned the nightly specials. The place was pretty busy for a Saturday night. Sunday was usually the big night in Chattaloo, when all the families went out for supper after the evening church services.

"Any leads on Paul's murder?" Nolen asked from the counter. "Newspapers ain't partin' with a word."

Lyle gave Nolen an official smile, tinged with smugness. "And neither am I."

Elwood Skoogs walked in and glanced at the busy counter, noting with an expression of chagrin that all the stools were taken. His short, squat frame and large belly made his arms look too small. They barely reached his thick waist. Lyle gave a thought to inviting him to join him, but having dinner with the Lee County medical examiner didn't bode well with his appetite. Elwood had the annoying habit of sharing his day's work over a meal.

"Hi there, Lyle. Mind if I join you?"

Well, the decision was made for him. If Lyle had second thoughts, he didn't show it. Or at least he didn't think he did. His mother didn't raise a barn bunny, after all. He waved for Elwood to take the seat across from him.

"Busy tonight, ain't it?" Elwood said absently, perusing the menu.

"What brings you 'round this end of town, Elwood?"

"Wife has her women friends over playing some fancy card game tonight, so I'm in no hurry to get home. She was pretty mad at having to cut our vacation short. So I visited a friend out this way until his wife gave me the old heave-ho. And I remember this place having good food and the prettiest waitress in town," he said as Rachel sauntered over to take his order.

"Why, thank you," she said, pink tinting her cheeks. She wrote their order on her pad as if she were signing an autograph, in big, loopy handwriting. Lyle thought she could easily be a movie star with those big blue eyes and loopy blond hair that matched that writing of hers.

"Thank ya, boys," she said with a wink and departed with a swingy little step, moving in tune to the Alan Jackson song on the jukebox.

Elwood leaned back and lit up a cigarette without asking if Lyle minded. He did. Apparently Elwood *was* raised a barn bunny. Lyle only asked him to refrain from smoking when the food arrived, but Elwood didn't get the hint and lit up as soon as he'd wolfed down his burger and fries.

"Sounds like you people have quite a case this way, what with the sheriff's own son gettin' killed."

Lyle glanced around for nosy eavesdroppers, then whispered, "Well, not to be pushy, Elwood, but we're pretty anxious to get that autopsy report from you, I'll tell you that."

Elwood straightened up a notch. "I delivered that report yesterday, right to your office."

Lyle leaned forward into the cloud of smoke. "What do you mean? I didn't hear about no report."

Elwood's bushy brows furrowed together. "You didn't? That's mighty strange. No one was up front, so I left it at the front desk, but I called Carl later to let him know. He said he'd take a look at it right away."

"What did it say? I never saw it."

"Pretty strange, if you ask me. Paul had been dead for a few hours before Marti found him. We figured it was seven that morning. It wasn't the knife that killed him, though. His heart wasn't pumping anymore when that knife was plunged into him. Broken neck was what did him in, poor kid. Then the sick bastard that did it stabbed him once he was already dead. Now, why do you think someone would go and do that?"

Lyle couldn't figure it out. Why hadn't Carl released her? Maybe he had some other evidence to tie Marti in with the murder. "Don't want to start rumors, but maybe there's more to Marti's involvement than that."

"Not with Marti. I saw her at breakfast that morning, up at Bad Boys Diner. She was working the breakfast shift. And as I recall, she was in a pretty good mood, too. Not like someone who'd just killed a person. Paul was killed during her shift."

Lyle stood up and dumped some wadded up ones on the table. "I gotta let her out of jail. If she should be free, she could sue us for keeping her longer. If I can't find that report, will you be able to get me another copy?"

"Sure. Look around, I'll stop by before heading home."

Lyle rushed back to the station and searched both his and Carl's desk, but turned up nothing. Why would Carl keep it from him? Maybe he hadn't read it yet. Yeah, that had to be it. After all, the man had just lost his son. His mind couldn't be completely on his job.

Lyle was still searching when Elwood walked. "Did you find it?"

"No. I'm afraid I'm going to need a copy."

"No problem. Wife's playing cards tonight. Got nothing but time on my hands."

They drove over to the medical examiner's office the next town over. While Elwood went into the file cabinet, Lyle wandered around out front, looking at the secretary's family picture collection. Couple of fat kids, fat husband, fat dog. Skinny secretary. Hm, figure that. Then he saw the scrawled note on top of her in-basket. "Send Sheriff Paton another copy of coroner's report on

Paul (son). He lost it. (What a dip.)" Lyle breathed a sigh of relief when he realized that Carl had just misplaced it and probably hadn't even read it yet. Well, he'd be proud that Lyle put everything right. It was nearly ten o'clock by then, but at least Marti would spend the night in her own bed tonight.

Elwood was right about the time of death, and he was also one of her alibis. If she was working, she would have plenty of them. A phone call to the cook and Priscilla verified that Marti hadn't left anytime during her shift.

Marti was sitting on the bottom bunk reading a magazine he'd given her earlier. She looked up at him blandly.

"Well, little lady, it looks like you're off the hook. We've got some papers to process, and then you're outta here."

Her expression was a mixture of joy and disbelief. "You found the real killer?"

"No, but we've got proof you didn't do it. I just got hold of the medical examiner's report, and Paul had been dead for hours before you found him."

"Thank God! I knew he had been dead for a while!" She shivered. "He was cold and stiff." Then her expression changed to panic. "Lyle! I've got to get out of here and stop Jesse from racing!"

Lyle quickly processed her paperwork, feeling a bit guilty for Carl's mistake in losing the report in the first place. Now she seemed frantic to get out and keep Jesse from doing further damage to his person. Lyle knew too well how painful broken ribs were.

"Why don't you use the phone here?" he offered.

"Thanks." Marti called information for the racetrack, then called the number. She didn't say anything, just wrote something down. Frustration settled on her pretty features and she hung up. "Darn! It's just a recording! Maybe I can catch him at his room. Can I?"

She pointed to the phone, and he nodded. No answer there. He wished he could help her, but he couldn't leave the station. He'd tried the sheriff's house earlier, but there'd been no answer. She grabbed her bag of possessions and headed to the door.

"I've got to go to Georgia tonight. If Jesse should call here for me, will you please tell him I'm out and not to race. Thanks!"

With that she was out the door, and Lyle realized he could help, even if in a small way. Marti was on her way back in.

"My car isn't here," she said.

He held up the set of keys for his police car. "I'll get you to your car in a big hurry."

He found a spot on the bleachers amid what looked to be a noisy crowd of racing enthusiasts who got there early like he did to get a good seat. Everything had gone well, just as planned. And Jesse was pole position, primed for a quick start. Damn, the kid was good. It was too bad, but it had to be done, he reminded himself. Too late now, anyway. Too late, too bad.

It should happen sometime after the tenth lap, maybe the twelfth. Hopefully he hadn't gotten a little overzealous and cut too much. Then he could get back and console the widow, who would still be in jail. He had once loved somebody else, many years ago. Marti would be her for him now.

"Jesse, are you sure you wanna do this?" Harry asked. "You looked like hell yesterday after qualifying."

Jesse leaned against the hood of the car, willing the blood to his face so Harry would shut up. "I got the pole position, didn't I?"

"I didn't say you raced like hell, I said you looked like hell. And you don't look so great now. How do you expect to get by with a lousy grapefruit for breakfast?"

"I had toast, too. I always eat light on race days, you know that."

"It's different this time. Did you take your pain medication?"

"Of course not. I'll get by, Harry. It's just painful right now. It'll pass."

"Pass my ass! You were like this all day yesterday. I

should have the infirmary black flag you." At Jesse's indignant expression, Harry raised his arms. "Okay, you wanna kill yourself, be my guest. I just got a bad feeling that your judgment isn't going to be so great out there today. I see the expression every time you climb in this car. But go right ahead and do your thing. I know you're gonna anyway."

"Harry, can't you see I don't have any choice. I've got to get Marti out of there, and this is the rest of the bail. I'll be okay."

Harry leaned against the car and slid his hands in his pockets. "You gonna walk the track?"

"Not today. I've been here before."

"You always walk the track, Jesse. No matter how many times you been at a place, you always walk it."

"Harry, are you going to fight me all morning on this? 'Cause if you are, I'd rather you just go hassle one of the other drivers."

Harry's expression became stern, almost fatherly. "I don't want to see you kill yourself out there. And I ain't leaving, either. One of us has got to have sense, and it ain't you. Just remember, you don't have to do this. We can try to raise that money another way. And I talked to Chigger yesterday, gave him an update. He says you won't be letting him down if you don't race. I'm just telling you what he told me."

Jesse turned away from Harry and stared hard at the red and yellow Thunderbird, wishing the pain would go away. Crawling in was the worst part. Once he was in, then he was okay, after that moment where the pain was so bad he thought he was going to faint. Once his vision cleared again.

The excitement stirred through the crowd of drivers and mechanics as they readied their cars for the race. It was almost time.

Marti fought exhaustion throughout the night, stopping only twice to buy a superduper coffee and get gas. She should have asked Dean to drive up with her. Billy, Kati, and Helen were already up there. Now that the sun was coming up, she felt more awake. A glance at the rearview mirror showed bugged-out eyes and disheveled hair. No time to straighten up this time.

She got off at the exit for the racetrack, then prayed she was going in the right direction. A stream of cars was backed up for half a mile, and she knew she was headed the right way. She also knew she was running out of time. Once he was on the track, there would be no way to stop him. Short of walking out on the racetrack and waving her arms. That wasn't out of the question.

When she neared the entrance, she realized how far away from the track the cars had to park. Too far for a pregnant woman to run. She raised an eyebrow as the light bulb popped over her head. Sure, she could pass for nine months. She felt big enough! Whipping the car to the shoulder, she sent rocks and dirt spinning as she raced alongside the waiting cars. They yelled and shook fists and fingers at her, but she was readying her speech for the attendants who were patiently waiting to turn her back.

A man wearing a bright orange vest leaned down as she rolled the window down. "Ma'am, I'm afraid—"

"I've got to get to one of the racers! He's my husband, and I'm in labor. My contractions are fifteen minutes apart. Is there a way I can quickly get to the racers' area?"

His expression changed dramatically as he peered in at her belly, puffed out even more for the lie. "Sure, ma'am! See that road there. It'll take you 'round to the pits. The guys at the fence will let you in. I'll radio ahead."

"Thanks!" she yelled breathlessly as he moved the gate aside more so she could squeeze her car through.

She felt like a race car driver herself, beeping at people starting to cross the roadway, tearing around the corner. A garbled voice on a loudspeaker made her heart beat faster, made her foot press harder on the gas pedal. Almost there.

She pulled the car into a space and quickly made her way to the gate. Gasping and in a panic, the guy at the pits entrance didn't dare doubt she was a woman in labor. Her pelvic bone ached with the pressure of the baby, and running wasn't helping.

"I'm looking for Jesse West. He's one of the racers. Can somebody tell me where he is?"

The skinny man shrugged, looking at her belly. "What's the matter, honey? You in labor?"

"Yes!" she shouted, drawing attention from nearby crew members. "I've got to find my husband!"

"Never heard of him. What car is he driving?"

"Uh, Skeeter's car. No, that's not it. Trigger's. Chigger's! He's racing Chigger's car!"

"It's the red and yellow T-bird moving into position now. You'd better hurry, young lady. We're about to start."

"No!"

She ran past dozens of people, around empty trailers and revving race cars. Number 72 pulled into the inside lane on the track and stopped; other cars followed suit. The drivers had their helmets on.

"Harry!" she yelled at the familiar face. "Is Jesse in the car already?"

"Marti, what the he— wait a minute. You're supposed to be in—"

"I know! I've got to stop him."

"He's in there, all right."

Before Harry could comment any more, she ran, one more time. Two men started to caution her about going onto the track, but she paid no heed. Jesse was right there, across the track and the grassy area.

She wasn't able to yell to him until she was nearly within touching distance of his car; she hardly had enough breath to compete with the roaring engines. He looked in her direction as she reached him, and immediately pulled his helmet off and crawled out of the car.

"Marti, what in—"

She threw herself into his arms, leaning all her weight against him in exhaustion. His eyes widened, and he gave her a hug before pulling back in pain.

"What are you doing here? Are you all right?"

"I . . . out . . . report . . . Jesse, don't race! Don't have to."

She leaned over, gasping for air. Harry ran over to them, motioning for them to move off the track.

"I told the officials you weren't racing today. Dan, one of the crew, is going to remove the car from the lineup."

Jesse was too busy holding her to object, and Marti didn't want him to leave for even a few minutes. He wasn't racing. Thank God he wasn't racing.

They walked back to the pits, and a few seconds later, number 72 roared into the pit crew area, turning sharply as it weaved through small groups of people. As Dan pulled up to them and started to turn toward the trailer, the car didn't turn. It was coming right at them!

"Marti!" He pulled her out of the way as the car slowly kept coming at them while Dan frantically turned the wheel to the right. He slammed on the brakes and turned the engine off.

"I don't understand it!" Dan said, climbing out and kicking at the tire. "The steering went out on it. We just went over everything yesterday, and now the damn thing won't turn! I wasn't trying to run you over, honest."

"I know, Dan," Jesse assured him. "I could see you pulling on the wheel. What do you think is wrong with it?"

He shrugged, staring at the car as if it would tell him. "It's the darndest thing." Then his eyes widened. "Jesse, the steering would have gone out during the race. You could've been really—"

"Shh," Jesse said, covering Marti's ears and steering her away from Dan.

"And you think Paul wanted to tell you something? He wasn't just trying to finish the job?"

Jesse leaned back against the swinging bench, releasing a long breath of indignation. Marti had realized it was time to tell Jesse about Paul's strange visit in Donna's front yard. She waited until the day after their return from Georgia, when the rain started pouring down. Bumpus emerged from his forage through the bushes and shook off a thousand droplets of water. She'd known Jesse would be angry at her for hiding it from him, but she'd justified her reason. With a spear of panic, she remembered how well she used to justify her actions in the past. With Jamie.

"This is different," she said aloud.

"What's different?"

"I . . . Paul was. He was scared, kind of. Urgent."

"Like he knew he was in danger, maybe?"

She shook her head. "I don't know. He said it was going to sound crazy. Something he noticed the night someone tried to kill me. Not looking over his shoulder type of scared. Worried might be a better word."

Jesse stared at the rain dripping from the edge of the roof. "Maybe he was trying to cover his butt, or he had an idea who it was doing all this awful stuff around here."

"At first I wanted to think it was Paul doing all this, and now I'd be safe. But, Jesse, I don't feel safe. I mean, I look out the window at night and I can still *feel* someone out there. And Bumpus hasn't stopped barking. If only I could prove that Paul was the one, I could breathe easier. Everyone could."

When Marti pulled into her driveway after a trip to the grocery store, Kati's car was parked out front. She and Jesse were sitting on the couch, the unobserved late evening news the only light on in the room. Something was wrong.

Kati was staring blankly at something to the right of the television when Marti put her purse down and walked over to them.

"Dean's been picked up for questioning in Donna's rape," Jesse said blandly, as if he didn't quite believe it.

"Oh, no. Can't be." Marti sat down next to Kati. "How did they drag Dean into this?"

"He sent her flowers saying he was sorry about what happened. Her father reported it to the sheriff. Something about the way the note was worded," Kati said.

"Don't they know Dean's kind of strange by now?" Marti asked. After a moment of silence, she added, "What? You don't think he raped her, do you?"

"He did send her flowers before, remember?" Kati

turned to Jesse. "She came in the diner the week before she got raped, telling us about her date with Paul and the flowers Dean had sent her."

"Yeah, but you know why he sent her those flowers in the first place, don't you? Didn't Billy tell you?" Marti asked.

Both Kati and Jesse stared at her dumbfounded.

"Kati, Billy told him to get you jealous, wake you up some. Dean whispered it to me when we were at the races that weekend, but I had to promise not to tell you."

Kati stood up and paced in the blue glow from the television. "It doesn't matter anymore. Nothing matters."

"What are you talking about?"

When Kati didn't answer right away, Jesse clarified. "Dean was over at the house when Carl picked him up. Kati was so shocked about the flowers and everything else, she couldn't answer when he asked if she believed he was innocent. I guess he was pretty torn up about it."

"It doesn't matter," Kati said dully. "Everything's screwed up anyway."

"Kati, I think it does matter. You love that boy, whether you want to admit it or not."

"As a friend, maybe."

"No, as more than a friend. He needs you right now."

Kati kept pacing. "He'll never forgive me for not believing in him."

"You don't know that, do you? Go down to the station and wait for him to come out. Sheriff's not going to find anything on him."

Kati looked at Jesse. "Why couldn't I have believed in him like she does? No, I had to show a glimmer of doubt. It was the flowers that made me wonder. And he turned away and never looked back. I hurt him bad." The resolve on her face crumbled, and a tear slid down her freckled cheek.

Jesse put his arms around her. "Do you think he could have raped Donna?" Kati shook her head. "Then let's go down to the station and pick the guy up. Marti and I'll follow you down there. We'll wait with you until Carl's through, then we'll leave you alone with him."

Kati swallowed. "You don't think he did it?"

Jesse shook his head.

"You always make fun of him and say he's weird."

He kissed her nose. "We give him a hard time because we know you like him. And he is a little weird, but he's not a rapist. Right now, I wouldn't trust anyone else with my sister."

She hugged him, then slipped her arm around Marti as they headed out the door. "Thanks, you two. I just hope Dean forgives me."

"He will if he loves you," Marti said. And she was sure he did. Just like Jesse had believed in her when she was arrested. She looked at Jesse, realizing then how much having someone believe in you meant.

They only had to wait ten minutes before Carl walked out to drive Dean home. When Dean saw them standing there, he dismissed the sheriff and walked over, avoiding Kati's worried expression.

"Did you come by to give me a ride home or find out if they'd booked me?" he asked.

Jesse shook Dean's hand. "Hell, we knew you were too stupid to do something awful like that."

Dean gave a grudging smile. "Thanks. I think. I sent her flowers, that's all. Never even took her out or anything. That jerk was trying to make me confess to something I didn't do. But he didn't have enough evidence to hold me, so I'm out." He glanced quickly at Kati, then looked away.

Jesse put his arm around Marti's shoulder. "Well, my wife here is tired, so we're going to let Kati take you home. You don't mind, do you?"

Dean looked at his shoes, then back at Jesse. With a shrug, he said, "I guess not. That is, if she trusts that I'm not going to throw her on the ground and jump her."

Without any warning, Kati threw her arms around Dean, and he tentatively hugged her back. Jesse steered Marti to the truck. When they climbed in, Dean was holding on tight to Kati with his face buried in her curls. Jesse patted her hand as he turned the truck around.

"Ah, ain't love grand?"

"Grand," Marti repeated absently, still watching the couple now kissing on the sidewalk. Grand if you can treat it right.

Two weeks later, Marti and Jesse started Lamaze class together. The other six women in the class laughed about how they couldn't even think of making love to their husbands, making Marti feel like a pervert for wanting Jesse so much. Sometimes she wished he would just throw her on the bed and make wild, passionate love to her and forget about the first time. She had a feeling Jesse wouldn't forget that easily, but she'd caught him just looking at her in an interesting way a few times.

The baby moved almost all the time now, sometimes in three places at the same time. Jesse never seemed to get bored of feeling the baby move or hearing Marti tell him how many times he moved or how he hiccoughed while she was taking measurements at a new client's house. He listened with rapt attention, his hand on her belly the whole time. It seemed that the baby was all they had between them anymore. That was the way it should be, she told herself. He had a racing career, she had California. But somehow those words just didn't make the sense they used to.

She no longer worked at Bad Boys Diner. Jesse had insisted she quit when her ankles started filling up like water balloons. The heavier she got, the more decorating clients she seemed to get. They didn't even mind standing on the couch and measuring the height to the top of the window themselves.

During their evening Lamaze class, Jesse was attentive and friendly, helping her to breathe properly and massaging her back. As the seven couples laughed at a joke, Marti had longed to share that laughter with Jesse, but he hardly looked at her. Not really looked, anyway. Just that casual brush-the-surface kind of look.

Back at home, she took a shower and slipped into Jesse's robe. His scent in the terry cloth made her close her eyes, thinking about the time they'd made love. Her face flushed when she realized that was exactly what it had been. Making love. Love. She caught that look again in the steamed mirror, that one she refused to admit was there most of the time. Happiness. Real contentment. Silly, foolish girl, she chastised. For one thing, there was him. And for another, there was her.

Jesse hadn't asked her to stay since they had made love, not that she had any intention to stay. She never stopped thinking about leaving. Only it wasn't with longing and desperation anymore, but with a sadness that it was the only way she wouldn't hurt Jesse or his family. Remembering the expression on Dean's face reminded her too sharply of how Jamie used to look at her sometimes. She told herself it was for the best.

Marti emerged from the steamy bathroom, tucking her wet hair behind her ears. With a groan, she pulled it forward again. The canned laughter of a television sitcom drifted into the bedroom, and she walked to the doorway. Jesse was crouched over an upside-down Bumpus with his four legs up in the air as he patiently let his master clip his nails. Wearing his faded blue jeans and nothing else, Jesse was a sight to behold. His muscles moved beneath his skin as he gently held each paw and clipped the nails with precision. Something stirred in Marti, making her feel warm and tingly inside.

For no apparent reason, Jesse turned around. Her face flushed even more, and she hoped it was too dark where she was standing for him to see it. She wanted to shrug, to make light of standing there watching him; she wanted to turn around and go back in the bedroom, but she couldn't move. His gaze riveted her to immobility.

"What's wrong?" he asked finally, coming to his feet.

She put her hand on her belly instinctively, knowing it was the baby he was concerned about. At her movement, he walked over and put his hand next to hers.

"Are you all right?" he asked, concern making his green eyes seem deeper than usual.

Marti felt as though some unseen force was squeezing her heart. She lifted her gaze to him, feeling that all of her heart was there for him to see and there wasn't a thing she could do about it. He would hate her for trying to complicate his life, but she had no intention of doing that to either one of them. The warmth from his hand emanated to envelop her.

She closed her eyes and whispered, "The baby's fine."

When he touched her cheek, she opened her eyes again. "Marti . . ."

She shook her head and walked into the bedroom, feeling embarrassed and angry at herself for the tears that threatened to spill over. She could not love him, no, no, no. Sure, she had felt *in* love with him, infatuated. But this feeling that overwhelmed her was more than lust or puppy love. It reached from her heart to every place inside her, even places she didn't know existed.

She wanted him to hold her, she wanted to share evening walks down by the river, talks on the front porch swing, kisses anywhere and everywhere, even in the pits just before a race. Marti shivered, facing the bed, wrapping her arms around herself. She wanted forever, and she couldn't have it. Her weakness, his racing. No matter that they were married, that they shared a baby together. Her fingers trembled as she put them over her mouth—*shared* a baby? Yes, she had thought that. Oh, God.

Jesse was standing so close behind her that she could feel his body heat, feel his breath caressing her ear. He touched her shoulder so gently, she wondered how he could know she felt so fragile that even a regular touch would shatter her.

"Marti . . ." he said, the question lacing his voice like aged whiskey.

"Go away, Jesse. I'm fine."

She heard his breath hitch lightly, but he didn't go. Her heart was on a fine wire, balanced between wanting him to leave and wanting him to stay. She only knew one thing for sure: she wanted him. It would never work, it would never work. She chanted the words in her head.

Jesse ran his fingers across her cheek and into her wet hair, turning her gently to face him. His thumb grazed her skin as he looked at her, studying her eyes.

"Jesse . . ." she cried out softly, her voice thick with held-back tears. *Go away. It will never work.*

But he didn't go away. He kissed her, firm, yet gentle. His soft lips remained there against hers, as if he were contemplating the sanity of the move. A second later he kissed her again, this time with a little more pressure. She relaxed her lips against his, opening them slightly. He took her invitation and slipped his tongue in her mouth. A hot tear slipped down her cheek, then another. She squeezed her eyes shut, wishing that she could pretend things were different between them.

Jesse stopped kissing her, but his hand remained against her cheek. Remaining only an inch from her, his thumb stroked the wet skin where another tear had splashed against his hand.

"Marti, what's the matter? Tell me."

She shook her head, looking down. She couldn't tell him, not now or ever. Never in her life had she felt so caught up in a whirlwind of conflicting emotions and doubts. Maybe, possibly, she could believe in herself and forget her past. Maybe she could be happy here with Jesse and his family—her family now. But he had not asked her to stay, not from his heart. That had to be because he didn't feel the same way. Even if she agreed to stay, he might tell her that he'd changed his mind, and that would kill her. No, she had to keep her feelings from him, no matter what.

Jesse was sure he'd never seen a more beautiful woman, tears and all. He held her face, wishing to take away the pain that clouded her brown eyes. But she wouldn't answer him, wouldn't let him help her. God, but he wanted to take care of her, to protect her and cherish her. It went against everything that he'd been telling himself for the last few years, and especially the last few months. A woman would get in the way of his racing career, distract him, confuse him. Hell, she was already doing that.

He leaned back to get a better look at her, to put a little distance between them. Why did she look so darn sad? It was evident that she wasn't going to tell him. Maybe she didn't want to hurt his feelings by telling him how unhappy she was. He pushed away the twinge in his heart, grasping on an answer. Hadn't she told him before how much she wanted to get out of Chattaloo and go back to California? He knew she couldn't be comfortable being almost ready to pop. That must be it.

"Marti, this will all be over soon." He touched her chin, smiling. "You'll have the baby and be able to go back home to California before you know it."

Her lower lip trembled, and another tear slid down her cheek. She turned away from him and closed her eyes, hugging herself. Jesse heard Bumpus whine from the other room and realized that he was probably still waiting for the claw trimming to end. Marti moved away from his grasp and lay down on the bed, keeping her eyes closed. Her delicate hands were lying on top of her belly, rising and falling with each breath.

Jesse wanted to touch her, to somehow comfort her. Hopefully he had given her some hope that this would all be over soon, and she could go home. He didn't let himself think about her not being there in the house, sharing his bed. He couldn't let himself think about her staying since those strange feelings about her had started to intrude. Racing was more important than anything. Jesse walked to the doorway, watching her. Wasn't it?

During the next week, Marti kept to herself. She ignored the almost constant pain that gripped her every time she thought of Jesse. He had been giving her odd looks since that night she had cried in front of him. She'd caught him twice just staring at her, his head tilted thoughtfully. But she wouldn't allow herself to think about the future, especially not after what he'd said about her being able to go home to California soon. He wanted her out, the sooner the better. Then he could go back to racing on the weekends.

Donna was a great distraction every evening, fraught with her own anxieties and shame. Marti sat in her chair next to the windowseat. Donna's state of mind was open today. She could always tell her mood by whether the curtain was open or not. It was open.

"Did you kill Paul?" she asked Marti out of nowhere.

"Do you think I did?"

"I don't know."

"I didn't kill him. He was already dead when I got there. Somebody had broken his neck, then . . . oh, I'm sorry, Donna."

She shivered, then faced Marti. "It's all right. I wondered how he'd died. Nobody would tell me, and I didn't want to ask."

"Do you feel safer now that he's dead?" Marti fished for clues.

She shrugged. "I don't know. Maybe. Maybe I'd like to have done it myself."

Marti proceeded cautiously, glad that Donna was finally opening up. "Do you feel that angry, enough to want to kill him?"

She clenched her fists. "I don't know. Maybe to rip all his chest hair out, to gouge his eyes out, to—"

"Did you say chest hair?"

Donna's eyes widened, and she wrapped her arms around her shoulders. "He had hair on his chest. I didn't see it, but when I tried to push him away, I felt it." She looked at her hand in disgust.

Marti remembered feeling a mat of hair when she'd pushed away the man in her bedroom. She walked over to the desk where her sketch was still sitting on top of other papers and cards. "Is this what your scratch looked like? On your chest?" Donna nodded without even looking. "Then it was the same man," she breathed.

Donna was staring at the place where the ceiling met the two walls in the corner. "Paul tried to get fresh on our date, right there in his truck outside his house. That's all he wanted, you know." She swallowed hard, and hesitated, making Marti think she would go silent again. "I stomped home, through the patch of woods between our houses. I was almost home. He came out of nowhere. At first I thought it was Paul chasing after me. I'm not sure. He shoved me down hard, knocking the breath out of me. Then he dropped down on top of me, grinding his body into mine. . . ."

Donna choked on her words, pushing the awful image from her mind. Marti walked over and put her arms around the woman's shaking shoulders.

"You don't have to tell me," she said. "You can stop there."

Donna shook her head. "I need to tell someone. I keep having nightmares about it. Maybe if I tell you, they'll go away." She took a deep breath, staring at the corner again. "He was wearing a robe of some kind, and he threw it off. There was . . . nothing underneath. At first I thought it was a black guy, because his face was dark. But his body was white. He pinned me down and . . . and . . ."

She started crying again, and Marti soothed her. "That's enough. Don't say any more."

"I didn't do anything. I mean, I tried to push him away, to scream. But once he'd pinned me, I stopped fighting. I didn't want to die, Marti. I feel like I should have done more, but I was so scared."

Marti thought of the woman whose place she'd taken. She had probably fought her attacker, and now she was dead. "That was the smartest thing you could have done."

"There's something else I need to tell you. He only said one thing to me, and his voice was weird, low and dreamy sounding. He called me a different name. He said, 'Marti, the blood of my heart.' He called me Marti."

Those last words squeezed Marti's heart into a tiny ball of fear. It was definitely him.

"I didn't mean to frighten you," Donna said through her tears. "I thought you should know. I wanted to tell you before, but I couldn't. Why would he call me your name? And say those other words?"

"Maybe he was thinking about his attack on me." Marti's words seemed hollow as they left her mouth. The first Marti had seen her attacker as he stopped to help with her car problem. He probably worried that she would remember him. But why would he call her the blood of his heart? She shivered.

Then anger surged. "I don't want to keep living in

fear of this animal. If it was Paul, then I want us to be able to relax a little. If it's not, we need to know for sure. I can't stand this not knowing."

"What are you going to do?"

Marti stood. "I don't know." But she did. She had to get ahold of that necklace and try to recreate the mark on her chest. Running to her car was physically out of the question, but she moved faster than she thought she could. As she passed by Carl's house, she realized how easy it would be to get inside that house and find the necklace. Then she'd have her answer.

Still, she tried to find Jesse first. He wasn't at the house, Helen's, or at the garage. She didn't know where Debbie lived, or even where else to check for him. Going to the sheriff was obviously out of the question, and she didn't want to drag Helen or Kati into this. The sight of Carl's car parked in front of the station gave her the adrenaline to drive directly to his house. She would find that proof by herself. Even though Jesse would yell at her, he'd be pleased to at least have an answer. Besides, Helen would do the same.

It was barely light when she drove past Carl's house, with the sun's setting rays casting an eerie glow over everything. She pulled onto an empty lot on the other side of the street, parking behind a large fig tree. Carl's colonial home sat on two lots, giving it room on either side. She walked casually up to the house, keeping herself hidden by the shadows of trees.

People in small towns were not given to locking their doors, unless there was a ruthless rapist in the vicinity. But the sheriff wouldn't be afraid of such a thing. The front door was locked, but the back one was not. She slipped inside.

The rooms were dim and musty. The television played in some distant room, making her wonder if Carl was indeed at the station. She had to believe he was since his car wasn't out front. With so many rooms to choose from, she realized she had no idea where to start.

She doubted Paul had been buried with his necklace, which meant Carl would have it somewhere special, like in his bedroom, or in Paul's room.

A quick check of the downstairs didn't reveal a master bedroom, so she walked up the stairs and continued down the hallway. The second bedroom looked used; cluttered and dirty. Nothing like the rest of the house, which was immaculate in its appearance. Paul's room?

The chain and eagle pendant were lying on top of a tall chest of drawers, toward the back. Pulling her shirt down a little, she pressed the wings into her skin until it hurt. When she pulled it away, her body went cold. It was the same mark. Pocketing the necklace, she turned to leave.

Photos on the wall caught her eye. Old framed photos of Carl in his uniform, Carl in what looked like a graduating class of police officers, Carl and Paul on a fishing boat. Carl's room, then.

Behind one of the photos, she could see the corner of another one tucked away. Even from the small piece, she could tell it was older. Pulling the frame down, she bent the prongs and removed the backing. The small photo behind it was a younger Helen. Jesse's mother. It had been cut from what looked like a family photo. Why Helen?

She studied the boat photo, the pendants that hung around both of their necks: eagles. But Paul's chest was hairless. And Carl's was covered with curly fuzz. She shivered.

"Oh, my God."

Her heart pounded. Sweat clung to her forehead. Carl. It had been Carl all along. She had to get out of there. Even though she'd only been in the house for about thirty minutes, it felt like hours had passed. Now to find Jesse and tell him the shocking truth. Something caught her eye. Through the window, she'd seen a glint of light. She looked through the curtain. The sheriff's car sat out front! How long had Carl been home? Where could she hide? In the closet of one of the unused rooms until he left again! She would be safe there.

"Find what you were looking for?"

A cold fear blanketed her before she even looked up to see Carl standing in the doorway. Blocking her escape. Smiling.

Chapter 18

~

Carl's hair was disheveled, and his green eyes looked glassy. "Or did you . . . come to see me?"

Marti's heart pounded so hard it impacted her vision. Which way to go? Some reason for being there. To see him? To find something?

"I . . . wanted some answers."

Carl moved in closer, taking one step, then another. Without looking back, she tried to remember what was behind her. No escape, that she knew.

"Why don't you just ask me, Marti?" he said softly, enunciating each word carefully. "I would be glad to clarify anything for you."

"P-Paul. I wanted to know what happened." That seemed safest. Carl wouldn't be as defensive about that. But she was wrong.

"You thought you could come here and prove somehow that I killed him? That I shoved him through the attic entrance and broke his neck?"

Ice shot through her veins, paralyzing her body. "You killed him?" she stammered, wishing he had not confessed.

Carl took another step closer. "It looks like you already figured that out."

"No! I mean, I didn't know. I never thought you would k-kill your own son."

"It wasn't easy. He put up a fight, but down deep inside, he's a wimp. Down to the core. His mother made him that way, coddled him and fussed until she left."

The crucial link between emotion and sanity was gone, replaced only by a thread of wickedness. She could see it in his eyes, feel it in the room as it floated toward her like a sinister fog. The picture of Paul's broken body lying in the grass flashed in her mind, followed by the realization that the man standing before her had been there in her room not long ago. He had tried to kill her.

"Jesse knows I'm here," she blurted out, trying desperately to hide the fear in her eyes. Too late. He already knew she was afraid.

"Sure he does. And he's on his way over, right?"

Her nod faded at his knowing smile. Instead of the adrenaline she needed, her body felt weak. She watched him as a mouse might watch a snake, weighing her options, judging her next move.

Taking a deep breath, she relaxed her shoulders. "Well, I guess you're going to arrest me for trespassing. I wouldn't blame you. Let's go down to the station."

She started to walk by him to the door. If she could just make it to the door, she could run. The stairs would be too dangerous in her condition, but maybe she could make it to another room, lock the door and scream for help out the window. Just as she thought she was going to get by, he grabbed her wrist. With a swift movement, he pulled handcuffs from his belt and snapped one on her wrist. She wriggled, desperately trying to keep the other one away, but her strength was no match for his.

"You're not going to get away from me as easily as you did the last time. Pretending to die was clever, very clever. And then you got yourself released from jail before I wanted you out. But not this time, blood of my heart."

Those words sent chills through her body, but she kept her fear hidden. He touched her chin, and she jerked away from him. His finger remained poised in front of her, his expression hard. The cuffs were tight around her wrists, jangling every time she moved.

Stay calm. Something isn't right inside his head. He killed his son. He'll kill you, too.

Subtly, she sucked in a great big breath, and as he moved toward his dresser, she let out the beginning of a howling scream. His palm shot out and smashed her into the wall, crushing her nose. Blood trickled past her

lips and over her chin. The sharp pain made her eyes
lose focus for a second. In that moment, Carl reached
into the top drawer, but she didn't see what he took out.
The room spun as terror turned her brain in circles.
Then it was black, in and out of consciousness as she
dropped down to the floor. She tried to clutch at the
walls, but her shackled wrists could hardly move.

No, not now! Don't faint now!

That was the last thought she had.

Marti woke with a start, staring into blackness. Lucidity
eluded her for a few minutes as she struggled to figure
out if she was having a nightmare. Her mouth felt full of
cotton. It *was* full of cotton, she realized. Something was
in her mouth, and no amount of pushing with her
tongue would dislodge it. Afraid to move, she waited for
her eyes to adjust to the darkness. Patches of dim light
moved around in front of her, but she thought her eyes
might be playing tricks on her.

Marti turned over to touch Jesse, intent on waking
him. With a screech of metal against metal, she was
stopped abruptly. She jerked her hand again, but it was
attached to something above her. Icy fear rushed over
her, washing her with reality. She tried to kick, but her
legs were shackled. Her scream came out as a muffled
noise.

The more she jerked and twisted, the more the handcuffs bit into her skin. She was cuffed to a bed in a dark,
hot place. The baby kicked three times in quick succes-
sion, and she started to put her hand on her belly as she
usually did. But her hand stopped far short. Did the
baby know what danger he was in? she wondered. Could
he feel her terror?

A creaking noise made her instantly still. A shaft of
light shot up to the trusses several yards above her. She
was in the attic. Another pinpoint of light in a dark
reality. And no doubt, Carl was coming up some kind of
creaky stairs or a ladder. Coming to see her.

His silhouette loomed over her, reminding her vividly
of the night he'd broken in to kill her. Was he there to
kill her now? She didn't move, afraid to breathe. Sweat

trickled down her sides. He was just standing there, looking at her, or something. She kept her eyes closed, wishing he'd go away so she could think. She had to get out of there!

Carl reached up and pulled a chain, sending harsh light from a bare bulb hanging above her. The fixture swung back and forth on its chain, casting wild shadows around her. She blinked painfully. Carl stood there with a stupid smile on his face. He was still wearing his uniform, unbuttoned down to his hairy navel. It seemed absurd to her that he should be wearing a sheriff's uniform when he was going to kill her in his attic. She wanted to tell him so, but she couldn't say anything other than a muffle.

Carl glanced around with narrowed eyes, then stepped over an upturned cardboard box to pull a dusty rocking chair next to the bed. His pungent cologne and sweat mixed nauseatingly with the musty smell of the mattress beneath her. She swallowed, trying to push down the lump in her throat that felt like a tennis ball. He rocked back and forth in the chair, making the floorboards creak with every movement.

She was not going to plead. Even if he did remove the blasted, foul-tasting cloth from her mouth. Somehow she knew begging would just incite him. Maybe the first Marti had found that out.

When he leaned forward with his hand, she flinched. He didn't falter as he smoothed her damp hair back in the way a father might do for a sick child. Then he laughed, a low, rumbling laugh that shot fear through her.

"You're finally mine, Marti. I've wanted you for a long time, a long, long time. But you were always afraid of me. Why were you afraid of me?" He pinched her chin between his fingers, his expression fierce now. "Why?"

She just stared behind him, wishing to God that Jesse would suddenly pop out of the opening and snare Carl in a killing hold around the throat. Jesse. The thought of him injected a small amount of hope in her. Carl glanced behind him as if she were really staring at someone. When he turned back to her, he held his finger threateningly near her nose, which still ached dully.

"Don't even think about screaming, blood of my heart."

Those words chilled her. Carl pulled at the cloth around her head until it finally came out of her mouth. She now recognized the taste as something close to car wax. Her tongue felt like a withered prune.

"I am not yours," she stated simply, after moistening her mouth. "I'm Jesse's." Just saying his name gave her strength.

Carl's laughter sapped that strength. "Looks like you're mine now." It was frightening the way his expressions changed so rapidly. His eyes grew hard again as they surveyed her body. "But now I don't want you. You're fat! You repulse me!"

She flinched at the way he spit the words out. "Then why don't you let me go?"

That laughter again, fraught with evil. "Can't do that. You know too much. You and Jesse just kept snooping around. You couldn't let it rest, could you?"

His mention of Jesse made her suddenly afraid for him. Almost as scared as she was for the baby inside her. "You tried to kill me," she stated, remembering that he had actually killed Marti.

"Yes, I did." He said the words wistfully, tilting his head up. "But I didn't. And you know why I didn't? Because you are meant to be mine."

"Was Helen meant to be yours, too?" she ventured.

He turned to her, surprise on his face. "What do you know about her?"

"Just that you asked her to marry you, but she turned you down." Jesse had told her that after Bernie died, Carl had come around panting like a dog. Marti didn't mention the photo she'd found.

"Don't talk to me about Helen."

"You couldn't make her love you, could you?"

He leaned closer to her, so close she smelled the whiskey on his breath. "Are you calling me a failure? Huh?"

She shrunk back as far as the bed would allow. "No. You succeeded in killing your son, didn't you?"

He leaned back, placing his ankle on his other knee. "Yes, but that wasn't planned. He was going to squeal on his own father. He came in here accusing me of being the one who attacked you both times. Said if I didn't confess, he had enough evidence to interest the Fort Myers police."

Marti remembered Paul's desperate tone in his voice that night outside Dr. Hislope's house. He'd known. That had been his crazy revelation, that his own father was the one.

Carl leaned forward, pointing at his chest. "He was going to turn his own father in? Can you believe the loyalty? Even before he knew I wasn't his real father." Marti's eyes widened, and he seemed pleased to surprise her. "I married his mother because she told me she was pregnant with my baby. But when Paul was born, I knew—*knew*—somehow that he wasn't mine. I made her tell me who she'd slept with. I forced the bitch to tell me."

She wanted to keep the conversation away from her and Jesse. "B-but you forgave her?"

He smiled, showing his perfect teeth. "No. I made her life hell until she left, ran away one night, just like that."

She shivered. "You killed Paul, then tried to set Jesse up for his murder."

"I wanted Jesse out of the way, so I could have you. But he left without seeing the note, and you found it instead. You always did find yourself in the most interesting predicaments."

"How did you get his knife?"

"I saw it in his car the night I arrested him for beating up on Paul. I remembered that Bernie had given it to him, so I took it." He shook his head. "I never wanted to hurt Jesse, really didn't. He was just in the way."

Her body stiffened. "What do you mean, hurt Jesse?"

"Sending him to jail for life didn't seem so bad, but when that didn't work out, I knew I had to get him out of the way. First, to get you. Second, to get him off my trail. He was getting close. But you screwed up that, too, by getting out of jail early and stopping him from racing."

"The steering going out," she whispered.

"That's right. But you see, it all worked out for the best. You're here with me, and he's alive. Unless he starts snooping around here, that is."

Marti was left with the strange decision to either hope he did snoop or to hope he didn't.

Carl stood up. "I'm going to bring you something to eat. Don't want you thinking I'm a lousy host." His smile seemed almost normal then, not dark and sick. "Oh, and I took care of your car, too. Found it across the street. We wouldn't want to worry anyone, so I dumped it far away from here."

Her car; she'd forgotten about that. But now it didn't matter. "What are you going to do with me?" she asked, not sure she wanted to know the answer.

He looked thoughtful for a moment. "I'm not sure. I wasn't exactly planning to find you in my bedroom, you know. But you'll be the first to know when I figure it out." He tugged the gag back into place.

Jesse was frantic by ten o'clock that night. He didn't know whether to be angry or worried, but worry was quickly taking over. Sure, things hadn't been great between them, neither one of them wanted anything permanent. Would she stay out late just to make him crazy?

"Come on, Bumpus. Let's go for a ride."

He already knew she'd left Donna's earlier that day, but the woman was still too terrified to talk to Jesse personally. Dr. Hislope said that Marti hadn't said where she was going. Phone calls confirmed she wasn't at the diner, his mother's, or at any of her current clients' houses.

The street Dr. Hislope lived on was unlit, save for a few lampposts outside some of the homes. Jesse glanced at Carl's old colonial as he drove past. The patrol car sat outside; he wondered why there weren't any lights on outside. He was glad to see the sheriff home; Carl was the last person he wanted to report Marti's disappearance to. And it looked like the station was going to be a stop Jesse would soon be making.

The Hislope home was well-lit, but there was no sign of Marti's car. He knew that but wanted to see for himself. Then another drive through town. He even drove past the place where Marti had been attacked, and far beyond it. Nothing.

At eleven o'clock, Jesse caught Lyle heading home for the night. He filed a missing persons report, even though she hadn't been missing for the required period of time. Because of the previous attacks, Lyle complied. Behind his concerned face, however, Jesse sensed pity that Marti may have hit the road. That had entered his mind too, but he refused to believe she would leave like this. Something deep in his gut told him it was worse than that.

Marti watched Carl work feverishly to fill in the slanted walls with pink insulation, putting up drywall, installing an air conditioner unit. To anyone else, it looked like a man fixing up his home. She didn't want to think about the implications of what he was doing. It looked . . . permanent.

Her best guess was that it was Friday, two days. She had no way of telling what time it was. When the light bulb was off, she could see cracks of sunlight filtering through from the eaves. Then she knew it was day, but nothing more. Carl seemed to take enjoyment in keeping the time from her.

Rock music from the group Queen pounded through the small area, sometimes hateful and full of power, sometimes oddly whimsical. He played a CD from a portable player over and over again, hardly glancing at her at all. This was good, but she wondered what thoughts rambled through a brain that became more warped every day. There were lucid moments when he seemed to realize what he'd done. He cried for the son who was not his, even for the baby inside her he was distressing.

There were more moments when his eyes were glazed, emerald crystals hard and somewhere else. He looked at her, but she knew he was looking far beyond her. He would stare at her for half an hour at a stretch, just watching her, contemplating. Those were the times she tried to roll onto her side to relieve her stiff, aching back. She could only achieve a partial angle, and she felt like a pretzel twist, but it still relieved a little.

For the last day, though, he was relentlessly working on refurbishing the attic, closing in a small area with drywall, causing her to gag from the smell of paint. She breathed through the pillowcase while the paint dried, trying to filter the oxygen the baby was getting.

He left her alone for a while, then returned with a tray of food. He fed her well, pasta, fresh vegetables, and juice. He'd even bought superstrength multivitamins to replace her prenatal ones.

"I read that you need your vitamins," he'd told her many hours before. "I'm reading a book about pregnancy so I'll know how to take care of you. I want to take care of you."

She'd kept silent, fear pulsing through her. And now he set the tray down on a small table he'd brought up. It was a ritual, before he removed her gag to let her eat, he would grasp her chin and force her to look at him. Then he would smile with self-pleasure and remove the gag. This time he leaned over and unlocked one of her hands. She didn't comment on it, for fear he would realize he hadn't done that before and lock her back up again.

"Today I have turkey sandwiches for us, and carrot sticks. And this is for you, too." He held up a glass of some unidentifiable beige substance. "It's a protein drink for pregnant women. You're supposed to have one of these every day."

She wouldn't have eaten anything but for the baby who needed its nutrition. "What is it?" she asked.

"Milk, powdered skim milk, brewer's yeast, vanilla, a raw egg, half an egg shell, honey, and fruit juice." At her skeptical expression, he pulled a book out from beneath a legal pad. "Right here." He pointed to a paragraph on page twenty as if to prove his good intentions. It really was a book on pregnancy.

"Why are you doing this?" she asked, nodding toward the book. With a stiff hand, she took the glass he held out for her. He seemed to be waiting for her to drink before he answered, so with closed eyes and a grimace, she gulped it down. Trying not to think about egg shells and the raw egg itself, she finished the glass and handed it back to him.

He smiled at her, wiping some residue off her top lip. This was one of his semilucid days, she thought. He was there, yet acting as if their arrangement were perfectly normal.

"I want to take care of you, sweetheart. We're going to be a happy little family."

She cringed when he touched her belly. "H-happy family? You're going to keep me here after I have the baby?"

He leaned back in the rocker, putting his feet on the bed. "I'm going to keep you here forever, blood of my heart."

Her stomach turned, threatening to spew up the ghastly drink. "W-what about having the baby? I've got to go to a hospital." It was a hope that if he didn't kill her before she had the baby, that he'd have to take her to a hospital when she went into labor. She'd found herself practicing what she'd tell the doctor.

Carl tapped on the cover of the book. "I've got more of these to help. I don't want you to go to some sterile, uncaring hospital. You're going to have that baby right here, with me helping you every step of the way."

She tried to hold onto her own sanity. "What if there are complications?"

"There won't be any complications, sweetheart. Look at you, healthy as a horse. I won't let anything happen to you, or that baby of ours."

Ours. The word stabbed at her. "It's not *your* baby, Carl. It's Jesse's."

Carl smiled wistfully. "Yeah, Jesse's a good name for the baby, if it's a boy. We'll name him Jesse. He'll be my son, my blood."

She shivered. He was losing his touch on reality, little by little. This room was going to be her prison. For *for-*

ever. No, Jesse would come for her, any time now. She had to keep hoping.

As if Carl read her thoughts, he pulled out the legal pad and handed it to her. "I think it's time you wrote a good-bye letter to your husband. Tell him you decided to leave early, that you won't be coming back."

She eyed the pad he'd thrust at her. "No, I won't do it."

He yanked her hair behind her, jerking her head backward painfully. "You will do it. Do you understand me? I will make your life hell if you don't."

"You won't hurt the baby, Carl. He's your blood," she lied.

"No, I won't hurt my son. But I will make you miserable. I'll turn the air off, feed you the most disgusting, albeit nutritious, food I can think of, strip your clothes off and make you lie there naked. . . ."

As he spoke, her resistance hardened. Until she thought of something. Grimacing at his words, she said, "Okay, I'll write the letter."

Carl smiled, handing her the pad and a pencil. "And don't think about putting anything in that letter that shouldn't be there. You know what I mean, don't you?"

She nodded, but her mind was whirling. Carl dictated the letter to her, shoving her hand into action.

"Dear Jesse. I have decided to leave early because I'm very unhappy here with you. Go on! Write it! I want to start a new life in . . . where were you going?"

"Oklahoma."

"Okay, in Oklahoma. Uh, I'm sorry I couldn't say good-bye in person. Signed you."

"Can I tell him to say good-bye to his family for me? Since I won't be seeing them again? He would think it was weird if I didn't."

He gave it some thought. "All right, but nothing tricky."

She was taking chances, and she knew it. It was her only hope. She wrote, "Please say good-bye to Helen, Kati, Billy, and your dog, Caramel. I will miss them all."

Carl looked over what she had just written, and she prayed he didn't know Bumpus's name. It was the closest she could come to spelling out Carl's name, and the obviously wrong name might cause Jesse to look at it carefully. If he paid much attention after all the other words before it.

"Oh, no you don't," he said, shoving the paper back at her.

Her heart caught in her throat. "W-what?"

"You didn't sign it."

She breathed out silently when he folded the paper and stuffed it into an envelope.

"Fill out his address. I'll head north a bit and mail the thing today."

Her hands trembled slightly as she wrote Jesse's name. Would she ever see him again? Would he ever take her hand so casually and not know how warm it made her feel? Carl tucked the envelope under his hand and leaned back in the rocker, a smug smile on his face. He made her uncomfortable under his silent stare, the way his gaze swept slowly over her, pausing over her distended belly. His eyes were glazing more, as if he weren't really looking at her, but someone else.

"How are you going to explain having a baby all of a sudden, Carl?" she asked, wanting to break through to the small, sane part of his mind.

"You think I'm stupid, don't you?" He cuffed her to the bed again. "I've got that all figured out. Everybody knows I have a sister out in Texas. She hasn't been out to visit in a long time, but the folks around here remember her. Well, as times would have it, she got herself into a little fix. Pregnant, by a married man. What a shame. But her big brother, Carl, will help her out. He'll take the baby and raise it as his own. No one will know about you, of course. But little Jesse here will become my son. Unfortunately, no one will know he really is of my blood." He grasped her chin hard. "It would have been so much easier last time, Helen."

A chill crawled down her body. "I am not Helen."

"Helen, the blood of my heart. You knew how much I wanted you, loved you. But you wouldn't leave Bernie, not even when you were carrying my child. You loved him." His voice became gruff. "You were blindly in love with him. And you never told him Jesse was mine. *My son!* He went on believing that he had fathered that boy, and I watched him grow up hating me. Hating his own father."

"I don't believe you," Marti whispered, realizing what he was saying.

"Helen, I knew that boy was mine the moment he was born. I was there, visiting him in the nursery. You never knew, but I held him a few hours after he was born. He was mine. And when you gave him his first birthday party, I watched from outside the house, watched Bernie coddle and hug my son. But his eyes, his hair, they were mine. You couldn't deny it was my son." Carl's voice raised. "I won't let you deny that now!"

She cringed backward, reeling inside from his words. Helen had told her she'd made mistakes, learned from them. Before Jesse was born. She looked at Carl, his features. And she conjured Jesse's image for the thousandth time that hour. There were similarities.

Carl smiled, as if reading her mind, seeing her putting it together. "But we have a second chance, Helen. We have a new baby. This boy will grow up knowing his father. We can have that happy family together. You denied me twice, but you won't deny me now. I have wanted you for so long, lived for you, longed for you." His expression grew hurtful. "Every time I saw Jesse, it killed me right here, in my gut. But you ignored me, wouldn't even take my calls. And even when Bernie died in that car accident, you wouldn't come to me. I did it for you, because I knew he couldn't make you happy like I could. But you still wouldn't come to me."

A shard of fear sliced through her. "Y-you killed Jesse's father?"

Carl shot to his feet, slapping her across the cheek as he rose. "I am Jesse's father!"

The sudden, sharp sting brought tears to her eyes, and her throat felt thick. "I am not Helen! I am Jesse's wife, and this is Jesse's baby!"

Carl turned away and started the CD again, cranking it louder than before. She continued to cry, for everything she'd just heard, for what it all meant. The words to the ballad, "All Dead, All Dead" pounded through her mind.

Hope drained away. Jesse thought she was gone, and probably hated her. She wanted to die then, but there was always the baby to think of. What kind of life would he have? How would Jesse have turned out under Carl's rule? She shook her head, trying not to think about that. The baby must live, that was all she knew. He might live a normal life, out with other people, going to school. Maybe Jesse would see him one day, and maybe he would know, somehow, that it was his son. Would she still be up here in this attic room, a prisoner of darkness? Or would she be insane by then? Probably, unless Carl let her see the baby often. Then she would have a reason to stay sane.

Over the next many hours, perhaps through a long night, she thought about what Carl was insinuating. What he believed. He and Helen had an affair, and she got pregnant with Carl's child. Helen. The woman she believed in, the woman who had helped Marti start to believe in herself.

Marti grimaced as another cramp seized her insides. These were not the Braxton-Hicks contractions she had been feeling for the last week or so. This pain she attributed to something more emotional, more heartbreaking. She felt betrayed, let down. Helen, the woman she thought of as a mother, had cheated on the man she professed to love so much. How could Marti have been so stupid to start believing she could change?

The sound of the dead bolt turning pulled her from her agonized thoughts. Carl walked through the doorway he'd fashioned in front of the trapdoor entrance. He looked around with a smile at the eight foot-by-eight foot room, painted a cheery pink. His eyes were glazed again, far from lucid.

"I should be done with the bathroom tonight, Helen. Won't that make you happy?"

She glanced at the bedpan. Happiness was relative. "Yes, that will be nice," she said carefully.

Inciting anger in Carl was far too easy. And painful, as her cheek could attest many times. He now allowed her hands to remain uncuffed, though her legs were still shackled. The gag was gone, too, for a day's worth of hours now. With the room sealed and soundproofed, there wasn't a need for it. She was biding her time until he finally unchained her legs and let her roam free while he was gone. Then she would find a way out of this hellhole.

"You'll be able to wash yourself by tomorrow. Although I must admit, I enjoyed washing your hair . . . and your body."

She tried to blank out those times when he gave her a sponge bath. Twice now, and he took his time, talking about how they would make love when she wasn't fat anymore. Remembering Jesse telling her how beautiful she was got her through those moments, got her through all of them. It seemed like months since she'd seen him, and they hadn't been on good terms for a week before that. He'd probably ripped up her note and thrown it away, angry at her for not keeping her end of the bargain, taking his son away. Without seeing her clue.

Her internal clock estimated that it had probably been a day or so since he'd received that letter. Her well of hope was drying up. Soon everyone in Chattaloo would stop thinking about her. They'd forget about her. She pushed away the fear that threatened to seize her.

She glanced at the steel door, left ajar. Beyond that the trapdoor was open, and below was the hallway that led to the staircase that Paul had been shoved down. The cuffs jangled around her ankles as she moved them idly. She'd never get away from him. He teased her by leaving the door open, knowing she couldn't escape, knowing she'd think about it. He promised her a clock and a calendar, but every day he made excuses about why he hadn't brought them. He never promised her freedom. She rubbed her hard belly, trying to press away the fear at having the baby in the attic.

Sometime later, Carl emerged from the bathroom, a triumphant glaze on his expression. "After I clean it up, it'll be ready to use, sweetheart. Think about how you're going to show me your gratitude. . . ." He gestured at the whole room. "All this for you. I want to see some gratitude." He pulled his jeans up a bit, grinning wickedly.

As he turned toward the steel door, he stopped suddenly. With the door open, he could hear anything downstairs. He walked to the tiny door he'd installed high up in the roof, climbing a step stool to open it. Usually a heavenly spot of sunlight would shine in before Carl's big head blocked it. It was nighttime now, she knew. No sunshine.

Sometimes he'd remark that someone was parked outside and go down to answer the door. Once she'd screamed her head off, testing the soundproofing Carl said he'd put in. When he returned, he said nothing about her screams, so she knew it worked.

This time he said, "What the hell is he doing here?" The edge in his voice indicated the visitor was not welcome.

"Who is it?" she asked as she always did.

Usually he told her. This time he didn't. He walked out of the room, bolting the steel door behind him. She knew how long it took Carl to walk down and answer the door. About ten minutes was the minimum, depending on who the visitor was. Many hours ago, when Lyle had stopped by, she had twenty-five minutes. Long enough to try something.

Last time it took her fifteen minutes. She would have to be quicker this time. With her hands and weight, she scooted the bed closer to the tiny door, just beneath it, counting out the seconds. With her large belly, it was dangerous to get to her feet on the uneven support of the bed, but she managed it with the help of a nearby wall. She opened the door and jumped a little, getting a glimpse of the street out front.

A jolt of hope shot through her at the sight of Jesse's truck parked out by the road. Her heart jumped against her ribs, and she had to force herself to get the bed back before Carl might return. She was trembling as she maneuvered the bed back to its original spot, marked on the floor by her in pencil.

As soon as she reached the mark, the door unbolted,

and Carl stepped inside. Her heart was hammering inside, more from seeing Jesse's truck than getting the bed back in place in the nick of time. She swallowed hard, trying to regain her composure.

"Who was it?" she asked in a cracked voice.

"Just those darn Jehovah's Witnesses."

It was frightening how well Carl concealed the truth, both in his words and expression. If she hadn't seen Jesse's truck herself, she would have believed him. Then Carl locked the door behind him, and she knew he was concerned. He went to the window and opened the little door again, then closed it.

"They're gone." He knelt down beside her, grasping her arm. "Don't worry, Helen. I won't let anyone hurt you. I'll kill them first."

"I don't want you to kill anyone for me," she said, trying to reason with an unreasonable man. "Killing is bad."

The baby kicked her rib, causing her to flinch slightly. He was sitting so low inside her, pressing down on her pelvis. She could see Jesse's face light up in her mind, amazed every time the baby moved or kicked. Now she was able to put her hand on her belly, and she used the one under Carl's hand.

"I'll go make dinner," he said, his gaze empty.

"I can help," she offered. "I'm a good cook."

He smiled. "That would be nice. I always dreamed about that quaint little picture I had in my mind, you and me cooking dinner together, snuggling on the couch afterward."

Her heart squeezed inside her. "Let me help you. You're always doing all the work."

He pinched her cheek, causing her to flinch away in pain. "You must think I'm stupid." He looked around the attic. "Maybe one day, if you're real good to me, I'll get you a television. That's all of the world you'll ever see, Helen."

In an almost robotic way, he stood and walked toward the door. Hope drained away, filling her with terror and helplessness. She wondered for a moment whether he would forget to lock it, but he slowly closed it behind him and turned the dead bolt. As soon as he was gone, she scooted the bed over and peered out the tiny window. It was darker now, as if the clouds had moved over the moon. Still, she could see the road was empty. Jesse was gone.

Marti remained at the window, knowing Carl always took about thirty minutes to cook dinner. She rapped on the thick Plexiglas, wondering if anyone could hear. When the dead bolt clicked, she turned toward the door and prepared herself to get caught. And punished.

Chapter 19

~

*T*he door opened, and Marti's knees gave way as she sank down to the mattress. Jesse stood there, his expression a mixture of relief and fear as he rushed to her. She started crying, unable to talk for a few seconds.

"My God, Marti, are you all right? The baby?" He looked around. "The sick son of a bitch!"

She clung to him for a second, then came to her senses. "Jesse, he'll be back up in a few minutes! Does anyone know you're here?"

"No. I came on a hunch when I realized what Caramel might mean after knowing something wasn't right with the Oklahoma thing. I came here pretending to ask Carl if he had any leads on your disappearance, but he nearly ran me off. Marti, I've never seen a man look the way he did. Besides being sweaty and covered in dust, there was something weird about his eyes, something empty. Through the window I saw him run back up the stairs. Then I walked around the back and saw where he'd recently put an air conditioner unit in the attic. With one man and a house the size of this one, that seemed strange, so I snuck inside and went up the stairs. I ducked in one of the rooms when he came down from the attic, and when I saw that opening, my heart twisted inside." He looked down at the cuffs on her ankles. "I've got to get you out of here."

"You're not going anywhere with her," Carl's voice said in a deadly tone. He shut the door behind him.

Jesse rushed him, shoving him up against the wall. Chips of plaster rained down on the two. Marti felt helpless, chained to the bed. A sharp pain ripped through her stomach, and she grimaced, squeezing her eyes shut for a moment. When she opened them again, Jesse was looking at her. She shook her head, telling him not to worry.

Carl emitted a caterwaul as he twisted a distracted Jesse around and shoved him to the floor. Jesse moved just before Carl dropped down knees first, ready to crush him. They wrestled on the wooden floor until Carl had Jesse pinned with his legs. He reached for a pipe wrench lying in the bathroom and swung it high in the air as Jesse struggled to free himself.

A severe cramp seized her. She managed to scream, "Carl, you can't kill your own son!"

Both men looked at her with widened eyes. Carl's fingers trembled, and Jesse grabbed the wrench and lurched upward, tumbling Carl onto the floor. With the upper hand, Jesse beat Carl with his fist until he was no longer fighting back.

Marti doubled over in pain, reaching for the handcuffs her hands had been in. "Here, Jesse!" she said breathlessly. "Put him in these!"

He dragged Carl to the bed and cuffed one hand to the rail. Then he searched his pockets for the keys to the cuffs around Marti's ankles. Carl's head lolled about before his glazed eyes settled onto Jesse, right in front of him.

"I'm your father," he uttered weakly. "I just wanted another chance. You were never going to love me, but that baby would have."

Jesse gave him a disgusted look. "You are *not* my father, and I ought to kill you for saying it. I should kill you anyway." He slugged Carl in the jaw, silencing him.

When he found the matching keys, he freed her ankles and helped her from the bed. Her legs were stiff from disuse. She groaned, leaning on him, her pain too overwhelming.

"Marti, what's wrong? Is it the baby?"

She nodded quickly. "I think . . . I'm in labor."

"Oh, my God. Okay, come on."

He helped her to the door, locking Carl into the prison he'd made for her. Getting her down the ladder was the most precarious part. Her body was covered with beads of sweat. Jesse sat her down on the couch for a few minutes as he made two calls: one to the hospital and one to Lyle. Marti was in too much pain to listen to either call. Letting the phone swing on its cord, he rushed over and carried her down to his truck. He jumped in on the other side, threw the truck into gear and screeched down the road to the hospital.

"Hold on, doll," he said, squeezing her hand for a second. "God, I thought I'd lost you." He looked at her for a moment, then leaned over and kissed her. "You're going to make it through."

Marti warmed at the words and their intensity. She wanted to tell him that she loved him in case she didn't make it, but something happened before she could get the words out. She gasped as warm water gushed out onto the seat, filling the cab with the faint odor of chlorine. "My water broke!" She looked at him, terrified. "I changed my mind! I don't want to have this baby! Not yet!"

"How long have you been in labor?" the first nurse they saw at the hospital asked.

"I don't know. The pain's been there for a few hours. I thought they were Braxton-Hicks at first."

"When's your due date?" she asked, taking her blood pressure.

"June twenty-third," Marti and Jesse answered simultaneously.

"How accurate was your date of conception?"

"Very," Jesse answered wryly.

The nurse eyed him, then started to take Marti's temperature. "Thirty-four to thirty-six weeks is the hardest time to go into labor, for us anyway. Dr. Diehl will have to make the determination of whether to suppress your labor for another day. With your water broken, that could be tricky."

Dr. Diehl let Marti's labor continue, based on their reliable due date. At four o'clock the next morning, Eli Bernard West came into the world with a healthy wail. Their two Lamaze classes had helped minimally, but Jesse had done everything possible to make it easy on er. Easy was not a word she would use for the labor process.

"Jesse, would you like to cut the cord?" Dr. Diehl asked, a tired smile on his face.

He looked hesitantly at Marti. "Will it hurt her?"

"No, she won't feel a thing." He handed Jesse the scissors, and very gently he cut the cord. "Good job, son. Since the little fellow decided to come early, we're going to have to take him right now and run some routine tests on him. Now, don't worry, he looks perfectly healthy to me. You'll get to see him in a couple of hours."

"God, there's a lot of blood," Jesse murmured as the nurses started to clean Marti up. His hands were shaking.

"She's going to bleed for a while," one of them told him. "It's normal."

Marti felt overwhelmed as they wheeled her to her private room. Emotionally exhausted, happy, sad, she tried not to think about the last week of hell she had spent as Carl's prisoner. Jesse held her hand during the ride and sat next to her bed when she was settled into her room at last.

She looked dazedly down at her belly, smaller now. "I thought it would go flat again when I had the baby. What's in there?"

Jesse held her hand tightly in his, as if he were afraid to let her go. "I don't know, stuff I guess. Debbie was the same way, and she said she had to work at it to get it down. You'll be back to normal again."

"I need more of that sugar they were giving me intravenously. I'm so tired." Her voice sounded tiny and weak.

"You've been through hell in more ways than one. Go to sleep."

"No, I don't want to. Do you think the baby's okay?"

His green eyes studied her carefully as he reached up and stroked her cheek. "Yeah, he's going to be fine. Marti, you gave me the greatest gift in the world. There's nothing I could do to show you how much that baby means to me, or that you stayed until you had him. The money, well, it doesn't even come close."

Marti shook her head. She'd forgotten about the money. "I don't want your money, Jesse."

He looked surprised, and she remembered with shame how she had planned to take money he'd taken a loan out for.

"I mean it. I've got some put aside, from decorating. . . ." Her voice trailed off, and she fought the tears that threatened.

He didn't say anything for a few minutes, but there was so much behind his eyes, so much she couldn't explore. She placed her hand on top of his, still resting against her cheek. *I love you, Jesse.* Exhaustion tugged her into sleep, leaving her words unspoken.

After Dr. Diehl stopped in to see how Marti was doing a few hours later, the nurse brought Eli in. Marti didn't even see the nurse, just the tiny little person she held in her arms.

"He's just fine," the nurse said. "Had a little trouble maintaining his body temperature and glucose for a few hours, but now he's perfectly healthy. I'll be back in later to check on you."

Her heart felt so tight, she could hardly breathe. Eli's eyes weren't open yet, but he reached blindly at her fingers, clutching them tight. She just stared at him for a few minutes, feeling Jesse's warmth at her side, and his own awe of the tiny life in her arms.

"Hi, little guy," she whispered. He gurgled in response. *Oh God, how am I going to leave you and your daddy?* "You sure wanted to come out into this awful world, didn't you? What was your hurry?" She kept her tone light, though her voice sounded strangled with the tears she was fighting back. "Jesse, he's so beautiful."

When she looked up at him, Jesse was watching her. He looked more tired than she felt, with his wrinkled shirt and tousled hair. He had looked almost the same the first time she'd seen him. How different things were now. Marti handed Eli to him. Jesse's broad shoulders dwarfed the tiny being in his arms, but he cuddled the baby with supreme gentleness. He turned away from Marti and faced the window for a few minutes, bowing his head slightly.

The door opened, and Helen walked quietly inside. Her smile glowed when she saw Marti and Jesse with the baby. She walked up and gave Marti a hug.

"How are you, hon? What a thing to go through, being kidnapped and going right into labor." Her kind smile faded when she looked at both of them. "What's the matter?"

Marti couldn't keep the chill of her heart from reaching her face. "I'm just tired, that's all," she lied. Helen had severely disappointed her, and it made Marti doubt herself. She had a feeling that tucked away in Jesse's heart were a lot of questions, politely waiting to be asked at the proper moment. He handed Helen her grandson.

"This is your grandson, Eli Bernard West."

She cuddled him, closing her eyes. "You named him after your father," she whispered.

Jesse stood straight, right in front of her. "Yes, my father."

When Helen met his eyes, they were free of guilt or secret knowledge. "He would have been so pleased."

As hard as Marti tried to keep the thoughts at bay, she remembered Carl telling her that he'd arranged for Bernie's accident. She would tell them all that later, when Lyle came in to question her. For now she could only hope that Jesse hadn't given any credence to the words that had made Carl hesitate before lowering that wrench on Jesse.

Marti drifted slowly from the trenches of sleep, aware of a voice speaking softly near her. At first she irrationally thought Eli was already talking, but she dismissed that as she became more awake. She then recognized Jesse's voice and opened one eye a little. He was leaning over the plastic crib Eli was sleeping in, speaking in a thick voice.

"What are you going to do without a mama, little

man? When are you going to start asking me about her? And what am I going to tell you?"

As she fought to keep the tears at bay, her deep breath betrayed her wakefulness. Jesse swung around to face her.

"I didn't know you were awake."

"I just woke up," she said, swallowing hard. "Is he sleeping?"

"Yes."

He walked over to the side of the bed, and she longed for him to take her hand. He didn't. Instead those hands clenched at the side of the table next to her bed.

"Did Lyle come in and talk to you this morning?"

"Yes. He said he was sorry he didn't see it. He knew something wasn't right with Carl, but he figured it was Carl's way of mourning his son. I'll have to testify at the trial."

"So you'll be back in town then?"

"Yes," she whispered.

He leaned down, bowing his head for a moment. Expeling a long breath, he looked at her again. "He didn't . . . hurt you, did he?"

"No, he didn't hurt me. Or rape me. I was too fat, he said. Thank God for being pregnant," she said, trying to smile. "I found out that Carl was the one who had killed Marti, and attacked me, and raped Donna. When Donna finally admitted she'd had the same mark, I had to know if it was Paul. I thought Carl was at the station, so I snuck into his house to find the pendant. Not only was it the same mark, but I saw a picture of both Carl and Paul wearing the same pendant. And Donna said the man who attacked her had a hairy chest; in that picture, Paul didn't—but Carl did. He came home and caught me." She looked away from him, seeing everything happening in her mind.

"He handcuffed me to that bed in the attic. And then he built a soundproof room around me. To keep me there, forever. He was going to raise Eli as his nephew."

The thought made her shiver and bury her head, trying not to cry as she did in front of Lyle earlier that morning. Jesse put his arms around her, and she melted into his needed touch. He held her for a few minutes. Maybe biding a little time for the questions he was about to ask. Finally he moved away and steadied himself with the table.

"Marti, there's something I need to ask you. You screamed that he couldn't kill his own son, and he stopped. Then he said . . ." His voice faltered as she nodded slowly.

"Jesse, all I know is what he told me. He said he and Helen had an affair, and she got pregnant with you. I would have thought he was lying, but I'd found a picture of Helen in his bedroom, behind another photo." She took a deep breath. "He thought I was Helen. And he wanted to pretend Eli was you."

Jesse took her drink container and flung it into the corner, spraying water everywhere. She had never seen such betrayal in anyone's eyes, not even Jamie's. His body trembled as he struggled to stay in control. Marti was only glad that she hadn't caused it this time. She maneuvered to the side of the bed and reached out to touch him. He jerked away from her, putting his hand out as a shield.

"Don't." He looked out the window. "His blood. My blood. God, no. No!"

He stormed from the room, leaving her gripping the edge of the bed with all her strength. If she could have told him a lie to smooth it out, she would have. But it wouldn't have solved anything, and Jesse deserved to know the truth.

Jesse's insides were imploding, drawing into a tight knot. He didn't want to believe it. He would ask Helen, and if she said it was all an ugly lie, he'd believe her. His senses were swirling around him, making him wonder about his own sanity. He had gone crazy worrying about Marti, and when he'd received that note, he'd believed she had left him at first. Jesse shook his head, not wanting to relive those moments of pain. Almost losing her made him realize how much she meant to him.

Helen looked up as Jesse stormed into the house, his

face drawn. Kati's eyes widened as she flicked the television off.

"Is everything all right? Marti? The baby?" Helen stood, her face taking on a panicked expression.

"They're fine. Kati, leave." At her shocked look, he took a quick breath and added, "Please."

She glanced at Helen, then slipped on some shoes and headed outside. A few moments later, her car started. Helen remained standing, a few feet from her son.

"Jesse, what is going on?"

He didn't want to be standing there asking his mother this. But he had to. "Did you have an affair with Carl before I was born?"

Her face paled, giving him as much of an answer as her words. "How—"

"He told Marti. As a matter of fact, Ma, he's still obsessed with you. Did you know that? He made himself believe that Marti was you."

Her hand went to her mouth. "Oh, God."

"How could you do that to Pa?"

"It was only once."

"Once is enough."

"Let me explain, Jesse. I know it was wrong, but—"

Rage and hurt warred inside him. He turned, and, before he dumped it on her, walked out. The sky was clouded over, and he wished for rain, for lightning and thunder. Helen was standing at the door, crying out for him to come back. He couldn't bear to look at her another second.

Marti couldn't believe who she saw standing in the doorway during visitors' hour. Donna smiled tentatively, waiting for an invitation.

"My goodness, come in! You're out of the house!" Marti said with a smile.

Donna nodded, sitting down primly on the chair next to Marti. "I'm ready, I think. It feels good to be out. And now I know I'm safe. The town is murmuring about your getting kidnapped and everything. It must have been terrifying."

"Not as much as childbirth," Marti kidded, not wanting to talk about the horrible experience at Carl's house.

"I saw the baby. He's beautiful. Jesse must be so proud."

Sadness flickered through Marti's eyes. "There's a lot of other stuff going on, but he is proud. Eli looks a lot like him."

Marti was telling Donna about her daily routine at the hospital when she felt a presence at the door. Hoping it was Jesse, she turned to see. Helen stood there, even more hesitant than Donna had been. She was clutching her purse tightly, and her eyes were red and puffy.

"Donna . . ."

But Donna was already on her feet, taking note of the expressions on the other two women's faces. "I don't want to hog all your time, and my dad's waiting out in the hall for me. Call me when you get out, and we'll have lunch. At a restaurant!" she added triumphantly.

"Thank you for coming," Marti said as Donna retreated.

Helen shut the door behind Donna and took a seat. Marti had never seen Helen less than composed, and even under the circumstances, it left her feeling unsteady.

"Marti, I am so sorry that this happened to you. I'm sorry that Carl . . ." She faltered, then continued. "Jesse came to see me a little while ago. He didn't give me a chance to explain anything to him. You—you're a captive audience, so to speak. I don't know if I'll be able to explain it all to my son, or whether he'll even care to hear it. But for some reason, I feel I should explain it to you. Marti, I feel like I've let you down."

Marti swallowed tears fighting to escape. "You don't have to explain anything to me."

"I do. Remember when we talked about fidelity and making mistakes. I told you about the time after Billy was born and Bernie was racing all the time. Carl became a friend to me during those lonely months, and that's all I wanted: a friend. But I made a mistake and let things get too far one night. We had sex, and that's all it was. Once.

"After that, I told Carl we couldn't be friends, or anything else. I confessed to Bernie, and that wasn't easy. But I didn't deserve easy, and he didn't deserve to be lied to. It was hard, so hard to tell him, and he hated me for a week. But he forgave me and started spending more time at home. Carl kept pestering me, watching me. But I never saw him alone again, and I thought he let that die a long time ago."

Helen waited for some kind of reaction. Marti wasn't sure how she felt after her confession. She who had made mistakes, and hadn't confessed them or learned from them. But there was something she had to know.

"Is Carl Jesse's father?"

Helen's eyes widened. "God, no. It was close to the time he and I, well, you know. I was worried. So the doctor conspired with me and told Carl there was concern about some disease going around. He took Carl's blood, and we ran tests against Jesse's. There was no way they were related." Her expression lit up with worry. "He thinks Carl's his father?"

Marti relayed the moments when Jesse rescued her from hell. As her words poured out, she felt a deep relief. And forgiveness.

Helen stood, wringing her hands. "I've got to talk to Jesse, but I know right now he won't listen to me. It's a horrible feeling to know your son hates you."

"I don't think he hates you. He's just hurt and confused."

Helen looked at Marti. "I let you down, didn't I?"

She shrugged, feeling her face redden. "I don't know why, but I feel almost as hurt as Jesse probably does. You gave me such faith in myself not to make the same mistakes I'd made before. If someone like you can fall, how can I expect to stay on the path?"

Helen's eyes glistened with tears. "Because you're better than I am. No, listen to me. I didn't think it could happen to me. I was this perfect wife. You don't have those delusions. You're walking in with eyes wide open, ready to protect what means the most to you. You think your past gives you a disadvantage, but it doesn't. You already know what to look for, and what you can lose. You lost it once. Now you have a second chance to grab at love and happiness, and Jesse won't ever let you down. Maybe you both can learn from my mistake. He needs you, Marti. And if you'll admit it to yourself, you need him."

"I think . . . I could be true to someone like Jesse, but it doesn't matter. He has his racing, I have California. We'll just get in each other's way." God, how she wanted to believe that.

Helen touched Marti's hand, a soft smile on her face. "Whatever you decide to do, please don't leave until you say good-bye. You're like a daughter to me."

Marti's tears now flowed freely down her cheeks. "Thank you for explaining, when you didn't have to."

Helen hugged her, then started toward the bassinet. "Have to see the grandbaby," she whispered to the sleeping infant. "Eli Bernard West." She looked up toward the ceiling. "Do you see your grandson, my love? They named him after you. I wish you were here to hold him. And me."

The evening breeze was humid and warm, but Marti wrapped Jesse's robe tightly around her as she walked down to the tiny lake in the hospital courtyard. Jesse's cologne drifted from the terry cloth. The ducks were sleeping, tucked away in their hiding places, and the lake was deserted. She sat down on one of the concrete benches that surrounded the lake. Lights reflected on the water that shimmered as tiny fish moved just under the surface.

"The nurse said I might find you out here."

Jesse's voice washed over her like the breeze itself, comforting and familiar. She turned to find him standing in the shadows where the pathway started to circle around the lake. He was wearing a black T-shirt and jeans, and his hands were stuffed into the pockets. His hair wafted in the breeze, but she couldn't see his eyes clearly from where he stood in the shadows.

"I needed to get away," she said. "To think. I'm getting out of here tomorrow."

"I know."

He walked closer. She looked up at him, trying to keep her heart from hammering inside her. What she wanted to do was stand up and press herself against him, hoping his arms would encircle her and comfort her as she knew they could. But he was already lost to her, different. He crouched down in front of her so that his face was even with hers.

"Are you all right?" she asked in almost a whisper.

He leaned forward then, putting his arms around her waist and burying his face against her stomach. His hands felt firm against her back. She leaned forward, resting her cheek on his head, rubbing his back.

"Carl isn't your father," she said.

He didn't move for a few minutes, and she wondered if he'd heard her. Then he lifted himself up to face her again.

"I know. I talked to Ma a little while ago."

She reached out and placed her palm against his cheek, and he put his own hand on top of hers. He was her Jesse again, warm and real.

"Did you work things out with Helen?"

"Yes." He looked away for a second, running his fingers through his hair. "I'm sorry I got so mad in front of you."

She smiled faintly. "Well, I kept telling you to show your anger."

"Yeah, you did. But you had the reason for my anger mixed up when Mike came down for that visit."

"I did?"

"Uh-hm." He took both her hands in his. "I was mad at *you*, not at life's unfair circumstances."

"Me?"

"More at myself, really. I was mad because I'd fallen so completely in love with you that even racing didn't seem that important anymore. That scared me, because I'd already come so close to losing my dream." Jesse reached up and touched her cheek. "But I almost lost you, and that put everything into proper perspective."

Marti's lips were trembling when he lifted her to her feet. "I figured you were going to marry Debbie so she could watch the kids. I remember you saying something about her visit answering some question for you."

He smiled. "When I started falling in love with you, I kept denying it to myself. I told myself I just wanted to have you stay because I wanted someone to help with the baby. When Debbie offered me that, I realized that I wanted you to stay for a lot more than just helping raise our son. Still, it drove me crazy. And so did you."

Her heart was up in her throat. "Jesse, will you tell me again what your pa said about how you'd know if you truly loved someone?"

He said the words slowly, and his fingers tightened around hers. "Sorta a clenched gut, drop down to your knees and die for her feeling, and you ain't in love till you feel it."

Her stomach clenched inside at the intensity of his gaze. She nodded, a smile across her lips. "Yeah, that about sums it up. Your pa was a smart man."

Jesse took her face in his hands. "Marti, I know I asked you to stay for the wrong reasons before. But now I want you to stay for the most important reason, the only one: I love you. And this time I'm not going to ask you to stay, I'm telling you that you are staying. I'm not letting you go to California or Oklahoma or anywhere else. You are home, doll. Right here, forever."

"Is that a proposal?"

"You can take it any way you want, as long as you take it. And me."

"Oh, Jesse, I love you so much. And I'm going to make you the best wife you could ever want." She glanced up toward the star-filled sky. "I swear it on the Bible."

Epilogue

~

*E*li hobbled unsteadily down the slanted beach, intrigued by every pretty shell and bit of seaweed. Marti and Jesse walked hand in hand just behind him, their pants rolled up, but still not high enough to avoid the splash of the waves.

"You know," she said, taking in a deep breath. "Caterina seemed so dull to me a century ago. Well, it seems like a century. Now I see the wonder of it." She looked at Jesse. "The romance of it."

He swept her up into his arms and twirled her around, kissing her all the while. "As long as you don't see the romance while you're thinking about the rich, blond guy."

"Jamie? You've got nothing to worry about, darling."

He raised an eyebrow. "Hm, I don't know. I'm still not rich, and I'll probably never be able to buy an island."

She hugged him, laughing at his words. "Yeah, but you can give me a ride in your fancy new race car, and I get on television because I'm your wife and they like to do those family interviews in the pits."

He touched her chin, lifting it up for a kiss. "And you know I can't lose with my two good luck charms cheering me on."

Eli's squeal of laughter made them turn around quickly. A baby girl, about Eli's age, ran toward them with her hands poised for a hug. Eli, not knowing what else to do, sat down on the spot.

"Kayla, what are you doing, sweetie?"

Marti looked up at the couple walking from a path coming from the jungle. Her heart stopped momentarily, and she felt dizzy. Jamie and Hallie both smiled when they saw that their little girl had found a friend. Three Shetland sheepdogs followed behind, interested only in chasing each other. Marti clutched at Jesse's arm to steady herself.

"Hi, welcome to Caterina," Jamie said, casually offering a hand. "I'm the owner, and this is my wife, Hallie. This is our daughter, Kayla. We own this little place."

Jesse stiffened almost imperceptibly, but he accepted Jamie's hand and shook it heartily. "I'm Jesse, and this is my wife, Marti." He planted a kiss on her temple. "I think Eli's found a girlfriend, huh, doll?" He pointed to the babies, drawing their attention away for a second so she could gain her composure.

She had never seen Jamie so happy before. Looking at her old body was stranger yet, but she felt no ties to it anymore. Whoever the woman was in it obviously took good care of it. Marti had never seen it looking so fit. Jesse noticed, too, and she nudged him. More so, his eyes were on Jamie, the man who seemed to haunt Jesse sometimes. This trip had been his idea, so Marti could say good-bye to her past. Marti suspected Jesse also wanted to quell his curiosity about the couple he'd seen on television long ago. He put his arm possessively around her shoulders.

"How do you like it here so far?" Jamie asked in his owner's voice.

"It's absolutely excellent!" Marti replied, and the look on Jamie's face revealed that he still remembered her old expression. Hallie's old expression. "What's wrong?"

Jamie shook his head, putting his smile back on. "Oh, nothing. I knew someone who used to say that all the time. Just like that, same inflection and everything." He shook his head, as if to throw off the memory. "Where are you two from?"

"Florida," Jesse answered, watching Marti carefully.

"California, originally. Oceanview."

Again, Jamie's expression looked haunted for a moment. Marti found herself wanting to tell him who she was, but afraid that he hadn't yet forgiven her for the way she'd treated him. And what would his new wife think? It seemed he knew about her true identity. Marti noticed that Hallie was just as interested in the "coincidences" as Jamie was.

"Well, maybe we'll see you later on," Jamie said, starting to leave. "Tonight's Jamaican Night at BooNoo-Noos. Great food, limbo, that sort of thing. My wife's one of the best limbo-ers around, and I'm sure she'd be glad to show you a thing or two. In fact, you're welcome to sit with us for dinner. It sounds like we have a few things in common." His expression had a strange shadow to it as his eyes studied her.

"Maybe we'll do that." Marti smiled at him in a wistful way. "Things have changed a lot since the last time I was here."

Jamie's eyebrows drew together. "Oh, really? I don't remember seeing you here before."

She took in the water and palm trees with a smile. "Seems like forever."

"I'm glad you decided to come back."

"I am, too." She scooped Eli up in her arms, then spared an arm to link with Jesse's. "Isn't it wonderful when you can look at your past and know that you've learned from it without living in it? I hope you have a wonderful life, Jamie. Hallie."

She turned and walked away from them, Jesse at her side. Her lips were twisted in a huge grin.

"You are bad," Jesse said.

"No, I'm good. I meant every word I said. The past is gone forever. And I do want him and Hallie to have a happy life. I lost the island, but I got the West. And the West is a lot better." She pinched his cheek. "Besides, Jamie isn't my type."

To contact the author, please write to:
Post Office Box 10622, Naples, Florida 33941
A self-addressed stamped envelope appreciated
for reply.

Royd Camden is a prisoner of his own "respectability." But when he sees beautiful Moriah Lane—condemned by society and sentenced to prison for a crime she didn't commit—he cannot ignore her innocence that shines through dark despair. He swears to reach the woman behind the haunted eyes, never dreaming that his vow will launch them both on a perilous journey that will test her faith and shake his carefully-wrought world to its foundation. But can they free each other from their pasts and trust their hearts to love?

Evergreen

by Delia Parr

"A UNIQUELY FRESH BOOK WITH ENGAGINGLY HONEST CHARACTERS WHO WILL STEAL THEIR WAY INTO YOUR HEART."
–PATRICIA POTTER

ANITA MILLS
ARNETTE LAMB
ROSANNE BITTNER

*Join three of your favorite storytellers
on a tender journey of the heart...*

Cherished Moments is an extraordinary collection of breathtaking novellas woven around the theme of motherhood. Before you turn the last page you will have been swept from the storm-tossed coast of a Scottish isle to the fury of the American frontier, and you will have lived the lives and loves of three indomitable women, as they experience their most passionate moments.

THE NATIONAL BESTSELLER

CHERISHED MOMENTS

It only takes a second filled with the scream of twisting metal and shattering glass—and Chris Copestakes' young life is ending before it really began.

Then, against all odds, Chris wakes up in the hospital and discovers she's been given a second chance. But there's a catch. She's been returned to earth in the body of another woman—Hallie DiBarto, the selfish and beautiful socialite wife of a wealthy California resort-owner.

Suddenly, Chris is thrust into a world of prestige and secrets. As she struggles to hide her identity and make a new life for herself, she learns the terrible truth about Hallie DiBarto. And when she finds herself falling for Jamie DiBarto—a man both husband and stranger—she discovers that miracles really *can* happen.

ON THE WAY TO HEAVEN

TINA WAINSCOTT